HOME TO THE HILLS

After the Second World War, Ellen and her daughter Netta make the journey from Germany back to Scotland. Nestled in the hills of the Southern Uplands is the farm where Ellen grew up — the home she left to be with the only man she's ever loved. She is still haunted by her memories . . . and the secrets she dare not share with anyone.

Having grown up in Freiburg, farm life is new and exciting to Netta. Determined to be useful, she offers to help new shepherd Andrew Cameron. But doing so might put her bruised heart at risk . . .

The war took so much from Ellen and Netta — can the sanctuary of the hills offer them the hope of a new beginning?

DEE YATES

◆

HOME TO
THE HILLS

Complete and Unabridged

MAGNA
Leicester

First published in Great Britain in 2019 by
Aria
an imprint of Head of Zeus Ltd
London

First Ulverscroft Edition
published 2021
by arrangement with
Head of Zeus Ltd
London

A catalogue record for this book is available
from the British Library.

ISBN 978–0–7505–4873–1

Published by
Ulverscroft Limited
Anstey, Leicestershire

Printed and bound in Great Britain by
TJ Books Ltd., Padstow, Cornwall

This book is printed on acid-free paper

For everyone who enjoyed *A Last Goodbye* and wanted to know what happened next, this book will let you into the secret.

For my daughters,

Rachel, Wendy and Liz

who help to make the world a better place

Prologue

April 1939

It seemed as though they had been on the move for days. By the time they reached their destination they would have been.

To begin with, it was quiet at the station. The parents were told to wait outside. You could tell they wished it otherwise by the sad looks on their faces. Someone began to sob, others around joined in and soon, from far and near, nothing was heard but the sound of sobbing, spreading as if it were an infection. A distraught young girl was being comforted by a kind lady. The lady reminded the boy of his own mother, except that she looked worried, constantly looking round as if suspecting trouble. She opened the carriage door and gently persuaded the girl into the seat next to him, asking him to look after her, seeing as he was 'such a sensible boy'. The girl continued to sob for a while but once the train was speeding on its journey, she settled into a sulky silence.

At times they stopped in the stations of big cities to refill the coal wagon or top up the water. In between, they rushed pell-mell through the countryside, a strange landscape that he did not know, cottages and hamlets scattering before their path, smoke swirling past the window of their carriage. The lady who had helped to put them on the train came back, offering sandwiches from a paper bag.

1

They were dry and curling a little at the edges, but nonetheless welcome. The girl refused the sandwiches with a shake of her head. He wished that she would be a little more responsive when he tried to talk to her. His own sisters had always been good fun; he had never been able to stop *them* talking. But thinking about them was bringing hot tears to his eyes. He blinked them away and concentrated on the view from the window.

After several hours they stopped at another station. It was different here. The people on the platform were friendly and welcoming. They came into the carriages with cakes and sweets and drinks of hot chocolate and juice. This time the girl took some of the cake and a drink of juice. She still said very little but she seemed more comfortable with him, staring at the flat land that had now replaced the rolling countryside and scattered cottages.

The sea was stormy and rough, though it didn't much bother him. Perhaps he had inherited his father's strong stomach. He remembered his father once telling him that he had been a sailor a long time ago, though he hadn't enlarged on his experiences. The girl was ill on this part of their journey. He held her forehead while she was sick, mopped her face and gave her sips of water once she was still. The kind lady came and sat by them, telling him how well he was looking after her. He could see now that the lady was a bit older than his mother and her hair was greyer, but her friendly smile made him feel better, just like his mother's did.

When they disembarked, he looked around him

eagerly. Maybe now they had reached where they were staying. Maybe now he would be shown the house where he would wait for his parents to join him. But no. They found themselves once more on a train — and then another. They slept through a second night and woke hungry. The lady came round again with sandwiches and water to drink. His companion was more receptive now, no doubt feeling better after her bout of seasickness.

As they munched on their sandwiches, the train began to slow and together they looked at the tall brick chimneys and blackened buildings of an approaching city. She asked where they were going. He didn't know. She told him how much she was missing her mother and father. 'Me too,' he said and squeezed her hand. 'But we will see them again soon.'

1
New Beginnings

December 1945

By the time the Glasgow train pulls into the insignificant station, still forty miles short of its destination, darkness has already claimed the village and its surrounding countryside. In a few houses there is the wavering light of a candle, in others the flare of an oil lamp. The scant illumination gives to the cottages and bigger houses along the road a forlorn, uncared for appearance, even though Christmas is only a few days away.

A woman alights from one of the carriages. She is still young, no more than thirty, but her headscarf and sombre coat make her look older than her years. Turning, she heaves down a heavy suitcase, then offers her hand to another woman, just old enough to be her mother, who takes one leaden step and then a second onto the platform, before looking joylessly about her. With a sharp hiss, a cloud of steam envelops them as the train eases its way out of the station to continue its northward journey.

The exit, to which they make their way, is lit by a swinging overhead lamp, the undulations of which lend a ghostly appearance to the platform and waiting room.

'Wait here, Mother. I will ask the station-master to look after our luggage while we walk to the farm. If it is as far as you say, we cannot carry it all the way.'

The older woman gazes into the distance, as though trying to see a farm, a hill or even a field. She shakes her head slowly, seeing nothing but blackness. By the light of the lamp it is possible to make out her slim build, a face upon which lines of sorrow are etched but which fail to mask its lingering beauty, and a generous head of pale gold hair streaked with grey, curled into a low bun at the back of her neck. She turns at the sound of her daughter's footsteps.

'He says we can leave our case. He is on duty until ten o'clock. That will give enough time.' She delivers this information with an unusual accent, strange to the area in which they now find themselves. 'Come along, Mother. We will feel better when we can stretch our legs. And look, it is a full moon. See it beginning to climb above the hills? It will soon light our way for us.'

'I know the way blindfolded,' says her mother in a monotone. They begin to mount the steps out of the railway cutting in which the station is situated. 'But I wonder how much of that time *you* will remember. You were only four years old when we left.'

'Some things I remember — the sheep, Grandfather's games when work was finished,' the younger woman replies with a giggle. She takes her mother's arm as they join the narrow road that winds down into the valley. 'You will be pleased to see Grandfather again, will you not?'

Her mother gives a smile. 'Grandfather? Aye, it will be very good to see him. He at least will be

6

the same. Everything else is changed. Everyone is gone.'

'*I'm* still here.'

'Aye, thank God, you're still here.' The mother squeezes the arm that is linked through hers and plants a kiss on her daughter's cold cheek.

The moon is slowly climbing through the sky and the hills loom dark. They walk steadily and her daughter is right: the rhythm of their walking helps to dissipate the tiredness of the journey. They can hear the tinkling of a small river that runs through the valley to join its parent at the village. The weather is good for the time of year and there appears to be no snow on the hills. Not yet, at least.

After about half an hour they see in the distance a gleam of light. It marks the site of the farm towards which they are making their way. As the light becomes clearer, they turn off the road onto a smaller track that crosses the river by means of a ramshackle bridge. Here the mother pauses, looking about her in bewilderment. The daughter puts her hand on her mother's arm in encouragement and they cross slowly to the farmyard. The mother is hesitant, her eyes looking everywhere, as though remembering things that happened long ago but seem like only yesterday. She lifts her hand, knocks on the door of a cottage and steps back, anticipating the opener's surprise. The door opens and she herself is the one who is surprised. For the owner is a stranger, a man, and not one or other of the elderly couple she is expecting. He too registers surprise before his face breaks into a welcoming smile. For a moment the woman is speechless. It is left to her daughter to ask the obvious question.

'We're sorry to bother you. We have come to see Duncan and Margaret Simpson. They do still live here, yes?'

'They're no' here now, hen. Margaret moved to the village. She couldnae very well stay on in the cottage after Duncan died. The farm needed — ' He stops abruptly at a cry from the older woman who takes a step back, stumbles and almost falls. The daughter is at her mother's side in an instant and the unknown inhabitant of the cottage, shocked at the effect of his words, steps forward to help.

'I'm sorry, hen. I'd nae idea you knew the old man. Come in and sit yourselves down for a bit.' He and the younger woman each take an arm and steer the mother across the threshold and into the cottage, lowering her into an easy chair by the fire. The man disappears and returns with a glass of water, which he gives to the distressed woman. She is pale, eyes staring into the flames, tears spilling down her cheeks. Her daughter is at her side, an arm around her mother's shoulders. The man looks at the mother closely and a dawning look of astonishment crosses his face. 'Forgive me for asking but you have a look of Duncan. You're never his daughter?'

'Aye, I'm Ellen,' she says, her sobs diminishing. 'And this is Netta, my daughter.'

He claps his hand across his forehead. 'How stupid of me not to recognise you. I'm gey sorry to give you such bad news in this way. If I'd known you were coming . . .'

8

'No matter,' Ellen says, accepting a handkerchief from her daughter and mopping her face with it. 'I'm used to bad news. What other kind is there?'

The man frowns. 'Well,' he says slowly. 'The war is over. We must be thankful for that.'

'Aye, the war is over,' Ellen echoes. She looks up at the speaker and takes a big breath. 'Can you give me any idea how my father died?'

'Aye. It was a gradual decline. He was still working, though not really up to the job any longer. It was him that taught me the job of shepherd, of course. I was living next door to him in the other cottage. Duncan was determined to carry on as long as he could. He was still going out to the sheep until a week before his death.'

'It was all the life he ever knew,' Ellen muses.

'I'm sorry. I havenae introduced myself. My name's Finlay. Finlay Baird. Call me Finlay. I'm the shepherd here. But before we talk any more, let me make you both a cup of tea. You will need it after that walk through the valley.' Finlay sets the kettle on the stove, where it immediately begins to murmur as it reheats. 'Sorry it's a bit rough and ready but make yourselves at home. I won't be long.'

Netta's eyes follow him as he strides through into the kitchen and busies himself with putting out cups and saucers, taking the remains of a fruit cake out of a tin, checking the milk to make sure it isn't on the turn. He is middle-aged, of average height, and sturdy, looking as though he can easily withstand days of inclement weather in the hills. His eyes are deep-set, fringed with crow's feet and

9

they disappear into his face when he smiles. In the middle of his chin sits a deep dimple.

'Here you are, ladies,' he says, putting down the cake with a flourish onto a small table drawn up by the fire. He turns back, fetches the crockery, milk and sugar, and adds water to the teapot. He pours a little milk into the cups and tops each up with the tea with a dexterity born of experience. He passes a cup to each of his visitors and offers them a slice of cake.

'You did not marry?' Netta says, with a directness that brings a look of surprise to the man's face. She has removed her headscarf and he can see the same shock of unruly dark hair and penetrating blue eyes that he recalls from her childhood. He chuckles.

'I remember you well, lass. I was one of those called out to help when you got lost on the hills that snowy winter. You were lucky to be alive when we found you. No, hen, I didnae marry. I suppose it's this job — tucked away, miles from the towns and cities, miles from anywhere, ken. I wasn't always shepherding, mind. The last time we met I was with the gang coming to take over the building of the reservoir at the end of the Great War. I was only seventeen or eighteen, just young enough to escape being called up. Not that I would have been — they were needing the likes of us to finish the work that those German POWs had started.'

Netta glances anxiously at her mother who is listening intently to what Finlay is saying.

'Did you no' think they made a good job of it then?' Ellen asks.

'The Germans? Aye, they did. But there was

10

a lot of work still to be done. There were certain things they were no' allowed to do — using explosives, for example.' He pauses. 'I heard one of them was killed by a landslide while they were building the retaining wall. Is that right?'

'Aye,' says Ellen with a slow nod of her head. 'Oliver Tauber was his name. He's buried in the churchyard near the village.'

'So how is it that you came to live here in the shepherd's cottage?' Netta asks.

'Och, I liked the look of the farm work and I like the countryside hereabouts — so wild and out of the way. I started to help out on the farm as an extra pair of hands, when building stopped for the day. They needed help, shorthanded as they were after the war ended. I helped the farmer here — Kenneth Douglas — and I helped your grandfather after your father was killed and you had all moved away.'

Netta glances again at her mother.

'Kenneth and Elizabeth Douglas,' Ellen says, eyes wide with interest. 'Are they still here? Do they still run the farm?'

'Aye, still here, though the work is a bit much for him now. I try to take as much of the burden off him as I can.'

'So you became a shepherd full-time?'

'Aye. Kenneth offered me a job here. Duncan couldn't manage on his own, so they took me on. I stayed in the cottage next door and moved into this one when Margaret moved out. There's a bit more room here. Not that I need it. But the view from the window is even better than next door.'

'You've worked here right through *this* war

11

then?'

'That's right. I would have been on the border-line for enlisting anyway. Too young for the first war and almost too old for the second. In any case I was needed here.'

'Does anyone else help besides you?' Ellen asks. 'After all, it's a big farm and acres of ground to cover, and Kenneth sounds as though he'll no 'be up to doing much walking.'

'There's a shepherd interested in coming to help around lambing time next year.' Finlay lifts the lid of the teapot and stares into its dark interior.

'Just enough for another cup,' he says and gives each of them a refill. 'So, ladies, what have you been doing all these years? It's a gey long time that you've been away.'

Ellen's cup clatters into the saucer. She takes a breath to begin speaking but Netta interrupts. 'I think this is a subject we must leave for another day. My mother is very tired. We have travelled a long way and need to find Margaret. Can you tell us where she is? You have been very kind and we do thank you for your hospitality.'

'Nae bother, hen. As I said, Margaret's back in the village. She has a wee railway house there, just the right size for one, though I've no doubt she'll be more than pleased to see you both. Now, give me a minute and I'll check with Kenneth that I can use the motor car, so I can give you a lift. You cannae go walking all that way back to where you started. Give me a minute or two.'

While he is gone Ellen walks slowly round the room, pausing at the stove, glancing into the kitchen, where an old stone sink has pride of place, running her hand across a row of dusty farming magazines on the bookshelf. 'Nothing has changed,' she says quietly. 'And everything has changed. It is both a comfort and a distress to be here.' Her voice catches in a sob and, when she turns, her daughter can see tears sparkling in her mother's eyes. 'It's just the same as when you were born,' Ellen says, looking across at Netta. 'It's just the same as when I was looking after Josef.' She smiles sadly.

'You looked after Josef here?'

'Oh, yes. This was where I first met him.' Ellen doesn't elaborate and they sit, each thinking her own thoughts.

'Someday you may tell me about your time here with my father?'

'Someday. Not now. When we have settled, maybe. For now we need to concentrate on you so that you can make something of your life.'

'You also, Mutti. You have many years left to you.'

'No, Netta. My life is over, but for you this is a new beginning.' Ellen glances towards the door. 'Let's go. I can hear Finlay with the car.' She takes a last look round the room and walks to the front door, from where she can see the car headlights piercing the blackness of late evening. Her eldest daughter follows in silence.

2
Old Friends

December 1945

By the time Ellen and her daughter reach Margaret Simpson's door, having called at the station for their suitcase, it is ten o'clock. The cottage is in darkness and there is no response to their knock. An owl hoots nearby and they jump at the sound.

'Try again, Netta. She was always one for going early to her bed.'

Netta knocks again, louder this time. A light wavers in a window and they hear someone approaching.

'Who is it?' a voice calls.

'Margaret, it's Ellen . . . Ellen Simpson.' Her voice trembles in anticipation.

There's a pause. 'I don't believe it. Ellen Simpson, you said?' They hear keys jangling in the lock and then the door is scraped back and Margaret is standing there, ghostly in her nightdress, curlers in her white hair, eyes wide as she stares at Ellen. 'What are you doing here and at this time of night?' Her glance switches to Netta. 'And this is never wee Netta! Well, come away in. Is it just the two of you?' She glances over Ellen's shoulder into the blackness.

'Just the two of us.' Ellen steps across the doorway and into Margaret's welcoming arms.

14

Margaret rocks her to and fro like a child. Netta can see that her mother's shoulders are shaking with sobs and she looks at Margaret who smiles in reply. 'You have the look of your father and no mistake,' she says to Netta. She takes a step back and holds Ellen at arm's length. 'Come into the room. You look gey weary. You too, Netta. Come and sit yourselves down. I wish I had known you were coming. Why did you no' send word in advance?' They follow Margaret's diminutive form into the living room.

'It has been difficult,' Netta replies. 'We did not know if we would be able to get away and then, when we could, there was no time to let you know. And we did not know about Grandfather. We have come from the shepherd's cottage, where Finlay Baird told us he had died.'

Margaret nods slowly. 'I had no way of letting you know he was going downhill. I wrote to the address you had left all those years ago but there was no reply, so I guessed that you hadn't received the letter.'

'The house was bombed. We had to leave,' Netta says.

'I miss him a lot. But I must be thankful that we had nearly twenty-five happy years together. Years that we never expected to have.'

'When did he die?'

'October it was, 1942.'

'Three years ago — and to think we never knew.' They all stand wrapped in thought.

'But what am I thinking of? Sit down, both of you, and get warm. When you are rested and feel stronger, you can tell me what you have been

15

doing. For now I will make you some supper and arrange where you are to sleep.'

'Please do not concern yourself. Mother and I can find a guest house perhaps. You have no room here.'

'Nonsense. We may be crowded but we will be cosy. You are staying with me.'

★ ★ ★

Netta can barely remember her grandmother Margaret, being so young when they had left the family farm. She is not, in any case, her real grandmother. *She* had died giving birth to her mother. Duncan had brought up Ellen alone and only married Margaret just before Netta and her mother departed. But Ellen has talked often of Margaret and her kindness. The fact that her mother has had the best night's sleep in months and is now resting again after a morning that included numerous cups of tea and a gentle stroll to the shops is witness to the long-term affection between them.

Netta is drawn to the farm that she saw only by moonlight yesterday. While her mother rests, she once again takes the smaller side road that peels off the main road and winds down into the base of the wide valley. Bare hills run along either side, grooved in places by burns that make their way haphazardly to the river meandering westward to join the Clyde. She scans the hilltops but can see no snow, only scattered flocks of sheep, dotting the hillsides to their upper limits. She remembers looking at the snow on the highest mountains of their last home on the day they left to return to

16

Scotland. She remembers how David loved to walk in the mountains, relishing the freedom. She remembers the day when he was no longer able to do so. Her heart clenches at the memory and she looks into the distance in an attempt to distract her thoughts.

She can see the farm up ahead, sheltered behind and to its western edge by a line of conifers. The shepherds' cottages patrol the valley, the farmhouse nestling behind, looking over an untidy assembly of outbuildings. So engrossed is she in the home she can barely remember that she fails to see the elderly man approaching her along the road. With the aid of a stick his bowed legs are managing to step out purposefully, defying his obvious advanced years. The hand that grasps the stick has knuckles swollen and deformed with arthritis. But in his tanned and weathered face, his eyes sparkle with life as he comes to a halt just in front of her.

'You seem gey interested in my farm, young lady,' he says with a smile. He looks at her closely, then shakes his head in disbelief. 'Well now, if I'm not mistaken, you must be young Netta, Tom's daughter. Finlay said you had called last night, though I would have recognised you, even if he had not told me of your visit.'

'Yes, I am Netta. And you — you are the farmer here. Mr Douglas, is it not?'

'Aye, Kenneth Douglas.' He holds out his hand and shakes hers warmly. 'Well now, what a welcome surprise. Will you no' come up to the farm and meet my wife? I was making my way back, as it happens.'

17

'I would like that a lot. Thank you.' Netta joins the farmer and they cross the river bridge together.

The man looks at her again and smiles. 'You look so like your father,' he says. 'He was a good worker here. I couldnae have managed without him.'

The farmer pauses and raises his head to look at the hilltops. 'Things got difficult later on, of course, but it was wartime and things have a way of getting difficult when war is on.'

'Yes, they do.' She stops and looks at the farmer. 'Everyone keeps telling me I look so like my father. Will you tell me about him? Only Mother was always reluctant to say much. She is here with me, you know. We are with Margaret Simpson.'

'Aye. Finlay told me. You must come in and tell my wife how Ellen is.

Elizabeth was hoping to see her. Are you planning on staying in the village?'

'Here is the only place my mother knows,' Netta murmurs. 'She is in a bad way at the moment. It has been a very difficult time for her. I hope we can stay, even if it's only long enough for my mother to find some peace.'

A soft lowing comes from a shed to their right. Netta puts her head round the opening of the barn and sees half a dozen cows, each in her own stall.

'My ladies,' says Kenneth. 'Just enough of them to keep us all supplied with milk.'

In the perimeter of the farmyard a number of chickens are pecking in the addled grass and there are others wandering in and out of a second smaller barn. On the fence a brightly coloured cockerel glares at her and angrily flaps his wings.

She gives him a wide berth. Kenneth Douglas opens the farmhouse door and stands back to allow her to enter.

'Elizabeth,' he calls. 'Come and see who I have here.'

His wife puts her head round the door of the sitting room. She smiles at Netta but it's clear she does not recognise her. She comes slowly across the room towards her husband.

'Elizabeth's eyesight is no' so good,' Kenneth says quietly, by way of explanation. He raises his voice a little. 'It's Netta Fairclough. You remember — Duncan's granddaughter.'

'Of course. Finlay told us.' She puts out a hand to indicate the chairs. 'Come away in and sit down. You'll take a cup of tea with us?'

'Thank you very much.'

'Is your mother not with you?'

'No. She is very tired. She has not been well. Perhaps when she is better . . .'

'Yes, you must bring her when she is better. Kenneth, keep our visitor entertained while I make the tea.' Elizabeth shuffles from the room.

Netta, who has sat down at Elizabeth's invitation, stands again and steps over to the piano to admire the farming trophies, which are arranged along its top.

'There havenae been the shows recently, of course,' explains Kenneth. 'But now that the war is finished, we hope things will get back to normal. Not that I'll be likely to win anything this time, with your grandfather gone and new shepherds coming to learn the ropes and help out. Your father now — he knew what he was doing

19

with the sheep.'

'Tell me about him.' Netta's eyes sparkle. Here at last is an opportunity to find out more about the father she never knew. 'He wasn't from these parts, was he?'

'Nay, lassie. He came up from Yorkshire. He wanted to learn about the Scottish Blackface breed. They're different down there in England, the sheep. But there's none as hardy in the bad weather as our Blackies. So, the plan was, he came up here for a year or two, maybe longer. But of course it was 1914 and the war started — the Great War, that is — and eventually he joined up. I was sorry to lose his help. He was good at his job and could always be relied on to go out in all weathers to see to the sheep. Plenty of energy he had, to carry on when us older ones had had enough. Of course we assumed that when the fighting was over he would return and we would carry on as before.' Kenneth pauses, shrugs his shoulders.

'So did he not?'

'The war changes fighting men, especially that war. It damaged them. They were never the same again — the sights they saw, the conditions they had to put up with. He was injured, of course, in the leg, but it was his mind that was altered. He was always the quiet sort, getting on with the job, taking himself off for long walks into the hills when work was done. But once he became a soldier ... '

Kenneth's reminiscences are interrupted by the arrival of the tea. It doesn't escape Netta's notice that Elizabeth has got out the best china teacups. It has been a long time since Netta drank tea in such style.

'I was telling Netta about her father's time here with us,' Kenneth says to his wife.

Elizabeth shakes her head slowly. 'Such a shame, how he went.'

'What do you mean, 'how he went'? How did he go?'

'Well, as I was saying,' Kenneth continues, 'being at the Front changed him. When he came home on leave, he was morose, more silent than usual, never smiling, always finding fault. He gave your mother a hard time when she was only trying her best. Then he would go back to join his regiment after his leave was over and your poor mother wouldn't hear from him for months. She never knew whether he was alive or dead until suddenly he would appear again. And then, in the new year, not long after the war had ended, he disappeared again — and so did you. We found you, thank God.

After several hours, it must have been. That winter was bad and any longer out in those conditions and you wouldn't have survived. It appeared that your father had taken you from your bed and gone out into the night.'

Netta stares at the farmer, shocked into silence.

'You know about your father's death?' Elizabeth says.

Netta gives a small shake of her head. 'I know he died in the snow while out looking for sheep. Did it take long to find him?'

'I'm afraid so,' the farmer continues. 'It was spring before the snow melted enough. It was your grandfather who found him out on the hill-side. He must have fallen through a snow pocket. It's like that, the snow. It distorts everything out there, so you don't know where you are. He knew the hill as well as me but, even so . . . ' Kenneth shakes his head slowly from side to side and stares through the window as though picturing again the broken body of Netta's father at the foot of the gully that fateful morning.

'I had no idea it took so long,' Netta says slowly. She frowns. 'So he had taken me with him — is that what you are saying?'

'It seemed that way. But no-one really knows because we never saw him alive again.'

'It must have been awful for my mother. Is that why she decided to leave here?'

Elizabeth glances at her husband. 'I think you need to ask your mother about her reasons for leaving,' he says enigmatically.

'Oh, I have done, many times. She seems reluctant to tell me.'

The farmer hesitates. 'Sometimes things go wrong in a marriage that are difficult to talk about. Especially to your own children. Tell me, are you married?'

Now it is Netta's turn to hesitate. 'I was . . . was about to be. But my fiancé died.'

'Oh, my dear,' Elizabeth says. 'I am so sorry.'

'Yes. That is something I too cannot talk about. Not now, anyway.' Her eyes sweep the room before fixing on the clock on the mantelpiece. 'Goodness, it is getting late. My mother will wonder where I am. I must get back.' She gets up quickly from her seat.

'Well, my dear, you must come again soon,' Elizabeth says, 'and next time, bring your mother. I was aye fond of her. It will be lovely to see her again.'

* * *

It *is* something that Netta cannot talk about. But she has no control over her dreams and that night Netta dreams about a young man. He has gone walking in the mountains. It is late. He has not yet returned. Her panic is growing. And then she hears him calling and she shouts in reply, 'Over here, come over here.' But he doesn't hear her; he just goes on shouting her name. And then she sees a wall of fire threatening to engulf him and she screams and screams over and over again.

She wakes in a cold sweat. Her mother is sitting on the side of the bed gently shaking her. 'Netta, wake up. You were dreaming. You're here, in Margaret's cottage. We're safe.' Ellen kisses her daughter's damp cheek.

Netta hauls herself up from the pillow and shivers. 'I am so sorry, Mutti.

I didn't mean to disturb you. It was bad — a bad dream.'

'Yes, you were calling David's name.'

'And he didn't come . . . he didn't come.' Netta twists out of her mother's grip and flings herself down onto the rumpled bedcovers in a paroxysm of sobbing. Her mother sits, a hand resting on her daughter's shoulder until, at last, Netta quietens, sits up slowly and looks at her mother, a twisted smile on her face. 'I am sorry, Mutti. It is much

23

worse for you than it is for me. I will not be like this again.' She blows her nose and wipes her eyes. 'There! No more tears. It must have been this afternoon, talking with Kenneth Douglas about father and his time on the farm. Then Mrs Douglas asked me if I was married. And I had to think about all that again when I would rather not.'

Ellen stares across the darkened room as though she too is seeing scenes from her former life. 'I suppose we cannot avoid questions about what has happened to us, turning up as we have out of the blue. I wonder if I have done a very stupid thing, coming back to this place. I did it because it's the only place I know. I did it so that you might come to have some of the happiness I remember. But I suppose it can never blot out the evil.'

'Only time will tell, Mutti. But we *must* talk about the past — your past here in the valley. There are so many things I don't know. I cannot live here when everybody knows more about our story than I do.'

'You are quite right. I wasn't thinking straight. Of course you must know more. But it is late now and we both need to sleep. Tomorrow I promise I will speak of the past. Perhaps it will do us both good to talk of these things. Some of them, at least.'

3

Addressing the Past

December 1945

Ellen glances up as her daughter enters the kitchen. Netta looks tired. There are dark rings under her eyes and she is paler than usual.

'Here, Netta, sit down at the table and let me pour you some tea,' Margaret says, fussing round in the small kitchen. 'And have a bowl of porridge.'

'Just tea, please. I am not hungry.'

Her mother frowns. 'Are you no' feeling well, sweetheart?'

'I am well, Mother. It was only that I could not sleep.'

'I thought we might go for a walk into the valley this morning. Would you manage that?'

'Yes, of course,' Netta says, 'and I *will* have some porridge in that case, thank you, Margaret. I will need it if Mother and I are to walk.'

Ellen nods in agreement. She has lain in bed considering their night-time conversation and has come to the conclusion that the surroundings of the valley will assist her as she tells her daughter the difficult tale of her past.

★ ★ ★

25

'Mr and Mrs Douglas will be pleased to see you,' Netta says as they set out.

'They must have known you from being born and watched you grow up. We are calling to see them, aren't we?'

'Aye. We'll call in at the farmhouse if we're no' too tired to get that far.

And yes, they did see me grow up.' Ellen hesitates, then continues, as she has decided she must. 'I was born in the shepherd's cottage, where Finlay stays now. My father was shepherd on the Douglas farm the whole of his working life. He always lived in one of those two cottages. And when my mother died giving birth to me, he brought me up on his own as well as looking after the sheep. So quite often he needed someone to help look after me. Margaret lived further along the valley then. She was married and had a wee lad, a bit older than me. She often used to pop in with Iain when Father was busy with lambing and clipping. Elizabeth helped Father as well. She and Kenneth had no children of their own and I think that was a great sadness for them. I remember she used to make a big fuss of me and make me special cake and buy wee presents. But generally it was just him and me. I mind how he used to take me to market with him, sitting by his side on the wagon when I was big enough and, before that, between his knees when I was too wee to balance.'

'You and Grandfather must have been very close.'

'Aye, we were close,' Ellen says with a smile, gazing into the distance. Then her smile fades.

'I suppose it couldnae have been easy for him when Tom came to stay and began to take an interest in me. Not that he showed any signs of it upsetting him. And I think he must have been glad to have someone helping with the shepherding.'

'Did you love Father very much?'

Ellen pauses. 'I was very young when Tom came to the farm — only fifteen. Think what your feelings were at that age. I hadnae had much to do with boys, not since I had left school. I suppose I was flattered that he took an interest in me. But I'm not sure I knew what love was at such a young age. And I don't know if he really loved me. He was a good man, your father, but we weren't right for each other. Maybe we should never have married.'

'Kenneth was saying how the Great War seemed to alter Father, so he was much moodier and easily angered when he came home on leave.'

'Yes, that was true.' Ellen peers ahead to where the cottages can now be seen in the distance, one of which had been Tom's home while he had been shepherd. 'Tom didn't enlist in the army at first of course, not until two years after war had started. And yes, it did alter him. He had nightmares about what had happened at the Front. It must have been playing on his mind all the time, day and night. And it did make him very moody and bad-tempered. I tried to help but nothing I did seemed to make any difference.

'And then, one day, when Tom was with his regiment fighting at the Front, German prisoners of war arrived in the valley. They had been brought

27

in to carry on the work of building the new reservoir. It had been started before the war but all our own men had gone off to fight. I guess that they would have waited till the war was over but extra water was needed to be piped to the growing towns further north who were making munitions.'

'And one of the prisoners was Josef?'

'Aye.'

'But surely you wouldn't have had anything to do with them. They were the enemy. My father was risking his life fighting them.' Netta glares at her mother and Ellen sees in the look echoes of Tom's anger. Ellen's stomach lurches, but she is determined that she will not shirk the responsibility of telling this story.

'Listen and I will tell you what happened. One day, soon after the men arrived, the English captain in charge visited the farm and asked me to look after a man who was very ill. What could I do? He would have died if he had been left. I thought he was going to die while he was with me. It was Josef, of course. I nursed him as best I could. I did nothing that I shouldn't have done.' Ellen hesitates then, reminding herself of her decision to be honest about her past, takes a deep breath and continues. 'But as the days went on I couldn't help being drawn towards Josef. I tried to fight against my feelings, to stay detached. But he was so gentle, so kind, so . . . different.' Her voice catches and she pauses as she looks at her daughter. 'You know yourself what Josef was like.'

Netta remains silent.

'Anyway, he recovered and rejoined the other POWs laying the railway tracks and building the

28

road. Soon after, your father came back on leave. He was very angry when he found out that the valley he loved was full of Germans — and even angrier when your grandfather let slip that I had been nursing one of them in our home.'

'That doesn't surprise me. I might have felt the same.'

Ellen pauses, reluctant to tell her daughter the extent of Tom's anger, not wanting to turn her against him. She sighs and goes on. 'Yes, but his reaction was extreme. He went off again back to his regiment and stopped writing to me. I was sick with worry. I didnae know whether he was alive or dead.'

'Couldn't his letters have got lost? After all, sending letters back home must have been a difficult thing to organise.'

'Yes, that's true. But it wasnae just that. He . . . well, he hit me. At first I tried to think that the war had turned his mind, that it wasnae his fault. But when he came home again, the same thing happened.'

Netta comes to an abrupt halt. 'This is true, that he hit you?'

'I'm afraid it is. I didnae want to tell you. It's no' a nice thing for a child to learn about her father. But I need you to understand how it was that I let myself become attracted to Josef,' Ellen pleads.

Netta is stunned into silence by this unexpected revelation of her father's behaviour.

'Of course, eventually the armistice was signed. Josef and I knew that it would be the end of our friendship. He left the valley along with his fellow prisoners. I had to try and rebuild my marriage for your sake, if nothing else. And then your father disappeared — and so did you. Thank God we found you the next day. Any longer and you would have been dead. Your father was no' so lucky. We didnae find his body until spring. I knew then that he must have tried to take you because I discovered your wee boots in his coat pocket, the boots that should have been on your feet when we found you.' Her voice rises in anger. 'I couldnae forgive him for that —risking your life in that dreadful weather, planning to take you away from me.'

'So you got in touch with Josef?' Netta whispers.

'Not at first. But one day I met the captain who had been in charge of the prisoners. He was in the valley, helping to sort out the handover to the men who had returned from the war. He had a letter from Josef that he had kept ever since the prisoners had gone. It had Josef's address on it. You can guess the rest.'

'It was a risky thing to do.'

'What? Following him to Germany?' Ellen shakes her head slowly. 'Not really. We both knew what we felt for each other. Grandfather had recently married Margaret — her husband had died a year or two before — so he didn't need me to stay and look after him.'

'Would you have followed Josef if you could have seen into the future?'

Ellen's face takes on a bleak look. 'For Josef's sake, yes,' she says. 'For me, I don't know.' Her voice is no more than a whisper. 'I had no idea what I was taking you into.' She pauses before continuing, 'But I loved him so much, I would have followed him anywhere.'

They are level with the farm now and only have to cross the valley base with its small river bridge. Ellen stands still and turns slowly, studying the strip of flat land to the south of the river.

'Here.' She gestures wide with her hands. 'All round here is where the prisoners were camped. We could see them from the window of the cottage.

They came in August and September, two hundred of them, put their tents up here on this small patch of grass and camped. That winter the weather turned bad, too bad for them to stay in their tents. They moved further up the valley and had to build proper huts to live in before they could continue the job of laying the road and the railway.'

'There is no railway now,' Netta says, looking ahead.

'I think they only built it to take materials up to the reservoir. It must have been taken away again.'

'Shall we walk on and see the reservoir?'

'No, not now. It's a long way. Perhaps another day. Let us call on Kenneth and Elizabeth.'

★ ★ ★

The door of the farmhouse is flung open while the two women are still approaching the farm.

'Kenneth spied you on the other side of the river,' Elizabeth says in excitement. 'This is a day I never thought to see. Come in, come in.'

Ellen steps over the threshold and Elizabeth hugs her warmly. Then she stands back and looks at her, screwing up her eyes. 'I hope you don't mind me saying, my dear, but I fear the years have taken their toll.'

'There have been hard times,' Ellen says, 'but it is very good to be back among friends. And I hope the return to Scotland will be good for Netta. She is badly in need of a little happiness.'

'Come through into the living room,' Elizabeth says, 'and I will put the kettle on.'

Ellen follows her through and stops so suddenly that her daughter almost collides with her. 'You still have the piano,' she says, her voice choking, and extends her hand to stroke the polished wood. She lifts the lid and gently presses one or two of the notes. 'Do you remember the day that Josef played this?' she says to Elizabeth, then turns to her daughter, tears coursing down her cheeks. 'Josef was recovering from his illness. He saw the piano and asked if he could play a tune. We had no idea how beautifully he could play.'

'Aye,' agrees Elizabeth. 'I ken well the day. Do you play, my dear?' She turns to Netta.

'No, I never learned.' Netta looks at her mother. 'My sister Eva and my . . . ' She hesitates, seeing Ellen's look of anguish. 'No, I never learned. Always too busy getting into trouble.'

'Nonsense, Netta.' Ellen summons some control over her emotions, as she sees her daughter's struggle. 'You were never any trouble. Right from an early age you were always too busy helping me. I don't know how I would have managed without you.'

'Do sit yourselves down. I won't be long.' Elizabeth Douglas bustles off into the kitchen.

'So the reservoir is finished now?' Ellen asks

Kenneth.

'It is indeed. It was officially opened in 1932.' Kenneth pauses and a smile comes to his face. 'Why don't I drive you along to see it after we have had some tea? Elizabeth,' he calls out to his wife, 'shall we have some sandwiches with our tea and then we can show our guests the changes in the valley?' He turns back to them. 'I think you will be pleasantly surprised with what you see.'

* * *

'And what of young Josef?' Elizabeth begins, when they are seated round the table. 'Your father said that you and he were married.'

'Yes we were,' Ellen says quietly.

'Josef was a kind man, a gentle man. Very different from some of his fellow soldiers, I should imagine.'

'Yes.'

'But he has not come back with you?'

'He died — more than three years ago.' Ellen pauses before continuing in a low voice, 'He . . . well, as you know, he was never very strong.'

'I'm so sorry, Ellen. We did not realise.'

'No, I had no way of letting my father know.'

'So did you no' have any more children when you —'

'I am sorry, Elizabeth,' Netta interrupts quickly, 'but talking about such things only upsets my mother. We have come back to Scotland to try and forget.'

Elizabeth is taken aback by Netta's rebuke.

33

Ellen puts out her hand and rests it on her daughter's forearm. 'Netta has always felt the need to protect me,' she explains. 'She doesn't mean to appear rude.'

'Of course. I should have thought,' the old lady says. 'Such troubled times we have all been through. To have two such awful wars within a lifetime is more than a body should have to endure.'

'Let us hope that the peace negotiations will mean an end to this idiocy,' Kenneth says.

'Yes, indeed,' agrees Elizabeth. 'And you, Ellen, will be feeling the loss of your father.'

'We didn't know about Grandfather until Finlay told us,' Netta says. 'Margaret wrote to us in Germany but we didn't get the letter.'

'He had a long life,' Ellen says, her eyes sparkling with tears. 'Not always a happy one but a long one, with a lifetime of doing what he enjoyed. So much better than many during this dreadful time.'

* * *

'I suggest,' says Kenneth, after the meal is finished, 'that I hitch up Princess to the wagon and we ride to the reservoir that way, rather than shut inside the car and not able to see so well. That will give you a better idea of how big it is. The day is dry and no' too cold for us to do that.'

The huge retaining wall of the reservoir rears up in front of them as they approach. The various huts that once sheltered the German prisoners during the two years of their labours in the valley are no more, cleared away and replaced by green fields and a cluster of dwellings. Ellen stares ahead, seeing the one-time buildings with their high, barbed-wire perimeter fencing. Her eyes take in the steepness of the valley side beyond the reservoir embankment and, at its base, the stells, untidy and broken in places but still adequate to provide shelter for some of the flock in inclement weather.

Along the top of the wall runs a narrow road and they stop at its centre and see the water stretching into the far distance, bigger by far than Ellen has imagined it would be.

'Margaret lived here,' she says, pointing across the ripples to a point east of where they are sitting. 'Her farm was on the land that was to be flooded, so she and her family were told they would have to move and they would be given land higher up, away from the water.'

'But that would have meant starting again.'

'Aye, it would. And then they lost their only son in the war . . . and Robert, her husband, took ill and died.'

'And she married Grandfather?'

'Well, yes, eventually.' Ellen turns to the reservoir again. 'It's huge. I never thought of it being so long.'

'Aye,' says Kenneth. 'It's made a big difference to the folk living in the towns north of here.'

'I like it,' says Netta decisively. 'It's beautiful, almost like pictures I've seen of lochs. And all the trees around it look as though they've been there forever.'

'One of the conditions of building the reservoir was that trees were planted on the surrounding hills. Aye. They made a good job of it, the Scots and the Germans together. Let's hope in years to come they'll learn to live together without all this stupidity that we've had to put up with.' Kenneth gives the horse a flick with the whip and she sets off back the way they have come.

'Are you planning to stay here?' Elizabeth asks as she dismounts. Kenneth is continuing to the village to offload his remaining two passengers.

'I think we would like to,' Netta replies, looking to her mother for confirmation. 'But we will have to find somewhere to live. We cannot stay with Margaret. Her cottage is much too small. The other problem is that we lost everything in Germany. We have nothing but a few clothes and a very little money, which we cannot use in Scotland. I need to get work, so we can pay our way.'

'Did you have anything particular in mind?' Elizabeth asks.

'I will do anything,' Netta says, her head held high. 'I cannot afford to pick and choose.'

'Then would you consider helping me in the farmhouse for a start? It is getting too much for me, especially with my eyes not being as good as they were. And when it comes to lambing and clipping later in the year, there is so much extra baking and looking after the farm labourers to do that I don't know how I will cope.'

'I would like that very much, but we will still need somewhere to live — and a landlord who is prepared to wait a little time for his money.'

'I have a new shepherd starting who will need

36

the other cottage, otherwise you could have had that,' Kenneth says, considering. 'But leave it with me,' he adds cheerily. 'I think I know just the place.'

4
Refuge

December 1945

The cottage sits on the floor of the valley about a mile east of the farm. A short distance from its door the river meanders past, carrying the surplus from the neighbouring reservoir. Whether it is its position in the valley base or the fact that it has been empty for some time is uncertain but the building is damp. Its walls are discoloured and, where there is wallpaper, it hangs in soggy shreds. Netta wanders with her mother through the rooms, seeming barely to notice the pervading air of mustiness and neglect.

'This is wonderful, is it not, Mutti? It will suit us very well. We will make it cosy in no time.'

* * *

Ellen and her daughter pass Christmas Eve with Margaret in a quiet celebration of Netta's thirtieth birthday.

'You were your mother's special Christmas gift,' Margaret says.

'It seems so long ago,' Ellen remarks. 'Another life entirely.'

'Not *that* long ago, Mother,' says Netta, attempting to lighten the sombre tone of the conversation.

In Margaret's cramped but cosy cottage they recall some of the happier memories of Netta's early life. Netta, who has not heard these stories, is entranced by them and feels special in a way she never has before.

★ ★ ★

The day after Christmas Kenneth Douglas calls for Netta in his car and together they drive to a nearby village where a farmer has recently died. Intending to take over the property, his son, or more accurately his daughter-in-law, is keen for a quick removal of some of its more ancient contents so they can be replaced with modern furniture. Netta therefore acquires, at no cost, two beds, a huge wardrobe, a chest of drawers, a dresser and numerous pieces of kitchen equipment. The next day Finlay hitches the horse to the wagon and rides with Netta to pick up the furniture, the size of the articles necessitating three trips to the farmhouse. Netta is anxious that the wardrobe may be too tall but, although it takes persuasion and a bit of brute force, it is eventually in place in what will be her mother's bedroom.

Prior to them moving in, Kenneth delivers a pile of logs and a bag of kindlers and Netta sets a fire each day in the living room and also keeps a fire burning in the kitchen range. The result is a marked reduction in the dampness and an aroma of pine that replaces the former odour of neglect in the small rooms. She also washes and hangs out to dry the curtains that have been left at the windows, the weather remaining blustery but snow-free while the improvements are underway. Now, with the furniture in place, she stands back and gazes at the transformation with a smile of satisfaction. She cannot wait to show her mother the result. With a donation of bedding and towels from Kenneth and Elizabeth and a generous supply of food, which Netta insists that she will repay in work, there is nothing to stop them from moving in. Except her mother's fear.

Ellen seems reluctant to leave Margaret's small cottage in the village. It being the first stopping place after their long journey back to her homeland, she is finding it hard to leave a person she loves and whom she has recently found again, to start afresh in new surroundings. It is Kenneth who makes up her mind, arriving after breakfast in his car and escorting her into the seat next to the driver as though she is royalty. Netta takes her place in the back seat and they drive sedately and in silence through the valley to their destination.

Netta watches as Ellen enters the cottage and is gratified by the look of pleasure on her mother's face. She steps over to her and puts an arm round her shoulders.

'We will be happy here, will we not, Mutti? This will be a new start for us.'

Ellen turns to her daughter. Her eyes brim with tears. 'Thank you, Netta,' she says. 'I wouldnae be able to face living without you by my side. You are the best daughter anyone could hope for. We will make a good home for ourselves here.'

★　★　★

40

An invitation comes from Kenneth and Elizabeth to join them for Hogmanay. Ellen would rather stay at home. She recognises, however, the need for her daughter to get to know their neighbours, few and scattered though they are, so agrees to attend. Margaret too is invited, as are Finlay and two farming families from nearer the village.

It has turned colder now and overnight there has been a sharp frost. Ellen and Netta set off to walk to the farm, having assured Kenneth the day before that this is what they prefer to do. The sky is cloudless but in these short days not long past the winter solstice, the sun fails to rise above the steep hills on their southern side. The base of the valley remains in shadow throughout the hours of daylight, bare branches of trees and grassy banks on the valley floor sparkling with frost although it is early afternoon. Against the whiteness, the sheep appear bedraggled and dirty. They look up as the women's approach disturbs their feeding, and scatter haphazardly at their approaching steps.

Finlay opens the door of the farmhouse.

'Come in out of the cold,' he begins. 'I saw you walking along the road. How are you settling in? Is the cottage drier now? Are you finding it lonely, so far away from us?'

Ellen steps into the hallway. Netta, uncertain which question to answer first, follows her.

'We're fine, thank you, Finlay. The cottage will suit us very well, I am sure. We only moved in two days ago, remember, so there has been no time to feel lonely.' They follow the shepherd through into the living room where a cheerful fire is lighting

41

the faces of the guests. Margaret is already there and smiles a welcome, clearing a space on the sofa for Ellen to join her.

'Let me introduce you to everyone.' Kenneth comes over to them. 'This is Angus and Moira Scott from Netheredge Farm and here, Billy and Isobel Black from Five Trees Farm. Both farms are our nearest neighbours. And here — this is our new shepherd, Andrew Cameron.'

Netta turns in surprise to see the man standing at the back of the room behind the sofa. He is tall, over six feet, and, like the other farm workers, tanned from a life lived at the mercy of the elements. His ginger hair, worn longer than is fashionable, falls over pale blue eyes, beneath which is a serious face that breaks into a smile as he nods to Netta.

'How're you doing?' he says and holds out a hand. 'Why are you looking so surprised? Have we met before?'

'No.' Netta feels a blush coming to her cheeks. 'We came only a few days ago. No, I thought Finlay said you were coming for lambing. I know nothing about lambing but is it not a bit early?'

The assembled company laugh at her comment. 'Yes,' says Kenneth. 'It's gey early. The sheep don't lamb until April in these parts. Andrew's not moved in yet. We've invited him over to meet everyone.'

'Where are you working now?' asks Angus Scott.

'Over west at the moment.'

'So what has decided you to move this way?' the farmer asks.

'Och, the farm hasnae been doing too well

42

— no' managed to increase production as the government wanted farms to do.' He shrugs. 'It's tenanted and the farmer is older and no' so well. He was threatened with losing his living before the end of the war but now he's decided to give up the tenancy anyway. I've been selling his ewes on so they're settled in new homes before lambing. I'll hopefully be moving over here in a few weeks, once I've made sure my boss is as happy with the situation as he can be. It'll be a wrench for him giving up a lifetime's work. As for me, I've been a travelling shepherd for a while and I fancied a change of scenery.'

'So you're staying with Kenneth for a day or two?'

'Andrew's staying with me,' Finlay says, stepping forward. 'We've been out on the hill together. I've been showing him the territory. And I'll say this for him: Andrew's a good walker. I've been struggling to keep up with him.'

'And do you like what you've seen?' Angus Scott continues.

Andrew looks round at the group, his eyes resting momentarily on Netta before replying. 'Aye. I like it very much. It's very different from where I am now but I was ready for a change.'

Now that everyone has arrived, Elizabeth calls them to the table and begins to serve the meal. Netta looks in consternation at the plate of food she is handed.

'What is this?' she says. 'I do not think I have tasted this before.'

'Try it,' says her mother. 'It's haggis. It is a speciality in Scotland.'

'Where have you been all these years that you havenae tasted haggis before?' asks Isobel Black. 'I thought Kenneth said that your mother used to live on this farm.'

'And so she did,' Kenneth says hastily, 'but that was many years ago. I doubt Netta will remember that time.'

'Well, I hope you have been somewhere well away from the effects of the wretched war,' Isobel continues. 'Such a time we have had of it — shortages of this and that, orders from government to work harder than we are already doing, nasty Germans dropping bombs on nearby Glasgow. Tell me, my dear, where have you been?'

'Germany,' replies Netta.

There is an uncomfortable silence around the table. Everyone stares at Netta, one or two seeming to think that it is some kind of a sick joke. But Netta is not laughing and neither is her mother.

'Ah!' says Isobel at last. 'I had no idea. How dreadful for you.'

'It was my decision to go,' says Ellen with effort. 'Things were different then. Everyone got on well together . . . or so we thought.'

'Tasty haggis, this,' Billy Black says, scooping another forkful off his plate. 'I don't suppose you've any left over. I wouldnae like to see it fed to the chickens.'

He holds the plate out to Elizabeth, laughing, and the rest of the guests are quick to join in.

★ ★ ★

44

'I'm sorry, my dears. Isobel Black can always be relied upon to put her foot in it,' Kenneth says, as he drives Ellen and her daughter back to their cottage later in the day.

'Don't apologise, Kenneth,' says Netta. 'People are bound to be curious. We turn up out of the blue after years away. It is to be expected, is it not, Mutti?'

'Aye, it will be some time before people get used to us being around. We will just have to put up with it.'

'It *will* take time,' Netta says when Kenneth has driven away and the two women are hanging up their coats and preparing to go to bed. 'People may talk about us for a while but it will die down, you wait and see.'

'I do hope so. I want you to settle and make a life for yourself here, and it won't be easy if folk are gossiping behind our backs.'

'Well, we must show them we are made of stern stuff,' replies Netta.

'Isn't that what you used to say? And meanwhile I will start working for Elizabeth. She and Kenneth at least are very accepting and helpful. So let us sleep for what is left of the night, and the morning will be the beginning of a new year and the beginning of a better life for us.'

5
New Year

January 1946

Netta hastily throws a scarf around her shoulders.
She is only just dressed and has been cleaning out
the dying embers from the kitchen stove, when
the knock comes at the door. Who can it be at this
early hour? She grabs the lamp and holds it high
as she swings the door open.

It is Andrew Cameron who looms out of the
greyness of early dawn. In his hand he is carrying
two lumps of coal and a half bottle of whisky. She
stares at him, perplexed, in consternation as he
steps over the threshold.

'A Happy New Year to you both,' he says with a
smile. Netta continues to stare at him. He laughs.
'I see you don't know this wee custom that we
have in Scotland.'

'Ah, we have a first-footer,' exclaims Ellen,
stepping into the kitchen. She is smiling broadly.
'I had forgotten about first-footing. We used to
have it on the farm when I was a wee girl. And
what's more, it is a tall, handsome stranger, if not
particularly dark — and not so much a stranger,
seeing as we met last night. Won't you come in
and have some breakfast now that you are here?'

Andrew glances over his shoulder towards the
farm. 'Well, Finlay is expecting me back to go a

last walk with him before I leave, so I had better not stop. I have to say though that you ladies are about bright and early considering what a late night it was.'

'I am starting work this morning for Elizabeth,' replies Netta, 'so I myself am hurrying.'

'In that case, may I escort you to the farmhouse?' Andrew makes a theatrical bow.

'I am more than capable of making my own way but, yes, it would be good to have your company.'

* * *

They walk together as the sky brightens and the undersides of the clouds begin to turn pink. By the time they reach the farm, the sunlight has touched the tops of the hills and is oozing down their sides like liquid honey. Netta watches, fascinated. She takes a deep breath of satisfaction. It feels good to have a job to go to. All week she has been busy making their cottage as clean and cosy as possible and, although it will need to be decorated when the weather improves, it is time to do regular work that will give them an income. She dislikes being beholden and intends to pay Kenneth and Elizabeth for the food they have supplied and then discuss the amount of rent with the farmer in whose cottage they are staying.

'So you will be helping at the farm permanently?' says Andrew, after the silence has lasted several minutes.

'I hope so — that is, if I do a good enough job. I have always been used to housework, so it will not be hard for me. And, anyway, I need to make

47

a living and there is not much else for which I am qualified.'

★　★　★

Elizabeth will not hear of payment for the food and, to Netta's dismay, the farmer's wife takes her along to the spare room that afternoon, where piles of clothes are laid out on one of the beds.

'I need you to look through these,' she says, pointing to the assortment of dresses, skirts, jumpers and outdoor coats. 'I have far more here than I will ever wear. Kenneth has said more times than I can remember that I need to clear out the cupboards. I'm afraid some of them are a bit old-fashioned, even for your mother, but I know how little you have brought with you, and these at least will keep you warm until your circumstances improve.'

Netta, stoical though she is, feels herself close to tears. 'You are so kind to us. How can I ever repay you?'

'It is payment enough to have you back with us. Your mother was always a delight to have around and it is so good that you are both here now.'

'Well, I am very grateful. I will take just a few things today and maybe some more tomorrow. It is true that we arrived with almost nothing.'

'Kenneth will take you back to the cottage to save you carrying things.'

'No, I wish to walk,' Netta replies adamantly. 'I must begin to be independent.'

'I think you already are, my dear, but do as you wish.'

48

Netta chooses two warm coats, one for her and one for her mother, and a selection of jumpers. She is thinking of the early months of the year in the country in which she grew up and remembers the snow and icy conditions. They need to be prepared for the same here. After all, she now knows of her father's demise in the deep snow that followed the ending of the Great War.

As she makes her way back in the gathering dusk, she is dimly aware of two figures coming down off the hill to her right. It is Finlay and the new shepherd.

'Good to see you again,' says Finlay. 'After the excesses of last night, I thought maybe you would be nursing a sore head.'

'I think it was not me who drank to excess,' Netta replies with a half-smile. 'And anyway, I have started working for Elizabeth, so I was at the farm early this morning, as Mr Cameron will tell you, to clear up the remains of the excess!'

'So you will be helping at the farm. Good. Then we can rely on the good hot dinners to continue into the future!'

Andrew is silent during this exchange of conversation.

Netta turns to the younger shepherd. 'And you are still here, Mr Cameron. Will your sheep not be missing you?'

'I return tomorrow. There are no trains on New Year's Day. Another of our quaint Scottish customs. And please call me Andrew.'

6
Stepmother

February 1946

'I can't believe how you've transformed this damp empty building into such a cosy cottage — and in only a few weeks.'

Margaret has been collected by Finlay from her house in the village and he will return for her when he has finished his work and before darkness falls. She looks around in admiration. 'It's a while since anyone lived here.'

It was 1919 when I married your father and moved out of my old farmhouse that's now at the bottom of the reservoir. The Steeles were in this cottage then — Ronnie and Elspeth. She died around the time this last war started and him not long after. Devoted to one another they were. I don't think he wanted to go on after he had lost her.'

Margaret shakes her head to dispel any gloomy thoughts, takes a seat to the side of the stove and looks at Ellen, who is putting cups and saucers onto a tray and finding something delicious in a nearby cake tin.

'It's so good to have you back in the valley,' she goes on. 'When you left to go to Germany, I didnae think I'd ever see you again. I missed you a lot — and wee Netta.'

50

'It was only because you married Father that I felt able to go. I could nae have gone and left him on his own.' There is a long pause. 'I was away a long time but, even so, I expected everything to be as I had left it when I came back. In the later years, I was nae able to contact him but I still assumed he would be here just the same when I returned. Isn't that ridiculous?' She pours the tea and sets the tray on a table between them.

Margaret smiles, her thoughts travelling back through the years. 'We were childhood sweethearts, you know, but then we grew up and fell in love with other people. He was gey fond of your mother. He missed her dreadfully when she died having you.' She sighs heavily. 'But when there's a wean to bring up, you have to get on and do what has to be done.'

'Aye,' says Ellen. 'I ken that.'

'You were very brave to go to Germany. What age were you — eighteen? And with wee Netta a toddler and baby Eva to look after.'

'It didnae feel particularly brave. I loved Josef and he loved me. We wanted to be together. That was all I cared about.'

'How did you manage that journey all alone? Were the Germans no'difficult to get on with, after all those years of fighting?'

'I think they were as tired of fighting as our men — those that were left.

Yes, it was a hard journey with two young daughters and days and days of travelling. Freiburg is in the very south of Germany, ken. But it helped a lot having Netta and Eva with me. A wean's a wean, whatever country you might be in and people played with them as they would their own. I wrote the name 'Freiburg' on a piece of paper, and showed that to people so they knew where we were going. That way maybe it wasnae so obvious that I was British, as I didnae have to try and talk. That's what I thought anyway.' Ellen shuts her eyes. 'Looking back on it now, it seems a very selfish thing to do, leaving like that. Father must have been worried sick about me. But I remember thinking at the time that now he had you, he wouldnae need me so much — and I knew that Josef needed me.' She looks at Margaret. 'I don't like to think about that journey now but at the time all I could think of was seeing Josef again. And it was worth it!'

'Did you have somewhere to live when you arrived?'

'Yes, he rented a wee house in Freiburg. It's a very beautiful city, though it was damaged during this war, our house included. The buildings are very old in the city. Down the sides of the streets run wee streams, *Bächle*, in channels cut into the road. When we were walking along the street, we could hear them tinkling a tune, as though they were welcoming us. There is a saying that if a man falls into a *Bächle* he will marry a woman from Freiburg. It must be true the other way round because I fell into one the first time I went for a walk and I married a man from Freiburg!' She giggles and Margaret can see an echo of the girl that Ellen used to be.

Ellen looks into the glowing coals of the stove. 'We were very happy there for a long time . . . and then things slowly went wrong.'

'You mean you and Josef?'

'No, not me and Josef. Everything around us. We weren't allowed to live our lives.'

'And then he became ill?'

'Yes.' Ellen hesitates. 'And then he died. You know how bad he always was with his chest. I'm sorry, Margaret. I don't really want to talk about this anymore. You see, it seems as though everyone who has ever been connected with me dies — my mother first, then Tom, my first husband, then . . . well, then Josef, and now I arrive back to find my father is no longer here.'

'Yes, my dear, but he was old. It is to be expected when we get old. You have Netta and I can see that she cares very much for you. But what about young —'

'Sometimes I think that if it wasnae for Netta, I wouldnae be here,' Ellen interrupts. 'Anyway, like I say, I would rather not talk about it anymore. Let me show you around the cottage so you can see what we — or should I say Netta — has done with it.'

Ellen takes her stepmother into each room, describing what changes have been made to rid the house of its uncared-for facade. She pushes open the back door with difficulty, for the damp has caused the wood to swell and stick, and they look round the barren garden, discussing the possibility of finding plants that might grow in such a windswept position. In the distance they can see the reservoir embankment. Ellen stands gazing at it, leaving Margaret to wander round the decaying vegetation in an attempt to identify the various bedraggled bushes. She is only roused from her contemplation by Margaret's gentle touch on her arm.

The short day is already beginning to fade and dusk is blurring the edges of the rounded hills that enclose the valley. They retreat indoors and Ellen puts a match to the hurricane lamp. In the distance she can see the lights of a car. She watches as it slowly draws near to the cottage along the stretch of road, the building of which contributed to the ill health of her Josef all those years ago.

'Do you remember when the POWs were here, Margaret — the months they took building that road?' Ellen nods in the direction of the approaching car. 'My Josef started building that with the rest of them and then he was taken ill and I looked after him. I should be glad. It meant that for all those weeks he belonged to me and no-one else. If nothing else, coming back here reminds me of that one spark of happiness in a difficult time.'

The car draws up and stops. It is Finlay, come to collect Margaret for home. Netta too steps from the vehicle and opens the front door. 'Your chariot awaits, Granny Margaret,' she says, helping her mother's visitor into her coat.

'Come again soon,' Ellen says, hugging her. Margaret climbs into the pickup and it sets off. She waves to mother and daughter, arms around each other as they return her wave, backlit by the soft light of the living room.

* * *

Netta is woken by the sound of her mother moving around in the living room. She lies in bed, reluctant to get up and put her feet to the cold floor.

She will wait a few more minutes before beginning her day. Maybe her mother will bring her in a cup of tea. But no tea arrives and, as Netta lies there, she hears the door of the cottage open and quietly close again. Netta sits up and puts a match to the candle on her bedside table. The light flares and illuminates the clock. It is four-fifteen. What can her mother be doing?

Netta tugs on her dressing gown and goes through into the living room. There is no sign of her mother. Checking in her mother's bedroom and finding it empty, she hurries to the door, noticing as she does so that Ellen's coat and boots are missing. Worried now, she throws open the door and peers out. The night is dark with no hint of moon. She takes a few steps, casting her eyes in the direction of the farm, but cannot see her mother. Turning, she sees a wavering light in the distance. It must be Ellen and she must be making for the reservoir.

Netta runs into the cottage, pulls on the clothes that she had left in readiness for the day ahead and snatches her coat from the peg. After stepping into her boots, she slams the door behind her and chases after her mother. She has no lantern with her but her eyes gradually acclimatise to the darkness. At first she cannot see where her mother has gone but as she chases along the path, she again sees the light. Ellen is at the base of the embankment now, picking her way across the valley floor.

The light wavers and disappears. Netta calls her name but there is no reply. She calls again, louder this time, and the next moment sees the lamp held high and the side of Ellen's face lit up in its glow.

'Mutti, what on earth are you doing? It's the middle of the night. You shouldn't be out here. You could have fallen, broken your leg, anything! What do you think you are doing?'

'I was remembering that time. I had to come and see the place again.'

'But what place? There is nothing here, only a broken-down sheep shelter.'

'Here. This place.' Ellen's eyes are wild. 'This was where Josef found you after you had gone missing from your pram. But of course you will not remember.'

'No, Mutti. I don't remember. Come and sit on these stones and tell me.' Netta takes the lamp from her mother and balances it on the ground. Then she sits next to her mother and puts an arm around her shoulders. 'Tell me,' she says again.

Ellen begins slowly. 'We came to see Margaret. She was living on her farm then, where the reservoir is now. It was the day that there was a landslide. It had been raining a lot, you see. On our way back, the embankment gave way. It was a sea of mud. I left you in the pram and ran to help and when I got back, you weren't there. The men helped me look. I was frantic. The river you see . . . it was very high after all that rain.

'It was Josef who found you here, in the stell. You were fast asleep on the grass. Everyone was rushing around and there you were, asleep.' Ellen's voice rises in a hysterical laugh before she bursts

56

into tears, which rack her body. Netta holds her in silence until the sobbing diminishes.

'But why would you want to come out and see this place again and why at this time of night, Mutti? Why not wait until daylight?'

'Margaret and I were talking about Josef today. I wanted to feel him near me again. I thought I might find him here.' She starts to cry again. 'You see, that day I hadn't seen him for a long time. I had not been well and had been staying indoors. I missed him and when we met, he told me that he had missed me too. It was a day that was both awful and wonderful. I wanted to feel it again.'

'Mutti, you must promise me not to do anything like this again. If you do want to chase after a special memory, then tell me and I will come with you, although I would rather it wasn't in the middle of the night.' Netta smiles at her mother and Ellen chokes on a laugh in reply.

'I'm sorry, Netta. It was stupid of me. I thought that coming back here might bring him close again.' She shakes her head. 'It doesn't seem to work. Nothing works. Don't worry. I won't do it again.'

Netta picks up the lamp, takes her mother's arm and together they stumble across the tussocky grass towards the path and their new home.

7
Shepherd

March 1946

Netta is not long in bringing the neglected farm-house into some kind of order. Within a month carpets are swept, floors mopped, papers gathered into tidy piles, journals arranged on bookshelves, china washed and replaced shining in the cabinets. Kitchen utensils are scrubbed, brasses polished and silverware treated until it sparkles. Elizabeth entreats her to stop, have a cup of tea, put her feet up for a break, but she will not, determined to reimburse the farmer's wife for the generosity lavished on her and her mother during the early weeks of their stay. It is only when the job is completed to her satisfaction that she feels able to relax a little.

It has snowed during the early weeks of the new year but now it is an exceptionally mild March day. Netta wanders outside after clearing up the dinner dishes. Finlay is in the barn examining a group of ewes who will soon lamb. Netta leans on the gate, watching him. He looks up at her, rests a hand on the gatepost and heaves himself up with a grimace. His florid face breaks into a grin.

'Our next group of mothers-to-be,' he says. 'It should be a good lambing this year unless the weather changes. Open the gate for me, hen, so they can get back to the hill.'

Netta swings the gate wide and the sheep skitter out of the pen and across the barn to the open air. 'Will they not get lost?' she says, her brow creasing.

'No, hen. They're born and bred on the hill and they can find their own way back, nae problem.' Finlay looks at her closely. 'I suppose you won't remember when you stayed here as a wean?'

'I left when I was only four. I do not remember anything about the sheep, only that they were everywhere. I don't remember much about Scotland, just small things, like a picnic with my mother and playing with my grandfather.'

Kenneth comes into the barn. 'How are they looking, Finlay?'

'Good, boss. I was telling young Netta here, they should make a good lambing.'

★ ★ ★

Andrew lifts his hand in farewell to his cousin Hughie and watches the pickup as it turns onto the single-track road and disappears into the distance. Beneath him the waters of the loch boil as *The North Argyll* eases away from the shore to cross Loch Linnhe at the Corran Narrows. It is a journey of minutes but its short passage marks the beginning of a new episode in the shepherd's life, one that he is anticipating with pleasure. He enjoys Hughie's company but each visit serves to reinforce the fact that there is no place for him on the family farm.

Once off the ferry, he turns north and begins to

walk towards Fort William, sticking out his thumb whenever he hears a vehicle approaching.

He doesn't have long to wait before one slows down and a voice calls,

'Where to, Andrew?'

'Ach, Hamish. Good to see you. Are you going to Fort William?'

'Where else would I be going along this road, pal? Put your bag in the back and sit in.' The farmer indicates the passenger seat next to him.

'Where are you off to then?' he asks as the truck pulls out of the lay-by.

'Quite a way from here. Lanarkshire, in fact. There's a shepherding job vacant and I thought I'd see what it's like working in the southern hills for a change.'

'Had enough of these parts, have you?'

'Old Willie Fergus McClean over at Drimnin where I've been working, he's decided to retire, so I want to try my hand somewhere else. I've been down the once to meet the farmer and see the set-up. It's no' so different from here in that there's a lot of land and very few people to tend to it. Suits me that way.'

'It amazes me how you spent all that time in Glasgow and still prefer the peace and quiet. It's a wee bit different in the big city, I should imagine. Too many people and not enough space for them all. Not at all to your taste, I would have thought.'

'Aye, it's crowded right enough and plenty of folk with no' enough food in their bellies.' Andrew casts his eyes over the grey water of the loch to his left. 'I shall miss all this,' he sighs, indicating the

60

water and the craggy hills beyond. 'But it's beautiful where I'm going. Miles of hillside to walk every day. Nae chance of sitting with my feet up!'

'And the girls down there, are they as bonny as round these parts?'

Andrew laughs but a picture of one of the guests at the Hogmanay party comes suddenly to mind. 'The only girls I'll be concerned about when I get there are the thousand or so soon to give birth!' he replies with a grin.

The truck pulls in at the station and the shepherd heaves out his bag from behind the seat. 'Thanks for the ride, Hamish. I appreciate it.'

'Nae problem, pal. Enjoy your stay. I'll see you when you get homesick.'

Andrew smiles and slams the door. He glances at the station clock. It is showing five to ten. Good! Just time to get a cup of tea in the station café and then he'll be on his way.

* * *

The sun has set by the time Andrew steps off the train, bright golden edges to the undersides of the western clouds all that is left of the glorious picture that he has been enjoying from the carriage window. He hopes it is a good omen for this next phase of his life. From what he had gathered during his last visit, it's more often raining!

Slinging his bag over a shoulder, he climbs the steep flight of steps out of the station. The approach of spring means that there is still enough light for him to see his path, though he must hurry if he is to reach the farm before night envelops him

61

completely. It feels good to be released from the confines of the carriage and he strides out along the narrow road that takes him into the valley. From the river rises the incessant piping of oystercatchers, newly arrived from their wintering grounds on the coast. On the flat land of the valley bottom and on the sides of the hills into the distance he can make out the pale shapes of the sheep, some still having their last mouthfuls of grass before settling down to sleep.

Were it not for the light from the farmhouse guiding him the last mile and a half, he might have missed his turning altogether and gone deeper into the valley, perhaps ending up at the cottage he had last visited on New Year's Day. He thinks of the two women who live there, the quiet older woman who says little but appears to have suffered much, and her daughter, Netta. The memory of how self-contained she was, how abrupt, how unwilling to accept even a modicum of courtesy makes him smile. But his smile fades as he remembers with admiration and empathy how protective she was towards her mother.

'Andrew! It's good to see you.' Kenneth Douglas extends a hand to the shepherd. 'Come away in. We had assumed you had put off your arrival until tomorrow, with the hour getting so late. Everything is ready for you though. But we could have met you at the station if we had known.'

'Och, I needed to stretch my legs and get used to these hills I'll be climbing tomorrow.'

'Aye, Finlay's looking forward to you joining him. The ewes are doing well with this good winter we've had. There'll be plenty of work to be done in a few weeks and all hands needed on deck to do it. I'll take you straight round to your cottage. Netta's been busy making it as comfortable as she can. In fact, it's true to say that she's turning into an indispensable member of the team,' Kenneth concludes, nodding emphatically.

★ ★ ★

The cottage is indeed cosy — much more so than when he had seen it on his last visit, when it was clean but bare. A fire has been laid, a vase of snow-drops placed on the table and, in the kitchen, there are enough supplies to keep him going for several days without needing to venture out to wherever the nearest shop is to be found.

'I think you'll find you have everything you need.' Kenneth Douglas looks round with satis-faction. 'Netta's proving a real godsend, so she is, with my Elizabeth no' able to do so much around the place. She'll be round in the morning, will Netta, to check on you,' the farmer adds mis-chievously.

'You'll have a daily supply of milk,' he contin-ues. 'We make butter when there's milk to spare and you'll get some eggs now the hens are coming back into lay.'

The door opens and it is Finlay.

'Good to see you, pal.' He goes up to Andrew and claps him on the back.

'I've something to eat waiting for you next door. You must be starving.'

'That's very good of you.'

'Not my doing, pal. It was Netta. She prepared

a mutton stew earlier on.

It's keeping warm in the range just now.'

'Right then. I am, as you say, really hungry. Lead the way.'

'We're away off to the top of the hill in the morning to check on the ewes,' Finlay tells Kenneth, as they leave the cottage. 'We'll start early, see if we can get round all of them during the day. As much as anything it will give Andrew a feel for the land.'

'Good. Let me know if there are any problems. I'll see you lads sometime tomorrow then.' The elderly farmer turns down the track away from the cottages to return to the farmhouse.

'And now to eat. You'll need all the energy you can summon for tomorrow morning's stroll.'

★ ★ ★

Andrew sleeps well. He is up and dressed and has had breakfast by six o'clock and Finlay opens his front door to find him sitting on the low wall in front of the cottage. Dawn is breaking and, in the south-east, the sky is brightening to yellow.

'You're an even earlier riser than me,' Finlay says, joining him at the wall. His border collie Jill stays close at his heels. Andrew holds out his hand and lets the bitch familiarise herself with his scent.

'A fine dog you have. Is she well-behaved?'

'Aye, as fine a lass as you'll find. She's been with me since she was a puppy and learned the job with no problem at all. She's all the woman I need!'

Andrew chuckles and the two men set off along the track that runs behind the cottages and joins

64

another that ascends the hill steeply. It's a steady climb and they reach the top just as the sun climbs above the top of the hills on the other side of the valley and bathes them in golden light. They stand to catch their breath and Andrew shades his eyes and looks eastward down the valley to where the reservoir can be seen sparkling in the new day.

'My word! That's a sight to behold. What an amazing view from up here.' He turns to look north and sees row on row of hills greying into the distance.

'It's not often that you get a sight like this,' Finlay says. 'More often it's raining or too covered in mist to see clearly. Must be a sign that you've come to the right place.'

'Well, I had my doubts about leaving the coast but this view is as good as any,' Andrew says, as they start off along the ridge that leads towards the reservoir. 'So how many sheep does Kenneth keep here?'

'There's about eleven hundred ewes, and thirty tups. If it's a good lambing there should be around one thousand five hundred lambs. Enough to keep us busy for a few weeks! What about yourself? What numbers are you used to?'

'Not quite so many ewes as that; just under a thousand ewes and their lambs. It's warmer on the coast of course, though just as much rain, right enough. The last farmer I worked for had a couple of cows, just for the milk and butter. I see there's a few more than that here.'

'Aye, just half a dozen — for the milk and butter, as you say. You'll find you get a supply of both, perks of the job, and eggs as well, fresh ones now the chickens are laying again. I reckon Elizabeth is glad of help with all that, now her eyesight's no' so good and she's not able to do the work she once did.'

'What about crops? There's not a lot of room to grow much.'

'Kenneth uses every bit of land he can. As you can see, most of it's not flat enough. He grows enough neeps and tatties, carrots too, to feed us all and enough turnips left over for the cattle. The rest of the land is for hay and corn, as much as he can grow, to feed the animals. We harvest in September onwards and hopefully there's enough to see them through the winter months.'

The track rises and falls, accommodating burns that have carved deep crevices into the upland slopes. Much of the hillside is bare but here and there is the occasional rounded stell, in which the sheep can shelter from the worst of the weather. As they approach the reservoir Andrew can see the cottage in which Ellen and Netta have made their home. Above the rough grass outside, washing is waving a welcome.

'How are they settling in?' Andrew indicates the cottage.

'Very well, I think,' says Finlay. 'I don't see much of the mother, mind. She keeps herself to herself. But Netta, she's always around the place. A great help to Elizabeth Douglas, she's turning out to be. But it's not just that — she's taking an interest in what goes on around the farm. She's asked Kenneth if she can come and watch the lambing. It's all new to her, ken. She was born here but they left while she was still a wean. She told me she grew up in a city called Freiburg. A beautiful place by all accounts but not a sheep to be seen.'

'She's returned to her roots, then,' Andrew says, nodding slowly. 'Maybe farming's in her blood.'

'This is the end of Kenneth's land,' Finlay says, coming to a halt. 'This line of trees up ahead marks the boundary. We'll stop here and have our piece and then make our way into the valley and up the other side. That's his sheep grazing those hills. That'll mean we'll do a circuit of all his land and you'll know which sheep are his and which ones not. At least that's the way it's meant to work but, you know how it is, there's always a bit of crossover.' Andrew smiles in agreement and they settle themselves on some large stones near the copse. Finlay delves into his knapsack for the packet of sandwiches they have been given for their lunch.

'Another thing Netta does well!' Finlay offers Andrew a sandwich.

'An indispensable lass indeed!' Andrew pours two cups of tea from the thermos flask and hands one to Finlay in exchange for the sandwich. They sit in silence looking eastward over the unmoving waters, in which the hills are mirrored to perfection. At last Finlay sighs and eases himself up from the slab of rock on which they have been sitting.

'We had better start walking again, pal.' He indicates the western end of the valley. 'If I'm not mistaken, the weather's about to show you its more normal behaviour. If we don't start off now, we're likely to get very wet. At least you've had a taste of what it looks like when the sun shines! Best not to forget it. There'll be little enough time to sit contemplating the scenery when lambing starts.'

* * *

A couple of hours later the two men are standing in slanting rain at the top of the hill on the opposite side of the valley from the farm. At this distance it has the appearance of a doll's house. The in-by to one side of it is filled with sheep and Andrew can just make out two figures on the perimeter of the field. As they descend the hill, the figures become clearer and Andrew can see that they are the farmer and Netta Fairclough.

'There's Netta learning the job,' Finlay remarks. 'She's usually to be found around the sheep when her work in the farmhouse is done. Though I don't think you've any reason to be worried yet,' he adds laughing.

'Och, I'm no' worried,' Andrew replies softly. 'She'll likely keep me on my toes and not let me get away with anything, if present showing is anything to go by.'

* * *

Andrew walks the hill regularly with Finlay, sometimes together, sometimes splitting the job between them to allow time for the other farm jobs that need to be done. The weather remains overcast but warm, and the two men consider that lambing will be as comfortable as lambing can be if the present conditions persist.

Kenneth comes out of the big barn, Netta by

68

his side, as the two shepherds descend together to the farm. He sees them approaching and waves. Finlay goes over to join him.

'Well, boss, I've walked Andrew round the flock so many times now, he knows where they all are. There's nothing to do but keep an eye on them and wait for the lambs to start arriving. Would you mind if I take the pickup and drive into Lanark. I've had word that my elderly uncle's no' so well and I'd like to see him. I ken he's not long for this world.'

'By all means, Finlay. In fact, if you're going that way, would you call in at the market? I was planning to go myself. We need to get well stocked up on supplies: some more serum for lamb dysentery, and a good amount of Cooper's fly dip.'

'And we need more tubs of cobalt and copper lick,' Finlay adds. 'They're running low. I better get moving straightaway then, or market will be closed.' He walks briskly back to where Andrew is standing surveying the sheep in the nearby field. 'Will you check on those sheep before you finish for the night?' he asks the younger shepherd, indicating the field with a nod of his head. 'Make sure they're all comfortable. I've a couple of errands to do in Lanark.'

'Nae problem. We'll meet again in the morning.'

Andrew approaches Kenneth and Netta who have resumed their previous conversation. Kenneth is talking about the cows and the need for their twice daily milking. So intent is Netta on listening to what the farmer is saying that she doesn't notice Andrew's approach and jumps

69

when he suddenly appears at Kenneth's side.

'I'm sorry, I didn't mean to startle you.' Andrew smiles at Netta before turning to the farmer. 'I've come to check over the ewes.'

'Have you had much experience of milking?' Kenneth asks the shepherd, indicating the cows in the nearby field.

'Not on a large scale, but the farmer I was with kept a couple for milking and he left those for me to deal with.'

'Perhaps you'd like to take that on here. I've been doing it but it seems a gey long way down to that milking stool now and even further to get up again. I was thinking Netta here might like to learn the job. The animals often respond better to a woman's touch, I've found.'

'No problem. I'll start in the morning. Will you be here early, Netta? We can make a start together if you are.'

'Yes, I will be here early. I will enjoy learning that.'

'Good. I'll get on and check these ladies then. Do you want to lend a hand, Netta?'

'Er, I would, but my mother has been alone for several hours. I need to go back and make sure that she is well.'

'Of course. And I won't ask you if you need an escort home!'

Netta smiles in spite of her best efforts not to do so, nods to the two men and sets off along the narrow track that leads to the road. Andrew shrugs his shoulders. 'She's very protective of her mother,' he comments, as he releases the catch on the gate and enters the field.

70

'Aye,' Kenneth says. 'But she's all Netta has ... and Netta is all that Ellen has. So it's hardly surprising. They're very protective of one another.'

8

Recruits

April 1946

Finlay has spent two hours with his Uncle Willie and, driving home afterwards, he doesn't think it likely that he will see his uncle alive again. The oldest of three brothers, he has outlived them all. Finlay's father, James, was a good ten years younger than Willie, and Willie had always taken it upon himself to look after James. Even so, James had succumbed to the bullets of the aggressor on the battlefield of the Somme. Willie, scarred as he was by the action he had seen in that dreadful war, nevertheless returned and began to watch over the son as he had once done the father.

Finlay wipes a tear from his eye and reaches deep into a pocket for a handkerchief, taking his eyes momentarily from the road in front of him. And when he looks up again, there, not more than five yards in front, is a sheep. He brakes violently, pulling down hard on the steering wheel with his left hand. The pickup, slow to respond, hits the animal a glancing blow before skidding off the road, turning onto its side and sliding down an embankment to come to rest in a flurry of decaying vegetation. The sudden silence is broken only by the plaintive bleat of the dying ewe.

Andrew sits at the window, stirring his second mug of tea and reflecting that he and Finlay should be able to split the walking today, perhaps walk one side of the valley each, to make things a bit easier. He marvels that Finlay has done the job single-handedly for so long. It's obviously some time since Kenneth Douglas has been able to climb the hills. He is now confined to helping in the environs of the farm.

Andrew sees Netta crossing the river and making her way along the track to the farm. He glances at his watch. It's time they were starting work. The older shepherd is bound to make an appearance soon. Perhaps he and Netta will get on and milk the cows, by which time Finlay will be here to allocate their duties for the day. He puts down his mug on the windowsill and leaves the cottage. Netta looks up as the wind catches the door and slams it shut.

'Finlay's having a lie-in,' Andrew says by way of greeting. 'Must be all this fresh air and exercise.'

Netta smiles. 'It's certainly fresh today. Quite a struggle coming up the valley with the wind in my face.'

Andrew takes a peek at her glowing cheeks and windblown hair and considers saying how lovely she looks, but he guesses that such a comment would not be well received and instead turns and indicates the cows. 'We'll get on with the milking while we wait.'

'Good. I've been looking forward to this,' Netta responds eagerly. Andrew picks up a bucket and milking stool and she follows him into the barn. She watches as he lowers himself onto the stool, places the bucket beneath the cow, takes a damp cloth to clean the udders and finally begins to massage them gently and rhythmically. A steady stream of milk trills into the pail.

'Your turn now.' He staggers up off the stool. 'This is where shorter legs are an advantage.' He laughs. 'It's too far down for me on that stool.' They move on to the next cow and Netta copies what Andrew has done. It takes no longer than a minute or two for her to learn the amount of pressure necessary and soon a second bucket is filling with the creamy liquid. They take turns until the job is completed. 'They're contented ladies,' Andrew says, forking hay into the feeding troughs. 'It's not always so easy. You must have the magic touch!'

'There's still no sign of Finlay.' Netta glances again at the shepherd's cottage. 'Perhaps he was late getting back from Lanark, if he found his uncle poorly. I'll go and knock on his door. If he was late back, maybe he has overslept.'

In a couple of minutes she has returned. 'There is no answer. I don't like to go in.'

Andrew frowns. 'I will,' he says, straightening up.

The door is unlocked and he enters the cottage. Everything is neat. The fire has not been lit. The bedroom door is open and the bed made. Andrew frowns again, indecisive. He decides to call at the farmhouse where Kenneth, perhaps, has more information. As he is leaving, he notices a car approaching through the valley. He can see that it's not the pickup that Finlay took to drive to Lanark. Perhaps he had a breakdown and has had to borrow a car. But as it draws nearer, Andrew sees to his consternation that it's a police car. He glances at Netta. She has seen it too. They stand side by side watching the vehicle draw nearer.

'Kenneth Douglas?' enquires the officer as he steps from the car.

'I'm Andrew Cameron. I work here. Has something happened to Finlay?'

'I'm afraid so, sir. Could you take me to Mr Douglas? Is it him who's in charge?'

'Aye. He's the farmer. Come this way.' They set off quickly, Andrew and the police officer, with Netta hurrying to keep up, a step or two behind.

Kenneth has seen them and is coming down the path.

'I'm sorry, sir, but I've come to report an accident. The pickup registered to you has been found this morning. It's come off the road and was discovered lying in a ditch. It appears that the car hit a sheep on the road.

The driver must have swerved to avoid it and turned over.'

Netta gasps. 'What about Finlay? Is he all right?'

'The gentleman who was driving has been taken to the hospital, ma'am. He's taken a bad break in his arm as well as cuts and bruises. And he's been out there all night, so he's gey cold.'

Netta takes a deep breath. 'Thank goodness it is no worse.'

'Is he being kept in the hospital just now?' Kenneth asks.

'That I don't know, sir.'

'I need to go and see him for myself . . . but of course I can't,' the farmer says, clapping a hand to his forehead. 'I have no car.'

'I'll take you, sir. I'm going back to Lanark myself.'

'Thank you. That will be very helpful. Andrew, can I leave you in charge of the sheep? Netta, will you go and tell Elizabeth what has happened? Say I'll be back as soon as I can.'

'Yes, of course,' replies Netta, as Kenneth climbs into the passenger seat of the car. She and Andrew look at each other in shocked silence, before Netta makes her way up to the farmhouse and Andrew turns back to attend to the sheep.

* * *

It is late afternoon before Kenneth returns. Andrew has done the round of the hills on both sides of the valley. He is busily checking on the sheep in the field, all of whom seem to be unperturbed by their imminent motherhood. Kenneth climbs slowly out of the car and limps over to the younger man.

'Not an easy car to drive,' he says by way of explanation. 'I've borrowed it from a friend until mine is repaired . . . if it can be.' His face becomes serious. 'I've seen Finlay. He's in a bad way at the moment. They're keeping him in for a day or two. It turns out he took quite a bang on the head and they want to make sure he's all right. He cannae remember too well just now and he's suffering

76

with headaches. The doctor reckons they will settle, given time.'

'And the rest of him? How badly is he injured?'

'Cuts and bruises . . . and his arm is broken in two places. They are operating on it now to put the bones back into position. It means he'll be out of the reckoning for six weeks at least and maybe longer.'

'For the whole of lambing then,' Andrew says reflectively.

'Do you think you can manage? I'd willingly help but my days of bending down to lamb ewes are unfortunately over.'

'Well, Finlay has been the only shepherd here since Ellen's father died, so I should be able to step into his shoes for a few weeks, even if it is lambing time.'

Kenneth hesitates. 'There is one possibility that might make things a wee bit easier. Suppose we ask Netta to help you — cleaning the ewes, feeding the pet lambs, that kind of thing. She's obviously keen. You could teach her how to do the inoculations. You might even teach her to lamb. She's a clever woman and very determined if she sets her mind to something.'

'Aye.' Andrew smiles. 'I ken that.'

'Come up to the house with me and we'll tell the ladies about Finlay, and see what they think of my idea.'

* * *

Andrew watches Netta's face light up when they tell her what Kenneth has been suggesting. But then her smile fades as she looks at Elizabeth.

'But what about my job here? I don't think I can manage to do the housework and cooking *and* help with the sheep.'

'The housework will wait for a few weeks and I should be able to manage the cooking. Unless, that is . . . .' There is a pause.

'What? You mean,' Netta says with dawning realisation, 'you mean, unless my mother would like to help.'

* * *

Netta's eyes sparkle as she tells Andrew what had taken place when she arrived home.

'I explained to my mother how we would find it hard to manage. She was upset when I told her about Finlay. She says she would like to go and visit him while he is in hospital. I think she feels sorry for him living on his own, having to look after himself. And now this has happened, she sees it as a chance to help him.'

'So has she agreed to come and help while lambing is underway?'

'Better than that. She suggested that she comes to help long-term, either with the housework or with the cooking. And it will be very good for me to have her around and to know she is not on her own all day.'

'I can see I *will* need to be careful or I might find myself out of a job,' Andrew jokes.

'Not at all. I was not suggesting that.' Netta

looks embarrassed. 'Though I would like you to show me some parts of what you do. I do find it interesting.'

'And so I shall. But first we need to tell Kenneth and his wife that your mother has agreed to help and that she wishes to see Finlay. I suggest that once we have done that, we go and see how the ladies-in-waiting have survived the night.'

★ ★ ★

Finlay arrives home six days later in the ambulance. Ellen is waiting for him at the door to his cottage. He smiles at her and she takes hold of his good arm and steadies him as he limps indoors. A fire is lit in the grate and a kettle of water simmers on the hob.

'Sit down here and get warm,' Ellen says, guiding him to the armchair.

He looks at her gratefully.

'I didn't expect such a welcome.' He looks round the room. 'And everything is so neat and polished.'

'Are you ready for a cup of tea? The kettle's just come to the boil.'

'Aye. I would like that — as long as you have one as well.'

★ ★ ★

'That's it. Just support the lamb. Pull gently. Well done!' The newborn slithers out onto the straw. 'Now, clear the afterbirth from around its face and nose, so it can breathe. Encourage it to stand.' Netta follows Andrew's instructions, while the mother staggers to her feet and turns round to lick her lamb. Within a minute the newborn lamb is tottering drunkenly towards its mother and nuzzling in for a first feed. Netta looks up at Andrew and her face is radiant. He grins back and his heart unexpectedly misses a beat.

'Well done,' he says. 'You're a natural.'

It is the first ewe that Netta has lambed. In the last few days Andrew has shown Netta how to turn the ewes onto their haunches and clean the udders ready for the lambs to fasten on and feed without problems. He has taught her how to inoculate each lamb after birth to reduce the risk of dysentery. And she has watched him as many as two dozen times as he has guided the lamb out of its mother into the waiting adventure of the outside world. But this is the first time he has stood back and let her do the lambing.

Another two ewes are in labour now, one of them taking longer than Andrew thinks right. He goes over to her and sees that all four legs are beginning to protrude through the opening. Quickly he kneels in the straw and begins to push the legs back.

'She can't lamb like this,' he explains. 'There isn't room. The blood supply to the lamb will be cut off and it will die. We call it hanging.' Netta watches carefully as the shepherd pushes the legs back into the womb and then delves deeply to disentangle the front legs and bring them forward, together with the head. The birth progresses quickly now and the lamb is soon being tended by its mother.

The other labour seems to be going well.

'You attend to that one,' Andrew says to Netta and she goes over and waits by the sheep's side until she sees the legs and head protruding. Again she steadies the lamb as it is born and frees its nose and mouth. The sheep stands to lick her lamb but soon lies down again.

'It's tired her out, poor thing,' Netta says.

'It's not tiredness. See the ripples in her abdomen. There's another one in there. Just stay with her.' Netta waits but no lamb appears. She looks up uncertainly at Andrew who kneels down to examine her. 'The problem with twins is that one or both can get the wrong way round and then the birth doesn't progress.' There is silence while he tries to make sense of what he is feeling. 'Right! I've brought the legs round together so they're straight ahead. One was bent backwards causing an obstruction.' He pulls steadily and the second lamb is soon lying wetly in the straw. Netta cleans it and the lamb struggles to stand. Soon the twins are vying hungrily for nourishment from their mother.

'Will there be enough for both of them?'

'There should be. Sometimes I'll put a twin onto another mother that's lost its lamb. But at the moment we don't have any, thank goodness — though there are bound to be some in time.'

Andrew straightens up. 'I need to set off onto the hill to see what's happening with the rest of the sheep. You're welcome to join me, if you think you can stay the distance.' There is a hint of mischief in his voice. Netta doesn't rise to the bait, saying only that she would like that. 'Very well. Then I suggest we pick up our piece and we'll be off.'

82

9
Losses

April 1946

Netta checks Andrew's lambing bag while he goes to have a word with Kenneth. The bag that he takes with him is big — large enough to carry two lambs, should it be necessary. She adds a fresh flagon of milk, checks for lambing oil and soap and makes sure there is enough cord and a length of wire. Jill, Finlay's border collie, shut in one of the sheds, senses the preparations and is barking incessantly. At first reluctant, having been reared and trained by Finlay, she is gradually forming a bond with the new shepherd. Andrew's soft voice and unruffled commands are bringing her round and she stays close to his heels as he sets off with Netta to climb the hill behind the farm.

A strong breeze is coming from the west and bursts of sunshine chase one another across the hills in front of them. They make steady progress, checking the ewes as they go.

'What will happen if they lamb at night?' Netta asks. 'You cannot be everywhere at once!'

'You actually find that very few lamb during the hours of darkness. As long as I am up and out early, I should be ahead of them. Of course there will always be one or two that don't stick to the rules and it's inevitable that we lose a few lambs. But there's nothing we can do about that, not when they are scattered so widely over the hillside.'

'I can come with you regularly . . . if you do not mind having me to accompany you,' Netta, says, with a half-smile.

'You do realise how early you will have to be out of your bed every morning?'

'That will not be a problem. I have always been an early riser. I will be with you at half past five tomorrow. Is that early enough for you?'

'Perfect. We will check the field, milk the cows, have breakfast and then set off on our rounds.'

Netta smiles widely and, to Andrew's surprise, takes off at a run across the hill. He watches her as she slows to a walk. There is a spring in her step that has not been there before. When she was first introduced to him, she seemed like a woman older than her years, carrying the weight of the world on her shoulders. Now he glimpses a younger woman, carefree even. She turns and waits for him and when he reaches her, he sees the sparkle in her eyes, eyes as blue as the sky reflected in the water of the distant reservoir. For the second time that day his heart skips a beat.

'You look happy at the thought of all the hard work ahead. You willnae mind the long days and getting your hands dirty?'

'Not at all. I have been always used to hard work. And it is a beautiful valley in which to be busy.'

'Well, I have to say that you being here makes it looks even lovelier,' he dares to say.

84

It is as though a cloud has crossed the face of the sun. Her smile fades and she turns away and looks at the view. 'Come along,' she says briskly, stepping away. 'We must not be too long. I need to get back and see how Mutti is.'

'I think your mother will do very well looking after Finlay,' Andrew says slowly. 'I can see that she is someone with a lot of love to give.'

Netta hesitates. 'She always was,' she replies thoughtfully, 'though she feels now that she has none left to give — that 'the reservoir has run dry', as you say. In the last terrible years she has lost everyone she has ever loved.'

'She has not lost *you*,' Andrew reminds her.

'That's what Mutti says.' Her voice is softer now. 'But I am all she has. That is why I need to look after her.'

The two proceed in silence down the slope of a hill. Ahead of them a scattered flock are quietly grazing the new grass. Andrew and Netta walk among them, checking for problems. But there are none. They make their way down to the river, where Andrew suggests they sit and have their lunch. They find a rock on the banking. The recent rain has swelled the river and Netta watches its progress over the stony bed. Andrew pours tea from the flask into two metal cups and hands one of them to her. She is lost in thought.

'It's strange,' she says suddenly. 'This noise — this chattering of the water — I remember it from when I lived here as a little girl all those years ago. My mother used to walk along this way when the weather was kind. I always wanted to run, but if I was tired, she would put me in the other end of

85

the pram and warn me not to kick my baby sister. We would stop by the river, like we are now, and play in the water and have a picnic. I hadn't thought about it till this moment.'

'Are you well settled in your cottage?' Andrew asks, indicating the small dwelling clearly visible in the base of the valley. He unpacks the sandwiches and holds them out. She takes one.

'Yes, it is good. We are happy there. Very peaceful. It is so wonderful to have a place of our own again.' There is a long pause and then she says,

'You see, when we were in Germany — in the later years, that is — we didn't have a home. We were put in an *Ilag*.'

'In an *Ilag*?'

'Yes, it's an internment camp for enemy aliens.'

'I'm sorry, I don't understand,' Andrew says. 'Would the Germans not let you come home when there began to be trouble?'

'Of course, you do not know what had happened — how we came to be in Germany. After my father died, my mother decided that we would all go to Germany. She had looked after a German prisoner-of-war during the Great War and they had fallen in love. Of course my father was still alive then and so nothing could come of it. But after my father died, we all went to Freiburg and mother and Josef were married.'

'But surely that would have meant you were treated differently if your mother was married to a German?'

'My mother was married to a German *Jew*. *He* was the one who was treated differently.' She pauses, stares out towards the reservoir, screws

86

up her face, looking as though she regrets having started this strand of conversation. With a sigh, she continues. 'He was taken away from us at the end of 1938. There was a terrible move by the Nazi Party against Jewish families and businesses. It had been building up over the years but in the November it was worse. Businesses were set alight, as were synagogues. Many Jewish men were taken away. Many of them came back to their families — at least for a while — but not Josef. He didn't come back.

'Things got worse and worse. Families disappeared. My mother was worried that if we stayed where we were, the same would happen to us. We went into hiding — some friends took us in. We thought we would be safe with them and we were, for a while. We heard that the Nazi soldiers had taken over our house. It seemed, though, that they knew where we had gone and one day they came after us and captured us.'

Netta pauses and a great shiver passes through her. 'They tried to put us in a concentration camp but my mother objected. She said we were British and it was an offence, what they were trying to do. And so, thanks to my mother, we were considered enemy aliens and avoided being sent to one of those awful camps. Instead they sent us to an internment camp. It was not as bad as it sounds. It was a large house. It must have been part of an estate at one time. There were people there from several countries, all considered aliens. The men in charge of us were older — they had fought in the first war — and we were treated quite well on the whole. There was usually enough food and from time to time there were even Red Cross parcels arriving from abroad, so we didn't starve.' There is a long pause before she says in a monotone, 'It was nothing like the awful conditions in the concentration camps, which news reports keep telling us about.'

Andrew refills her cup. 'So you were there until the end of the war?'

'Yes, we were. And then we were freed by the Allies and we returned to Freiburg. We needed to find Josef. We knew that when he came looking for us it would be Freiburg he would come to. But our house in Freiburg — it was a lovely house in a beautiful city — had been bombed early in the war, in 1940. We were told it was a mistake; they said the city was bombed by our own Luftwaffe!

'Our house had gone and so had all our possessions. We stayed with our friends, to start with, the ones who had given us shelter before. There was very little work to be found. I managed to get a job in a café, which gave us just enough money to rent a room. Then the café closed down. There was no money, you see; nobody had any money to spend eating out. That was when we decided to return to Scotland.' She looks across at him and shrugs her shoulders. 'So now you know. But enough about me. How are you settling in? Is it very different from where you were before?'

'I've no' been here long enough to find out really.' Andrew gets up while he is speaking, packing the remains of the picnic into his bag and slinging it over his shoulder. 'We had better continue walking while we talk, in case there is work waiting for us back on the farm.' He is wondering

88

about what happened to her stepfather, and also her sister, whom she has not mentioned as being with them in the internment camp. But perhaps she will tell him when she is ready.

'Yes, it is milder on the west coast,' he says, answering her question. 'I think the weather will be colder here. And, of course, it *is* different. I was shepherding under war conditions when I was there on the last farm. We were expected to do a lot with a little. The farm was fairly similar to this, only smaller. The farmer was on his own, no family. He wasnae getting any younger and, in the end, he decided to retire.'

'Do you come from a farming family?'

'Well, I do in a roundabout way. My father was a schoolteacher in Oban but he went off to fight in the Great War and never came back. I was only eight when I lost my dad. My mother struggled to make ends meet and then at the end of the war she was struck down with the flu that devastated the country. She died too, when I was just eleven. My uncle took me in, my dad's older brother. He's a tenant farmer over west. The trouble was, he had two boys already and they were beginning to work with my uncle. I got on well with my younger cousin, Hughie, but there was really no job for me on the farm. I'd seen enough of shepherding though — and done a bit too — to know that's how I wanted to spend my life.

'And then I fell out with Stewie, my elder cousin, and I decided on the spur of the moment that I would go off to Glasgow and make my fortune! I didn't, of course — make my fortune, that is — but Glasgow was the making of me. It made me realise how much love and care I had been given by my uncle and his family. Things were really grim in the city and got grimmer as time went on. There was poverty and hunger and bad housing. I was lucky to get a job but I did — in shipbuilding. Would you believe I helped to build the *Queen Mary*! I was still there when she was launched in 1934. But the problems all around were impossible to ignore and early on I become friendly with some of the Quakers in the city. They were trying to establish better working conditions. There was such a lot to do and we sometimes felt that what we were doing made very little difference. But looking back now, I can see that we must have helped quite a few families to find their feet again.

'Anyway, in 1935 I think it was, I decided to go back to my roots. I missed the countryside and thought there might be a job back home for me now. I turned up at the family farm. They were pleased enough to see me but there was still no work to be had. So I found work on another sheep farm where a second shepherd was needed. I was new to the job but what I'd learned at my uncle's had stuck and I soon picked it up again. Later I decided to become a travelling shepherd, going from place to place, wherever a shepherd was needed. Which is how I came to be here. And very glad I am that I came.'

'Are you a Quaker now?' Netta asks in the direct way he is coming to expect.

'Well, I used to go to their meetings and I agreed with what they believe, though I have not officially joined their number. I still have Quaker friends

90

in Glasgow and write to them from time to time. How can you not be drawn to a group that recognises something of God in every man and tries as they do to put their beliefs into practice?'

'I think there are a lot of us who find it difficult to see something of God in every man,' Netta says crisply. She swings away from him and strides out ahead. Andrew follows her in silence. After a minute or two she slows.

'So both of us lost our fathers,' she says, when Andrew is by her side again.

'I can hardly remember mine, and I think that the little I do know is what my mother has told me. He was the shepherd on the Douglas farm until after the first war. He died up there behind the farm.' She points to the hills that form a backdrop to the farm buildings. 'But you — you were eight. It must have been awful to lose your father at that age — and then your mother as well.'

'Did you get on well with your stepfather?' Andrew asks, choosing not to say more about the death of his parents.

'Yes, I did get on well with him. He was a lovely man.' She indicates the farm just ahead of them. 'Look, we are almost back. And, if I'm not mistaken, there is Finlay in the farmyard, making sure that everything is in order. I'll go on ahead and see how he is. Remember, he's been back at the hospital today for the doctors to check how his arm is mending.'

★ ★ ★

'Aye. I think they're pleased with my progress.' Finlay smiles at Netta as they climb the slope to his cottage, where her mother, in Finlay's absence, has been taking the opportunity to give it a thorough clean. 'They never say much, of course, only that I must go back in two weeks and they may remove the bandages and let me start using it — but not for farm duties, more's the pity. I'll go mad if I have to sit here much longer watching everyone else do the work!'

The door to the cottage is open and Ellen is preparing to leave.

'Ah, Netta, there you are. Kenneth has offered to give us a lift home as it's getting late.'

'That will be very welcome. I've walked a long way today. Let me tell Andrew I am going.' She runs back down the slope to the barn, followed more slowly by her mother. She hears the engine of Kenneth's car spring into life.

There is no sign of Andrew at the pens. He must have been delayed near the road. Perhaps he has found another sheep about to give birth. Netta's attention is drawn to a sheep lying on her side in the corner. She hesitates then goes over to the car.

'You go ahead, Mutti. I need to find Andrew to help with a sheep in the pens. I'll get a lift later.'

Netta opens the gate of the pen and in an instant is kneeling by the distressed sheep. She has seen enough to know that the labour is obstructed and the ageing mother exhausted with her struggle. Netta's heart beats fast. Her eyes sweep the lower hill but there is still no sign of Andrew. Dare she try and lamb this one herself? Has she seen and done enough to manage this birth? She looks at the sheep again. If she is left much longer, she may well die.

Pushing her arm deep into the womb opening, through which two legs are emerging, her hand encounters the lamb's head. It is bent back on its neck. With an effort she pushes back the extruding legs and bends the head forward, so that it lies between the legs. Almost miraculously the lamb slithers out into the straw. The mother lies quietly, gathering her strength. Her lamb is unmoving, seemingly lifeless. Quickly Netta cleans its mouth and nose, rubs its body with a handful of straw, and, when there is still no response, picks the lamb up by its back legs and swings it round twice. Mucus streams from its mouth and it gives a sharp bleat. Netta places it in the straw and its mother staggers to her feet, nudging her infant until it stands swaying and, with another sharp cry, totters to its mother and starts to suckle. Netta looks up with a sigh of satisfaction and there is Andrew gazing at her from the far side of the pen, a bemused smile on his face.

'I thought you were going home for your tea,' he says calmly, 'though I think this sheep is not the only one to be glad that you are still here.' He opens the gate and steps over to her side. For a moment she thinks he is going to put his arm round her but instead he drops to his knees in the straw and examines the lamb. 'You've done a good job there, lass. I'll make you my partner yet!'

'You weren't back and I didn't like to leave her.'

'A good decision, especially as I was delivering twins on the hill.'

* * *

'Stay for some tea,' he says to her later, when they have cleaned up the sheep and are leaving the pen. 'I'll walk back with you afterwards, if I'm allowed.'

Netta hesitates. It is late now and she is hungry.

'That will be good,' she says.

10
Market

April 1946

Towards the end of the month Andrew asks Netta if she would care to accompany him to the market to stock up on supplies. Neither of them has been there before and it will be a break from the rigours of lambing. The day is overcast as they set off in the second-hand pickup that has replaced Kenneth's irreparable one. Low clouds hug the line of hills on either side of them and they proceed in silence out of the valley and along the road to Lanark.

Farmers are standing in groups, busily discussing the coming months and an anticipated increase in livestock prices. The gloom that settled on the industry in the difficult days of the war is lifting and an air of optimism pervades the atmosphere. Andrew and Netta pass between the groups, a few of whom nod to the shepherd and shoot a puzzled look at Netta. 'You're causing quite a stir.' Andrew smiles. 'They're no' that used to women here, I can see.' They join a long queue snaking back from the store.

'What do we need to buy?' Netta asks. 'It seems to me as though the sheep can look after themselves up there in the hills. Do they have many problems?'

'No' so many, not in a good year anyway. But we'll need to dip them to protect against ticks and flies. Then there's the licks — you'll have seen the tubs out in the fields — they prevent the diseases caused by the pasture being too rich or more often not rich enough. The copper, for example. We give it to the pregnant ewes to prevent something called swayback in their offspring. That can affect the lambs when they're just a few weeks old. You see them staggering about or unable to walk or even to get up in some cases. In a bad case the lamb will die. So it makes sense to prevent it, rather than wait until it happens. I'll buy some more tubs of the copper lick today and get some dip in readiness.'

'New to these parts, are you?' asks a voice from behind them. The pair turn and are confronted with a burly man with a bristly moustache and deep-set steely eyes.

'Aye, I'm assistant shepherd over at the Douglas farm. I came at the beginning of the year. My name's Andrew Cameron. And this is — '

'Aye, I've heard of you,' the man interrupts. 'Roddie McCann's the name. How's Finlay Baird? We all heard about his accident.'

'He's doing well, but it'll be several weeks before he's fit enough to work, so it will. Meanwhile Netta here has stepped in and . . . she's now an important member of the team.'

'Aye, you sound as though you have a willing pupil on your hands, pal,' the farmer says, giving Netta a look of condescension. 'Be careful or she'll be taking the job from our boys who've just returned from the war.'

'I don't think that's likely, Mr McCann,' Andrew says evenly. 'From what I've heard, shepherds and other farm workers are hard to come by, especially up in the hills. Where's your farm, may I ask?'

'A few miles away, west of Lanark.'

'And do you have your full complement of workers back with you?'

'My sons came back, thank the Lord, though I lost a couple of my farmhands. It's sure to get better now there's no longer the threat of the enemy contaminating our land.' There is a pause. 'Just a minute,' the farmer says slowly. 'Are you no' in the valley where the Germans were drafted in during the first war? Gey hard to get rid of the contamination in that case.'

'You forget,' says Andrew, 'it was partly their efforts that brought enough water to the villages and towns to the north of us.' He shoots an uncomfortable look at Netta who is staring intently at the farmer.

'On their side now, are you, pal? I should watch your tongue if I were you, or you'll no' make many friends round here.' The farmer glances round at the interested crowd of onlookers who have half-heard the conversation and have drawn closer to listen.

Netta can keep silent no longer. 'Have you ever thought that there were Germans who had no wish to fight, just as there are some thoughtless and unkind British only too willing to speak evil of them?'

The farmer steps back in mock surprise. 'I'm sorry, hen. I'd no intention of causing offence.'

Netta looks the man up and down and turns on

her heel to walk away. Then she stops and turns back to face him. 'And if I wish to become a shepherd, there is nothing you can do to stop me!'

She walks swiftly out of the building. Once outside, she begins to tremble and has to sit on a nearby low wall until she has her shaking body under control again. A minute later Andrew is there. He sits down at her side and nudges her with his shoulder.

'I'll say this for you, lass. You're no' lacking in courage and that's a fact. That Roddie McCann's a bully, and I could see there was more than one in there pleased to see him spoken back to.' He gives her a wry smile, which turns into a chuckle and the next minute they are both laughing uncontrollably. 'Tell me,' Andrew says, when he can speak again, 'did you mean what you said to Roddie McCann? Are you really thinking of becoming a shepherd?'

'Let's just wait and see.' Netta looks at him with a cheeky grin.

'All the same,' Andrew replies, 'it's probably best if you steer clear of him in the future!'

'I meant what I said to him about the soldiers.' Netta is serious now.

'There were some who didn't agree with what was happening — although there were plenty more who saw to it that the life of our family was changed forever . . . and not for the better.'

Netta has no wish to go back inside the building and Andrew has still not made his purchases. While he does so, she walks along the High Street and buys three-pence worth of cinder toffee to give to her mother on their return. She is thinking how difficult she is finding it to bring to mind one kind German, her stepfather aside, although she knows in her heart of hearts that what she said must be true.

★ ★ ★

'What happened to your stepfather?' Andrew asks, when they have left the bustle of Lanark and are several miles down the road. 'You said that the life of your family was changed forever.' She is silent for so long that he knows he has made a mistake. 'I'm sorry. I had no business to ask such a personal question. Please forgive me.'

'No, there is nothing to forgive. As you pointed out, it is I who raised the subject.' There is a pause and she lets out a long sigh. 'My stepfather died in a concentration camp.'

11

Appassionata

February 1942

Josef swung the spade onto his shoulder and stumbled outside, struggling to catch up with his workmates who were already snaking across the strip of addled grass to the gate. Half a dozen soldiers were chivvying them to speed up or half the working day would be lost. Josef raised his eyes to the horizon, where a faint blur showed the beginning of dawn. Hardly the loss of half the working day, he considered. A nearby guard shoved him in the back with an order to hurry up. He tried to run a few steps but the exertion brought on his cough and he slowed down again until he had caught his breath.

This daily trudge to work, a journey that took upwards of an hour, gave him ample time to think about his family, how they were coping, if they were safe, whether they had enough to eat. But such thoughts weighed on him so heavily, they almost seemed to grind him into the ground. Better to save them for night-time when his cough prevented sleep and he could give way to the emotions that he had kept at bay during the hours of daylight.

So instead he thought for the hundredth time of the irony of the situation and his mouth grimaced in the approximation of a smile. Twenty-five years ago he had been a prisoner-of-war in a foreign country, put to work in helping to build a road and a railway that would, in turn, provide the access for the excavation of an enormous reservoir. Every morning he had been marched out with his fellow prisoners in every kind of weather to undertake the task. Now, here he was, a prisoner in his own country, made to do the same work, though where the road was to lead to was anyone's guess. He doubted whether the prison guards themselves knew.

And it was there that the similarity ended, for in Scotland they were given ample food and good shelter, their captors were fair and one or two of them even kind. In his present 'lodgings' the food consisted mainly of watery soup of dubious description, together with a small ration of stale bread, which had to be guarded against theft by one of the other inmates.

The best way to avoid this was to eat it all at once and go hungry for the rest of the day. The alternative, saving some of it for later in the day, gave a high risk of its being stolen and the recipient having to endure even greater hunger for the next twenty-four hours.

When Josef had first been admitted to the camp, there was room enough for them all. But gradually, over the three years of his incarceration, more and more of his countrymen had been brought here. They were now sleeping two or three to a bed. His poor health did nothing to endear him to his bedfellows, his worsening cough meaning that none of them got the sleep they needed. And they received nothing but abuse at the hands of the guards.

If Josef had been able to see himself in a mirror, he would hardly have recognised the ageing man who confronted him. No-one would have guessed him to be fifty-two. His brown curls had faded to lanky grey strands that hung around a face so lined and devoid of colour that he looked years older. He had never been tall but his stooped posture and emaciation made him appear even smaller. It was the first war, 'the Great War', as they called it, that had been the cause of his chest trouble — the torpedoing of his submarine, the floundering around in the water, choking on the oil that had spilled from the intestines of their doomed vessel. If it had not been for the ministrations of Ellen, he would, in all likelihood, be dead — buried like his compatriot Oliver Tauber in that tiny graveyard near the valley in which Ellen lived.

Ellen. How he had loved her from the moment he had regained consciousness after being carried on the stretcher into her cottage. He had tried to keep his feelings under control, knowing that she had a husband already and that, at any time, he might return on leave. And return he did and made it very clear that Josef was not wanted, neither near his wife nor in the country. And then came the end of the war and the abrupt ending of their time together.

Except that it wasn't. He remembered her letter, the one the captain had given him before the prisoners had boarded the train to return home, the letter telling of the birth of her daughter Eva. *Their* daughter. His heart thrilled as he thought of the later one she had sent after her husband's death, telling him that she was planning to join him in Germany. What he had thought was the end of his happiness was only the beginning — although what had followed brought a persistent flow of guilt at the suffering it had caused.

The sharp pain of a rifle butt brought down smartly across his shoulders shook him abruptly from his reverie. He stumbled and almost fell. The ground beneath his feet was icy, sparkling in the newly risen sun. He looked around him, confused, his memory still in that deep Scottish valley that had seen the awakening of his passion.

'Get along with you, or you will forfeit your dinner break,' the guard growled.

'*Not a big loss*,' Josef mumbled to the man walking next to him, though knowing that he must eat the meagre rations in order to have even a modicum of strength for the day's work. He tried to keep up with the man but lagged behind again and was rewarded with another slap of the guard's rifle. He knew he should have kept his mind on the walk, instead of allowing it to wander onto thoughts of his family. If only someone could tell him how they were.

The man, who was called Frank, offered him his arm to help him along and Josef took it gratefully. The two had struck up a friendship over the months. Frank had arrived over half a year before, a university professor of music who had lost his job in 1935 and then, after living a ghetto existence for the first three years of the war, had been rounded up with hundreds of others from his hometown. He was a big man, sturdy, and better able to manage the back-breaking work to which they were subjected. Gentle, despite his strength, he was a ready listener and slow to give his opinion.

Their fellow prisoners were already starting work on the road to nowhere, as they called it. They had learned how to prepare foundations; some carried stone from a nearby quarry, breaking it into usable pieces with a pickaxe and laying it as evenly as possible on the prepared ground. They were not allowed a rest, even for five minutes, until dinner time, when they could stop to eat their dry bread, drink their water and go off to relieve themselves, though never out of sight of their guards. The only way to get through the day was to think of the night's sleep that awaited their return.

'Hey, Josef.' Frank paused his digging and turned to him. 'Did you know that the orchestra has to perform tonight? You are to play the piano. It's a concert for the guards.'

Josef sighed. Gone was the possibility of an early night. He loved the chance to play his music but he was so weary that he would willingly forego his greatest pleasure for the chance of a night's sleep. However, it did mean that he could take his mind off the exhausting work and lose himself in deciding what he would play.

For as long as he could remember he had played the piano. Before joining the navy in 1914 he was on the verge, at the age of twenty, of becoming a concert pianist. He returned when war ended, expecting to continue where he had left off. For a while it looked as though he might succeed.

But the country was in a sorry state. There was no money to spare for people to spend on concert-going. Germany was struggling to hold its head up after the harsh edicts of the Treaty of Versailles ordered it to pay huge reparations. No-one was interested in the musical talent of a young pianist in Freiburg. He starred in occasional concerts with local orchestras, but never became as well known or played as often as he had dreamed that he would.

When Ellen and the girls joined him after the war, Josef knew that regular income would be needed in order to support his young and growing family. He began to teach music, giving lessons to young piano students in his house. It brought in just enough money to feed and clothe them. From time to time there was extra money from his concert performances. They got by — and they were happy. They rented a small house in Freiburg, the children went to school and Ellen became a 'Hausfrau'.

But times were changing. The National Socialist Workers' Party was in the ascendancy and with Hitler's rise to power, hatred aimed at the Jews — long simmering beneath the surface — flared into open hostility. In 1933 Josef was told that he could no longer teach music. He was not alone. Jewish conductors and musicians were being banned from orchestras, Jewish singers losing their jobs, as were those Jews involved in the arts, literature and the theatre. Wherever he turned, he could see that Jews were suffering. Germans were ordered to boycott Jewish shops. Netta had by then left school and, unable to train for teaching

105

as she had wished to do, had begun working in a café run by friends from their local synagogue. For a while the business continued, her employers determined not to give in to pressure, but within a few years they were forced, along with thousands of others, to close their business. Jews were forbidden to attend cultural events. Jewish pupils were expelled from school. Everywhere that Josef looked, the net was closing in.

He realised now, and the realisation brought bitter regret, that he should have attempted earlier to take his family and leave the country — go to England, to America, anywhere that would give them a life of freedom. But he, like so many of his fellow professionals, Frank included, saw the rise of the Nazi Party as a temporary phenomenon. Things would change — the Social Democrats would take control again, the contribution of music and the arts that he and others gave to the welfare of the German people would surely be recognised. As time went on, it became clear that this wasn't the case. By the time Josef accepted the inevitable, it was too late.

Strange then it was, that, from his incarceration in Dachau, Josef should be allowed to play his music again. It was what kept him alive, that and the bittersweet memory of his family, whom he had not seen for more than three years. His Ellen, so loyal and loving and with such determination that she would keep going, whatever the odds. He knew that, with her, the children would be in safe hands.

They had come at night, the soldiers. They had done their homework well. They knew which of the houses were occupied by Jews, which of the businesses were theirs. They had smashed the windows, ransacked the interiors. The synagogue was burned to the ground. And Josef, along with dozens of other men, was taken into what the Nazis called 'protective custody'. Many of them eventually returned to their homes — but not Josef. He had no idea why they kept him. He asked but they couldn't — or wouldn't — tell him.

His favourite composer was Beethoven. His was the music that he played when given the choice and it was his music that he would play tonight. He had been told not long before his capture that for a Jew to play music by a German composer was an insult to the German people — it was no longer allowed. But he set his mind on Sonata number 23, 'Appassionata'. He would play it for Ellen, not for the Nazi soldiers who would, in all probability, not recognise it. It was their music, his and Ellen's. When he played it to her, it was his coded message of love.

The occasion was special. A visitor, a Nazi soldier of high ranking, was seated in the front row, along with the officer in charge of the concentration camp. The first piece, a Haydn string quartet, was greeted with polite applause. When Josef sat down to play, he could see that he had the Nazi officer's attention. The room went silent as he started to play. The music was dramatic, arresting. When he began the beautiful and subtle second movement, his surroundings receded into the background and he thought only of Ellen.

He remembered the look on her face, the first time that she had ever heard him play. He was

107

convalescing and she had taken him for a walk and they had called at the farmhouse. He had glanced over the shoulder of the farmer's wife and there stood a piano in the living room. His fingers had twitched with longing and Ellen had asked if he could be allowed to play it.

He had played this second movement of 'Appassionata' and when he looked up, Ellen's eyes were full of tears.

'Stop playing! Stop this at once!' a voice roared. Josef started. He looked round in a daze and his fingers stalled on the keys. 'How dare you play this music,' the visiting officer shouted. 'All Jews have been expressly forbidden from sullying the name of our great German composers. Take him away. I wish to hear no more of this.'

'My apologies, Herr Meyer,' the commandant of the camp grovelled. 'I had no idea that this is what he was playing. He will certainly be punished for this.' He indicated to the guards, two of whom came forward and, catching hold of Josef by the arms, dragged him backwards from his seat and across the floor to the exit. What little fight there was in Josef's body left him. It was as though his message of love had been cast into the mud and Ellen was lost to him forever.

'Why did you do it?' Frank said to him later, as he climbed into the bunk he shared with Josef. Josef was sitting hunched on the side of the bed. 'Didn't you realise what trouble it could get you into?'

'I am going to die. My lungs are getting worse. Some days there is no breath in me. It is only a matter of time. Why should I not hasten the day and put myself out of my misery? I will never see my Ellen again. This music was the only way to bring her close. For a moment there I could feel her wrapped in my arms. It is enough. There is nothing more I can do for her.'

Frank stared at him speechless, unable to contradict Josef's words, which were almost certainly correct.

'There is something, Frank,' Josef said with a gasp. 'I almost forgot.' He fumbled his hand into the inside pocket of his jacket and pulled out a crumpled sheet of paper.

'Take this for me.' He handed the paper to Frank. 'It's a letter for Ellen. I wrote it a while ago, when things began to look bleak. Look after it for me. And when this war ends, make sure that she gets it, will you?'

'But what makes you think that I will get out of here?'

'You're a strong man, Frank. If anyone can get out of this hellhole, it's you. Take it. Do as I ask, if it's humanly possible.'

The door was flung back and hit the wall with a crash. The camp commandant stood in the opening. Two guards were on either side of him.

'Josef Kessler,' he shouted. 'Come over here.' Josef staggered to his feet and, nodding once to Frank, walked slowly over to the commandant. 'You have brought the good name of this camp into disrepute. You will be punished.' A murmuring arose among Josef's fellow inmates. 'Silence, or you will all receive the same punishment. I will not have disorder in my camp.'

'And he won't tolerate being shown up for the

109

idiot he is,' Frank whispered beneath his breath, as the guards seized Josef and dragged him outside. Frank folded the letter carefully and slid it into his inside pocket, holding it in place long enough to feel his heart miss a beat as the gunshot rang out in the darkness.

12

Opening Up

April 1946

'Only a few 'stragglers' left to lamb now,' Andrew says to Netta, as they make themselves as comfortable as they can in their usual riverside spot.

Netta pours tea and passes Andrew a sandwich. 'I was talking the situation over with Finlay yesterday. It's been a fair lambing, though why more than the usual number of ewes have failed to achieve a pregnancy is a mystery, given that the winter was so mild.'

'The lambs are all growing well and not many were lost.'

'No, indeed and if this spell of good weather continues and the grass grows well, they should fetch a decent price at the market.'

'So what comes next?' Netta asks, gazing along the valley, the sides of which are dotted with sheep and their offspring.

'A wee bit of a lull and then clipping will start. After that, into September, there will be the sales.'

'No' so much of a break then.' Netta gets up and balances on the stones at the edge of the river. 'Will Finlay be able to help with the clipping?'

'I hope so, although it's no' easy to hold down sheep when they've a mind to get away. He mustn't risk it until the doctor is satisfied that his arm is

111

properly mended.'

'Do you want to show me how it's done? I may be able to help.' She glances sidelong at Andrew.

Andrew looks sceptical. 'It's back-breaking work, so it is, but I've no objection to you trying, if that's what you want.'

'I'd like to try, if you'll show me.' Netta steps from one stone to another but her foot skids on its mossy surface and the next second she is ankle deep in the water. Andrew jumps up, laughing, and grabs hold of her hand to steady her as she steps onto the banking. As soon as she is safe she snatches back her hand, a rising colour coming to her face, and sits back down on the stone. 'Let us hope I make a better job of it than I do of balancing on the stones,' she says, tipping water out of her boot.

'Just what you used to do when your mother brought you and your sister here for picnics, was it?' Andrew says smiling.

'Yes, though she always had a change of clothes, just in case, I seem to remember.'

'What happened to your sister?' Andrew says tentatively. 'You mentioned before that she was a baby in the pram when you were here.'

'Eva. Yes, she was three years younger than me.' Netta pauses and gives a half-smile. 'Actually, I used to assume she was my sister but later on, as she grew up, I thought she was probably my half-sister. She had such a look of Josef, it was impossible to ignore! I had two sisters in fact. Anna was born in Germany three years after Eva.' She takes a breath, as though to say more, but closes her mouth again and the words remain unsaid.

112

'I'm sorry. I shouldnae ask. It's upsetting you.'

She hesitates. 'Yes, it is upsetting me — but sometimes it is best that these things do not stay hidden. Better that people know about the bad things that happen as well as the good. Do you remember how I said my stepfather had been taken away at the end of 1938 and we never saw him again and that later we went into hiding but the Nazi officers came and found us anyway? It seemed they knew where everyone was. It was impossible to hide from them. They came into the house one day and took hold of my mother but my sister Eva ran over and tried to drag her away.' Netta is talking slowly now, her eyes fixed on the distance, as though picturing the scene she is struggling to describe.

'The officer turned and shot Eva at point-blank range and then he shot Anna too. She had been standing just behind Eva.' Netta's voice rises uncontrollably. 'They shot them dead right in front of our eyes, without any word of explanation.' She covers her face with shaking hands, screwing her fingers into her eye sockets, as though to blot out the image of her sisters' blood spilling onto the floor.

Andrew is appalled. He goes up to Netta and puts his arms around her and this time she doesn't pull away but nestles her face into his shoulder and weeps.

'And what about you? Did they threaten you as well?'

'I was on the other side of the room when the soldiers burst in,' she sobs.

'I stood there. I didn't move. It haunts me now

that I should have done something, should have tried to stop them.'

'And get yourself shot as well? No, you did the right thing. It meant that your mother was not entirely alone in her ordeal. So it was then they took you both away?'

'Yes, but we kept insisting that we were British, not German and not Jewish. We had our papers with us to prove it and our friends said that what we had told the soldiers was the truth.'

'I suppose it would have looked bad if they had shot two British women for no reason,' Andrew says slowly. He has kept his arms around Netta during this explanation and she begins to free herself now, brushing away her tears with the sleeve of her jacket.

'How did you learn of your stepfather's death?' Andrew asks cautiously.

'Did you hear of it from the German authorities?'

'I believe records were kept. But, no, not from them.' Netta sits down on the stone again and sighs. 'When the war eventually ended, Mother and I went back to our friends who had sheltered us before. I told you about them, didn't I? I don't know how we would have managed without their help. We had no-one else to turn to. Our house had been bombed and we had lost everything. They took us in again. We had no money and hardly any clothes but they said it didn't matter — they would look after us for as long as we needed. You see, we didn't know where Josef was, or if he was alive. Unless we were there, he wouldn't find us when he returned. We tried to make enquiries but

114

what was one among so many thousands dead?

'And then, one day, there was a knock on the door. A man was shown into the room where we were sitting — a tall man, thin although he might once have been well-built. He said his name was Frank Wasserman and he had been with Josef in the concentration camp. He had been looking for us and neighbours had told him where we were staying. He had a letter from Josef for my mother. He had kept it in his jacket pocket since 1942, given to him by my stepfather before he was taken out and shot. The news was not unexpected but my mother was distraught. I suppose that, underneath it all, there had remained a tiny hope that he might still be alive and yet return to her. At least she had a letter, which was more than a lot of poor families had. And, no, before you ask, I have not read the letter. I believe it reiterates his feelings for her. They were always very close.

'When we came back to this valley, people naturally began talking about her time in the valley as a child and a young woman, about her marriage and what a decent man her first husband was. It made me angry at first, angry that she had not tried harder in her marriage. When I learned just how difficult it had been, I understood better. I wondered why she should want to come back here to be reminded of my father — but, of course, it was also the place where she and Josef met. Bittersweet, is it not?'

There is a long pause before Andrew says simply, 'Thank you. I understand better now.'

'Those friends in Freiburg who we stayed with,' says Netta, 'they are also Quakers, like your friends in Glasgow. I was possibly a little sharp when you spoke of the Quakers before. They are good people. Things would have been even worse, were it not for their help.'

'If we don't get back home soon,' says Andrew laughing, 'things *will* be worse for you. Your wet feet will lead to double pneumonia.' He offers her a hand to pull her up but she springs up nimbly, ignoring his help, and climbs the incline onto the road that her stepfather helped to build, pausing to wait for him as he clambers up to join her.

13
Different Perspectives

May 1946

Netta climbs steadily until she is out of breath, then sinks down suddenly onto a stone by the side of the burn. There has been no rain for weeks and the water is low and sluggish, idling over the assorted pebbles forming the base of the channel. When her breathing has slowed, she reaches down to rest her hand on the barely damp clumps of waterside plants, yet to come into flower, before raising her eyes to the vast landscape of hills and water, feeling its loneliness.

Loneliness is a feeling not new to her. It has been with her all her life or, at least, as long as she can remember. The loneliness of seeing her mother dote on a younger sister. Netta loved her sister, of course she did, but her mother's subtle preference was not lost on the older daughter. Then came the journey to Germany, leaving behind all that Netta knew and loved, for a man she could not even remember. She had learned to love Josef for himself, as well as for the need to stay in her mother's affections, but, even so, there was always the recognition that he came first in her mother's life.

He was first, the rest of the family second and herself the last. Or so it seemed to her.

The wind stirs her hair and blows a strand of it across her face. She reaches up and brushes it away from her eyes. David loved her hair. He loved the thickness of it, used to run his fingers through it and then kiss her. That was as far as their courtship went, both sets of parents on hand to make sure they behaved correctly. But he was hers and she was number one with him — until his disappearance, that was; his disappearance and that of so many others. Everyone she has ever known and loved, she has lost, apart from her mother. She is still here, though Netta has come to accept that she will never be number one with her.

And now Andrew has disappeared — and she has no idea where. He has gone without saying anything to her. Finlay passed on the news to her that morning, saying that Andrew needed to leave before everyone was up in order to catch the early train. He had not told him *where* he was going but Finlay assured her that it was only for a few days and he would certainly be coming back.

Netta can't help thinking that it is all her fault. She has been so offhand with Andrew at times, cutting him off whenever he attempts any demonstration of friendship. Where has he gone? Is it true what Finlay says, that he will definitely be coming back? Perhaps he won't be needed now that Finlay is on his feet and ready to start work. She stares down the hillside towards the empty shepherd's cottage. In reality nothing about it has changed but to her it looks desolate and forlorn. Its appearance gives her an involuntary shiver. Is she to be as lonely here as she has felt all her life?

She clambers to her feet and resumes her ascent.

There are wild pansies here, delicate violet-blue petals quivering in the breeze that is always present at this height. Up and up she climbs, not stopping until she attains the summit. She stands, taking in huge gulps of air. To the north, hills stretch like waves on the sea, green-blue fading to misty purple. In the east the reservoir reflects the clear blue of the sky and to the south there are more hills stretching to the horizon. Sheep graze the fields in all directions. If the good weather continues, the lambs will do very well. She smiles.

She's beginning to think like a shepherd herself.

She does love it here. She is beginning to feel settled — as though she has come home. Everyone on the farm here has been so kind to her and her mother.

But where on earth is Andrew?

* * *

It's a spur-of-the-moment decision to visit his friend in England. Lambing is finished, clipping is still some weeks away and Finlay's injuries are well-enough mended for him to supervise work around the farm. Jack has written to Andrew recently to say that he has left Scotland and moved to take up a job as bursar at a Quaker school in Yorkshire.

When Andrew calls in at the local railway station after the day's work is finished, it is to find out that the distance, no more than one hundred and fifty miles as the crow flies, will take him all day to accomplish by train. This means that he will need to take four days off to achieve a two-day

119

stay with his friend. Kenneth Douglas agrees that if he leaves early on Saturday morning, he will be back late Tuesday afternoon, in time to attend an important local branch meeting of the Farmers' Union and then, the following day, prepare the ewes that are to go to the Thursday market.

Unusual though it is for Andrew to come to such a quick decision, he has missed the regular contact with Jack and is keen to see him in his new surroundings.

He closes his eyes against the glare of the early morning sun. It is another beautiful day and he relishes the opportunity to have some time off and enjoy it. It is strange to be travelling north when he needs to go south but this train, after calling at Glasgow, will take him on to Edinburgh, from where he will catch a train to cross the border into England. He has never crossed the border before and is excited at the thought of seeing this new part of Great Britain, a part that he has been told is as picturesque as his own Scotland. Now he will have the chance to decide for himself.

Andrew rests his head back and gives a sigh of satisfaction. It was a good decision to move to his present job. He gets on well with the farmer and the shepherd, although, due to his accident, Andrew has not yet worked closely with Finlay. But with the size of the flock and the large area they graze, he has no doubt that there will be plenty of work for two men, if not more. He thinks of Netta and his face creases in a smile. In the short time he has been working at the farm, Netta has shown herself to be a hard worker and an apt student. She has been up and waiting for him, no matter how early the hour; she has matched him step for step on the high hills and has never complained of tiredness or asked to be excused any part of the jobs in which she has been involved. He doesn't know whether it is merely that she enjoys the work or that she is trying to push to the back of her mind the horrors of the past decade.

In Glasgow and then Edinburgh he is caught up in the busy morning rush to work and it is not until the train is steaming south with the North Sea lapping at the rocks far below and spreading in a glistening sheet to the eastern horizon that his thoughts return to Netta. They are a mixture of admiration and intrigue. The admiration is for the way she has coped with so much loss in her young life and is now trying to rebuild her life and that of her mother in a place to which her mother has chosen to return. Where would Netta choose to be, he wonders, if the choice could be hers?

He is intrigued, he supposes, because, beneath the brittle shell within which she protects herself, there must be a vulnerable woman, craving love and attention. He wants to understand her. At times she seems to open up to him, not hiding from him what she has been through. But as soon as he attempts any closeness, even as little as a helping hand to steady her from falling, she reacts like a startled rabbit or like the sheep who scatter down the hillside in alarm at any unexpected disturbance. He is in all likelihood expecting too much of her. After all it is only a few months since he first set eyes on her and he recalls how direct and even abrasive she was then. And now he has seen her skipping across the hillside like a young girl. He gives a chuckle at the thought, causing the man opposite him in the carriage to look up in surprise from his book and give a smile in return.

'Sorry,' Andrew explains. 'Just contemplating humankind . . . or, more precisely, womankind.'

'Nothing better on a beautiful day like this,' replies the man, 'as long as you don't bother your head with trying to work out what makes them tick. I gave up trying to do that long ago.'

Andrew grins. 'You may be right.' There is a pause, each man seeming to consider whether to continue a conversation. 'Actually,' Andrew says, 'I'm visiting a friend of mine who's moved to a school in the North Riding of Yorkshire. Do you know that area?'

'Can't say that I do. I'm a bit of a city person myself.'

'Me neither. This is the first time I've ventured across the border. My friend has only moved recently.'

'He's a teacher then?'

'No, he's the bursar. When I first knew him, he worked in the city — Glasgow, that is. He's a Quaker, if you know who they are. They did a lot to help the poor and destitute in Glasgow.'

'Is that where you come from?'

'No, I'm from the west. Argyll. I was brought up on a farm but when I was old enough, I decided to have a taste of city life. I got a job in the shipyards. It was interesting enough but not what I wanted long-term. I'm a shepherd at heart. Anyhow, I had met Jack while I was in Glasgow. When he wasnae at his job, he used to help with some of the families who were destitute or near to destitution, the

122

Irish families in particular — find them work, sort out their finances, get the little ones settled in school. That kind of thing. I started going to the Quaker meetings with him. An impressive group of people, the Quakers. They do a lot of good but never seek the limelight.'

'They didn't do themselves any favours by refusing to take up arms,' Andrew's fellow traveller says.

'They may have been pacifists but they were still in the thick of the combat — working on the front line to rescue wounded, driving ambulances and such like. You can't say they lacked courage.'

'No, you're right there.' The man looks around as the train begins to slow. 'Durham. This is where I get out.'

'I need Darlington and change there for Middlesbrough,' Andrew says.

'That's the next stop. Well, enjoy your visit . . . and I hope all goes well with the lady who was filling your thoughts!'

★ ★ ★

Andrew phones Jack's office from Middlesbrough Station, while waiting for the short bus journey that will take him the last few miles of his journey. His friend is there at the bus stop to meet him as he steps down into the soft air of early evening. They shake hands warmly.

'I can see you are back where you should be,' Jack says. 'Sheep are obviously suiting you!'

'And you look happy as well, considering you've just taken on a job that's completely different from

123

the one you're used to.'

'Not completely different. I'm still dealing with money, though in a slightly different way. The children though — they're a bit of a shock to the system! They keep me on my toes and no mistake. This way. You can see the school there in the distance.' He steers Andrew onto a road bordered with hawthorn in full bloom, its heady scent filling their nostrils. It runs through a farm, corn bending like green waves on the sea, filling the land to the left side of the track. On the opposite side is a field of sheep, unlike any Andrew has seen before. On the far side he can see a group of children outside a barn, filling buckets with water from a hosepipe.

'This is the school farm,' says Jack. 'Students are encouraged to come and help — but only if they want. It's surprising how many do. There's a fair number interested in agriculture as a career. The school used to specialise in farming, though not so much now.'

They reach the river that runs through the village. On its far side a stretch of green fronts the school, which is square and sturdy, pale grey in the setting sun.

'It's a bit of a change from working in Glasgow,' Andrew states.

'It is, though it's not without its problems. The children here are boarders. Most of them don't see their parents all term. It's not easy for them to adjust. And there are a few who have had even bigger headaches. But we'll talk more about that tomorrow. You must be starving. There's a meal waiting for us inside. Let's go and eat.'

124

'A number of children here came as refugees. You may have noticed one or two of them — the ones who are still struggling a little with the language.'

Jack is picking up on the conversation of the previous evening. Andrew looks at him with interest. It is Sunday morning. He has gone with his friend to the Meeting House and now they are out for a walk. They have climbed steadily and until their lungs are bursting. At the top of the hill they stand and look south, the North York Moors a colourful counterpane of fields and hedges spread out below them as far as the eye can see.

'So these children came from Germany with their families?'

'From Germany and from Austria too. Some came with their parents; others made the journey alone. Several of them, I believe, have never had contact from their parents since leaving. I've been told that some of the children here were from mixed marriages — a Jew marrying a non-Jew, that is. Maybe that made it easier for them to leave.'

'So it's presumed that in the cases of those who have had no contact with their parents, their parents will have been killed?'

'That's right. I believe records have been kept of many of the deaths, so relatives are informed where possible.'

'It must have been hard for the children who left parents behind. Hard for them and hard for the parents,' says Andrew. 'I mean, I've never been a parent but what a decision to have to make, to send your child away, not knowing whether you would see them again.'

'Did you ever hear talk of the Kindertransport?'

'Aye, we did get some news in the 'wilds of Scotland', though it often took a long time arriving.'

Jack sits on a large flat stone, one of many heaped at the summit of the hill, and invites Andrew to do the same. For a minute the two men gaze in silence over the peaceful fields. 'I suppose I got to know more about the Kindertransport,' Jack continues, 'because various Quaker groups were involved in organising it, and in supporting it financially. Children as young as four were brought over. The upper age limit was seventeen, so most of them were of school age. A guarantee of fifty pounds per child was needed to allow them to enter Great Britain — so they wouldn't be a burden on the state. The Quaker Meetings supplied much of this money. Glasgow sent money — I know that. Manchester Friends formed a committee, the Manchester Quaker Refugee Committee, to help bring children safely over. But the German Quakers must have had the riskiest job. Right under the noses of the Nazis they arranged for children to be put on the trains that transported them up to the Dutch ports. From there, boats took them across the water to England. Then, at this end, they were met and allocated foster parents or went to camps or boarding schools. Quite a number of them now have left school and gone on to university or to other training. The organisation has arranged work permits, helped them find employment and, some of them, British nationality.'

'I have a woman working with me who has come

126

with her mother from Germany,' says Andrew. 'She was telling me that they had near-neighbours who were Quakers and who sheltered them when their house was bombed. The Germans came and took them away after a while and they were interned as enemy aliens until the end of the war. They went back then and the Quakers looked after them until they decided to come over here.'

'Did they lose family?'

'Aye. Her stepfather died in a concentration camp and her two sisters were shot. Netta and her mother are Scottish, one of her two sisters was Scottish and the other one half-German Jewish.' Andrew shakes his head.

'Netta and her mother were exhausted physically and mentally when they arrived. The farmer found them somewhere to stay — a cottage down the valley. Cramped and damp, but they like it a lot.' His eyes fix on the distance but it is another view that he is seeing. 'Netta's taken an interest in the sheep,' he says with a smile. 'The local farmers don't know what to make of her!' He looks at Jack. 'Come to think of it, neither do I!'

'You are attracted to her, this Netta — I can see that.'

'Aye. She's . . . Aye, I am. She's straight-speaking but a bit of an enigma as well!'

'I'm planning to be married myself,' Jack says.

Andrew looks at him in astonishment. 'You've surely no' met someone here already?'

'Do you remember Beth in Glasgow? When you were there, she would have been about twenty-one or so. Before I left we felt it was right that we married . . . but I was moving down here to this job and we decided to wait until I had moved, to see if we still felt the same for each other once we were apart. And we do. So I will be travelling up to Glasgow during the summer holidays and we will marry in front of the Friends at one of their meetings.'

'I remember her well.' Andrew looks at Jack with admiration and the faintest tinge of envy. 'Knowing you both, I'm sure you'll be ideally suited and very happy.'

★ ★ ★

The following day, his last, Andrew is left to his own devices in the morning, as Jack has work to do in his office. He wanders into the village, admiring the attractive stone cottages reflected in the smoothly flowing river, thinking how different it looks from the ruggedness of the land that is now his home. He returns in time for lunch, which he will take with the students in the dining room. Jack meets him there and they sit together surrounded by the nervous chatter of those shortly to take their School Certificate exams.

One student, a fair-haired girl with an infectious smile, realising that he is being left out of the conversation, turns to him. 'Are you coming to teach here?' she asks.

Andrew laughs. 'I'd no' make a very good teacher. No, I'm a shepherd up in Scotland.'

'Is that why you were staring at the sheep on the farm yesterday?'

'Oh, did you see me? I noticed some of you hard at work while I was taking it easy. It's Scottish

128

Blackface on the farm where I am now. I've never seen those that you have here.'

'You mean the Swaledales? They're all over around here — a hardy breed like the Blackface. Freda likes them best, don't you?' She turns to the girl next to her.

'I was allowed to have a go at shearing them last year,' Freda replies. 'I didn't make a very good job of it. The first one looked more like a moth-eaten carpet!' Her dark curls shake as she laughs. 'Dorothy's better at it but she's been brought up to it.'

'Not really,' her friend says. 'I never used to take much notice when I was younger.'

'So you come from a farming family?' asks Andrew.

'*I* do,' says Dorothy, 'but Freda's parents live in Manchester. Not much farming there. It's all cotton mills and smoke.'

'Were your parents farmers?' Freda asks Andrew.

'I lost my father in the war when I was only a lad, and then my mother died just after war ended, so I was brought up by my uncle. He's a farmer and so are his sons. I've spent a lot of my life as a travelling shepherd. Just now I'm on a farm in the south of Scotland with thousands of Blackface, all of them out on the hill.'

There is a long pause. Freda looks down at the ground frowning, her thoughts seemingly far away. When she looks up at him, her eyes are glistening with tears. 'I'm . . . I'm sorry about your parents. I shouldn't have asked.'

'Of course you should. And don't be upset. It was all a very long time ago.'

Another pause. She looks at Andrew, then grins, shaking her head. 'Thousands! I don't think I could manage to shear that many!'

14
Manchester

April 1939

It was the middle of April but you could have been forgiven for thinking it was still winter. The day was raw, fog seeped menacingly between the tall black buildings and Gwen shivered as she stood beside Peter in the austere railway station. Their small group was clustered inside the entrance awaiting the arrival of the London train. The group had worked together with others from London and abroad to ensure the safe travel of the children. Now that they were nearly here, Gwen's apprehension grew. The Meeting had felt unanimously that this was the right way forward, that what they were doing was for the ultimate good of the children. But as the minutes ticked by, she kept thinking of the parents left behind, bereft of their children. What must they be feeling?

In truth, Gwen had no idea what it must feel like to have a child, nor to undergo the torture of losing one. She and Peter had been married for fourteen years and no child had resulted. She was now fast approaching forty years of age and recognised that her chances of having a baby were diminishing fast. Peter said that she was not to worry on his account — he loved her and the addition or not of a child would not alter that. At least

131

it meant that they were able to help in whatever way the Meeting felt was right, unencumbered by children of their own. He was right of course, but it didn't take away the yawning hole in her life.

A shrill whistle heralded the approach of the London train. Amid clouds of steam, the engine crawled to a stop. A guard approached a carriage and flung open a door. One by one a group of assorted children stumbled down.

They ranged from the very small to the nearly adult. Around the neck of each hung a label, with a number written on one side and their name on the other, and each carried a bag or small suitcase. Most of the younger children clutched a doll or a teddy bear, many looking as dishevelled as their owners.

It was clear that some of them had just been woken from their sleep and they looked around bleary-eyed and disbelieving at the unwelcoming gloom of the railway station.

One small girl began to cry loudly, looking around in vain for her mother. A woman who had followed the children from the carriage went over and put an arm around her. The woman walked over to the waiting group, her arm still comforting the tearful girl, and asked which one was Peter Halliwell. Peter stepped forward and shook her hand.

'I'm Mary Goodwin from the London Meeting,' she said. 'I'm pleased to meet you. I have twenty-five very tired children here. They have been travelling for several days. Some are related, others have come on their own. Obviously it would be desirable if those who are related could

132

stay together.'

'Of course we will try to do that.' Peter nodded. 'We have a hostel that can take sixteen children and the rest we will share out between us.' Peter turned to the group who had been waiting silently. 'Shall we each take the child or children who we think will best fit into our particular circumstances? Remember that this is a temporary arrangement. Things may well change in the future.'

A woman approached and smiled at a taller girl who looked to be around fourteen. 'Would you like to come with me?' The girl hesitated, frowning.

The woman took her hand and gently steered her over to where her husband was waiting. Other women began to do the same, some with husbands, others alone.

Gwen looked at the young girl. She had quietened now, her sobs intermittent. She was studying the adults, two dark plaits framing a thin face with liquid eyes fearful and ready to spill over again. Gwen's heart lurched. She had a fleeting memory of the death of her mother when she herself was about the same age as this vulnerable child, looking so lost on the platform. She crossed to her and took her hand.

'Would you like to come home with me?' she asked. The girl stepped backwards away from her. Gwen took a deep breath. ' *Willst du mit mir nach Hause kommen?* ' She smiled. ' *Wie heisst du?* '

The girl paused. '*Ich heisse Frieda.*'

'Willst du mit mir kommen, Frieda?' *Gwen repeated.*

'*Samuel auch?*' She turned and went over to a

boy in early adolescence. *'Das ist Samuel. Wir sind zusammen. Er muss mit mir bleiben. '*

Gwen glanced at her husband but he was engaged in sharing out the remaining children. *'Jawohl,'* she said to Frieda. *'Er darf mit uns bleiben.* Samuel may come too.'

'Thank you,' said Samuel in immaculate English, causing Gwen to glance at him in surprise. 'You are very kind.'

*   *   *

'We can use the study as a bedroom,' Gwen said, as Peter negotiated the busy streets of Manchester. 'After all, it may be only for a short time.'

'If it turns out to be longer, we will be a little crowded,' Peter said, smiling. He had been somewhat taken aback by the appearance of two children at his wife's side when he had finished finding accommodation for all the others, but, looking at her excited face now, he could see that it was the right thing to do.

'The boy speaks good English,' Gwen said, 'but of course he will have learned languages at school, just as we do here. It will make things easier for him to fit in.'

'And mean that I won't have to bring out my rusty German quite so much!' Peter replied.

'Oh, I think you will or little Frieda won't understand you.'

'We need to be careful what we say. Remember that the boy will be able to understand you. Let's talk about everything later when the future is less uncertain.' Gwen glanced in the rear-view mirror.

Samuel was gazing out of the window at the tall buildings and gave no indication of having heard them. He turned to Frieda who was also intent on the view from the window, and said in German, 'These buildings need a wash. They are very dirty.'

'They are black!' she replied, laughing and snuggling close to him.

They left the city centre and drove north a short way to a part that had solid rows of stone houses with small front gardens and long narrow back gardens of colourful flowers trumpeting the onset of spring. Peter pulled up outside one of these houses and turned off the car engine. 'Here we are. This is your home for now.'

Samuel nodded and translated for the girl. She stared at the row of houses.

'Come along,' Gwen said briskly. 'Let's go inside and find some breakfast. You must be hungry.'

'I hope that you do not give us hard bread.'

'Hard bread? Oh, you mean stale! No, I promise it will not be stale. I made it last night so it would be fresh for your coming.'

The house seemed smaller with all the extra bodies inside it. There was a living room at the front and a large kitchen behind it with a bathroom built on the back. Upstairs were two bedrooms and a tiny study, almost full with books and a large desk.

'This will be your room, Samuel,' said Gwen. 'We will move the desk outside and put in a chair that will let down into a bed. There is not a lot of room but we will be cosy.' Samuel opened his case and drew out some money, which he handed to Gwen. 'What is this?' she asked.

'It is ten Deutschmarks. Frieda has the same. It is to pay for our food.'

'No, Samuel. You keep this. Peter and I do not need money. What else do you have in your case? Is there anything that you need to show us?'

The boy reached for a document. 'This is a paper with my name, my address, my birthday and the names of my parents. I will keep it safe.' He placed it back in the case and shut it firmly.

Gwen turned, and Frieda was standing there in tears. ' *Was ist los, Frieda?* '

Frieda said something so interrupted by sobs that Gwen couldn't understand.

'She says there is no room for her father and mother when they arrive,' Samuel interpreted.

'Don't worry. We have a big room downstairs. They can stay there. Let us put your case in the bedroom and then I will show you.'

The big room lacked the cosiness of the rest of the house, for it was rarely used and, as was the Quaker custom, had little in the way of ornaments and pictures. Samuel stepped inside, however, and his eyes lit up.

'*Es gibt ein Klavier!*' he said and went up to the piano against one wall.

'Do you play the piano, Samuel?'

'Yes, I learn the piano.'

'Well, you can have lessons, while you are staying with us, if you would like to do that.'

'Yes, I like. Thank you.' He turned to Frieda and addressed her. She shook her head. 'Frieda does not wish to play,' he said.

'What does Frieda like to do?'

The two young people chatted rapidly in their

own language. 'She asks, do you have a garden? She likes to play outside.'

'We have a big garden at the back. After we have had something to eat, we will go and see it.'

* * *

Frieda wandered down the path of the long thin garden, turning at the end to look back at the house. It was a friendly-looking house, she decided, comfortable grey stones and red window frames with a red back door. Outside the door were tubs containing herbs. She didn't know the names of the herbs but she recognised the colours and scent of some of them as being like those in her own garden at home. Elsewhere the garden was alight with spring flowers: crocuses beginning to fade, daffodils in full bloom, tulips about to burst open.

Her parents would like it here, she thought, her mother particularly. She was the one who looked after the garden at home, her father being much too busy in his shop. At least he had been until he had been forced to close. Just now he had been taken by the soldiers to help them with enquiries — at least that was what her mother said, though she looked so sad that Frieda wondered if there was more that her mother wasn't telling her. Anyway, her mother assured her that it would not be long before she and Frieda's father would be able to travel to England, so they could all be together again.

Frieda sighed. She shut her eyes so she could count the days she had been without them. Was it two or three . . . or even more? It felt like more. She frowned, trying to remember the journey but found she couldn't. It was all mixed up in her head. All she could clearly remember was being with Samuel. He was her brother now. That was what brothers did — they looked after their little sisters and brothers. And he was very good at looking after her.

She squinted up at the house again. There was her bedroom window with its view over the garden. She wondered if she would be able to sleep tonight. She hoped so, for she had slept only in snatches during their long journey and she was very tired. Her eyes travelled to the left, to Samuel's bedroom window, and there he was, peering out. He waved to her and his face disappeared. The next minute he was coming down the path towards her.

'Mrs Halliwell says that she will take us for a walk to see the neighbourhood and introduce us to some of her friends who have children.'

'Do they speak the same as Mrs Halliwell? If so, we won't understand them.'

'It may not be easy at first but I will help you. I speak some English and we will soon learn more.'

* * *

There were many streets with houses much like theirs, and presumably with similar long gardens at the back, though they could not see them from the road. Mrs Halliwell needed to buy some food, so Frieda and Samuel accompanied her into the grocer's shop and introduced them to the man behind the counter. He nodded to them but didn't look particularly friendly. He muttered something to Mrs Halliwell and shook his head.

'What is he saying?' Frieda asked Samuel.

'He says he doesn't know why it is necessary for us to come to England. Why can't German parents look after their own children?'

'I don't understand either. But soon Mother and Father will be here and then they will be able to look after us.'

Along the street past the row of shops, Mrs Halliwell stopped in front of a brick building with an entrance at each end, one marked 'BOYS' and the other 'GIRLS'. 'This is the school,' she said. 'For now they are on holiday. It is Easter. Do you understand, Samuel? Er — Ostern.'

Samuel frowned. ' Ostern . . . oh, Christlich. Ja, ich verstehe. *I understand.*'

'After the holiday I will go to the school and ask them if there is a place for you both.'

'That will be good,' Samuel said. 'We were not allowed anymore to go to the school in Germany.'

'I didn't know that. When did you stop?'

'In November. It is six months now.'

'I see. Well, next week I will go and talk to the school. The most important thing to do when we get back home is for you both to write to your parents to tell them you are safe and let them know where you are.'

Samuel translated this for Frieda who smiled broadly. 'Yes, I will do that straightaway. They cannot come until we tell them where we are.'

15
School Days

April 1939

Arranging for a place in school was not as easy as Gwen had imagined. The local school agreed to take Frieda. She was eight years old and the children were there until they had sat the eleven-plus exam, when they went either to a grammar school or to a secondary modern. Whether or not Frieda's English would be sufficient for her to take this exam remained to be seen.

Gwen pointed out that to predict what the situation would be in two years was impossible. Hopefully by then Frieda would be back in her own country and going to the school she was used to.

Samuel was more of a problem. He was fourteen and had been attending the '*Mittelschule*' since he was nearly nine years of age. If he had continued his education in Germany, he would have been preparing for entry to the '*Gymnasium*'. How would the authorities adapt his schooling from a three-stage system to a two-stage one, especially when he was well past the age for taking the exam that was meant to decide the ability of the child and the type of education for which he or she would be best suited in the future?

140

The sensible solution, it was decided, was to put him into the secondary modern school.

The problem caused by Frieda's separation from Samuel was twofold. Not only was she bereft of his company but, on a practical level, she no longer had him to act as interpreter. For her first week at the local school she was miserable. During the second week, however, she made a friend and life became more bearable. Her English vocabulary was growing fast and the friendship was such that the two girls succeeded in understanding each other even without the use of words. For a short time each day Frieda was able to forget that there had been no letter from her parents in reply to hers.

Samuel, on the contrary, enjoyed being at school. What was more, he could understand much of what was said in the lessons and was quick to grasp what he was being taught. To start with he had enjoyed his days at school in his homeland; that was until he, and one or two others in his class, started to be singled out, made to sit in separate desks away from his fellow pupils. The teachers had begun to insist on the whole class giving the Nazi salute, firstly at the start of the day and later, with each change of teacher. New books were issued, the old ones collected in. History books emphasised how the Germans had been treated badly, biology books talked of racial superiority, worthy and unworthy races, and in science they were taught about shooting and aviation, about the need for German youth to be ready for war and, worst of all, that the Jews were a racially inferior people.

Samuel had even seen a book entitled *The Jewish Question in Education*. It contained guidelines for the identification of Jews. He was appalled. He couldn't understand why this should be happening.

But now he could leave all this behind him. He was in England. He was safe. He had heard little talk of politics, discrimination and war.

At the end of his second week of the summer term he opened the front door, threw his satchel down on the floor and, muttering a few words to Gwen to let her know he was back, passed on through the house and into the back garden. Gwen paused in her preparation of tea, put her head round the kitchen door, frowned at his abandoned school bag, for he was always well-mannered and thoughtful when it came to tidiness, and went back to what she was doing.

Samuel knew that he would find Frieda in the garden — and there she was, working away at the little plot she had been given. The soil was marked out in lines with string, small channels following the straight lines, and she was adding seeds as evenly as she was able along the indented soil.

'Carrots,' she said, smiling up at him. 'Tomorrow, if the weather is fine, I will plant potatoes. We will have good meals when I have finished growing them.'

'We have good meals now,' Samuel replied and went to sit on the garden seat where he could watch her working.

'I read a whole page of my book to the class today,' Frieda went on, 'and understood most words.Peggy and I were allowed to choose pictures to cut out because we had both finished our

142

reading.'

'Good.'

Frieda glanced at Samuel. 'Did you read in class?'

'A bit.'

Frieda gave a huge sigh. 'Well, did you play with your friends?'

'Not today.' He got up from the seat. 'Has there been a letter?'

'No. No letters.'

Samuel walked slowly towards the house.

'Aren't you staying to talk?'

'Later, maybe. I have homework to do,' Samuel called back before disappearing indoors.

When Peter came in from work, his face was grim.

'What's happened? Is it more bad news?' Gwen asked.

'I'm afraid so, the latest in a long line. Six weeks ago appeasement talks were abandoned. Now Britain is bringing back conscription. The threat of war is drawing nearer.'

Gwen put down the cutlery and went over to her husband, putting her arms around his waist and laying her head against his chest. 'What will you do?'

'If it comes to it, I'm not fighting. There will be plenty of other work needing to be done, just as before — but I'm not fighting,' he said finally and bent to kiss the top of her head.

Gwen looked up at him. 'Perhaps that's what is wrong with Samuel. He must have heard about this too. Darling, will you call the children for tea? It's all ready to put out.' She loosened her hold and turned back to the oven.

Samuel stood up from the table and asked to be excused. He had hardly said a word during the meal, unlike the first week and a half of term when he couldn't wait to tell them what he had been learning at school.

'Has anything happened, Samuel?' Peter asked. 'Only you are very quiet this evening.'

Samuel shrugged.

'Has anyone said something to you?'

He shrugged again and looked at the floor. 'They say I do not belong here.'

'Who say so? Your friends?'

'My 'friends' say they are not my friends anymore. They say their fathers and brothers must become soldiers because of what my country does. They say I am a filthy German. I try to explain that Germany does not like me but they do not listen. What can I do? They do not want me here and my country does not want me there. And we have no letter from our parents, Frieda and I.'

Frieda, who had been staring at Samuel during his outburst, burst into noisy tears. 'Maybe *they* don't want us either,' she sobbed to Samuel.

'But of course they do,' said Gwen, putting her arm around the young girl. 'They love you very much. It must have been the hardest thing in the world to put you on the train and let you come here.'

Frieda stopped crying suddenly and looked up at Gwen. 'Did you have any children?'

'No, we were not fortunate enough to have children of our own.'

144

'So we are like your children at the moment?' Frieda said hopefully.

'Yes, just for the moment, until your parents can have you back.'

'I have an idea,' said Samuel, brightening. 'It might help Frieda, even if it does not help me now. We can use your name, so we sound English, not German — Frieda Halliwell, Samuel Halliwell. This is a good idea, yes?'

Gwen looked at Peter expectantly. Her husband nodded slowly. 'That may be a very good idea while the political situation is as it is. It may or may not help you at present, Samuel, but it can do no harm. If you use my surname, it may also be best if we shorten your name to Sam. Frieda is a name that is common in this country anyway but maybe we will spell it the English way — F-r-e-d-a. Will you explain to Frieda what we are saying and ask her what she thinks?'

'Freda Halliwell . . . Freda Halliwell. Yes, English name.' She turned to Samuel and spoke rapidly in her own language.

'She says she will be Freda Halliwell and you will be her mother and father. When her parents arrive, she will be Frieda Schäfer again.'

Gwen looked at her husband and they exchanged a nod and a smile. It was a plan that would suit them all very well.

★ ★ ★

Sam began to listen more closely to the news on the radio and took to reading the daily paper, or as much of it as he could understand. It seemed

145

that Britain and France were making pacts with Greece and Turkey, while Germany, teamed up with Italy, were negotiating with the Soviet Union. Whatever became of it, he, Sam, was in a difficult position — a German boy in an English school.

Following the teatime conversation, Peter had made an appointment to see the headmaster of Sam's school. Without apportioning blame, he told the head what had been going on in the playground at school and how it was affecting Sam. He explained their decision for Sam and Frieda to 'adopt' Peter's surname, in the hopes that they would appear less obviously German. The headmaster, while acknowledging that this was a good idea, wished they had done so before Sam had started at the school. Still, what was done was done and they had to make the best of it.

The best of it, as far as Sam was concerned, meant that things continued much as before. The form teacher was sympathetic and asked the boys how they would feel if they were made to flee from the country in which they grew up, leaving all the friends they had made for a country where they knew nobody and the people they did get to know spoke a different language. The boys nodded in sullen agreement, but in the playground the language of war that they were fast learning from adults at home and in the street, as well as from the radio and newspapers, dominated. No matter how inconspicuous Sam tried to be, the alienation continued.

His only consolation came from the piano. Peter, true to his word, had found a piano teacher who would come to the house and give Sam lessons.

Hidden in the seat of the piano stool was a stack of sheet music, and Gwen pulled out more from the bottom of a cupboard. Sam spent a Saturday morning in rising excitement, as he carefully went through the music, sorting it into piles — music that he had seen before and was able to play, pieces that looked as though he could learn with practice and others that were much too hard at the moment but he could try later.

His music teacher, John Baxendale, who had in his younger days attended the Royal Manchester College of Music, was astounded at Sam's repertoire. He came weekly to hear what Sam had been practising and to help him with new pieces that he was keen to try. He found himself moved by the music the boy was playing, for Sam poured his emotions into it, more emotions than seemed likely a fourteen-year-old boy would possess.

* * *

One evening at the beginning of June, Gwen and Peter sought out Sam in the garden. He had finished his homework, spent three-quarters of an hour on piano practice and was now making the most of the long days leading up to the summer solstice. Freda had insisted a chair was put at the side of the herb garden, which had expanded considerably since her arrival. She had also endeavoured to teach Sam the different herbs and their uses. But for now he was merely enjoying their individual fragrances drawn out by the evening stillness. He turned at the sound of footsteps.

'I hope we're not disturbing your peace,' Peter

147

began.

'No, of course not. Please have my seat, Mother.'

'We've brought some out for ourselves, thank you, Sam.'

'It is a beautiful evening, is it not?' Sam said, as Gwen and Peter made themselves comfortable.

'It is,' replied Peter, 'and you will be finding it a lot more peaceful than in the playground at school.'

Sam glanced at him and looked away. 'Yes, it is true. It is not easy. Still the other boys do not like me there. But maybe it is not so bad now,' he added doubtfully.

'We have an idea that might help,' Peter went on. 'You must tell us honestly what you think. There are some schools in England that are run by Quakers — you have been with us to Quaker Meetings, so you know a bit about them. We have made enquiries and there is one in North Yorkshire that has taken boys like yourself who have had to leave their country. We have been told that these boys are very happy at the school. We think that it would suit you well.'

'But North Yorkshire? How do I get back to your home at night?'

'It is a boarding school, Sam. You will stay there during term and come home for the holidays at Christmas, Easter and in the summer.'

'But a boarding school must be very expensive. I have no money.'

'You do not have to worry about that. The Friends have agreed to pay, if you agree that is what you would like to do. Of course we will take you there to see it first.'

148

Sam was silent, considering. 'Yes, I would like to be at a school where I can make friends and not worry all the time. But Freda . . . I think she will miss me very much.'

'Yes, she will,' Gwen said. 'But it is different for her. She has friends at school and the children there are not old enough to understand all the unsettling things that are going on in the world at the moment. In any case, she will come with us when we take you to see the school and, when she is old enough, she will have the chance to go there also.'

'And you think my father and my mother will agree for me to go there.'

Gwen glanced at Peter and back to Sam. 'I'm sure they would be very happy.'

'Then I will go and see it. Thank you. When are we to go?'

★ ★ ★

The following weekend they packed a bag for an overnight stay and set off on the Saturday morning. Freda had not yet been told of the plan for Sam to go to boarding school. It had been considered best to wait until they had arrived and looked round the place, for they felt sure that she would love it too.

It was a long drive and mid-afternoon by the time they arrived. The school was set to one side of a small village surrounded by rolling hills. Out in the fields they could see children playing. Others were walking in twos and threes along the road and Sam searched their faces in an effort to judge how happy they were.

While Gwen and Peter went in to talk to the headmaster, Sam and Freda went for a walk in the school grounds.

'I like it here,' said Freda.

'Would you like to come here when you are old enough?'

'Oh, yes. It seems a friendly place and the countryside is beautiful. A lot better than smoky Manchester.'

Sam laughed. 'Well, we've come today to look round because there's a place for me here, if I want it.'

'You mean, to go to school *and* to live here?'

'Yes, I would have to live here during the term and come home for the holidays.'

Freda looked crestfallen. 'I would miss you,' she said in a small voice.

'And I would miss *you*. But things aren't going well for me at the school I'm in and Peter and Gwen think I would fit in here much better. And you have your friends at school. Maybe if I come here, I will have friends too.'

'Yes. Yes, that will be good.'

They had reached what looked like a farm entrance. Ahead of them was a big barn, its doors wide open. Inside they could see sheep being shorn and, if they were not mistaken, it was one of the pupils who was doing the shearing. They stepped up to the door to see if they were right. It was indeed a pupil, his sleeves rolled up, holding down a complaining ewe and calmly clipping the wool from the ewe's back. A farmer stood by directing operations. He looked over and winked

150

at them.

'You two coming to the school one day? If you're interested, we could do with more help on the farm and that's a fact.'

★ ★ ★

It was settled. Sam would finish the term in Manchester, spend the holidays with Gwen and Peter, then travel to his new school for the beginning of the autumn term, the first week in September. He would work towards his school certificate exams, and he would continue to have piano lessons with the help of a teacher arranged by the music master.

Peter and Gwen joined the two children on the green outside. 'Freda,' Gwen began nervously. 'We have arranged with the headmaster that Sam is to come here to school after the summer holidays.'

'Yes, I know, and in two years' time I am coming to join him and learn to shear sheep,' Freda said with a huge grin, leaving Gwen speechless with surprise.

It was just as well that this arrangement had been reached, for seven weeks later Hitler marched into Poland and the Allies declared war on Germany. Had he not moved, Sam's journey through the city school could have become even more difficult.

16

Hostility

May 1946

'A telegram's arrived from Andrew,' Kenneth says to Netta. She is in the kitchen preparing the afternoon feed for the pet lambs. 'There's been some kind of delay on the railway line and he's not going to be back in time for the local Farmers' Union meeting tonight.'

A wave of disappointment runs through Netta but she merely shrugs her shoulders and continues stirring the milk.

'I know Andrew planned for you to go with him,' Kenneth says. 'I wondered if you would care to go with me instead. I think we need to be represented and Finlay's arm isn't strong enough to let him drive.'

'Yes, I would like that.' She indicates her soiled working clothes. 'I will need to go home first and get changed out of my working clothes.'

'Good. I'll pick you up in the car at half past six.'

Netta makes her way to the lambing shed with the bottles. There are a couple of dozen lambs needing to be fed, the majority of orphans having been fostered onto ewes who have lost their lambs. She is adept at giving them the bottle and works steadily, not allowing herself to give in to her disappointment. But later, on the long walk home, she cannot stop her brain from reasoning that this is how she had known it would be. He has decided to go elsewhere to farm, somewhere he can more easily find friends. She blames herself for acting so coldly every time he has offered her the hand of friendship. For that is all he has done. There has been no overstepping the mark. He has been nothing but a true gentleman.

Clouds have rolled in from the west during the afternoon and it begins to rain when she is still fifteen minutes from the cottage. By the time she opens the door and steps inside, she is drenched.

'Poor girl,' says Ellen. 'Go and get changed while I get the meal ready. You're surely not going out again in this weather.'

'Kenneth is calling for me. Andrew won't be back and Kenneth said he would go himself and offered to take me with him.'

'I wouldn't have thought a Farmers' Union meeting was that important that you have to go out again on an evening like this.'

'It is important,' Netta says, a little more emphatically than she feels.

'Farming is suffering — everything is suffering after the war. It will take a long time for industries to recover. It is necessary to support them when they are trying to help us.'

Ellen's eyebrows are raised in surprise. 'I had no idea that you felt so strongly about the farm. That is good. I am very proud of you. Well, go and get changed quickly if you don't want double pneumonia, and I'll have your tea ready.'

Netta cannot prevent a small smile as she

remembers Andrew's identical words after she had slipped off the stone and soaked her feet in the river.

Her smile fades just as quickly as she thinks how much more fun it would be if he, rather than the ageing farmer, was taking her to the meeting.

* * *

Netta scans the crowded room and sees only two other women and one of those is sitting at the front preparing to take notes. Several of the farmers nod a welcome to Kenneth and stare at Netta as she takes her seat. She sees Roddie McCann across the room, just as he recognises her. He leans over and whispers into the ear of his neighbour who looks up in Netta's direction with a small shake of his head.

The meeting begins. The main topic for discussion is how to provide help for those farms that have suffered financially as a result of being unable to increase production during the long years of the war, some of them because farm labourers had been called up to serve in the armed forces. The conversation goes to and fro. Kenneth stands up to point out the value of travelling shepherds who will spend anything from a year to several years to help out on a farm. He has, he says, taken on a shepherd from Argyllshire who is proving a godsend to the farm.

'I would like to point out . . . ' says a voice, that of Roddie McCann. He rises to his feet. 'I would like to point out that the history of this farm is not one we should think fit to follow. This farm

154

collaborated with the enemy in the First World War. It let them into the valley. It even paid them for their help.'

Kenneth rises to his feet. 'I think you'll find that what the Germans were doing there was nothing to do with the farm. They were prisoners of war, brought in to help build the reservoir. Work had been stopped because our men were sent off to the front.'

'To be killed by the Germans!' another farmer scoffs.

'And the enemy were paid a good wage for their work, so I've heard,' a third farmer speaks up.

'They were paid the same wage as our men would have received, so that the reservoir could be completed and water supplied to the factories that were making guns for us to shoot the Germans,' Kenneth Douglas responds.

'Are you telling me that the farm had no contact with the POWs?' Roddie McCann stares at Netta. 'From what I've heard there was rather a lot of contact between the farm and the visitors.'

Netta stands up suddenly and faces Roddie McCann. Kenneth puts a hand on her arm in an effort to persuade her to sit down but she shakes him off.

'You have no idea what you are talking about,' she says. 'Perhaps you were still in nappies when the Great War was taking place.' She looks around at the farmers, each face registering surprise that a woman is interrupting their meeting. 'Who among you has even visited the valley and the new reservoir?'

Silence falls and the men look round at one

another, some embarrassed, one or two with a half-smile on their faces, as though amused at what is developing.

'My mother worked hard on that farm with her father. He, my grandfather, was widowed when she was born. He brought up my mother single-handedly. When a shepherd came up from Yorkshire, he eventually married her. I was the result. That farm, like all hill farms, was hard work and even harder when my father went off to fight.

'The men who came were prisoners of war, as you have been told. Some of them had been rescued from the sea when their submarine was torpedoed. I suspect that many of them had no more desire to fight than our men. They were brought to the valley to take the place of our own men who were away fighting, in order that the work of building the reservoir could continue. Some of them were unwell as a result of their experiences. One was very unwell. The British captain in charge of them came to my mother and asked her to nurse him. She too would receive a wage. She did this — she nursed him back to health, although as a result of what he had suffered in the water, he was never strong.

'When the war ended, he went back to his homeland and my mother prepared, like every other woman whose husband returned from the war, to rebuild her marriage. But then, as some of you may know, my father was killed in the snowy conditions of that winter following cessation of hostilities. The following year my mother decided to join Josef Kessler in Germany. They had become friends while she was looking after

156

him.'

A couple of young men at the back of the crowd jeered but a look from Netta silenced them.

'My stepfather was a gentle soul. He hated fighting and everything to do with it. He was a musician — a pianist. He had had a promising career before the war and when he returned to his homeland, he resumed his profession. After the war, and the death of my stepfather, my mother decided to come back to the valley. We are both living there now and helping on the farm.

'This farm has as honourable a history as any other. If you want to take exception to the reservoir, then do it with the people who govern our country and who planned its construction, not with the farmer who happens to have had his living disrupted by the enterprise. But before you do, just think where you would be now without fresh water coming out of your taps to ease the day-to-day work on the farm and to fill your bath at night so that you can soak away the aches and pains of the day's hard work.'

Netta goes to sit down, then changes her mind and begins to make her way past the row of legs. Suddenly from the back comes the sound of applause and the next second it is taken up by a substantial number of farmers in the room. She is hurrying now, her way blurred by the tears she cannot check, and she doesn't see the tall man standing at the open door until she collides with him. He takes hold of her and steps backwards with her held fast. The door swings shut behind them and she looks up into the face of Andrew. He is smiling broadly.

'If you are going to make a habit of this, I shall have to write a label to fasten to your back, 'Farmers beware!' or something like.'

'Andrew! How did you get here?'

'By train, as planned, only a later one. And I've come straight to the meeting, rather than go home first. I'm starving, I don't mind saying, but I wouldn't have missed this for the world. You were brilliant.' He smiles at her in admiration and then his smile slowly fades as he bends to kiss her lips.

17
Aftermath

May 1946

Rain is lashing the windscreen, making it difficult to see the way ahead, as Kenneth manoeuvres the car along the flooded road.

'What kind of weather is this to bring back from Yorkshire, pal?' Kenneth grunts, not taking his eyes off the road. 'We needed rain but not in bucketfuls!'

'It was beautiful down there, and the scenery too. And very good to see my pal Jack again. It's a lovely school he's in.'

'Teaching, is he?'

'No, he's the bursar — he's looking after all the finances. But he's quite involved in the welfare of the children as well. They even have a farm attached to the school. The children can help on the farm, if they're minded. They have several fields, a herd of cows and a few dozen sheep — Blackface like our own and a Yorkshire breed, the Swaledale. A hardy breed by all accounts and nice-looking too.'

Netta studies the back of Andrew's head from her seat in the back of the car, where she has insisted she would prefer to sit. She pays little heed to their conversation. Her body is still thrilling to the memory of the unexpected kiss outside the door of the farmers' meeting room. If her mind was in turmoil at the end of the impromptu speech, it is doubly so now.

Kenneth Douglas had not waited until the conclusion of the meeting, worried about the after-effects of Netta's outburst. He had encountered Andrew in the lobby, looking uncharacteristically flustered. Netta was just disappearing through the doors to the outside.

'That girl is too outspoken for her own good,' Kenneth had muttered as he went after her.

'Judging by the applause that followed her, I would say she got it about right. And I have to admit, she's a lot braver than I would have been.'

'Have the sheep been giving you any problems while I've been away?' Andrew says now.

'There've been no problems that I know of. Finlay's been walking around getting his strength up and giving Netta orders. She's been doing all the work, haven't you, lass?'

Netta drags her thoughts back to the here and now. 'There's not been so much work. The pet lambs are all doing well. In this weather I would think they'd be better off in the shed than those out on the hills with their mothers. They've had too little water the past week or two and now they have too much!'

'Aye,' says Kenneth. 'It's to be hoped that this wet spell passes over as quickly as it has come. Still, better now than when it's time for clipping.'

They continue in silence, each of them staring out of the windows at the beating rain. When they arrive at Netta's cottage, Andrew says he will see

160

her to the door but she says she can manage perfectly well and jumps out, slamming the car door and splashing through puddles and into the cottage.

'She's a mind of her own, that one,' Kenneth says, shaking his head in amusement.

'Aye.' Andrew sighs. 'And I can't even begin to fathom how it works.'

★ ★ ★

Rain is still pounding on the windows as reluctant dawn insinuates itself around the curtains. Netta has been awake all night — at least that's what it feels like. She sits up, swings her legs out of bed and goes to the window. To the side of the cottage the river is wide and wild, escaping its usual boundaries. She gazes along the valley towards the farm. It is invisible from the cottage but she pictures its grey stone walls and surrounding collection of outhouses and barns. In her mind's eye she sees the two white cottages nearby, hunkering down into the hillside, one occupied by Finlay, the other sheltering the man who kissed her a few short hours ago, and is doubtless still fast asleep.

She tiptoes downstairs, lifts the kettle onto the hotplate and, while she waits for it to heat, fetches the milk jug, sniffing its contents to make sure it isn't on the turn, for the weather remains warm despite the heavy rain. The kettle boils and she pours water onto the tealeaves, carries the pot to the windowsill and collects a cup and saucer. She pours a cup of tea and sits at the window to ponder on what she must do.

Two hours later she enters the barn to check on

the remaining pet lambs.

The rain has eased during her walk but her boots have been insufficient to protect her feet from the saturated fields. She takes off her raincoat and shakes it, then takes off a boot and upends it to allow the water to escape.

'Och no! Wet feet again! You seem to be making a habit of it.'

Netta spins round to see Andrew putting the lambs' feed into bottles.

'I was trying to save you a job.' He indicates the milk. 'I thought you might leave a bit later — waiting for the rain to ease, maybe.' She takes a breath to reply but he goes on, 'I would have driven the wagon over for you, if I didn't think you would refuse the lift.'

Netta looks at him sharply but cannot stop a smile from breaking out, try as she might. 'You look awful,' she says, 'as if you've slept in the hay all night.'

'Well, thank you very much for the compliment — though I've seen you looking tidier.' She glances down at herself. She is covered in mud and, when she puts her hand to her hair, she can feel it lying in rats' tails around her face. He opens the gate to the pen, where the lambs are scrambling to be the first to get to the bottle.

'If the rain keeps on,' she says meekly, 'I'm sure Mutti would like you to collect her.'

'Nae problem. I'll go as soon as we've finished these . . . that's if you've no objection to me helping.'

'Of course not. To tell you the truth, I didn't sleep too well myself.'

162

'Did you no'? What was the problem, hen?' he says softly.

She looks at him closely, unsure whether he is mocking her, takes a breath to begin saying what is on her mind, then thinks better of it and merely says, 'Oh, I'm beginning to regret what I said at the meeting last night. I don't want to make things difficult for Kenneth when he's been so good to us.'

'I'm sure you've no' done that. You were setting the record straight, being honest. We all need to know the truth and separate it from the rumours. What you said is all to the good. I'm certain most of them saw it that way. I for one am very proud of you.' He turns back to the lambs and offers a bottle to the nearest who begins to suck on it greedily. Netta stands for a minute looking at his figure bent over the lamb, and goes to join him, offering her bottle to a restlessly impatient lamb.

★ ★ ★

Over the next week Netta and Andrew appear to play a game of cat and mouse. She is the mouse, diligently avoiding being where he is, apart from first thing in the morning when they are usually in the company of Finlay handing out the work for the day. One morning it is dry, the first for days that Netta hasn't undergone a drenching on her way to work. She and her mother walk briskly to the farm, glad of the improved weather but not confident of its lasting. Clouds are low on the hills to either side of them and there is no glimmer of

163

sun or even blue sky to lighten their steps. In the distance Netta can see Andrew in conversation with Finlay and the farmer. Despite all attempts not to react to his appearance, her heart misses a beat. She accompanies her mother up to the farmhouse, ignoring the men, and enters the kitchen where Elizabeth has seen their approach and has a cup of tea poured and waiting for her.

'A long walk planned for you today, Netta,' Elizabeth says, passing her the tea. 'You are to walk with Andrew to the furthest hefts. I have a piece here ready for you and him. You'll likely no' be back till late this afternoon. Let's hope the rain keeps off today.'

* * *

Netta follows Andrew as he climbs through rough grass interspersed at times with stretches of heather. At the top of the hill they pause to catch their breath. The low cloud has moved away to expose the interlocking hills as they fade into the horizon. Andrew glances at her before turning eastward and making his way along the ridge of hills. It is a way they have been before, on a day of racing sunlight and shadows, chatting companionably as she learned the basics of looking after sheep. But today they say little, Netta following in Andrew's footsteps as he makes his way across the springy grass with Jill bounding ahead.

After two hours' walking they reach the boundary of Kenneth's land. The sheep are scattered thinly at the tops, more numerous on the lower stretches. Andrew goes about them, Netta following as he

164

checks the lambs for pulpy kidney, this being more common, he explains, when the weather has been good, with richer growth of grass than is often the case.

'Occasionally we find the lambs dead,' he says. 'Other times they just have no bounce in them and find it difficult to stand. Moving them to a poorer pasture usually works. There's no problem with these, though we'll need to come back and check again.' She listens closely to what he is saying.

'We'll stop here and have our piece,' Andrew says, indicating a spot against a nearby wall, which might offer a smidgen of shelter, should it come on to rain again. Netta finds a stone and sits down, unpacking the knapsack and taking from it the flask and several tattie scones wrapped in waxed paper. She offers one to Andrew and he takes it with a grin.

'I'm ready for this,' he says, biting into it. 'I'm nearly as hungry as I was that night I arrived late for the Farmers' Union meeting.'

Netta casts a glance in his direction and feels herself reddening.

'Aye,' Andrew says. 'We cannae go on ignoring what happened that evening. Look, I'm sorry if I got it wrong, only I like you a lot. In fact, I find you intriguing and would love to get to know you better . . . and I was beginning to believe you might feel the same about me. Now though, I think I'm just no' very good at detecting the signs and all I've done is upset you. So I'm sorry and I wouldnae like this to get in the way of our friendship. I promise you that — '

165

'Please stop. Don't say any more. It's not your fault. You weren't to know.'

'Weren't to know what?'

'I am engaged to be married.'

Andrew's shoulders sag and his face loses its habitual colour. He looks away down the valley.

'I'm sorry. I should have mentioned it before but I never thought that this . . . ' Her voice trails off.

Andrew hesitates, then turns his head, looking at Netta in confusion. 'May I ask who you are to marry? Do I know him?'

She shakes her head. 'No, you don't know him. His name is David. He's German. We were engaged on my nineteenth birthday. In 1934.'

'In 1934!' He stares at her in confusion. 'But that was years ago. You didnae marry?'

'We couldn't. David was Jewish. Soon after we were engaged the authorities brought in a law that Jews were not allowed to marry non-Jews. We didn't break off our engagement — it is after all a promise and I did not intend going back on my promise — but of course we kept it secret. We thought surely things would get better. But they didn't. They got worse. By the time Mutti and myself went into hiding, David had been rounded up, taken away. Our Quaker friends found out that he had been taken to a concentration camp. We have heard nothing since.'

'So you don't know whether he is alive or . . . not. But when was he taken?'

'It was 1939.'

'Seven years ago! Surely he would have got in touch by now.'

'I told Kenneth and Elizabeth that he died. I think that must be the case but I don't know that for sure.'

'And do you still love him?'

'I promised that I would be faithful to him. If I go against that promise, I will have betrayed him. Suppose he comes back looking for me — what would I do if . . .'

'I see.' Andrew stares into the distance.

'I'm sorry, Andrew.'

Andrew frowns. 'Yes, so am I.'

★ ★ ★

'I didnae tell you how I spent my time in England. Do you no' want to hear?'

They are riding the horse and wagon homeward from the Lanark market, where they have bought supplies for dipping the sheep after they have been clipped. Andrew is determined not to let his feelings get in the way of his friendship with Netta, so is attempting to push his disappointment to the back of his mind.

'Of course. Kenneth told me you had gone to meet a friend.'

'That's right. Do you remember me speaking of my Quaker friends in Glasgow? One of them, Jack, moved to Yorkshire in England. I stayed with him. It's a bonny place, Yorkshire. Moors and fields and sheep, like around here — though not at all like here. It's greener and the hills are not so steep — most of them anyway. There are sheep like ours and sheep that are different too. Jack's working in a school — a boarding school.'

'A boarding school! Poor things. I wouldn't like that. I enjoyed school but I wouldn't like to be separated from my parents all term. How long can the children stay at the school?'

'Until they're eighteen, though some leave at sixteen.'

'Now that I *would* have liked, the chance to stay on till I was older. When I was at school, they wanted girls to learn how to be good housewives, nothing more. I wasn't interested in that then.'

'They have a school farm,' Andrew goes on. 'The children can help on the farm if they want, though it's not compulsory.' He pauses, directing the horse onto the side road into the valley. 'I said I'd go again sometime. Give them a hand on the farm, if they want. You could come too, if you'd like, have a few days' holiday.'

'A busman's holiday, more like,' Netta says, smiling. 'But maybe, some day.'

* * *

Ellen is sitting on a bench outside the farm when Andrew approaches. She has cleared away after dinner and has decided to enjoy a few minutes in the sunshine, which has been in such short supply in the latter part of the month. She smiles at Andrew. She likes him very much. She finds him thoughtful and kind. She is glad that he is willing to teach her daughter about shepherding and grateful for the friendship they share. Having been concerned about how Netta would settle in such an out-of-the-way place, her mind has been put at ease by his friendship with her daughter. True,

168

in the last couple of weeks Netta has been quieter than normal but it is unusual for her daughter not to speak out if there is something on her mind. Perhaps she is imagining a problem that doesn't exist.

'May I sit down?' Andrew indicates the bench.

'Of course. Come and join me.'

'I only have a minute or two.' He glances towards the barn. 'I wanted to talk to you while Netta is busy. She's tidying the sheds at the moment, ready for them to get in a mess again when we start clipping!'

'There's nothing wrong, is there?'

'Not at all. Well, nothing to do with work. I just wanted to ask . . . well, I wanted to tell you . . . I think a lot about your daughter.'

'I was wondering if that might be the case.' Ellen smiles at Andrew.

'Have you told her how you feel?'

'Aye, and well, one evening I kissed her.'

Ellen nods her head slowly. So that is what has been making Netta quiet.

'I see — and how did Netta react?'

'She seemed to like it at the time, or so I thought. But ever since then she has hardly spoken to me and then, when we were on the hill the other day, she told me about David.'

Ellen looks at him with sympathy, considering how to reply, but Andrew continues.

'It seems strange to me that it was all a long time ago and yet she still feels bound to him. And she doesn't even know whether he is still alive.'

'Which is why she feels bound to him, I would guess. The sad fact is that he most probably died

169

years ago, like my husband. I believe she told you about Josef.'

'Yes, she did. And it must have been awful for you hearing that he had died. But the years before must have been bad as well, when you didn't know what was happening to him.'

'Very true.' Ellen pauses, her eyes taking in the distant hills. She sighs.

'At least when we know, we can grieve and then in time may come the chance to start a new life.'

'Is that what you are finding — that you are beginning to start a new life?'

'Yes,' Ellen says slowly. 'I believe I am at last.'

'This is why I wanted to talk to you. Netta has told me you had Quaker friends in Germany. I too have Quaker friends in Glasgow. Do you remember me having a few days off recently? I went to see one of my friends, Jack, who has moved to Yorkshire. He was telling me that some of the Quakers in Germany were able to find out information about what had happened to relatives in the camps. Some helped to take children and families away from danger during the war. It may be that their organisation has contacts with their members abroad. With your permission, I could ask Jack if he could write to them and ask for any information they could find.'

Ellen is silent for so long that Andrew's heart sinks. Not only does he realise that he has made a mistake in asking but he knows too that gone is his only hope of opening Netta's eyes to the reality of her fiancé's death. He wants it for her and, if he is honest, which he has always tried to be, he wants it for himself too.

'It may be possible,' Ellen says eventually. She has gone very pale and is having difficulty keeping her voice under control. 'I have heard that there are lists now of those who perished in the camps.' She turns to Andrew. 'Yes, please try. We will not say anything to Netta just now — it may come to nothing — but yes, I would be very grateful if you would try. His name was David Kleinman. His home was in Freiburg — I will find his address later — and he would have been born ... ' She pauses to calculate. 'He would have been born in 1909, I believe. When they were engaged, he was twenty-five.'

'Thank you, Ellen.' A sudden smile lights his face. 'I will let you know as soon as I hear anything.'

'Thank *you*. And tell *me* first if you manage to find out any information. And, please, Andrew, be gentle in your dealings with my daughter. She may appear tough on the outside but she is more fragile than she looks. And she has been through a lot.'

★ ★ ★

Ellen sits on in the sunshine after Andrew has left. All around her on the hills is the bleating of lambs calling to each other and to their mothers, followed by their mothers' low-pitched grumbles in reply. The ewes are bulky with wool, eager, she imagines, to be shorn of this winter surplus. Her mind goes back to the time when she would help out at clipping time. As soon as she had left school at fourteen, she would be called upon to gather and roll the fleeces, help to make dinner for the workers, serve them afternoon mugs of tea and homemade cake, and do a hundred and one jobs of fetching and carrying as each day required.

And of course Tom was there. Tom, her first husband, who had flattered her with his attentions but had secretly loved another. Tom, who had turned her away from him and into the arms of another because of the way he was with her. Tom who had met his death on the hills behind the farm during the freezing conditions of that first winter after the war — and given her the freedom to go and find Josef. How young she was then, how oblivious to the dangers and the suffering that would follow.

Josef hadn't been able to believe his eyes when he opened the door and she was there, standing on the doorstep with two children, the second of them his own Eva. She smiles now at the memory of it — his astonishment turning to joy as he took hold of them as though they would disappear again as suddenly as they had appeared; his inability to let them out of his sight; his first fumbling attempts to cradle his wee daughter in his arms.

They had been happy beyond her wildest dreams. For years they had been happy raising their young family. And then came the bad times, not all at once but one by one. Injustices that neither he nor any of them deserved, until life became one hammer blow on another, an unending nightmare.

Ellen opens her eyes, which have been clenched tight. The sun is still shining, the sheep still grazing the hillside with their young — sheep that can have no idea that within a month or two they will be bereft of their babies after such a short time

172

together. She gets up slowly from her seat and goes into the farmhouse, closing the door firmly behind her.

18

Clipping

June–July 1946

Finlay is upset on two fronts. First, the weather is not at all settled. There have been days of sunshine though fewer than they would like. And there have been many more than they would like of cloud and rain. The trouble is that it alternates from day to day, and it is much easier to clip sheep if it is dry. They decide, therefore, that, starting with last year's lambs, the ewe hoggs, they will bring the sheep into the big barn to dry off for a day before they are clipped. It means supplying them with food, which is not in plentiful supply, but there is no other way round it.

Finlay's other problem is his arm. It is mended but not as well as he would have liked. There is stiffness and pain in his elbow and it no longer has the movement in it that it possessed before his accident. He expresses his concerns to Andrew one morning as they walk down to the farmyard.

'I'm going to give it a try, pal, though I might not be as fast with the clippers as I used to be. I'm used to getting through fifty before lunch and another fifty afterwards.'

'Aye, me too,' Andrew agrees. 'All we can do is see how we get on. Kenneth is not nimble enough anymore and it's not really a job for a woman.'

'What isn't?' Netta has appeared behind them.

Andrew can't resist a smile. 'Caught out again! I was just saying to Finlay that clipping's no job for a woman.'

'And is that the result of observation or have you merely made it up?'

'I've made it up, of course. I'm sure women are equally as capable of using the clippers. It's just that sheep don't keep still for you when they're being clipped. They toss and turn and try to escape. It's hard work with one — by the time you've done twenty your back hurts fit to explode.'

'Well, why don't you show me how to do it and let me have a go. Even twenty a day would be a hundred and twenty a week. It would all help.'

Andrew looks at Finlay. Finlay shrugs his shoulders. 'How can we resist such a woman? If you're willing, Andrew, you give Netta some lessons and I'll see how many I can get done myself.'

* * *

Netta watches closely as Andrew methodically clips the ewe, starting with the belly and then turning her and separating the wool from the skin of her back, so that it falls in an unbroken fleece onto the floor of the barn. He lets go of the ewe and she scrambles to her feet and makes off to the far corner of the barn. He takes another ewe from the shedder and repeats the process before handing the clippers to Netta.

'Your turn now.' Andrew sends another ewe along to where Netta is waiting. She takes the sheep by the horns and twists her onto her back as

175

she has seen Andrew do. Then she begins to clip, slowly and steadily. The result, Andrew agrees, is good. The ewe looks a little moth-eaten and the fleece rather ragged but, for a first go, it has potential.

His arm is, as Finlay suspects, too painful for him to clip more than three or four sheep. He discusses it with Andrew and they decide that Finlay will walk the hill with his dog Jill and fetch the next batch of ewes down to be penned up in the barn awaiting the coming day's work. Later in the day Ellen, leaving the small barn with a basket of eggs, comes across him sitting on the bench staring moodily across the valley. He looks up as she approaches.

'I feel so useless,' he says, before she has a chance to speak. 'I thought this arm would be fine by now — and look at it.' He tries to straighten his elbow and winces with pain. 'What good is a shepherd who can't clip sheep?'

'There are plenty of other jobs you can still do. There's nothing wrong with your legs, after all. If Andrew and now Netta are clipping, they will need you to encourage each sheep through the shedder to be clipped. And you can put them through the dip.'

'Aye. There's still that.' Finlay sighs. 'But I'm only forty-six. I've years ahead of me yet that I still need to work.'

'When I was young, I used to massage my dad's back and then later, when I was married to Tom, I did the same to him. I do know what it's like, this job. It gives you aches and pains before your time. So, if you would like, I can try out some gentle

176

massage on your elbow — give it the hot water treatment and then try and free up the muscles and get it moving properly again. How does that sound?'

'It's got to be worth a try — if that's all right with you. I don't mind admitting I've been getting quite down about it, feeling as though I'm not fit for anything except the scrap heap.'

'You're fit for a lot more than that. We'll start tomorrow. I'll come early and work on it for half an hour or so.'

* * *

Netta is dog-tired. Clipping has taken more out of her than she cares to admit, even if it did give her a great sense of achievement. She has tried her best not to upset Finlay for she knows that he would dearly have liked to do more himself. He is happier now, however, for Ellen's treatment is making a noticeable improvement. Netta has gone with him over the last few days checking the lambs on the further hills, while he has sung her mother's praises and shown her how much more he can use his arm. Lamb sales are not far away and he is pleased to see how the lambs have progressed, although, given the spell of good weather after lambing, he would have been upset if it had not been so.

Kenneth has driven her mother home while Netta has been out on the hill, so Netta walks. After the heat of the last few days, which ended yesterday in a spectacular thunderstorm, it's a cool clear evening. The river is still high as a result of the rain, flowing swiftly and silently along its path.

She wonders what Andrew is doing. The majority of the clipping has fallen to him. If she is tired, he must be doubly so. He has been even quieter than usual, keeping himself to himself just recently. Has she done something more to upset him? She thinks how good it would be if they could spend some time together when they are not working, though wonders at the same time whether this would be wise. What does he do when work is finished? Maybe he borrows Kenneth's car and goes into Lanark or another of the nearby towns. It would not be unusual if he had friends, a girl maybe, whom he spends time with. She frowns at the thought.

Ellen has tea prepared and Netta, hungry after the day's work, is ready to eat. When they have finished and are sitting at the window with a pot of freshly brewed tea, Ellen asks her how her day has gone.

'All well. We checked on the last of the lambs, Finlay and I. They should fetch a good price at market.'

'And Andrew? What was he doing?'

'I don't know. I haven't seen him much today.'

Ellen pauses. 'He's a good man.' Netta looks at her mother, wondering where this conversation is going. Ellen gets up and, going over to the bureau, brings back a piece of paper. 'I think you should read this, Netta.'

Netta takes the paper from her mother. The writing is in German. She glances up at her mother, perplexed, then back to the paper. It's

178

a list of names of those from Freiburg who are known to have died in the extermination camps. She glances down the list quickly and then again more slowly, scanning each name. And there it is:

DAVID KLEINMAN, DATE OF BIRTH
24TH AUGUST 1909, DIED 24TH
FEBRUARY 1942, BUCHENWALD.

Netta's heart clenches. She swallows, reads it again. There is no mistaking it. She knows this to be his date of birth. This is the information that has so long eluded her.

After the initial shock, she feels, strangely, only calm. She sits in silence, taking in this news that is no news. She has known for years that it must be so.

'More than four years ago,' she murmurs at last, 'and it is only now that we come to hear of it. I thought that this would be the case but it is good to know for sure. But how did you come by this piece of paper? Who sent it to you?'

'It is Andrew who found it out. He was concerned that not knowing the fate of David was hard for you. Better to know than be in the dark about such things.'

An unwarranted surge of indignation courses through her veins. 'Better for him as well,' Netta says. There is an edge to her voice.

'He admits this — and he feels bad about it. But his concern is for your welfare.'

Netta's face shows a flicker of scepticism. 'He has spoken to you then?'

'He is an honourable man. He came to me and

179

told me about his feelings for you. He suggested he might be able to find this information through a friend he has in England.'

'Yes, in Yorkshire. He told me about him.' Netta stares out of the window and her mother watches her in silence. 'I need to go and talk to him,' she says decisively to her mother. 'Don't wait up for me.'

★ ★ ★

It is not until she is walking through the valley towards the farm that Netta's tears begin to flow. They are not because of the loss from her life of the man who asked her to marry him; she is, if anything, relieved to be free of this commitment, although that release is tinged with guilt. No, she is weeping for the needless loss of a young life that, like so many others, held such promise.

There is no answer to her knock at Andrew's cottage, which is in darkness. At her second knock Finlay opens his door.

'Ah, Netta,' he says. 'Andrew's no' in. I think he's away up the hill for a walk.' He indicates the steep rise behind the farm. 'He often strolls up there after work.'

'Thank you, Finlay. I'll see you tomorrow,' Netta calls, as she sets off through the farmyard to take the path that crosses behind the farm buildings and the lower field, before turning sharply uphill. Her tiredness of earlier is forgotten as she climbs. The sun is disappearing at the western end of the valley and the tops of the hills alone show that it is sunset. When she has climbed halfway she stops and scans the valley and there is the reservoir, liquid gold in the reflected light. She gives a deep sigh and resumes her climb.

She cannot see him at first. He has walked along the ridge of the hill and is seated, still as a statue, in the shelter of a wall. She stands, as still as he, looking at the outline of his face, his long body, legs bent, elbows resting on his knees, his eyes seemingly fixed on the distant horizon.

'Andrew,' she says. He doesn't hear her. She steps closer. 'Andrew.' He starts and jumps up.

'Netta. What are you doing here? Is something wrong?' He looks behind him down the hill towards the farmhouse.

'No, nothing. I needed to see you. Finlay told me where you would be. Do you mind if I disturb you?'

'You won't disturb me any more than I already am.'

'May I sit down?'

'Of course. Sit here on this stone.'

'Why are you disturbed?'

'Has your mother shown you the list?' He lowers himself down beside her.

'She has.'

'I am so sorry about your fiancé. I don't know if it was the right thing to do. I just thought it must be awful for you not — '

'It's all right, Andrew. You did the right thing. I suppose I knew already.

It is a relief really to be free of the burden of my promise, although to say so makes me feel bad.' Her words are choked with tears. 'But it was many years ago and, though I loved David then, I was very young and I am not the same woman now.'

Andrew is at a loss for words and hangs his head, while Netta weeps silently. When she is calm, he says, 'It is not only telling you this news that disturbs me.'

'No?'

'No. I feel bad because I did this in part because I care about you and I like to think that you might feel the same about me in the future.'

'I might. This news has altered everything. But you must give me time, Andrew.'

'I know that, and I will give you time, I promise. I will not pester you.' He turns his head to look at her. 'Friends then?'

'Friends.' She smiles, then gives an involuntary shiver.

'Are you sure you're all right?' He looks at her anxiously.

'I'm cold, that's all. After the warm weather we've had, I'm not really dressed for this cool evening.'

'Here, let me put this coat round your shoulders.' He takes off his jacket and drapes it round both of them, giving each a modicum of warmth. It is almost dark now and in the new-moon sky, stars are blossoming around them.

'Let's have no more secrets,' he says after they have sat in silence for a while.

Netta pauses. 'No more secrets.'

They sit in comfortable silence. There is no sound, only their breathing and the occasional breath of wind through the islands of long grass dotted across the hillside. Then slowly they become aware of a glow on the northern horizon, a strange jade coloration of the sky. Andrew suddenly wakens from the trance-like state that his nearness to Netta has produced. He sits up straighter and stares ahead.

'What is that light?' Netta asks.

'It's the aurora,' he says, excited. 'The Northern Lights. How strange to see them now, in July. It must be this sudden cold spell that has caused them.'

They watch in awe as shafts of light shoot upwards from the horizon and the green intensifies, while balls of brightness roll across the stretch of sky. Andrew looks at her and sees the magical light reflected in her eyes. Gradually the light fades and her eyes are again pools of darkness.

'I don't believe in omens,' says Andrew, still looking at her, 'but I think this must be a sign — a lucky one.' With a sigh, he tears his gaze away and glances around. It is almost night and they must take care on their downward path if they are not to sprain an ankle on the irregular ground of the hillside. 'We must go. What will your mother say, you staying out till this hour of the night? Take my hand. I know the way.'

And, just this once, Netta puts her hand in his and lets him guide her down the hill and back to her home.

★ ★ ★

Her mother is sitting in the darkened room, awaiting her daughter's return.

Netta closes the door softly behind her and strikes a match to the candle on the table.

'Are you all right, Netta?' Ellen says quietly, making her daughter spin round in surprise.

'Mutti! You shouldn't have waited up for me.'

'I couldn't sleep. I was worried about you.'

'You needn't have been. Everything was OK.'

'So Andrew was at home, was he?'

Netta sinks down into a chair facing her mother. 'No, actually he was at the top of the hill behind the farm. I had to go and find him. Finlay said that Andrew often climbs the hill after work. I didn't see him at first, he was so quiet — just sitting staring at the sky. It was beautiful up there. So much sky, so many thousands of stars.' Ellen smiles but says nothing. 'We talked about David,' Netta continues, 'and about what Andrew had found out. And . . . and he told me that he likes me very much. I said he must give me time because finding out for sure about what happened to David . . . well, it feels disloyal to suddenly switch my affections to someone else.

'And then the strangest thing happened. The sky in the north became green and shimmering. Andrew said it was the Northern Lights. He said it was unusual to see them at this time of year. They were beautiful — out of this world. I wish they had lasted longer but they soon faded and disappeared.' She gives a small laugh. 'Andrew says it is a good sign. I wish you could have seen them too, Mutti.'

Ellen laughs outright. 'I think I would have been a wee bit in the way!'

'Perhaps. But for now we have agreed to be friends. Is that not the best thing, Mutti, to get to know him better?'

184

'Of course, Netta, that is the best thing. I wish I had been as sensible when I was young.'

'Yes but I am twice the age you were then. I *should* have learned to be sensible!' Netta pauses. 'I know Andrew would like us to be more than friends but he has promised to give me time.'

'Yes, he seems a very patient man. And a good one. But there is no reason why you should not be happy now as friends. Just because we have lost so much does not mean that you should lose even more.'

'But what about you, Mutti? How can I be happy if you are not?'

'I am learning to be content. That is something for which I am very grateful. It was the right decision to come back to the valley. We have friends here. They have made us welcome and given us work. I have peace. What more can I ask? To see you loved by such a man would be very good but to see you with a friend you can talk to and spend time with, that will make me happy enough.'

Netta sits forward in her seat and the candle throws her face into relief and casts a flickering shadow on the wall behind her. 'Mutti, he said tonight that we should have no more secrets.'

Ellen looks at her daughter. 'I agree that you should not have secrets in the future if your future is to be with him,' she says slowly. But our lives here are better than we could have imagined. Let what happened in the past stay in the past.' For a minute or two there is silence between them, broken only by the soft murmur of the stream and the persistent piping call of a group of oystercatchers further up the valley.

Ellen takes a deep breath. 'You should plan to go out somewhere, the two of you, not spend all your time together working. Lambing is past, and clipping too. Finlay can do more on the farm now. There is nothing to stop you from having a day out every now and then.'

'Well, Andrew has said that he would like to visit his friend in Yorkshire again and he asked if I would like to go with him.'

'That's a lovely idea. Will you go?'

'Maybe. We'd wait until the sales are out of the way though — it's the lamb sale in August and the Blackface ram sale in September. Then they put the rams out with the ladies for a few weeks. He thinks that would be a good time to go.'

Ellen laughs. 'For a city girl, you're sounding very knowledgeable about sheep! It suits you.'

'I enjoy it,' Netta says thoughtfully, 'more than I ever thought I would.'

19
Auctions

August 1946

In the third week of August the first of the lambs are separated from their mothers. Ellen tries to busy herself in the farmhouse but she cannot ignore the plaintive calls of the sheep as they search in vain for their offspring. By the evening she is exhausted by this distressing reminder of thwarted motherhood and the next morning amazed, as ever, to see the ewes grazing as if the past twenty-four hours had never happened.

Finlay takes the first Blackface lambs to sale at Lanark market. It is a dull overcast day as he steers the wagonload of lambs out of the valley towards the market town. Kenneth Douglas is in the seat next to him, keen not to miss this first day of the lamb sale and anxious to see if the prices are higher than they have been during the lean years of the war. Netta watches the horse and wagon disappearing into the distance.

'Our turn tomorrow,' says Andrew coming up behind her. 'Kenneth has said that you and I can take the female lambs to Lanark.'

She beams at him. 'I'm looking forward to it. Will there be many lambs to be auctioned?'

'Tens of thousands each day. Have you no' been to an auction before?'

187

'Never.'

'Prepare to be educated then! But for now, our next job is to sort out the older ewes that are going to be sold as cast ewes. They'll go to farms on lower ground and used for, maybe, one more lambing. And then there are others that we'll sell off for mutton. Let's go and look over the ladies and sort out the ones that are past breeding.'

★ ★ ★

It's all new and exciting to Netta. Seated beside Andrew as he steers the horse and wagon into one of the few empty spaces outside the auction hall, she looks at the sea of lambs penned up and waiting to be sold. Sales have already been in progress for two hours and satisfied customers are driving away from the auction site, some of them with wagons hitched up to tractors. Andrew examines them with interest.

'Did you know that Kenneth is considering investing in a tractor? It will make our journey to and from market much easier, as well as being useful for harvesting the small amount of crops that we are able to grow. It'll no' be any help on the slopes, of course, but that's hill farming for you. A lot of the lowland farms have them already.'

'Have you worked with one before?'

'No, not over west. Mostly farming's on a smaller scale than here and, anyway, the farmers can no' afford them.'

Andrew ties up the horse and gives her a bag of hay and they encourage the lambs into an empty pen, before making their way into the auction ring and finding a seat. The auctioneer is in full swing with his sing-song patter. Groups of lambs are chivvied in, sold and encouraged out to their new owners with almost unerring precision. Occasionally a more adventurous lamb will make a bid for freedom but she is quickly put in her place again. As the time for their lot draws closer, the pair return to their lambs and move them from pen to pen until they are next in line for the ring. Andrew has told Netta that it is necessary for her to accompany him into the ring in case any of the lambs try to escape.

Their entrance in the ring is accompanied by a sudden hush in the audience. Andrew grins at Netta, knowing that the farmers are unused to female help in the ring. Mostly their help comes from their wives and takes place behind the scenes. True, several, short of manpower during the war years, have had land girls working on the farm. But for the most part, farmers have dispensed with their services and they have been dispatched back to the towns and cities from which they had been glad to escape.

Netta blushes crimson but acts as though she doesn't notice the effect that her appearance has on the farmers. She encourages the lambs to move round the ring as she has seen the other farmers do and when one tries to jump the low wall, she tackles it so abruptly that she draws cheers of appreciation from one or two of the younger clientele. Once the purchase is made, she chivvies them towards the exit, looking up as she does so, at the men seated nearest to the exit gate. There she recognises the face of Roddie McCann. He is looking at her with ill-disguised hostility. She gives him a wide smile and disappears into the vast hinterland of satisfied farmers and shepherds.

* * *

Kenneth is well pleased with the first two days' sale. Prices are well up on the previous year and continue this way for the remainder of the lamb auctions. In September he sells a hundred and forty ewes, some for further breeding and the rest for mutton, and in the following month the best of the Blackface ram lambs are put up for auction. The farmer, as he has hinted, rewards himself and his employees by investing in a small Fordson tractor. He also gives Andrew and Netta a few days' break to visit Andrew's friend in North Yorkshire.

20
Holidays

December 1940

Freda stood impatiently on the platform of Manchester London Road Station, awaiting the Middlesbrough train with its precious cargo. Sam's school had broken up for the Christmas holidays the previous day and he was now thought old enough and sensible enough to journey alone, although, as he had reminded Gwen and Peter in a letter two weeks before, it would not be the first time he had travelled unaccompanied, and the first time it had been for three days, compared with the three hours that this journey was due to take.

'The train is late, Mummy,' Freda said, turning to Gwen. 'Where is it?'

Gwen glanced at the large clock over the arrivals and departures board.

'It's not that late. Remember, when there's a war, the trains may be used to take soldiers where they're needed and that's considered more important than passenger services. And it may be too, that there has been damage to lines from some of the earlier bombing.'

'Will Father be here this evening or is he working?'

'He will be with us this evening. He doesn't

191

have to work till Sunday night.'

'Good, because Sam will want to tell him all his news and to hear all that Dad's been doing.'

A disembodied voice began to announce the arrival of the Middlesbrough train. Freda ran to get as close to the exit barriers as possible. After a couple of anxious minutes, there was Sam, heaving his case out of a carriage and walking up the platform towards her with a huge grin on his face. Freda jumped up and down in excitement and, as soon as Sam had handed in his ticket and was coming through the barrier, she ran up to him and threw her arms round him. He stopped to greet her, causing a good-humoured collision among the following crowd, who smiled at the affection shown between the two young people.

Gwen's heart swelled as she watched the two together.

'Hello, Gwen.' Sam kissed Gwen on the cheek and she hugged him warmly.

'Sam, it's so good to see you again. And you are looking very well.'

'It's all the fresh country air. A little different from here, if you don't mind me saying.' His eyes took in the smoky station with its grey walls and greyer people.

Outside, the city looked as down at heel as the building they had just left.

In the mid-afternoon gloom there was no hint that Christmas was a mere five days away.

'There were bombs,' Freda informed Sam. 'Have you remembered your gas mask?'

'Yes, I have it here.' Sam indicated the cardboard box suspended round his neck and tucked beneath one arm. 'And, yes, I was here, remember, when Manchester was bombed. It was at the end of summer. There was one in Middlesbrough even before that but now it's quiet again.'

'It is quiet here too. I wish there were no bombs anywhere. I don't understand it.'

Gwen and the children joined the queue for a bus. Petrol rationing meant that they now used the car as little as possible. They arrived home to find Peter already there, having just come off shift. The kettle was coming to a boil and the teapot warming. He turned with a smile as they came in and stepped over to Sam, giving him a welcoming hug.

'How's work?' Sam asked.

'All pretty routine at the moment, thank goodness. How about you?'

'Not routine at all! I have exams when I get back to school, practice exams before the real thing in the summer. There's a lot to learn but I'm enjoying it.'

'And the piano?'

'Definitely the best thing! I take Grade Six in the spring and Mr Davies thinks I will do well.'

'Well, our piano has been gathering dust while you've been away, so I hope you'll show us what you can do.'

Peter had applied for a job with the ambulance service just before the onset of war, and had been accepted, extra recruits being needed for the anticipated coming hostilities. He underwent six weeks' basic training, which enabled him to work as a medical orderly or a porter. After the bombings in August and September he was put on air raid duty and helped to provide accommodation for those bombed out of their homes. Recently though, with a cessation of hostilities, at least in their part of the country, he was back in the hospital working as a porter. His wage was much less than in his previous work as a teacher but his conscience told him that this was the right thing to be doing. He was also to be on stand-by in case of further attacks.

While Freda was at school Gwen now helped at the children's hostel in the city. It was the home to which a group of the refugee children had been taken on their arrival in Manchester. Like Sam and Freda, most of these children had heard nothing from their parents back in Germany. All too few had had happy reunions when one or both parents had managed to make their way to Britain but it was feared that the rest had died or been killed. The younger children, perhaps because they did not have such a store of memories, seemed more able to adapt to the absence of their parents than the older ones. Neither Sam nor Freda spoke much about their families now. After more than a year passed, neither of them continued to write for there had been no reply to any of their correspondence.

All four relished their time together. They sat in the living room before a cosy fire, the blackout blinds shutting them away from the unenviable reality of the outside world, swapping stories of what had been happening in the last three months. The decision to use Halliwell as a surname had been a good one for both Sam and Freda. Freda was happy at school. The younger children, who

194

understood little of war, treated her as one of them. She had rapidly learned to speak their language, even picking up some of the local dialect along the way.

'Only two terms to go and then you will be joining me at school,' Sam said, turning to Freda. 'Are you looking forward to it?'

'I am. I want to work on the farm. Is it the same as when we first visited the school because I'm really looking forward to helping with the sheep?'

'The farm's even more important now than it was then. The food that it grows is used in the school, and some of our meat too.'

'Have you made friends at school, Sam?' Peter asked.

'Yes, I have some good friends. It was awkward at first not joining until the fourth year but I do have some friends in the class now. Thomas and George. And I've made friends with some in the years above who are refugees like us. Mr Harris told me that there have been refugees who have now left school and gone on to university or other study. He says there's no reason why I shouldn't do so.' His voice rose in excitement but then he paused, his face taking on a look of bleakness. 'My parents in Germany would be really pleased for me, don't you think?' There was silence in the room, broken only by the crackle of burning coals in the fireplace.

'Have you any idea what subjects you would like to take for your Higher School Certificate?' Peter asked. 'What does your form teacher think?'

'I seem to be best at languages ... and Mr

Davies, my piano teacher, says I must definitely take music.'

'And you, is that what you would like to do?'

'Oh yes, music is my favourite.'

★ ★ ★

On Sunday evening, two days after Sam's arrival home, they were startled by the heart-stopping sound of the air raid sirens. Freda was in her night-clothes about to go to bed. She cried out in alarm and ran from her room to the top of the stairs. Sam, who had been curled up by the fire, deep in a book, stared around him in bewilderment. 'Come on, Sam. We need to get to the shelter quickly,' Gwen said, taking hold of his arm and dragging him from the room into the corridor. 'Freda!

Quickly, downstairs!' She grabbed coats from the rack in the hall and opened the front door. They could hear the sound of aircraft overhead as they stumbled after Gwen along the unlit road, Freda holding tightly to Sam's hand. Beams of light tracked across the dark sky in an attempt to pick out the aircraft. Gwen pushed the children ahead of her down into the shelter.

Several families were there already, making themselves as comfortable as possible in the enclosed space. Gwen smiled and nodded to them. They were neighbours and, although she knew none of them well, she had passed the time of day with them on many occasions. The mattress and covers that she had left down there since the last alert were damp and cold. She dragged from the corner of the room a tall oil heater, took a match from the box that had been left in readiness on the top of the heater and attempted to strike one. The matches were damp and refused to ignite. After several fruitless attempts she was saved by the appearance of an elderly man at the top of the steps. He was sucking an empty pipe and when he saw her problem, he smiled, fished in his pocket and drew out a matchbox.

'Jimmy Braithwaite,' he said and smiled, passing her the box of matches.

More people joined them in the shelter. It was crowded now. Gwen sat with Sam and Freda on their mattress. The sirens began to wind down and there was silence in the shelter as everyone held their breath and wondered what would happen next. Then, in the distance, came the sound of an explosion, followed by another, then a third. Freda nestled into Sam and hid her face in his shoulder. The bombing continued, though further away now. Freda lifted her head and listened. She gave a huge sigh and turned to look at Sam.

'Do you wish you were back at school, Sam? You would be safe there.'

'Maybe, but I would be worried about what was happening to the rest of you.'

'I don't think school is any safer than anywhere else,' a mother with her two children, a boy and a younger girl, suggested.

'Sam's school is in the countryside,' Freda explained. 'Maybe there are no bombs there.'

'He used to go to our school,' the woman's son, a boy called Richard Wainwright, said. 'He's German, aren't you?' There was a sudden hush in the shelter and everyone looked in Sam's direction.

'Sam escaped from Germany before war started,' Gwen started to say. 'He doesn't want this war any more than —'

'I bet his father is up there in one of those planes dropping bombs on us,' Richard Wainwright interrupted.

'Come on now. You don't know that.' It was Jimmy Braithwaite, who had given Gwen the matches.

'Well, if he's not up there, he will be shooting our men on the ground, or torpedoing our ships bringing supplies,' the boy continued spitefully.

'My father is doing none of those things. He was taken prisoner before the war even started,' Sam explained.

Richard was not going to let the conversation drop. 'A convict then! What had he done?'

'He had done nothing. He was taken prisoner because he is a Jew.' There was another silence, while this information was absorbed. Freda began to cry. Sam put his arm round her to comfort her. 'You see, you're upsetting my sister now.'

But Freda had heard the bell of an ambulance as it raced past. 'I'm thinking of Peter. He is out there driving, with all those bombs falling around him. Will he be safe?'

'I do hope so,' Gwen said. 'It's a dangerous job but so is fighting, which is what this poor lad's father is no doubt doing.'

'Why is your husband not on the front? Is he unfit?' Richard's mother turned to Gwen.

'No, he is a conscientious objector. He will not fight because he believes it is wrong.'

'So he will let our menfolk go to fight but not go himself!'

Jimmy spoke up again. 'Now, now. I think we need to stop all this arguing. This lady's husband is doing a dangerous job, driving round the streets in this.' He gestured to the door of the shelter and, as if in confirmation of his words, a huge explosion sounded nearer than any that had gone before. 'And I happen to know,' he continued, 'that this lady and her husband have done a lot to ease the plight of refugee children caught up in this terrible conflict. So let us stop picking on a husband and wife whom it is good to have in our neighbourhood, and on two children who have suffered enough already. And, apart from anything else, it looks as though we will be here for the night, so we'd better get some sleep.' The old man lay down, turned slowly onto his side and pulled the blanket over him.

Mrs Wainwright gave a half-smile in Gwen's direction. 'Happen he's right. And *you* can stop your accusations, young man,' she said turning to her son. 'It's time you were asleep. I've jobs lined up for you in the morning.' She gave him a none too gentle cuff round the ears and threw him a blanket.

★ ★ ★

The all-clear went at five o'clock the next morning. No-one moved. It was as though they didn't wish to be confronted with the picture that might await them outside. In any case the children were all asleep and it seemed wrong to disturb them

199

when the evening before had been disturbed enough for them all.

At seven o'clock, there was a frantic knocking on the door before it burst open to reveal Peter at the top of the steps.

'Are you all OK in here?' He swept his torch around the fusty room, stopping as it lit up Sam and Freda on the mattress and Gwen sitting at the side of them.

'Yes, lad, all present and correct,' the old man said, putting a match to the hurricane lamp, which threw ghostly shadows round the walls as it spluttered into life.

Gwen went to the bottom of the steps and Peter stepped down into her arms.

'Goodness, you look as if you've been busy.' His face was smeared with soot and his clothes bloodstained and muddy. 'Was it bad last night?'

'I'm afraid it was. Hundreds dead, they estimate, and many more injured. The danger is past now, though I would prepare for another night in here. They often come back the next night to finish what they started.'

They all staggered out from their semi-underground dwelling into the crisp pre-dawn morning. The stench of burning filled their nostrils but in the darkness the buildings around looked solid and untouched.

Peter turned to Gwen and the children. 'I must go back. There are more buildings yet that haven't been cleared. It's likely there'll be more injured or worse in some of them. You go home and rest. I'll be in later.'

It was dinner time before Peter got back home.

200

He was too exhausted to eat. Gwen made him a pot of tea and took it to him as he sat soaking his weary bones in the few inches of bath water allowed. 'It was dreadful,' he said. 'Whole families wiped out, others horribly injured. You must go into the shelter again tonight, warnings or not. At least I will know you're safe and not worry about you.'

'I don't think the children will be too keen,' Gwen said. 'There was a bit of nasty banter going on about them being German. I was proud of Sam though — he put them right on one or two points!'

Peter took a sip of his tea. From below came the sound of piano playing.

'Mm. 'Moonlight Sonata'. Very appropriate.' He sat still in the bath listening. Gwen opened the door a fraction so they could hear better. Tears came to her eyes. Sam, as usual, was putting his heart and soul into the music. She tiptoed downstairs. Freda was asleep on the sofa. She went up to Sam and put a hand on his shoulder. He paused, turning his head, his eyes like hers, brimming with tears. She looked at him questioningly.

'I don't think they will be coming, my parents — do you?' he said. 'I am very afraid they are dead.'

★ ★ ★

The bombs came again the next night. Sam and Freda, as Gwen had predicted, were reluctant to enter the shelter again but they were sensible children and saw the necessity of it. This time they were better prepared. Each took a book to read and they carried down extra blankets, as the night was another cold one. Mrs Wainwright and her children were there again, as were several others who had been there the first night.

They were beginning to think they could have stayed in their beds when the wailing siren began again. They lay in silence listening to the bombs exploding as they hit the ground. They were far away, in all probability aiming for the industrial areas of the city. But then came a much louder crump and another, and they could feel the shelter vibrate in answer to the explosions.

None of them slept much that night. As it grew light, they emerged into the freezing morning. Their houses were intact, but they could see in the distance the shells of houses that had been shattered by the bombing. Acrid smoke blew towards them from the devastation. They learned as they made their way back to the house that the nearby area of Piccadilly had been hit.

'Perhaps there will be no trains,' Freda said, squeezing Sam's arm, 'then you will have to stay with us longer.' He smiled in reply but said nothing.

Peter was late coming off shift again. It was almost dinner time when they heard a knock. Sam went to the door and opened it. Outside stood an ambulance driver.

'Hello, lad. My name's Gordon. I work with your dad. May I speak to your mother?'

Sam looked at the man's concerned face and turned to find Gwen. She was coming down the hall.

'I'm sorry, Peter's not back yet,' she said.

'I know. I've come to tell you he's been injured. There was an explosion — it must have been a gas leak or something. He was just helping to load a stretcher into the ambulance. It caught the side of his face. I'm afraid he's suffered some burns.'

Sam put a protective arm around Gwen's shoulders. 'Where is he?' she whispered.

'He's in the hospital. They took him to theatre, to clean the wound. He's bandaged up now. I'll take you to see him if you'd like.'

'He isn't blind, is he? Please tell me that his sight is OK.'

The man hesitated. 'We hope he's all right but we won't be sure until he's properly round from the anaesthetic and talking to us.'

★ ★ ★

Peter came home from hospital ten days later, his face still heavily bandaged. His left eye had been so badly damaged that it had been removed in order to save the sight in his good eye. The left side of his face had borne the brunt of the explosion. Elsewhere there were bruises and cuts but nothing that wouldn't be gone within a week or two.

Sam had laid and lit the fire and the room was cosy for Peter's return. He had also chosen a piece of welcoming music and, as Peter came through the door into the living room, 'The arrival of the Queen of Sheba' burst forth from the piano, breaking the tension and making them all laugh.

'It is so good that you are home,' Freda said, kissing his good cheek. 'I have baked some special rock buns for your return.'

'It's very good to be back. I only hope I won't look too ugly when all these bandages are removed.'

'Well, you never were a picture book,' said Gwen, putting on a sad face, 'so I suppose I can put up with a few more wrinkles or whatever is under the packaging.'

'I don't want to go back to school and leave you like this.' Sam sat down opposite Peter.

'If you're looking for a way out of taking those exams, I'm afraid it won't work.' Sam pulled a mock stern face and they all laughed again.

There was a knock at the door. 'I'll go,' said Freda, jumping up.

'I hear the trains aren't running into Piccadilly station since the bombing,' Peter said to Sam. 'Have you thought how you'll get back to school?'

'Your friend Gordon, he says he'll take me to a station further up the line. That is very good of him, is it not?'

Freda came back into the room carrying a cake tin. 'It was that lady from the shelter — you know, Richard's mother. She brought you this. I asked her to come in but she wouldn't.'

Inside was a fruit cake and, on top of it, a piece of paper, folded in half. Peter took it up and held it close to his good eye, reading it out loud:

'For a very brave man. With apologies, from Kathleen Wainwright, Richard and Susan.'

* * *

Sam's journey back was long and slow. Rain fell without stopping and the landscape was as grey as his mood. He wasn't looking forward to the exams that awaited his arrival but what occupied his thoughts for the majority of the journey was that not only had he lost one family but he had been and still was in danger of losing a second. His adoptive father would not be able to drive an ambulance again and it was likely that his recovery would be slow and painful.

And who was to know whether more bombs would fall on Manchester and put the lives of not only Peter and Gwen at risk but also that of Freda, his beloved sister? It was with a heavy heart that he climbed the steps into the school, where his friends were waiting to greet him.

21
A Visit

November 1946

Netta gazes out of the train window, seeing the fields and scattered farmhouses through the haze of swirling smoke. A rising tide of excitement courses through her body. She cannot help but compare this journey with that taken only ten months ago, when she had accompanied her mother on their sad journey away from the country that had changed beyond recognition, back to the old country that seems to be the same as it has always been. Her mother has told her that she is pleased with Netta's decision to have these few days away. Netta senses that she is hoping for her daughter's friendship with Andrew to develop into something more.

'So, this Mr Sadler, you say you were good friends?'

'Jack. Call him Jack — he prefers that. Aye, we met when I was working on the Clyde. He used to help some of the men get into work, try and house their families, that kind of thing — and all that as well as his job. We became good friends. We've kept in touch ever since I left Glasgow. He and Beth married in July, during the school summer holidays. I remembered her a wee bit from my time in Glasgow back in 1935. She was only young then, of course, but even then she and Jack got on well together.'

'But didn't he invite you to be best man if you were such good friends . . . or at least invite you to his wedding?'

'Weddings between Quakers are no' like that. They are quiet affairs — they take place during one of the morning meetings. Of course there are those of the meeting who will talk to them before the wedding takes place: make sure that they are well prepared for marriage, help them decide what they are going to say, make sure the correct legal documents are in place. But there's no fuss, no bridesmaids or best man, no wedding breakfast, nothing like that.'

Netta considers all this in silence, then smiles. 'I'm looking forward to meeting them,' she says simply.

★ ★ ★

Andrew has phoned ahead, as on his last visit, and both Jack and Beth are waiting for them at the bus stop. By the time they arrive it is twilight and a crescent moon is shining bright and clear above the dark hills. It is unusually warm for November. The group walk between the school fields in the gentle air, so unlike the normal brisk chill of the Scottish Uplands. Their talk is animated and friendly, Netta relieved to find that the newlyweds are a normal couple and not the other-worldly creatures that she had imagined them to be. She is excited by the delicious sense of freedom that these few days' break are giving her, an experience that has not been hers for a very long time, if ever.

Jack and Beth stay in a small cottage in the grounds of the school. It is here that Andrew and Netta are taken when they arrive. Beth has prepared a lamb casserole and after they have eaten they sit around the fire and exchange news of the last few months.

'So you are Andrew's enigma,' Jack says, turning to Netta. She frowns at him, not understanding. Jack grins, his dark unruly hair flopping over his eyes. 'He was singing your praises when he was here before, saying how good you are with the sheep.'

'So why am I an enigma?' Netta asks, turning from one to the other of the men. 'What's so strange about me being interested in sheep?'

'Nothing.' Jack laughs. 'The trouble with Andrew is that he's lived so long in the exclusive company of sheep that he's forgotten what humans are like!'

'Nonsense,' says his friend. 'Netta and I get along just fine now. We understand each other well. We have no secrets from one another, do we, lass?' Netta shrugs, clearly embarrassed by the conversation.

'Well done indeed to Netta for working this transformation.' Jack chuckles.

'So, Jack. Tell me how your job is going. Are you still happy with your decision to move? And what about you, Beth? Have you been given a job here?'

'Beth has a job as deputy matron. It was too much for just one person, so it's worked out better this way. And, as for me, yes, I love it here. It's so good to be away from the big city and breathing

208

country air, but, apart from that, it's a job I love. These young people — they've all got such a lot to offer, so much potential. I've just seen the first of those I've got to know leaving school. Some of them have gone on to further study at university, a couple to agricultural colleges, several others to work in outside jobs — gardening and such like.'

'What about you, Netta?' says Beth, studying their guest. 'Where are you from? Not a native of Scotland, surely?'

Netta pauses before speaking and glances at Andrew. 'I *am* actually a native of Scotland but my mother took me to live in Germany when I was just four, so I don't have a Scottish way of speaking. We returned nearly a year ago, back to the place where my mother was born.'

'Was it a good decision to come back?' asks Beth.

'Yes, a very good decision. We are making a new life for ourselves.'

'And learning the job of shepherd!' Jack laughs.

'Oh, I shall never be like Andrew. It's in his blood.'

'It is in your blood too, hen,' Andrew reminds her. 'Did you no' tell me that your father was a shepherd and that he was originally from Yorkshire?'

'Yes, he was. He came up from the West Riding to learn about Blackface sheep.'

'And fell in love with Scotland?' asks Beth.

'I don't know about that. He died in the hills in the snow,' Netta says simply. 'It was all a long time ago. I don't remember much about him. I was only wee.'

'I'm sorry,' says Beth. 'I had no idea.' There is silence before Beth says, in an effort to lighten the conversation, 'Tomorrow we will take you to see the farm — that's if it's no' too much like 'carrying coals to Newcastle', as they say in these parts. I confess to knowing very little about farming. I am Glaswegian through and through!'

'Jack, what were the names of the two girls I met last time, who were involved with the farm?' asks Andrew.

'Oh, you mean Dorothy and Freda. They're still here. They're in the sixth form now, studying for their Higher School Certificate. They still love helping on the farm, Freda especially. Dorothy was brought up on a farm in Yorkshire, so it's all routine for her but Freda loves the novelty of it. She loves to get her hands dirty looking after the chickens and the sheep, though she tells me she's not so keen on the cows. We'll no doubt see them tomorrow. Freda came from Germany, Netta. You will be interested in meeting her.'

Beth gets up from her chair to clear the teacups away. 'We have morning school,' she explains, 'so we had better get to our beds. We will have to leave you to make your own amusement for a few hours tomorrow. If you fancy walking, there's a lovely hill called Roseberry Topping near here. It will give you a good view of Yorkshire.'

* * *

Beth is right. The view from the top of the hill is stunning, even in this late autumn time of the year. Andrew and Netta, used to climbing the hills

210

of their valley, have no trouble in coping with the steep incline.

'The view is nearly as good as ours in Scotland,' Andrew concedes, adding that this is not the first time he has climbed it, having done so with Jack on his last visit. They stand side by side gulping the air back into their lungs. Andrew, pointing out landmarks, tentatively puts his arm round Netta and she moves closer. Together they take in the views that contrast so much with the ones they are used to. As if it is the most natural thing in the world, they turn to one another and she tilts her face upward for Andrew to kiss her. And then she pulls away and challenges him to a race back down the hill to the start. She has gone before he has a chance to pull his coat back on and he follows her laughing, amazed again at this girlish side to her character that occasionally bubbles to the surface.

After lunch, taken in the refectory with the high-spirited pupils, all of them relishing the one and a half days of weekend freedom that await them, Andrew and Netta walk hand in hand along with their friends across the green to the farm. It is quiet now, compared with Andrew's last visit. Ewes are grazing in the field accompanied by a fine-looking tup. In the distance they can see a small herd of cows. To one side of the barn is a chicken run and a girl with a basket is searching for eggs. Andrew can see by her dark curls that it is Freda. She turns at their approach and beams.

'Mr Sadler said you were paying us a visit.'

'Freda, this is my friend Netta. She has come to

211

inspect what you have on the farm. She is a hard task-master, mind, and will tell you if she doesn't like what she sees.'

'Nonsense,' laughs Netta. 'I wouldn't do any such thing. And anyway, it all looks neat and tidy and everything in its place. Your sheep are quite different from the ones I've been helping to look after.'

'How were your exams?' Andrew asks. 'You were very nervous about them last time I was here.'

'They were not so bad as I thought they would be. I passed them all. My best marks were in languages and biology.'

'And what about Dorothy?'

'Not so good on languages! She was good in biology and geography. You'll see her later. She's gone into the village to get a haircut just now.'

'Is that the farmer over there with the cows?' Andrew asks, indicating a man in the far field.

'Yes, that's Mr Thwaites.'

'Do you mind if I go and have a look? We've a few cows on the farm — just for milk, ken, but I'm no' so good with cattle. I would like to pick his brains.'

'You go on,' says Netta. 'I want to stay here and look at the sheep.'

'And we'll go and prepare a meal,' says Beth. 'You'll need it after a day in the open air.'

'You forget, dearest. A day in the open air is what they have every day, and not always in weather that's as kind as today!' Jack says laughing, as they turn to retrace their steps towards the cottage.

'He's grand is Andrew,' says Freda, turning to watch him striding out along the path to the far field. 'Is he your boyfriend?'

212

Netta pauses to consider. 'Yes, I suppose he is.'

'You don't sound too sure. If I was in your shoes, he would be mine!'

Netta smiles. 'I'd better make sure I don't let him escape in that case!'

They walk up to the fence and stand gazing at the flock in front of them. 'I sheared ten of them this year,' says Freda. 'I'm getting better at it but I need more practice. How many did you shear?'

'I told Andrew I'd try to do twenty sheep a day. At first I made a poor job of it. I'd done none at all before this year. I made it to twenty later on. I was only helping because the older shepherd on the farm broke his arm earlier this year, so he's not been able to do so much. Andrew, though, he clips about fifty at a go. He's very good at it.'

'Will you and Andrew be married?'

'Oh, it's much too early to talk about things like that.' Netta laughs, seeing a reflection of the same forthrightness she is accused of using herself. 'I haven't known him long and he certainly hasn't asked me.'

'I hope you do.' Freda picks up her basket and resumes the search for eggs. She turns to Netta, hesitates. 'You don't talk a bit like him, do you? I understand you. I have trouble understanding some of the words Andrew uses. Don't you come from Scotland?'

'Yes, I do. But I lived in Germany for most of my life. My mother and I only came back at the end of last year.'

Freda looks at Netta with interest. 'We were born in Germany, me and my brother,' says Freda, 'and then we came to England. I don't remember it

213

very clearly now. It was a long time ago.' She pauses, pondering. 'It was a long time ago,' she says again slowly. 'I remember it was a horrible journey.' She shakes her head as if to dispel the memory. 'But we grew up in Manchester. My parents are still there.'

'And what about your brother? Is he at school?'

'Oh no. He finished school three years ago. We were here together for two years and then he left. He's living with our parents again at the moment. I'm glad about that. My father got badly burned in the war. He was driving an ambulance. It all happened only a few months before I was to start school here. I really, really wanted to come and join Sam, but I was worried about leaving Mum and Dad. You see, my father's never properly recovered. He needed a long time off work. I think the Quakers helped by giving them money when he couldn't work. Eventually he went back to teaching — that's what he was doing before the war — but he sometimes has to have time off when he is poorly. The injury left him with fits, something to do with the brain being damaged. I was just nine at the time, so I didn't understand that much about it. So it was good when my brother decided he would live at home again.'

'Do you have any other brothers and sisters?'

'No. My mum told me not so long ago that she and Dad couldn't have any children. They adopted Sam and me. She said she just saw us together and knew that we were meant for them. Isn't that wonderful! She says that the years since finding us have been the best years of her life. I feel the same . . . and so does my brother usually, though he used to wonder why our real parents didn't come and find us.'

There is a sympathetic silence. 'It's . . . it's a wonderful story.' Netta gives Freda a wide smile. 'So what does your brother do, now that he's back home with them?'

He's been studying at music college. The college is in the city, so it made sense for him to live at home. He's finished now. He plays the piano. He's very good at it! If he carries on being as good as he is, he might have the opportunity of playing in concerts and I will go and hear him and tell everyone that he's my brother! What is the phrase — 'bathe in his reflected glory'!' They laugh.

★ ★ ★

The next day, their last, Jack and Beth have decided that they will take their visitors to the seaside town of Whitby. They go by train through the beautiful Esk valley. Netta, save for her journey home from Germany, cannot remember seeing the sea and has certainly not been for a day trip to the seaside. She is entranced by the houses clinging to the sides of the steep valley and the many ships tied up along the harbour walls. She walks barefoot along the sand and splashes in the freezing water of the North Sea, trying to get Andrew to do the same but not succeeding. They climb the one hundred and ninety-nine steps leading up to the ancient church and the even more ancient abbey of St Hilda.

At last they find a seat near to the church, a precipitous drop to the sea some way in front of them. It has been a good day. They have enjoyed each other's company, have got on well together, and now they are taking a last look at the wide expanse of water before descending the steps and making their way to the railway station. The wind has got up and gulls scream and swoop over an angry, grey sea. Netta clasps her coat collar to her neck for warmth. Her exuberance of the last two days is exhausted and she is quiet and reflective.

'Thank you for entertaining us,' says Andrew. 'It has been a marvellous break, don't you think, Netta?'

'I have loved it,' Netta agrees. 'It will be hard getting back to work.' She hesitates, then sits forward and faces their friend. 'Can I ask you one thing that's been puzzling me, Jack? Freda was telling me that she and her brother had a horrible journey to England. But she said she didn't remember much of it. Can you tell me what happened?'

'I know a little of their story. They came across on the Kindertransport from Germany. Have you heard of the Kindertransport?'

'Yes, I've heard of it.'

'She was quite young, I understand, her brother a few years older. They finished up in Manchester. Peter and Gwen Halliwell adopted them. They are a Quaker couple who had no children of their own. The couple are quite open about this, so would have no objection to me telling you. Their children have been with us, one or other of them, for several years. Her brother left to go to music college before I started here. He's finished now — he'll be in his early twenties — and I understand he's doing well.'

'Yes, she told me so.'

'It's not unusual . . . ' Jack hesitates, before continuing, 'It's not unusual for these children, especially the younger ones, to be unable to remember their experience of leaving family and travelling such long distances. Whether it's really forgotten or buried deep in their memory we don't know. Whatever the reason, it's often better that way. It allows them to make a new life. Freda especially is growing into a contented and well-rounded young woman. Whatever horrors have been hers in the past, she has put them firmly behind her. As for her brother, she is hoping one day that she might go and hear him play in a concert!'

★ ★ ★

Beth brings a tray of teacups and a freshly brewed pot of tea into the living room. They are sitting round the fire, Andrew and Netta close together on the sofa, Jack and Beth in easy chairs on either side of the fire. Netta is struggling to stay awake.

'Actually,' says Jack, 'there is an idea I would like to discuss with you, Andrew. I have been thinking about it for some time — since you were last here, in fact — and I feel it right to mention it now.'

Andrew, who has also been feeling pleasantly relaxed, sits up and focuses on his friend.

'You may remember I said to you that the school had a special interest in agriculture and preparing students for agricultural college. It is less so now but, as you have seen, we have the

217

farm and a surprising number of students take an interest in helping on it. You've met Freda — she's an example, though I've no idea whether she wants to pursue the interest when she leaves.

'A good way, I feel, of students deciding what they want to do with their lives, would be for them to spend some time on a farm. Conditions are very different on a working farm from the small set-up we have here ... the numbers of animals involved, what happens at a market, how a farm is financed ...'

'Working in bad weather,' Netta adds.

'Yes, that too. Some of the children come from farming backgrounds, so they, of course, are used to some of these aspects of farming. Others come from cities or towns where life is very different. Freda's parents live in Manchester. Her previous experience of farming is what her mother serves up on her plate for dinner.'

'So you are wondering if we might have a student on our farm,' Andrew says thoughtfully. 'It's a really good idea. They could come for a short time — say five or six weeks or even less — to get some idea of life on a farm, or if they are considering it as a career, they could come as an apprentice and stay for up to a year and see the farming year from start to finish.'

'That is exactly what I was thinking.'

'I can talk to Kenneth Douglas, the farmer, about it. You realise it's not up to me at all. I've been there less than a year and it's by no means certain that I will be staying there.' Andrew feels Netta tense at his words. 'And there would of course be implications for the farm — financial ones, where to house the students and look after them, that kind of thing.'

'Yes, I have considered that too. Some of the children who came as refugees have no financial backing. But this needn't be a problem. The Friends have supported them through school and would be likely to continue to do so if this scheme got off the ground.'

'It's an exciting prospect. Leave it with me and I'll talk to Kenneth about it.'

'I know one person who would be pleased,' says Netta, 'and that's my mother. I think she would love to have someone young to fuss over again.'

★   ★   ★

'You are very quiet today. Are you no' looking forward to starting work again?'

Andrew and Netta are on the train to Edinburgh. So far Netta has said hardly a word.

'Of course I am looking forward to work and to seeing Mutti again. This is the first time we have ever been separated, as far as I can remember. I am anxious to see that she is all right.'

'Is that what is making you quiet or has something upset you? You seemed to want to be close to me. Are you regretting it now?'

They are alone in the carriage. Netta puts her head on his shoulder. 'It has been a lovely break.'

Andrew looks down and takes one of her hands in his own. 'You do know I think a lot about you. In fact, I think I love you. Actually, I know I do, even if I know nothing about anything except sheep! Do you think you might feel a wee bit the

219

same about me?'

Her mouth twists in a half-smile. 'Yes, I might . . . but you must give me time. There is so much to think about.'

'What more is there to think about? Is it really so complicated?' Andrew is finding it hard to conceal his frustration.

Netta answers with a shrug. Andrew keeps her hand within his and stares out of the window at the sea breaking on rocks at the foot of the cliff edge not many feet from the railway line. Whatever this weekend has done, it has failed to resolve the enigma that is this woman sitting at his side.

22

Hogmanay

December 1946

The sky is cloudless as Andrew and Netta walk through the valley towards Five Trees Farm, the home of Billy and Isobel Black. Their breath steams in the freezing air. Fields are white with frost. Each skeleton of long-departed grasses sparkles in the rays of the sun. Bare branches are silvered, hilltops tinged with gold.

Kenneth and Elizabeth have driven to the Blacks' farm in their car, taking Finlay and Ellen with them and picking up Margaret on the way. Andrew and Netta have agreed to do the essential farm jobs and follow on foot as soon as they can. The cows have been milked, any sheep checked that have given rise to concern and now, dressed in their best, they are on their way.

Isobel greets them at the door. 'What a beautiful day it is for this time of year,' she says, looking over Netta's head at the cloudless sky. 'I hope we don't have to pay for it later. Come in, the two of you, and let me take your coats. You'll find everyone in the living room, deep in conversation with the help of the whisky!'

Kenneth looks up as they enter. 'Ah, Andrew, there you and Netta are. I was telling everyone here about your wee scheme for getting schoolchildren

221

to come and help on the farm.'

'Well, yes, actually they wouldnae be children. They would come when they were in their final years at school, so they're really students — seventeen or eighteen. And the idea is that one, or two at the most — no more than that at any one time — would be gaining experience and finding out how a farm is run. It would only be for those students who are thinking of farming as a career.'

'But surely they will have come from farming families themselves and will go back to their family farms.'

'Not necessarily. Some are from the cities, a few from abroad.'

'It's a nice idea,' says Billy, 'but have you thought about the implications for Kenneth and Elizabeth?' He looks sharply at Kenneth. 'None of us is getting any younger. Suppose either Kenneth or Elizabeth should become ill — what would happen then?'

'Then Finlay and Andrew would need the extra help even more,' Ellen says in an excited voice.

'Yes, we would. The only snag is that my contract is only for a year, so I may not even be here at the time we are talking about.' Andrew looks at Ellen but avoids the gaze that her daughter turns on him.

'I hope very much that you will be here, Andrew,' Kenneth says quickly, clearly perturbed at the thought that he might lose his junior shepherd. 'You've worked harder than any of us this past year, what with Finlay being injured and me getting older.'

'Is that an official request?' says Andrew smiling.

'It is indeed. I would be very upset if you decided to go . . . and I'm sure I wouldn't be the only one!' he says, glancing round the room at the assembled guests and his eyes coming to rest on Netta. 'Then I am more than happy to stay. I look forward to another rewarding year with you all.'

'If I may make a suggestion,' Billy intervenes, 'why doesn't Andrew put together some plans — how these students would best spend their time, what they should pay for it, what would need to be provided in terms of accommodation and their general care. That would help you to decide whether it is a feasible undertaking.'

'I'm happy to do that,' Andrew agrees, as Isobel comes into the room and calls them in for dinner.

★ ★ ★

Late afternoon finds Andrew and Netta retracing their steps to the farm. The cows must be milked and Netta, who has enjoyed the company, is looking

forward to the peace and quiet of the cattle shed. Twilight is fast approaching and they hurry through the valley. Andrew has taken her hand and she has not pulled away. They say little. He walks her up to the farmhouse, where she has left her working clothes, and hurries to his cottage to change. Kenneth and the others will be back soon and will be taking her mother and her back to their cottage.

By the time Netta has milked the cows and taken the milk to the farmhouse, night has closed in. She sees Andrew closing the barn door. For a moment she stands still, watching him, deciding. Then she walks over to join him. Together they stroll down to the river bridge and stand close, listening to the comforting babble of the invisible river. Netta turns to him. Her heart is beating fast, but she must speak.

'Will you kiss me?'

'You want me to kiss you?'

'Yes, please.'

'Are you sure?'

'Oh Andrew, haven't I just said so?'

Andrew obliges before saying, 'And what has brought this about?'

'I'm really glad you're not leaving us.'

'Us?'

'Well, *me*.' She hesitates. 'You see, I didn't realise how much you meant to me until you started to say that you might not stay.'

'Is that right?' he says softly.

'Yes. You see, I care for you a lot.'

'Care for me?'

'You are *not* making this easy for me.'

'Am I no'?'

'What I am trying to say is that I love you.'

Andrew looks down into the river and back at Netta. He is not smiling now. Her heart lurches. Perhaps she has made a mistake. Maybe her reluctance has turned him away from her.

'I do understand,' says Andrew slowly, 'that you can't love me as you loved David but I'm prepared to accept that because I've never loved anyone in my life as I love you.'

'No,' she says breathlessly. 'You are wrong. What I felt for David is nothing like my feelings for you.

We were young. We were friends and we would probably have stayed as friends, no more, if times hadn't been so hard. I suppose I took comfort in knowing that he loved me, knowing that when the bad times were passed, the happy times would be there waiting for me. But of course, the bad times only got worse and everyone I loved was taken away from me. I suppose I didn't want to get close to you in case the same thing happened. And then you said you might be leaving and I thought, here we go again. I'm going to lose him, just as I lost all the others. So I knew I'd done the right thing and not allowed myself to love you.'

'And now?'

'Now I know you're not going and I'm so afraid that I've ruined everything by pushing you away.'

Andrew puts his arms around her and holds her close, bending his face to hers. 'I'm going nowhere,' he whispers and kisses her again.

In the distance the headlights of a car appear, like dragon's eyes piercing the darkness.

'Just as well.' Andrew sighs dramatically. 'I was just about to lure you up to my cottage and who knows what more might have happened then.'

23
Changes

February 1947

Ellen frowns at the sight of Elizabeth Douglas outside the front door in her dressing gown. Although
her elderly employer has been getting noticeably
more absent-minded in the last few months, she
has always been decorous in her appearance. She
would never be seen without being fully dressed
and her hair tidily brushed. This dishevelled
woman on the doorstep in a keen wind, peering
into the half-dark of early morning, is completely
out of character. She starts when she sees Ellen,
takes several uncertain steps on the frozen path
towards her.

'Have you seen Kenneth?' she gasps. 'Have you
seen him? He isnae here.' She takes hold of Ellen's
arm with a bird-like grip.

'Elizabeth, what are you doing out here? You'll
catch a chill. Come on in where it's warm.' Ellen
tries to coax her indoors but she resists.

'You've got to help me find him. He's not here.
He's been away all night.' She pulls away and
begins to totter along the path. Ellen's eyes sweep
the dark hills. But then she shakes her head.
Elizabeth is getting more confused than she has
realised. 'I'll tell you what I will do, Elizabeth,'
she says catching up with her. 'Come inside

226

with me and let me make your breakfast. Then I'll go down to the barn and see if he is there. Even if he isn't, Finlay or Andrew will know where to find him.' She puts an arm round Elizabeth's shoulders and persuades her into the house. She places the kettle on the hob and quickly puts together a tray with cup and saucer and a plate with oatcakes and butter, all the while making frequent checks on the old lady to make sure she is still in the room. When the kettle has boiled she makes the tea and sets the tray on a low table next to where Elizabeth sits staring out over the indistinct valley floor.

'There you are. You just stay here and keep warm and eat your breakfast. I'll go on down to the barn and find Finlay.'

Kenneth is with Finlay in the big barn. They are checking the stock and making a list of anything they might need before the lambing season is upon them. The wind catches the door and slams it shut behind Ellen and Kenneth turns, smiling.

'Looking for Netta, are you? She went straight out to walk the hill up at the western end.'

'No, I was looking for you. Elizabeth couldn't find you and she was getting agitated.'

Kenneth frowns. 'Aye, she's getting gey forgetful recently. Do you need me to come back with you?'

'No. I'll tell her you're here. I think that will settle her down.'

As Ellen reaches the barn door, she hears Finlay remark to the farmer, 'I think you ought to put your idea to the test, boss. Things are only going to get worse, then who knows what might happen.'

She closes the door softly, wondering what they have been talking about. They are surely not thinking of selling the farm. It has been their life. Or has there been a suggestion that Elizabeth should be admitted to hospital? She may be forgetful and easily upset but not more than many of her age.

Ellen does not have long to wait for her answer. She is sitting with Elizabeth in the living room, having a late breakfast, when they hear Kenneth in the entry. He kicks off his muddy boots and comes through to the room where the two women are sitting.

'Will you have some breakfast now, Kenneth?' Ellen asks.

'Aye. And a mug of hot tea would be good,' he replies, rubbing his hands together. 'The temperature's dropping. I thought the warmer weather was too good to last. Come, Elizabeth, let's go through into the kitchen. It's warmer there.'

Ellen makes porridge and sets down a plateful in front of Kenneth, together with tattie scones and a large mug of tea. He smiles at her and takes a mouthful of tea. 'I don't know how we'd manage without you, Ellen, lass. You've been a godsend, especially now Elizabeth is no' so well.'

Ellen looks at him sharply. *So they are selling up,* she thinks, her heart sinking.

'Recently I've got to wondering whether you'd be prepared to move in with us here on the farm,' Kenneth continues. 'It would be a weight off my mind when I'm out and about, knowing that there was someone always here to keep an eye on things.' He glances at his wife. 'And of course

228

there would be a rise in your wages for the extra it would involve.'

Ellen's first thought is relief that they are not going away, her second dismay at the prospect of leaving the cottage that she has grown to love. But even before Kenneth has finished speaking, she knows that she will accept his suggestion. Kenneth and Elizabeth have given her nothing but kindness for as long as she can remember and particularly since her sudden reappearance in the valley the Christmas before last.

'Of course I will . . . only I would like to keep on the cottage. It has been our home since we came here and anyway Netta . . .'

Kenneth interrupts. 'Of course we would like Netta to move here as well. We would not want her to be on her own. But you must keep your cottage on, if that is what you want to do.'

Ellen gives a wry smile. 'I am not sure how Netta will take the suggestion that she moves from where we are now into the farmhouse. Our cottage in the valley has become her wee retreat. I am going to need all my powers of persuasion!'

Beyond the window a flurry of snowflakes dances through the farmyard. Kenneth looks at Ellen and shrugs. 'Well, hen, if the weather is taking a turn for the worse, I suggest the sooner we see your lassie and explain to her the better, and then we can get you moved in.'

24
Weather

March 1947

Netta wakes early. The unaccustomed brightness in her room can mean only one of two things. Either she has slept longer than intended — but her alarm clock has not alerted her — or there has been a further fall of snow to add to what has already been falling on and off over the previous two weeks. If this is the case, she should be jumping out of bed, preparing herself for a walk that will take longer than the usual amount of time. She rolls onto her back and stretches out, her feet reaching into the cold depths of the bed. It is quiet, very quiet.

Netta has continued to be politely adamant that she will stay where she is, in the wee cottage near the reservoir. She can see the extra purpose given to her mother's life by caring for the farmer's wife. Having settled her daughter back in the valley of her birth, Ellen is now repaying all the support that she and her father had from Kenneth and Elizabeth in the times when life was hard for the young family. If Netta had gone with her mother, she would have found it difficult to stand on her own two feet. And that is what she wishes to do, even though she misses the companionship of her mother. She loves it here in the place that she has

230

made into a home. Here she can come and go as she wants, can spend the day doing all the things on the farm that she enjoys doing but leave the busy environment behind when she wishes to be quiet again.

Netta swings her legs out of bed and stands up shivering. She goes over to the window and, drawing back the curtain, gasps at the unfamiliar sight that meets her eyes. It has snowed heavily in the night and the wind has blown the snow into banks and troughs that were never there before. The valley is unrecognisable. And it is still snowing.

She fumbles to light a candle and pulls on her warmest clothes. In the kitchen the stove is still alight and she puts the kettle on to heat and throws coal onto the embers, closing the vents in an effort to keep the stove going and a modicum of heat through the cottage while she is away. Quickly she puts together some breakfast. She knows how foolish it would be to go out in such weather without food in her stomach. At last, dressed in coat, hat, gloves and boots and with a shovel in her hand, she opens the door and is met by a huge drift of snow, which has completely blocked the entrance. Fighting her way through with the help of the shovel, she steps into a world of whiteness. Everything is white — hills, valley floor, even the trees, their branches bent low under the weight of the snow. More disturbingly there is not a sheep to be seen.

It is dangerous to proceed in conditions such as this but what else can Netta do? She cannot sit in isolation in her cottage and leave everyone else to struggle. Her help will be needed at the farm, now more than ever. There are only the ageing Kenneth, Finlay with his still indifferent health, Andrew and herself. There is no-one else. Her mother will be occupied with Elizabeth and with the necessary job of providing food for them all. And she knows, if only in theory, the risks of this weather to sheep. They are likely to be suffocated if buried too long under the snow; if left without food, they will starve. There is nothing for it but to make her way through the valley to the farm.

If she can reach the road, Netta thinks, the snow is likely to be less deep. She struggles towards the river bridge, over which the snow has not settled, but on its farther side she sinks waist-deep in a drift and loses her footing completely, falling sideways into the deep snow. Laughing at the picture she must present, she fights to find her feet. But it is no laughing matter. Before she has reached the road her legs are trembling with fatigue. It is, however, as she has imagined. The way is slightly easier here. At least she can keep her footing on the even ground. Even so, in places it is thigh deep.

The sky is lightening now. Usually she would be approaching the farm by this time of the morning. When she looks up, it is to see that she is only a third of the way there. She struggles on.

* * *

Carrying a full pail of milk as he leaves the barn, Andrew glances down the valley. There have been several snowy winters over west during the years but never snow like this. He is not expecting Netta and has got on with the job of milking the cows, a job that is normally hers now. He stops so abruptly that some of the milk slops over the side of the bucket into the snow. He can see her in the distance. At least he thinks it is her. At times she seems to disappear completely before he spots her again. He sets down the bucket by the barn wall and steps out into the snow. By the time he reaches her, she can hardly stand.

'This is ridiculous,' he says, his voice shaking with emotion. 'You should never have tried coming out in this.'

'But the sheep — we need to rescue them. They will die in the snow.'

'And so could you. You're much more important than the sheep. They're going to have to take their chances. Anyhow, we'll talk of that later. Let's get you to the farm.' He bends down to where she is sitting in the snow and puts an arm round her waist. Haltingly they make their way to the farm. Instead of entering the barn as Netta had intended to do, Andrew steers her up the short path to his cottage.

'What are we doing?'

'You're having a mug of restorative tea and maybe a wee bite to eat, before you do anything . . . and I want no arguments.' His voice is stern, until he adds more softly, 'Every cloud has a silver lining.' Opening the door, he steers her in and sits her down in front of the fire. He pulls off her boots, which she hasn't the energy to do and throws wood on the fire to create a warm blaze. 'Now take off your wet things and get warm,' he orders.

'Or I'll get double pneumonia.' She laughs.

'Something like that,' he replies and cannot avoid a smile.

The tea, when it comes, is perfect. She wraps her fingers round the mug and gazes round the room. It is cosy in a non-cluttered kind of way: books stored in a pile on the top of the cupboard, coats hung on the back of the kitchen door, boots in a tidy row by the front door.

Andrew enters with Kenneth and Finlay. 'Well, what a woman,' the farmer says. 'We never dreamed you'd try and make it through the snow. We're all concerned about the sheep, of course we are, but we need to be sensible.'

Finlay stands by the door, poised for action. 'Andrew and me, we're going to try and get to the sheep on the lower parts of the hills — clear some snow away so they can get to the grass. We could even try to get some into the barn.'

Andrew shakes his head. 'I don't think that will be possible, seeing the trouble Netta has had getting here.'

'Maybe not . . . and we certainly won't get to those that are higher or those that are right down the valley. Not today anyway,' Kenneth adds. 'They'll either make it or they won't. In my experience the sheep are more resilient than we give them credit for. Though I have to say, this winter is turning into one as bad as any I can remember.'

'It was bad when I first came here at the end of the Great War,' Finlay ruminates. 'That first winter was terrible, when I was still helping with the reservoir. The first two winters of this last war were bad too.' He shakes his head. 'We'd already lost men to the front and then the snow came and there weren't enough workers to find the sheep. We lost a lot those years.'

'Aye, it could be bad over west — but not like this. I've never known it like this.' Andrew puts a hand on Netta's shoulder. 'Your mother knows you're here, by the way. I don't think she realised just how bad it is or she would have been more worried than she appears to be. She says you're not to go back to the cottage tonight.'

'Oh, but I must, then I can look after the sheep at my end. In any case the snow might be away by then.'

Andrew gives a short laugh. 'I don't think there's any chance of that. Anyway Finlay and I are going out to look for sheep. You're to stay here and rest and get dry.'

Netta jumps up from her seat. 'If you think I've walked through the snow in order to sit here all day, you're very much mistaken. I'm going to help you.' She takes hold of her still-wet boots and begins to drag them onto her feet. Andrew glares at her and then his shoulders relax, he looks at Finlay and shrugs.

'What can a man do?'

'Do what the lady says, I guess,' says Finlay.

'Well, you're staying with me then, OK? It's safer that way — and no arguments.'

'Sorry I can't get on the hill with you, pals,' Kenneth adds mournfully,

'but I'd be more of a hindrance than a help.'

'Could you get some feed into the barns, Kenneth? If we can fetch some sheep in, we will do.'

Slowly they make their way to the slopes at the back of the farm, where some of the sheep are gathered for shelter against a stone wall. Others are gathered along the side of the burn, where there is a hint of green showing along its edges. With the help of shovels the shepherds clear the snow from a large area of grass and the sheep immediately begin to feed. Very slowly they make their way across the hill, the snow at times waist-deep. It's exhausting work and after a while Netta, tired already from her earlier struggle, can do no more.

'Go back and make us another pot of tea, will you?' says Andrew. 'And we'll join you.'

It's half an hour before the two men enter the cottage, having found a half dozen sheep completely buried but thankfully still alive. All is quiet and when Andrew enters the living room, he sees Netta curled up in the chair by the fire, sound asleep. He stands still, looking down at her. Her hair is tousled from pulling her hat off and on, her face smeared with mud, her fingernails ringed with dirt. To him she looks beautiful.

There is no tea. Presumably she has sunk into the chair and fallen asleep before she has even thought to put the kettle on the fire. He goes into the kitchen, fills the kettle and brings it back to set it on the fire. Netta stirs but doesn't wake. He makes tea, brings mugs, milk and sugar, and pours the tea. He puts out a hand and rests it gently on her shoulders. She stirs, looks up at him.

'Tea, Sleeping Beauty.'

She smiles wearily. 'Beautiful I am not!'

'You are to me,' he says simply and passes her the mug.

Later in the day they all meet up again to discuss their plan of action. The snow has stopped falling but the drifts are deep and many of the sheep have not been reached. They can only hope against hope that conditions higher up the hill are such that areas of grass have been uncovered by the wind and the sheep have found enough to eat. Andrew suggests that he gets out the tractor and drives Netta back to her cottage, so that he can try and clear the road and judge how it will be in the morning. If it is passable, he and Netta can concentrate on finding the hill sheep in that end of the valley tomorrow.

It is a slow and difficult ride, one that he could not have done in the car and even the tractor is finding difficult. They proceed at walking pace, the tractor throwing out snow on either side of it to give them a passage through and, at times, slewing off the road dangerously near to the banking and the river below. As they reach the track to the cottage, the tractor hits a deep drift and stops abruptly. Andrew puts it into reverse but the tractor refuses to budge. He waits two or three minutes, then tries again but the tractor is embedded in the snow.

'It looks as though you are staying here for the night,' Netta comments.

'I can try walking back. After all, you did it this morning.'

'I was fresh out of bed. You've done a day's work — a day and a half if you feel anything like me. And, in any case, it snowed for several hours after

237

I walked to the farm. Come along. With any luck the fire will still be in and it will be warm.' Netta takes his hand and together they struggle along the track to the cottage. She pushes open the door and they stumble into the unexpected cosiness.

'Good. My plan worked. The fire has kept going all day.'

'Not just a pretty face then.' Andrew sinks back in the easy chair and closes his eyes. 'Do you have a spare bed, sweetheart?'

'Yes I do . . . if a spare bed is what you want.'

* * *

Though the sky is grey and heavy, there has been no more snowfall overnight.

Andrew stands at the door, stamping snow off his boots. He has taken a spade and dug out the snow from round the tractor as best he can. But there is no point in moving it at the moment. What they need to do is get on up the hill with their spades and begin to dig out the sheep. Dawn is a mere hint in the eastern sky but the snow will light the way enough for them to see where they are going. They cross over where they know the road to be and begin to climb.

'You make your way to the stell, sweetheart. That's as likely a place as any to find them. I'll go over to the burn and see if any have survived there.'

Although she cannot see it, Netta knows the rough whereabouts of the stell, the circular wall designed to give sheep some protection from the effects of the weather. She digs into a drift, encountering nothing but snow. Gazing round the valley to get her bearings, she tries again. Nothing. She stands irresolute. It is quiet, even the sound of the bubbling burn in the distance muted by the snow heaped all around. And then she hears a faint bleat. She listens and it comes again. She locates it to another huge drift. She begins to dig, at first with the spade and then with her hands, fearing to harm the sheep. The snow comes away softly, in huge scoops, and there suddenly her hand lights on the yellow-grey wool of a sheep's back. Digging madly, she makes a hole big enough for the sheep to escape and it skitters out, skidding on the steep slope of the hill. And then she sees others, huddled together within the shelter for warmth. She digs a small circle to expose some grass. The sheep emerge into the cold air, seemingly uncertain what to do, before staggering across to the cleared area and beginning to feed.

Netta looks towards Andrew in the distance and shouts. He turns in her direction, and gives her a thumbs-up when he sees the sheep. From where she is standing, she cannot see any sheep near the burn. She turns back to the stell, pauses, listening. And there is another unmistakable bleat. She repeats the process and in a few minutes more sheep stagger out from their cold captivity and make their way to the patch of grass. She listens again but can hear nothing more. She clears snow from the wall of the stell, so that she can make out the whole of its shape, and then begins to shovel away snow from its centre, digging with her hands in places for fear of damaging the ewes. And here she comes upon another but it is lying down and as she frees it of snow, she can see that it is stiff and cold. She tries to coax it to move but it is already dead. Nearby she finds another sheep lying on its side. It is gasping for air. She massages its face, grabs hold of its back, pulling it upright in an effort to encourage it to walk. At first it seems too exhausted to bother but as she persists, it struggles onto its legs and joins the others feeding.

By the time she has cleared the inside of the shelter, there are three dead sheep and thirteen that she has saved. She enlarges the area of grass, then turns again to see how Andrew is faring. He is further up the hill now and several sheep are grouped together in a cleared area. Picking up her spade, she climbs the hills towards him and sinks down at his side, unbuttoning the top of her coat and removing her hat.

'This is hard work,' she says, 'and hot. How many more are we going to lose before we can dig them all out? You have found some dead as well.'

'Yes, half a dozen already.' He indicates the area in which he had started digging and she sees a pile of carcases near the water. 'There's no air pockets down near the burn, ken. But sheep are canny creatures when it comes to sheltering. They're more likely to survive where there's a wall or a stell to trap the air. And the sheep can nibble away at any grass that's still showing, as well as the moss and lichen on the walls. They even nibble each other's woolly coats to get the goodness out of them. They're not half as stupid as they're made out to be.' Andrew sits on an exposed rock and loosens his coat collar. 'This is hot work — and thirsty work too. Pour a drink from the flask, sweetheart. We need to reserve our energy, if we are to keep this up all day.' They stand together sipping their tea and staring over the acres of land yet to be uncovered.

'There should be a wall running up the hill over there.' He indicates an area to the west of where they are standing. 'What I suggest is that you make your way over there and work along the edge of the wall where the drifts are deepest. Our most immediate concern is getting fresh air to them. Feeding can come later. If we can get a good number out, I will try and get back to the farm later and bring some feed for them. But first I need to dig a hole and bury those dead sheep. I cannae leave them all out here on the hill and we certainly can't get them all back to the dead pit.'

Netta has always stayed as far away as possible from the dead pit. It is situated a quarter of a mile downwind of the farm, a huge manmade hole, into which the casualties of lambing, old age and the weather are thrown, together with a quantity of lime. Even so, on days when the wind comes from the east, its evil smell reaches the farm and its environs.

'I hope Finlay is OK working on his own,' Netta says, staring back towards the farm and seeing nothing but white.

'Aye, I hope so too. It's no' so good seeing half your life's work threatening to disappear before your eyes. At least Kenneth's safe back at the farm and no' up here to see what's happening to his flock. Right, is that us ready to carry on? Are you sure you've enough strength?'

'Do I look ready to give up?'

241

Later they break from their work and have oat-cakes and cheese and the remainder of the tea. There are more dead sheep, though fewer than they feared. The snow has melted a little during the day and other sheep have succeeded in forcing their way out from their imprisonment. Perhaps it will not turn out so bad after all. They return to their digging after a short break. By four o'clock the dull day is getting gloomier. They must hurry if they are to get back to the farm, load feed onto the trailer and get it back to the sheep before nightfall. They make for the tractor and set off along the road.

Finlay has been working hard at his end but Netta is surprised to see her mother also in the yard, dressed in boots and a long mackintosh.

'I've been helping Finlay,' she explains to her daughter. 'We've brought some of the sheep into the barn. That way, if it snows more, at least we will know there are some that will already be safe and not needing to be dug out.' Ellen looks at her daughter's exhausted face. 'Are there many casualties at your end?'

'Some, though fewer than we feared. Knowing where to look is half the battle. The other half will be keeping them alive if it snows again. Andrew says they can last up to a couple of weeks if they're lucky. He's going back with food for them. I'll stay here for now and see if Finlay needs some help. Oh, and milk the cows. I had to leave them for Finlay this morning.'

'And then you'll all come and have tea with Elizabeth and me. No arguments. It's all prepared. Would you mind going down to Finlay's cottage to invite him for tea. And please don't try to get back down the valley tonight. Stay here in the farmhouse.'

When Netta has done all that she must in the barn, she makes her way up to Finlay's cottage. She can see that he is in. Light is spilling from the window to form an orange rectangle on the snow outside. Through the glass she can see Finlay sitting in his fireside chair, a glass in his hand. She pauses, a pang of sadness coming over her at his hunched and lonely demeanour. It occurs to her now how this must have been his way of life for many years, no company but his own. She recalls his words when they first met — 'I didnae marry . . . it's this job, you see'. She also remembers some words she had been reading in a book not long before, a book she had borrowed from Andrew. How did the words go? 'Better to have loved and lost than never to have loved at all.' Perhaps, for all the sadness that she and her mother had experienced, they were better off than this lonely man.

'Finlay!' She opens the door and calls out. 'You are invited for tea at the farmhouse. Mother says she will not accept a refusal.'

Finlay looks up, his eyes red from staring at the hot coals in the fireplace.

'That's gey good of her.' He adds a splash of whisky from the bottle in the fireplace to what remains in his glass and takes a large swig.

'You look sad, Finlay. Is it the sheep?'

'Aye, lass. It's the sheep.' He sighs. 'I've been working here on this farm for nigh on thirty years, improving the flock, and then all the good we have done gets wiped away in a single day of weather. And where's it all going to end, I'm thinking. We may not be done with the snow yet.' He swirls the whisky in his glass and finishes it in a single gulp.

'Look at it this way, Finlay. If you and Kenneth hadn't spent all those years with the flock, they wouldnae have been so hardy and even more might have been lost.'

He sighs. 'Aye, perhaps you're right, hen.'

But it seems little consolation.

* * *

He is right to be downhearted. Two days later the snow returns. For day after day it is relentless, blown on strong winds into huge drifts several feet deep. For days and days the farmer and his employees are housebound. Basic stocks of flour and oatmeal run low. Root vegetables, never abundant, have to be shared between the family and the cattle.

By the time the blizzards have blown through and the heaped clouds part enough to show welcome patches of blue, forty per cent of the flock will be lost and of those that remain, many will be in such poor condition that, when their lambs are born, they will not have the milk to feed them and they too will become victims of the devastating weather.

25

An Unwelcome Discovery

March 1947

Netta stomps up the path to the farmhouse, her boots heavy with mud. She is beginning to feel as though she will never be dry again. She enters, calling out as she does so. At least she will have a few minutes to warm up in the kitchen over a cup of tea.

The huge snowfalls of the previous weeks have given way to heavy rain.

The river through the valley, usually low and innocuous, is fast and menacing, filled with the overflow from the brimful reservoir. In several places the river has spilled over its banks and flooded the fields in the base of the valley. Sheep have made their way up the hillsides away from danger. If the water continues to rise, there will be difficulty getting from the farm to the road out of the valley. Already it is only just below the planks of the bridge.

Ellen flings open the door of the living room, the expected look of welcome on her mother's face being instead one of consternation.

'What is the matter, Mutti? Has something happened? Is Elizabeth all right?'

'It's not Elizabeth. It's Kenneth. He's disappeared. I thought this morning that he'd gone for a walk as he often does.' Ellen's voice trembles. 'But he's no' come back and Elizabeth is in a state and Finlay is out searching — and we cannae find him.' She puts her head in her hands and gives way to the tears she has been holding back all day.

'He hasn't gone out in the motor?'

'No, I've looked. The pickup is in its usual place, and he can't get far without it.'

Netta smiles at her mother. 'Don't worry, Mutti. No doubt he will be out somewhere checking the sheep. You know how anxious he gets at this time of year.'

'But he's no' had any dinner. It's not like him to miss his dinner. And he always comes in to check on Elizabeth and he hasnae been.'

'Has he been well recently? Has he said anything about feeling poorly?'

'Not a thing.'

Netta puts her arm around her mother's shoulders and stares out of the window at the hills on the far side of the valley. She has been over her patch as carefully as the ruts and hollows allow and has seen nothing amiss. The sheep have all looked as they always do, none of them needing her help. And there has been no sign of another human being in the expanse of hillside she has traversed. Finlay is still not back. She casts her eyes eastward, in the direction of the reservoir and can see nothing out of the ordinary. But that is where Andrew has gone and he has not returned either.

'I'm going to look,' she says, pulling away from her mother.

'No, don't go.'

'What? What do you mean, don't go? What should I do — stay here doing nothing while Kenneth is out there somewhere and may have had an accident? Leave him to die like my father?'

Her comment hits Ellen like a slap in the face. She steps back, staring at her daughter. 'Do you think that's what happened? That I left him to die? I told you what happened and that is the truth.'

Netta's shoulders droop. 'I'm sorry, Mutti. I didn't mean it like that, only you've made *me* worried now about Kenneth.' She hesitates. 'And about Andrew as well. He should be back now and he isn't. I will be careful but I must go and look for them.'

'I'm sorry too. I'm a bit on edge, that's all. And I don't want anything happening to you.'

'Nothing will happen to me. Could you put together something to eat and a warm drink to take with me? They'll no doubt be hungry when I find them.' She glances up at the sky. 'It looks as though it's coming on to rain again. The clouds make it so dark I shan't be able to see if I don't go soon.'

★ ★ ★

Netta searches the barn and the outhouses. Kenneth is not there and neither is Finlay. He must be still out on the hill. She makes her way over the bridge and starts to climb. She reckons that her best chance of seeing the farmer, if he is here somewhere, is to climb high and look down. Despite the rain, the snow of the previous weeks still lies in the hollows, evening out the sculptured

247

landscape, so at times her foot sinks deep into the mud beneath. She worries that she might turn her ankle over and be unable to proceed but she can see no alternative. How else will Kenneth be found?

She has reached the top of the range of hills now and turns towards the reservoir, which is just out of sight because of a slight curvature of the valley. But she can picture it there, spread out for a mile or more until the far hills enfold it. The wind has risen, flinging needles of rain into her face and numbing her hands. She picks her way slowly along, breaking the silence from time to time with Kenneth's name and sometimes Andrew's.

The sky is darkening now. Soon she will no longer be able to see her way. She sits abruptly on a jutting rock, taking gulps of air in an effort to steady her failing energy. The wind catches her wet hair, slapping it across her face. She pulls it back, catches it behind her ear, stares through the gloom to the river racing below. And then she sees him.

It is Andrew. She is sure it is him. Even in the encroaching darkness she can recognise his height. He is stretching his arms out. He bends over, then stretches again. What can he be doing? She stands quickly, shouts his name and shouts again. But her voice is carried away in the wind's frenzy. She begins to stumble down the hillside towards him and suddenly he sees her, staggers upward in her direction. She falls into his outstretched arms, unbalancing him, so he topples into the heather, taking her with him.

'What in heaven's name are you doing out here,

lass?'

'Looking for you. Well, looking for Kenneth. He's been missing all day.'

'I've found him.'

'Where? Where is he?'

Andrew holds her head against his chest and gently strokes her wet hair. 'He's there just below us. He's . . . he's dead.'

She gasps, sits up abruptly. 'How?' Her voice cracks. 'What happened?'

'I found him on the river bank, half in the water.' He nods towards a stretch where the river has spread widely over the floor of the valley. 'I've been carrying him from there — but I can't go any further. He's too heavy. There's no sign of injury that I can see. He wasnae near rocks. He's maybe fallen and been unable to get up. Or perhaps he's been taken ill and collapsed. We'll never know.'

'And you're sure he's dead?'

'Aye. It was still light enough when I found him for me to check. He had been dead for a while, I reckon.'

'Can I help carry him?'

'I don't have the strength to carry him any further, and I don't really imagine you do either. We'll walk back and bring the pickup as near as we're able to drive it . . . and get Finlay to come and help us.'

Netta staggers to her feet and they begin their slow descent to the unmoving body of the farmer. Andrew picks up his stick and plants it vertically into the mud, so it will mark the position of Kenneth's body. He takes Netta's hand and the pair walk as quickly as they are able through the drenching rain and gusts of wind that try to blow them back the way they have come.

* * *

Netta watches Finlay start the pickup and follows the car as it disappears with Finlay and Andrew into the distance. She takes a deep breath and makes her way to the farmhouse to deliver the sad news to the waiting women.

Elizabeth seems unable to take in what Netta is telling her. She gazes dry-eyed at Netta before turning to Ellen.

'What's she saying? I don't understand. Where's Kenneth? Why isn't he home?'

'Andrew has found him. He's dead, Elizabeth. He must have collapsed. They're bringing him home now, Andrew and Finlay. You'll see him soon. You stay here with Netta while I go and prepare the spare room for him.'

But Elizabeth follows Ellen, like a dog trailing its master, into the spare room. 'Why will they put him in here? This isn't where he sleeps. He doesn't like this room.' Ellen is crying silently as she makes ready the bed to receive the farmer. Netta leads Elizabeth back into the kitchen and sits with her at the table trying to calm her.

Eventually they hear a car approaching and the brakes being applied. Elizabeth gets up and goes to the window, her mouth gaping open as she sees the body of her husband in the car's headlights, as the two men carry him into the house. Netta puts her arm round the old woman's shoulders, feeling the quivering of her bony frame, but she cannot restrain Elizabeth as she follows Andrew and Finlay into the prepared room. They lay him gently on the bed and Ellen removes his muddy boots before covering him with a sheet, turning away and leaving the room without saying a word. Elizabeth goes up to the bed, dragging the sheet from her husband's face, running her fingers gently over his brow, his cheeks, across the sparse hair covering his head.

Netta looks at the doorway through which her mother has departed. She guesses that for Ellen it has brought back in vivid detail the ordeal of her discovering her first husband in the melting snow of that faraway spring.

26
Unforeseen Consequences

March 1947

For Finlay it is a relief to be driving to the village to inform the doctor. The atmosphere of shock and grief within the farmhouse is oppressive. Kenneth's death, coming on top of the loss of so many of the flock, is too much for him. He needs to escape and be alone with his thoughts.

As he passes the Blacks' farm he sees Billy himself crossing the farmyard. Billy hails him and steps over towards the car. Finlay brakes and steers to a halt.

'How's everyone?' Billy asks. 'It's been bad for us here but we've been thinking it must have been even worse for you with so many hill sheep.'

'It's been dreadful — the worst ever. We've lost a huge number of ewes and I wouldnae be surprised if we lose a lot of lambs in the next few weeks.' He pauses. 'But we've even worse news today.'

'How's that?' Billy asks, looking at Finlay's serious face.

'It's the boss. He's died. I'm away to fetch the doctor now.'

Billy looks at Finlay's face as if he can't believe it, before nodding his head slowly. 'When did this happen?'

'Sometime today. Andrew found him out on the hill. Looks as though he went out for a walk, maybe checking on the ewes. There's no sign of injury that we could see. We're thinking he must have collapsed and that was it.'

'Ah. A good way to go, perhaps. Yes, definitely. Tell Elizabeth I'm sorry for her loss. I'll call around and see her tomorrow.' Finlay puts the car into gear and Billy steps back as Finlay sets off again. Billy shakes his head slowly, his eyes following the lights of the car until it is out of sight.

Dr Ferguson is nearing the end of his evening surgery. As soon as his last patient has left the consulting room, he picks up his bag, hurries out to start his car and follows the pickup slowly into the valley. The sheep on either side of the road, caught in the headlights of the two cars, look up dazed but don't move from the comfortable position they have adopted for the night. Seeing them, Finlay hopes that Andrew has been able to free himself from the upset and upheaval at the farm to check on the welfare of the ewes in the barn. These are the lucky ones, the ones who are getting extra food to try and build them up for their lambing. On the hill there is very little decent grass left after the snows of the recent weeks and no growth of new spring grass visible. It is anyone's guess whether these ewes and their lambs will get through the next difficult weeks intact and healthy.

★ ★ ★

Ellen opens the door and Dr Ferguson crosses to the living room where Elizabeth is sitting gazing out of the window.

'Mrs Douglas,' he begins. 'I am so sorry to hear about the death of your husband. You understand that I will need to examine him before I say any more. I will come back to you directly I have finished.' He pats her hand and turns to follow Ellen into the spare room. Ellen glances quickly at the body and turns away.

'Do you need anything, Doctor?' she asks, uncertain as to what her duties should be.

'No thank you, Ellen. I will call you if I need anything.' Ellen goes to the door, closing it quietly behind her, glad to be out of the room. She walks slowly over to the window and stares at the blackness in front of her. But her imagination is back in Germany. She wonders if this is how Josef's body was handled after he was shot — and knows that it will not have been so. Since the cessation of hostilities, news has gradually emerged of the treatment of those who died in concentration camps, news so horrific that she can hardly bear to picture it. No peaceful lying in a comfortable bed with a clean white sheet to cover him. At least she was able to give her two daughters a funeral of sorts, even if it was done quickly and quietly. They were laid to rest. She imagines Josef's soul wandering the earth forever in search of her.

The quiet closing of a door behind her brings Ellen out of her reverie. The doctor is standing there. She leads him to the bathroom where she has left soap and a towel. He pauses and looks at her.

'It seems he did not suffer. However, there appears to be little indication of how he died. I need to speak to his wife — see if she can give me any hint of recent problems.'

'I'm worried about her,' Ellen confides in the doctor. 'Recently she has become very forgetful and at times confused. I have no idea what her reaction will be to Kenneth's death.'

The doctor looks at his watch, considering his best course of action. 'I think,' he says slowly, 'that, considering the time, I will just give Elizabeth my condolences and then return tomorrow morning to talk to her more fully. You must all be very tired. I will leave you all alone to try and get some sleep.' He reaches into his bag and pulls out a small packet. 'This will help Elizabeth to have a night's sleep. Dissolve the powder in a glass of water and get her to drink it about half an hour before she goes to bed. I won't keep you any longer tonight. You look exhausted.'

* * *

Dr Ferguson drives over as soon as morning surgery is finished. The rain has stopped and patches of cloud chase each other across a blue sky, giving an optimistic feel to the day, an optimism that is not shared by the group in the farmhouse living room. They are all here — Elizabeth, Ellen and her daughter and the two shepherds, all eager to throw any possible light on the reason for Kenneth's death. The doctor pulls up a chair and sits opposite Elizabeth.

'Now, Mrs Douglas, I hope you have had a

255

good night's sleep.' There is no reply and the doctor looks to Ellen for confirmation. 'So tell me, had your husband complained of being unwell recently? Any aches or pains of any kind? Had he lost weight?'

Elizabeth looks round at Ellen. 'He wasnae ill, was he, Ellen? He didnae tell me he was ill.'

'I live here now, Doctor, since Elizabeth has been unwell,' Ellen explains. 'He hasnae been ill at all, as far as I know. He's getting older of course, and cannae do so much on the farm as he used to. He leaves all that to Finlay and Andrew. But he still gets out of the house for a walk every day and supervises the work, am I no' right?' The two men nod in agreement.

'He's troubled with pains in his knees,' Elizabeth says slowly, remembering his one and only complaint.

'Yes, that's right.' Ellen smiles. 'He says — said — that it stops him walking as far as he would like.'

'The trouble is, Mrs Douglas, that I have to complete a death certificate and I'm not at all sure what —'

A loud knock on the front door stops him in his tracks and a voice calls out, 'May I come in?'

Ellen hurries out of the room. Billy Black is standing in the hallway.

'The doctor's here just now,' she says in a whisper. 'It's Kenneth — he's died.'

'Yes, I know. I met Finlay up the valley last night. It's only that I have some information that might help the doctor if he's mystified over what caused Kenneth's death.'

Ellen takes Billy through. He goes over to Elizabeth first and takes her hand. 'I'm sorry for your loss. Kenneth was a fine man and a good friend.'

'Mr Black has some information that may help,' Ellen says, turning to the doctor.

'Aye,' says Billy. 'We've been friends a number of years and he tells me things. A while ago he mentioned he'd been taking pains in his chest — not enough to worry you about, you understand. But he mentioned them again recently — said they were getting a wee bit worse, enough to stop him doing all the walking he would like. He mentioned too that he had been getting short of breath, especially climbing his beloved hills. I told him he should consult you about it but he was no' so keen. He reckoned it was all part of growing old and what would life be like without a little bit of hardship now and then. You know the kind of thing a lot of us say when really we ought to come and pay you a visit.'

'Indeed, indeed,' Dr Ferguson says. 'So it sounds as though Kenneth has been suffering from bouts of heart pain — angina, we would call it. This would fit very well with his good overall condition. And there is nothing to suggest a suspicious cause.' The doctor pauses, considering. 'The farmer was no doubt out taking stock of his sheep, as happens all over at this time of year, and he suffered a sudden heart attack.' He turns to Elizabeth. 'His death would have been very sudden, Elizabeth. It is unlikely that he would have known anything about it. I will need to refer his death to the coroner but I expect, given this information, that a death certificate can be issued without the

257

need to resort to further investigation.'

The doctor sits at the table and opens his case, pulling out a pad and beginning to write down all the details he has been given. Billy Black nods his goodbye to the group and turns to go. Ellen opens the door and sees him out. Once in the yard he turns to Ellen.

'As you will appreciate, the position regarding Elizabeth is somewhat delicate. She is not in the best of health herself and, in my view, unable to manage on her own. Are you happy to continue staying here with her?'

'Of course . . . but should we see someone to ask if this is in order? As far as I know Kenneth and Elizabeth have no relatives who can take charge of the situation.'

'No, indeed.' Billy Black proceeds thoughtfully. 'Fortunately, however, although Kenneth was not particularly protective about his own health, he did think of his wife in advance of his death. He asked me to go with him to see a solicitor and together they worked out a proposed plan of action to cover just such an eventuality as this. If you, Ellen, are prepared to stay here with Elizabeth for now, I will ring the solicitor and make an appointment to go and see him after the funeral. And I would be grateful if you could make yourself free to come along with me.'

Ellen looks at him in surprise. 'Do you need me to come along? I am perfectly happy to stay here and care for Elizabeth if that is what is decided. After all, this place, or at least the cottage, was all I knew for the first twenty years of my life.'

'I know that, my dear, but these things have to

258

be seen to be done properly, especially when there is the farm and all its land to be taken into consideration.'

'Of course. I hadn't thought of that side of things. Right enough, you let me know when the visit is arranged and I will make sure I can accompany you. Should I bring Elizabeth with me?'

'I will ask the solicitor but I think not. She is confused enough and I don't think a visit to the solicitor will make her any less so. We can explain things to her later. Let us hope that this spell of better weather continues, so that Kenneth's burial is not delayed.'

* * *

By the time of the funeral four days later, the frequent bouts of heavy rain have cleared the snow from all but the tops of the hills and ensured that the river level stays as high as it was when Kenneth's body was discovered. Kenneth is driven with due ceremony out of the heart of the valley that has been his home and workplace for so many years, and along to the church in the village where a large number of friends and acquaintances, most of them farmers, await his arrival.

He is buried in the graveyard from which a view of his hills can easily be seen and in which lie generations of local farmers, as well as Tom, his erstwhile shepherd and father of Netta, and also the German soldier who was killed not by enemy action but in the building of the reservoir that Tom had so much resented.

259

'Do come in,' says the solicitor, Martin McCrae. Ellen steps nervously into the room and takes the chair indicated. She has never been in such rooms before and feels herself very out of place. Billy Black sits in the chair next to her and gives her a reassuring smile.

'This won't take long,' the solicitor continues. He shuffles a wad of papers in his hand. 'There is no necessity at present to go into too much detail. Mr and Mrs Douglas came to me some time ago with Mr Black here and arranged for the guardianship of Elizabeth Douglas to be given to Mr Black in the event of Kenneth Douglas's death. Kenneth had realised some time ago that his wife was not in the best of health and not entirely capable of looking after herself. He suspected that he might not be long for this world.'

'I have said that I am happy to continue to help,' Ellen interjects. 'Elizabeth helped my father when I was young — my mother died, you see — and I would like to repay her for all her kindness.'

'Yes, of course you would. But you understand that there is a legal requirement for this agreement to be written down, so that no irregularities occur. I think that all we need to do at present,' he says, with a glance at Billy Black, 'is to say that Kenneth Douglas specified that, if you were willing, he would like you and Netta to move into the farmhouse, so that you, Mrs Kessler, would be able to look after his wife. This was, of course, if you were willing, and I understand that that is indeed what you have done.'

260

'I have, sir, but my daughter wished to stay in our cottage further down the valley. She is thirty-one, you see, and wanting her independence. But I am concerned about this. Her wage is not big and I doubt she will be able to stay there for long without help.'

'Indeed. However, Kenneth specified that, in addition to you living in the farmhouse, he also wished for an amount of money, that is five hundred pounds annually, to be given to you in addition to what you currently earn. This will pay for food and other necessities needed for the comfort of Elizabeth Douglas. And I think Mr Black will agree that we can put aside an amount for rent, so that your daughter can comfortably stay in the cottage. Is this agreeable, Mr Black?'

Billy Black nods his assent. 'In actual fact, Netta is now doing the job of trainee shepherd and I don't suppose her wages are reflecting that fact.'

'It seems that some adjustment is necessary in that case. May I leave that to you to correct, Mr Black?'

'Of course. I'd be only too pleased.'

'And what about you, Mrs Kessler? Does that all seem agreeable to you?'

'Yes, sir, very agreeable.'

'Good. Mr Black here will administer the money and you will tell *him* if it is insufficient for your needs. The other arrangement of which you should be aware is that Mr Black will oversee any repairs that are necessary to the general upkeep of the farmhouse and of the farm buildings, so do consult him if you think money should be spent on redecoration or other problems that may arise in the farmhouse.

'If there is a material change in your circumstances or Mrs Douglas's health should deteriorate, I will be happy to see you both again and review the arrangements. If you have any worries, talk to Mr Black. As far as the farm is concerned, Mr Black, are you happy to work with Mr Baird to ensure its continued smooth running?'

'Of course, and I will come straight back to you if there are any problems.'

'Good. I suggest we leave it for now. The rest can be discussed later, if Mrs Douglas should regrettably die.'

Ellen is shocked by the solicitor's words. She looks from one to the other of the men. 'No need to worry, Mrs Kessler,' Martin McCrae reassures her.

'It is my job to look at all eventualities, but we don't anticipate any trouble just yet.' He extends his hand and Ellen and Billy Black rise from their seats and shake hands with him. His secretary shows them out.

'Nothing to worry about, my dear,' Billy says to Ellen as they make their way towards where his car is parked. 'All these things have to be done properly, especially when money and property are concerned.'

'I didn't like to ask when we were in the room — but what will happen to the farm itself? I mean, I can understand that, at the moment, with Elizabeth alive, it is best to keep things as they have always been. But what will happen when she dies? They have no children to inherit the farm and I don't even remember any other relatives ever visiting. Will it be sold?'

Billy smiles at Ellen. 'Don't worry about that at the moment. I believe Kenneth has discussed it at length with Mr McCrae. Suffice it to say, all the farm's employees will be well taken care of.'

27
Letters

April 1947

25th April 1947

Dear Andrew,

I do hope you and Netta are both well. What an awful winter it has been. We have been snowed in for much of March and although the pupils have enjoyed it, there have been difficulties getting supplies into the school and trying to get the pupils outside to work off their excess energy!
Beth and I have been wondering how you have been coping with these conditions on the farm. It must have given you a lot of extra work. In connection with this, we wondered if you had had time to consider my proposal for students to gain experience of farming with you. If the farmer you work for is willing for it to go ahead, we could arrange for some students to be with you over the summer holidays.
Let us know what you think.

With our very best wishes,
Jack and Beth

★ ★ ★

Dear Jack and Beth,

My apologies for taking so long to reply to your letter. The season has, as you say, been awful. We have lost a lot of stock. Deaths are in their hundreds. We have lost both sheep and lambs. But everyone is suffering as much as we are. The only thing we can do is carry on. It will be a lean year financially but, as Finlay says, there have been others in the past and farmers have pulled round and built up their stock again.

An even bigger shock is that Kenneth Douglas, the farmer here, has died quite suddenly. He has been here all his life and his father before him. He has no family to carry on the farm but for now we are keeping it going between us for the sake of his wife and, if I am honest, for our sakes too. It would not be a good time to be looking for another job. It is maybe for the best that he is not here to see the full results of the awful weather.

Before Kenneth died we did discuss your proposal. He suggested I look into it and come up with some figures, which Finlay, the head shepherd, and I did start to do before the bad weather meant all our efforts were required in other directions. However, I have enclosed what we have worked out so far. Of course most of this was done before Kenneth's death but it will not materially alter the cost of the project — housing and feeding the pupils being the main expense. If anything, the losses we have incurred may make it easier,

265

*as we will be under less pressure, there being only
half the stock we originally had.*

*Let me know how soon you wish to send us
pupils and for how long, and we will arrange the
visit at this end.*

With every good wish,
Andrew

28
Ceilidh

May 1947

Ellen's memories of visiting an agricultural show
are hazy. She sits at the window seat in the early
morning sunshine, trying to recall how old she
had been when Kenneth and Elizabeth had taken
her and her father to a local show. She must have
been nine or ten, just old enough to understand
what was going on. What still stands out clearly in
her memory was the moment when a first prize
rosette had been attached to the pen containing
Kenneth's Blackface tup. She remembers the
farmer's face, a studied indifference attempting
to hide the pride of winning, and her father's grin
as he sipped the pint that Kenneth had bought
him afterwards in the big noisy tent crammed
with farmers. She looks at the wall over the piano
where the rosette, dusty from the passage of years,
still has pride of place.

There will be no such success in this year's
show, she thinks, with the awful weather of the
past winter and its devastating effect on the flock.

With the loss of dozens of ewes, many while still
carrying their lambs, and the poor condition of the
remainder, it will be hard to find good exhibits to
put in for judging. However, the situation they are
in is little different from the neighbouring farms,

although their elevated position in the hills has no doubt meant that their losses have been higher than others and their meagre store of grain and vegetables even less sufficient for their needs.

She had been surprised to find Finlay standing outside yesterday when she answered the knock at the door. She sees him usually only from a distance, as he goes about his work.

'Andrew suggests I invite you to the show tomorrow,' he had said. 'I can take you in the car, if that's OK with you. The only thing is, we'll need to leave early, to help Andrew prepare the sheep that he and Netta are showing and get them looking as good as we can in the circumstances.'

'That's a lovely idea, Finlay, but Elizabeth's no' safe to be left on her own all day.'

'Och no, we didnae intend to leave her here. She's to come too. She'll enjoy it, seeing all the animals, meeting with all her old acquaintances.'

'Well, in that case, thank you, Finlay. We would love to come!'

A thrill of excitement passes through her now as Ellen thinks of the day ahead. It is the first occasion in a very long time that she has anticipated with such pleasure. She glances at the clock on the mantelpiece. Seven-thirty — she must make a move if she and Elizabeth are going to be ready for when Finlay brings round the car.

★ ★ ★

Andrew and Netta have been up since the early hours. The days are long now, less than a month before the summer solstice. Even so, Netta has been awake since before dawn, listening to the familiar tuneless call of the oystercatchers as they gather along the river to search for breakfast. She doesn't stay in her bed for long. There is a busy day ahead — and an exciting one. She considers making a pot of tea but rejects the idea. She will set off for Andrew's as he has, in any case, invited her for breakfast.

The sky is golden as she walks through the valley, the sun shining on the hills, which have only in the last two or three weeks begun to turn green with new grass. The river chats companionably, its excesses of April replaced by a comfortable fullness. Splashes of celandine decorate the banks. Her shoes are soon wet with dew.

Andrew is in the barn. The show sheep, shampooed the afternoon before, are receiving a vigorous brushing. There are two tups, two gimmers and four lambs. Netta has oiled the horns of the adult sheep and, despite the inclement conditions of the last few months, the results are good and she is proud of her work. Andrew looks up as she approaches and grins.

'Nearly done. Breakfast is out ready, if you would like to make the tea. Give me five minutes.'

Netta enters the cottage. She loves the way it speaks of Andrew — his long raincoat with the faint scent of its owner, hanging by the door, his hats on the row of pegs, his shoes and boots lined up beneath, the orderliness of his living room and, daring to put her head round the door of his bedroom, the made bed and clothes on hangers in the wardrobe. Colouring slightly, she steps back and hurries to set the kettle on the range. She selects

269

two eggs, putting them in a saucepan of water, which she places next to the kettle. When Andrew comes through the door, all is ready.

He goes over to her and kisses her hungrily. 'I'm looking forward to today, aren't you, sweetheart? It'll be a chance to show that we have survived and have not let the weather get the better of us.' Netta passes him a mug of tea and they begin on the boiled eggs. 'What a marvellous day for the show. I've been to a few in my time that were very wet. It's no' much fun, a wet show. Animals and people finish up looking and feeling miserable!'

'I'm a wee bit nervous, not having done this before.'

'No need to be nervous. I'll look after you . . . unless you object, of course!'

They hurry through their breakfast and Andrew goes to get the sheep in the trailer while Netta clears away the breakfast things. And then they are off. Their spirits rise as Princess trots along the road. Andrew has decided that the horse needs some vigorous exercise, having necessarily been stabled for the earlier inclement months of the year.

'You know that they have a section for Clydesdales too at the show. Maybe next year we'll put Princess in for that. There's hardly been time to think about it this year.' He gives a contented sigh and turns to look at Netta. 'It's so good to have a day off to enjoy ourselves. We'll have to do it more often.'

Netta nods. 'I know Mutti's looking forward to it as well. It was a good idea of you and Finlay to invite them. And Elizabeth will hopefully recognise some old friends among the crowd and enjoy it too.'

'I'm hoping it will cheer Finlay up as well. He's been so down in the mouth recently. This disastrous year has got to him more than we realise. Let's hope for some successes today to make him feel better!'

* * *

Ellen is having difficulty keeping an eye on Elizabeth. They have watched the judging of the sheep. One of Kenneth's Blackface tups has won a third prize and farmers are busily congratulating Finlay on the result. When Ellen looks round, Elizabeth is wandering away in the direction of the horses who are being put through their paces up and down the field. Ellen watches from a distance as a woman approaches Elizabeth. She is middle-aged and smartly dressed. She says a few words to the farmer's wife and the two of them embrace before continuing to talk. Ellen gives them space to hold their conversation before walking slowly across the grass towards them. Elizabeth turns to her and smiles but it is left to the other woman to introduce herself.

'I'm Catherine, an old friend of Elizabeth's. It's good to see her out and about again after Kenneth's death. And you must be Ellen. She's been saying how you are looking after her now. Have you been at the farm long?'

'I was brought up on the farm but went away. I've been back now about eighteen months.'

'You're never Duncan Simpson's daughter?'

'Yes, that's me.'

271

'Well, I'm very pleased to meet you. My mother and Duncan knew each other when they were young. I was in your village but moved away when I married. My husband farms near here now. I'm about to have a bite to eat. Would you care to join me?'

The three women stroll over to the refreshment tent. Here the Women's Rural is in command. Plates of sandwiches and cakes cover the tables at one end and cups of tea are being rapidly handed out to meet the increasing demand. Judging has finished and everyone's thoughts have turned to food. Elizabeth and Ellen choose from the mouth-watering assortment on the tables in front of them. Ellen pays and they take it to one of the few remaining empty tables. Catherine makes her way towards them, nodding this way and that to acquaintances as she does so.

'I've no idea where my husband is,' she says. 'Probably in the bar area chatting with his pals. He may join us later. Who brought you today?'

'We came with the head shepherd in his car. My daughter and our other shepherd are here too but I'm not sure where at the moment.'

'Correct me if I'm wrong but did you not lose your husband in that bad winter after the war? The Great War, that is.'

'Yes, that's correct.'

'So you had no more children.'

'He died before we could have any more,' Ellen says evasively.

'I'm sorry, my dear, I've no right to be questioning you like this. It's just that so much has happened in the past few years that it's difficult to

272

keep tabs on it all. What's the matter, Elizabeth? Where are you going?' Elizabeth is getting up out of her chair and picking up her cup.'

'Shall I get you another cup of tea?' Ellen asks.

'I'm going to find Kenneth.'

'No, Elizabeth. Kenneth died. Remember?'

'No, he's in the tent, getting a drink. I'm going to find him.'

'I'll come with you then. I'm sorry, Catherine. She gets a bit confused.' Ellen gathers up Elizabeth's bag and coat and makes to leave.

'I'll come as well and give you a hand.' They all three leave the refreshment tent. Outside, Elizabeth calms down again, attracted to the horses, who are now at rest with their owners and being admired by a crowd of onlookers.

'Where's Princess?' Elizabeth says. 'I can't see her anywhere.'

'She's no' in the show. She pulled the trailer with the sheep, remember? Andrew said he wanted to stretch her legs because she had been stabled so much during the snowy weather.'

'I want Catherine to come and see her. Where is she?'

'She'll be tied up in the field at the back, and Catherine has likely other things that she needs to do.'

'Not at all. Come along, Elizabeth. Show me Princess. I'll look after Elizabeth for a wee while, Ellen. You go off and look at some of the stalls. We'll be over at the field when you need us.' Catherine takes Elizabeth's arm and steers her in the direction of the cart horses.

Released temporarily from the care of her

273

charge, Ellen makes her way to the industrial tent. Within are all sorts of arts and crafts — paintings on paper and canvas, knitted and crocheted baby jackets, embroidered tablecloths and runners, flower arrangements, vegetables of all shapes and sizes from big to enormous, cakes, shortbread, clootie dumpling, potato scones and a variety of carved sticks to be used by shepherds.

Ellen ambles from stall to stall, marvelling that farm workers are able to find enough hours in the day to do all this handiwork. Maybe she ought to consider trying her hand at some of these crafts. In Germany the handicrafts done by women and taught to schoolchildren were intricate and beautiful.

She had made some herself, all of course now buried under the heap of rubble that was their house. No, on second thoughts she would rather not. Too many memories would be sure to surface.

★ ★ ★

Judging over, Andrew and Netta are chatting to a group of young shepherds who, like them, have been exhibiting. The talk is of the trials of the previous winter, the low price that their ill-conditioned stock are likely to fetch and the high price that meat will cost in the shops. It's also about the ceilidh to be held in the village hall that evening.

'You must come along, the two of yous,' James McCann says. 'They're always good fun.'

'What's a ceilidh?' Netta asks.

'You've never heard of a ceilidh? Where have

274

you been all your life?'

'Netta only arrived in these parts eighteen months ago,' Andrew intervenes. Netta gives him a severe look but he continues before she has a chance to speak. 'We had wild ceilidhs over west when I was a shepherd there,' he goes on. 'What do you think, Netta? Shall we go to it? We'll have to go home first and do the milking, though we might ask Finlay if he would mind seeing to them this evening. It'll no' take him long and he'll probably be heading home soon with your mother and Elizabeth.'

'I don't think he'll be much help to anyone this evening,' a voice says behind them. Andrew and Netta turn round simultaneously to see who the speaker is and come face to face with the argumentative farmer with whom they had rubbed abrasive shoulders in the market some months ago.

'Andrew, Netta, I don't think you've met my father.'

'In actual fact we have,' Netta smiles. 'Good afternoon, Mr McCann. Nice to see you again.' She holds out a hand and, with only a moment's hesitation, the farmer takes it and gives it a single firm shake. 'As you see,'

Netta continues, 'here I am learning how to be a shepherd.'

Roddie McCann, lost for words, glances at his son who, along with his friends, is grinning. It appears they all know the farmer's antagonism to female involvement in farming. It is also clear that the farmer realises the wisdom of keeping his mouth shut on the topic.

'So what's keeping Finlay?' James asks his father. 'He's no' met with another accident has he? Becoming too disaster prone for his own good?'

'No, nothing like that. He's had one too many to drink, that's what. I don't think he'll be driving anywhere for a bit.'

★ ★ ★

Finlay is slumped on the grass inside the beer tent, propped against a tent pole. The farmers are keeping an eye on him but he has obviously been the focus of a few jokes and some mild banter. Andrew, however, is not laughing. He is attempting to control the irritation that has welled up through his body. This golden opportunity he has been handed to have an enjoyable evening with Netta after their weeks of hardship and disappointment has just as quickly been snatched away.

'Finlay, pal, what are you doing down there? You're meant to be taking the ladies home, not getting drunk. You've left me with a problem now. I can't drive the car *and* get Princess and the trailer back — and the cows need to be milked soon.' Finlay grins inanely but says nothing.

'Can I help?' It's James. He has followed Andrew into the tent to see for himself what has been happening. 'Why don't you let me bring the horse and trailer? I like horses. I'm the one who looks after ours at home, so I'm well used to them.' He looks round and catches Netta's eye. 'If you think I might make off with them, pal, Netta can come with me. Although, on second thoughts, I might

276

make off with her as well!'

Andrew forces a smile. 'Are you sure you don't mind helping out?'

'Well, look at it this way. If I help you get home, you and Netta will be able to come back this evening for the ceilidh and we get the pleasure of your company,' he concludes, winking at Netta.

And so it is arranged. Finlay is piled unceremoniously into the front passenger seat of the car, Ellen helps Elizabeth into the back and climbs in after her, and Andrew drives them out of the showground and towards home. Netta helps James to harness Princess and attach the wagon. She jumps up into the seat next to him and he too sets off along the road, directed by Netta. Andrew, now that the dilemma over travel arrangements has been resolved, is worrying about Finlay, wondering just what it is that has brought him to this state. James, meanwhile, is questioning Netta.

'I had no idea you knew my father. It's well kent that he's no' keen on women in farming. He's happy as long as they stay in the kitchen and get him his meals on time but any more than that . . . ' He shakes his head and smiles.

'It wasn't really that,' Netta replies. 'He made some comment about the Germans on Kenneth's farm in the Great War, how they were polluting the land. In fact, they were brought in as POWs to help build the reservoir. They didn't have an easy time of it at all. And then . . . ' She pauses before deciding to continue. 'And then I went to a farmer's meeting with Kenneth and your father implied that there was rather more contact between the Germans and those looking after them than there should have been.'

'Aye, I heard about that set-to but I hadn't realised that the person my father was having a go at was you. If it's any consolation, my father got a row from my mother when she got to hear about it. He can be a bit of a bully but she's more than a match for him!'

'So you're still living on the farm with your parents?'

'Aye. I've not found anyone I'd like to marry yet.' He glances at her with a twinkle in his eye. 'But I wouldn't be averse to a dance with you later if you're free.'

★ ★ ★

Ellen entertains James to tea and cakes in the farmhouse, while Andrew and Netta between them help Finlay into his cottage and put him to bed.

'I probably shouldn't do this,' Andrew says, diverting to the kitchen and peering into the pantry. 'Mm, I just felt I had to check. There are signs that he's been drinking a bit at home as well: a couple of half-full bottles of whisky and two unopened. It might mean nothing but I've never seen friends visiting, and no-one needs more than one bottle of whisky at a time.'

Andrew suggests that he milks the cows and leaves Netta to give the pet lambs their milk and check on the sheep that are still penned in the barn because of previous concerns about them.

'I can't go to a dance in my working clothes,' she says when she has finished. 'I will need to go home and change.' She indicates her soiled clothing.

'Right, we'll pick up James and drive down to your cottage. I can show him the reservoir while you pop indoors and do what you have to do.' He bends and kisses her. 'As I've said before, you look beautiful as you are but I suppose everyone will be in their glad rags tonight, so I had better let you do the same. Although I confess to being a little concerned about the lingering looks that James keeps giving you!'

★ ★ ★

Netta is exhausted. She has galloped and twirled, stamped and spun until she has no energy left.

'It is,' she claims, 'more tiring than clipping a field of sheep.' But she had not realised that dancing could be such fun. She has renewed acquaintances, made new friends and danced with half the men in the room. And now she is snuggled in the front seat of the car while Andrew drives slowly back to the valley. It is late but even now it is not quite dark. A scattering of stars decorate the night sky as they drive into the valley. In the west a quarter moon drops behind the hills.

They have been chatting about the evening but, as they near Netta's cottage, their conversation tails off. The car stops by the side of the track, the engine dies and there is silence, apart from the comforting murmur of the river, playing over the stones. Andrew gets out of the car, walks round and opens the door for Netta.

'I am to be escorted, am I? Are you afraid I

279

might not be able to find my way home?'

'Not at all. But I thought that there would be more chance of an invitation to come in if I accompany you.'

At the cottage he opens the door and stands back for her to enter. She takes his hand as she passes and he steps into the room and closes the door quietly but firmly behind them.

29
Visitors

July 1947

Ellen wakes up with a start. She thinks she has
heard a knocking on the door of the farmhouse. It
is dark. She fumbles with the matches, lights the
stub of candle on her bedside table and picks up
the alarm clock. Its hands show ten to twelve. She
knows it must have been a dream. She replaces
the clock, blows out the candle and turns over in
bed, pulling the sheet up around her neck. She
is on the cusp of sleep when she hears whispered
voices. Her eyes snap open. She lies, breath held,
and listens. There comes the whispering again.
She is not imagining things.

She swings her legs to the floor and wraps her
dressing gown round her.

The door to Elizabeth's room is ajar. It must be
Elizabeth who has been walking in her sleep. She
has taken to doing this on occasion. But no, she
can hear gentle breathing coming from the big
double bed that the farmer's wife still occupies
although the farmer is no longer there. Ellen's
heart skips a beat. If it is not Elizabeth, then who
is it at this time of the night? Maybe Finlay is
unwell or Andrew or even her daughter, come all
the way up the valley to seek her assistance. Lighting the candle again, she hurries to the front door

and opens it a fraction, peering round.

Two young women stand outside. By the meagre glow of the candle only their faces can be seen with any clarity, the rest of them being in shadow. One of them has a serious face surrounded by dark curls. The other, a fair-haired young woman, gives a wide smile.

'Happen this isn't a good time of night to disturb you but when Andrew didn't meet us at the station, we thought we'd best make our own way here.' She speaks with an accent once familiar but long forgotten, a form of words that raises goose bumps on Ellen's skin. Who are these women, not much more than girls? She stares at them, her brain refusing to engage.

Who was Andrew meant to be meeting at the station? He has said nothing to her.

'Maybe he didn't get the message.' It is the other girl speaking now, with the same accent, just slightly less pronounced. 'We're from the Quaker School in Yorkshire. We've come to spend six weeks on the farm. Mr Sadler arranged it with Andrew. Is he here?'

Ellen's face shows dawning realisation and the girls relax. 'Of course! Now I know who you are. Er, no, Andrew stays in the cottage over there along the track but he was planning for you to stay here with me. But I had no idea the date was decided. It's unlike Andrew to forget something like this. He's always so organised. Do come in.' She opens the door wide, stepping back so the girls can enter. 'Just a minute — I'll light the lamp and we can see each other better.' She carries the candle to the kitchen, strikes a match to the oil lamp and the light flares to illuminate the two girls. For that is what they look like, scarcely out of childhood, standing in the middle of the room, tired and dishevelled, clinging on to their suitcases.

'I'm Dorothy,' says the fair-haired one, 'and this is Freda.'

'I'm so sorry about this mix-up,' Ellen says. 'You must be exhausted. Take off your coats. I'll put the kettle on. Are you hungry? You must be hungry, coming all this way. Sit yourselves down. I'll find you something to eat. Young ones like you are always hungry.' She goes off to the kitchen, aware that she is talking too much, trying to get her brain to engage as she wonders whether the bedroom is ready and if there is anything else she needs to do at this time of night.

But no, she decides, the rest will wait until morning. For now she will feed them and show them their bedroom. She keeps the beds freshly made in case of visitors. Nothing else needs to be done. First thing in the morning she will go over to Andrew's, tell him that she has them in the farmhouse and get him to contact the school to let them know of the girls' safe arrival. He will no doubt be upset at his forgetfulness.

She lies awake until five-thirty then gets out of bed and pulls on her clothes. Her distress at their appearance on the doorstep has given way to a growing excitement. She goes over in her mind their unexpected arrival. They seemed not the least bit perturbed by their ordeal, considered it an exciting adventure to be retold and laughed over. It was the first time, they had said, that they had been allowed to go away on their own and they had thoroughly enjoyed their journey. The girls put her in mind of her own two lost daughters who were a similar age when they were taken away from her. Now these two have come and for the next few weeks she will have the pleasure of looking after them.

She opens the door of the farmhouse quietly and closes it behind her without a sound. She can hear Andrew in the barn. He is talking to someone. As she nears, she sees to her surprise that it is Netta. She must have risen early to be already at work. Netta looks up in surprise at her mother's approach.

'Mutti! What are you doing here so early?'

'I was wondering the same about you.' There is a pause. 'Anyway, I have news for you, Andrew. Your visitors have arrived — in the middle of the night, in fact.'

Andrew, who is crouched down examining the underside of a cow, straightens up, frowning. 'I wasnae expecting any visitors. Who do you mean?'

'The two girls from Yorkshire, Freda and Dorothy. They said it was all arranged, that the school had sent a letter, telling you of their time of arrival.'

'I havenae received a letter.' Andrew shakes his head slowly. 'I've had nothing in the post. Unless something's been delivered to Finlay and he's no' passed it on,' he says slowly. He glances at Netta. 'He hasnae been attending to things the same as he used to do.' He gives a quick shake of his head, looks at Ellen. 'So what have you done with them? I should go and welcome them.'

'I've a feeling they'll no' be up and around till

much later in the day. They were no' in their beds until one o'clock, by the time I'd fed them and introduced them to where everything was.'

'Oh dear, I'm going to be in for a spot of bother from Jack over this.' Andrew grimaces.

'I don't think so. The girls had quite an adventure, the way they tell it, getting the last train from Glasgow, finding their way through the valley. They've no intention of telling Jack or their parents for that matter.'

'Still, it shouldnae have happened. I must have a word with Finlay — see if he's been keeping the post back.'

'Go easy on him,' Netta says. 'He's still feeling sore about that episode at the show. Why not let me have a word with him?'

'Aye. Why not? He's more likely to tell you if there's anything wrong than he is me.'

'Perhaps. I think he's lonely. That's a lot of what's wrong — and my guess is he's still upset about the loss of half the flock that he's been helping to bring on over the years.'

'Maybe having some young pupils to show the ropes will give him a new interest.' Andrew nods towards the shearing shed. 'We'd better get on with the day's work while the sun shines. We've a hundred ladies penned up in there to clip. The girls can join us when they've had their night's sleep. I remember Freda telling me that she'd had a rather unsuccessful first go at clipping. That was a while ago. Maybe she's an expert now. Let's hope so, then we'll all have less to do!'

★ ★ ★

It's a merry gathering that afternoon. The two girls are not out of their beds until late morning and Ellen brings them down to the shearing shed where clipping is in full swing. Andrew looks up with a grin as he finishes an elderly ewe with a resigned look on her face, one who has done it all before and knows that there's no point in struggling. He straightens up and the ewe scrambles to her feet and makes off across the barn to the open field.

'Freda! Dorothy! It's so good to see you. I'm sorry about the mix-up last night. Jack's letter must have gone astray and I didnae realise you were on your way to us or I would have been at the station to meet you. So your walk through the valley will have acclimatised you to what life is like in this neck of the woods! I think you know most people. Netta you met last November.' Netta looks up from the ewe she is clipping and smiles at the girls. 'Ellen you met last night — you must have given her quite a shock! And this is Finlay, the head shepherd.' Finlay nods in their direction.

'I'm about to get dinner ready,' says Ellen. 'What I would suggest is that you all come and eat and then the girls can get acquainted with the sheep this afternoon.'

'A good idea. We've five left to do and then we'll be with you.'

Freda and Dorothy stand to one side and watch as the two men and Netta finish the morning's work.

'You told me last year that you weren't good at shearing, Netta. You look *very* good to me,' Freda says. 'I've been too busy with exams to be involved

286

much in the farm. But I'm going to make up for it now.'

'You can start by rolling the wool this afternoon,' Andrew suggests. 'Unfortunately the fleeces aren't good as a result of the poor winter. A lot of the sheep have been losing their wool over the last couple of months and we can't do much except tidy them up. Yet another loss to the farm, I'm afraid. But next year will hopefully be a lot better.' He glances at Finlay but the shepherd has his head down and doesn't return the look.

Ellen is reminded of the sheep shearing of her younger days: the long hours of sunshine, the camaraderie of the farmer and shepherds and the shared meals breaking up the long hours of work. Those were the days when all her life lay before her. Recalling them now brings a twinge of that happiness overlain with all the sadness that came later.

That afternoon the girls enjoy rolling wool, encouraging sheep down the runs to the floor where they are to be clipped and then being supervised as they try their hand at clipping. Freda is instructed by Andrew and Finlay oversees Dorothy. The head shepherd sums up Dorothy's effort by claiming that 'it can only get better'.

★ ★ ★

Netta knocks on the door of Finlay's cottage and is invited to come in. As she enters, she can't help noticing that the room is untidy. Dirty cups are dotted around, clothes lie in heaps on the chairs and the floor looks as if it hasn't been swept in weeks. A pile of papers sits precariously to one side of the easy chair. Finlay is sitting in his usual place by the fire, although the grate is empty. He has a bottle of whisky on the floor beside him and a glass in his hand.

'Take a seat, hen. I don't suppose I can interest you in a wee dram?'

'No thanks, Finlay.'

'What can I do for you, hen?'

'Er, it's a bit awkward really. You see, Andrew should have received a letter about the girls' visit but nothing came. If they had been less sensible girls, who knows what could have happened to them? We wondered whether maybe the letter had been delivered with some of yours and been mislaid. It wouldn't matter so much, only it's an official letter from the school, telling us the time of the girls' arrival. If this arrangement doesn't work well, they mightn't be so keen for us to have more pupils.'

Finlay bristles at the implied criticism. 'Are you saying it's my fault, hen? I'm no' the one who made the arrangements. Why not ask Andrew?' He glares at her before taking a gulp of whisky.

'No, I'm not saying it's your fault. It's just that Andrew's not had a letter. He wonders if a letter has maybe got muddled with some of yours.'

'My letters! Who's going to write me letters?'

'Well, farming magazines then. You get them delivered, don't you?'

'Aye, lass, I do,' Finlay says in a more conciliatory tone. He scratches his head, looking vacantly about the room.

'Shall I help you to look?'

288

'Aye, you'd better.' He sighs. 'I have been letting things slide a bit lately. The room is no' so tidy as it used to be.'

The letter, dated a month earlier, is sitting on the bookcase next to a pile of farming magazines. Finlay stares at it in disbelief. 'Aye, I ken now. It came through my letterbox by mistake. I was going to give the postie a row and I put it there until next time he called. It must have slipped my mind with everything else there was to do.'

* * *

Andrew is enjoying the luxury of a hot bath to ease his back after a long day's clipping, when a loud hammering on the door shocks him out of his reverie and he sits up so abruptly that water cascades over the end of the bathtub onto the floor. Who can it be at this time in the evening? He smiles at the possibility that it might be Netta come to keep him company. More likely it is Ellen with some question about the girls that she needs answered, he thinks. He grabs the towel, wraps it round his waist and paddles to the door. When he opens it, Finlay is standing there.

'I've come to apologise,' he says without preamble, stepping unsteadily into the hallway.

'Sit yoursel' down here.' Andrew indicates a chair. 'Give me a minute. I'll put some clothes on.'

'That letter,' Finlay begins when Andrew returns a minute later having hastily pulled on his work trousers. 'It was in the house all along. I remember it coming and I put it to one side to

289

give to you later and it must have gone clean out of my mind.'

'It's understandable. We've all been gey busy.'

'Aye.' Finlay pauses. 'But it's not just that.' With an audible intake of breath he continues, 'I've not been myself recently. I've been . . . well, I've been getting a bit too fond of the whisky. Drowning my sorrows, you could say.'

'It's been a bad year. Plenty of sorrows to drown.'

'Aye. You're not wrong there. The loss of all those sheep in the early months and then the boss dying. I was gey fond of the old man. But since Netta came round, I've been thinking about that letter and what could have happened to those two young lassies and, well, it's brought me up short. I'm meant to be the head shepherd here and I'm behaving like a . . . like a . . . ' Finlay puts his head in his hands and a sob escapes from between his lips.

The silence gathers round them. Andrew sits staring at the ground, his hands clasped in front of him. He is deep in thought. Eventually he speaks.

'It seems we've been given the opportunity to help young people like these two lasses, show them about farming and all that's involved. Aye, they learn it at school and at college but there's nothing like getting their hands dirty by working on the land. If all goes well over the next few weeks, I think you and I, with Ellen and Netta's help, could work with that training scheme we talked about at New Year — perhaps even talk to one of the agricultural colleges to see if they're interested in sending their students out to spend some time on the farm. After all, pal, we're not going to

290

get a bad year like this one every time. Next year the weather could be marvellous and the flock go from strength to strength. What do you think?'

Finlay looks up and gives a half-smile. 'The year that we have marvellous weather I've yet to see! But you're right, of course. I've just let all that's happened this year get on top of me. I think your idea is a really good one. I'm grateful that you consider me fit to take part after the way I've been behaving.'

'OK, let's work on it together, using Dorothy and Freda as guinea pigs. They know quite a bit already. Dorothy comes from a farming family and Freda's been helping on the school farm ever since she's been there, I think. The only snag, of course, is that we don't know what will happen to the farm eventually, now that Kenneth is no longer with us. But I believe it's safe as long as Elizabeth stays well.'

'And can I ask you to check up on me from time to time — make sure I'm no' drinking too much? In fact . . . ' Finlay gets up and goes to open the front door, picking up some bottles from the step and holding them out to Andrew. 'Look after these for me, will you, pal, and don't let me have them, even if I get angry with you! And now I better get to my bed and let you get to yours. Another heavy day of clipping ahead of us and I think the weather is set fair. Up with the larks tomorrow, and no mistake.' He goes out, slamming the door behind him and leaving Andrew lost for words and with an unopened bottle of whisky in each hand.

30
Proposals

August 1947

'We have the two of you here for six weeks. As you're the first, we would like to hear from you what you most want to do and see. You both come with experience gained from the small farm at your school. And you, Dorothy, come from a farming family and will know things I have no experience of. Obviously the time of year that pupils visit us will determine what they do and see. If it's at this time of the year, the students will learn about clipping and what we do with the wool. And they will see how we choose which lambs go to market and have a chance to come with us to the auctions. If they come earlier in the year, at lambing time, we will be very busy, but perhaps too busy to spend much time teaching. And the opportunity to do other things will not be there — going to market, for example.'

Andrew breaks off to take a gulp of hot tea and helps himself to a piece of shortbread. Freda and Dorothy are sitting with the two shepherds and Netta in the mottled shade of two silver birches. The morning is hot and this is their first break since starting clipping at first light. Both Andrew and Finlay have stripped off their shirts and Netta has a short-sleeved cotton blouse over linen trousers. Finlay takes out a large and none-too-clean handkerchief and mops his brow.

'And there was me telling Andrew that we never get good weather.' He laughs. 'I'm almost wishing for a few clouds!' He looks up into the blue, stretching unbroken from one side of the valley to the other.

'It's a good job we didn't try to visit earlier this year,' Dorothy says. 'We would never have made it in the bad weather. We'd still be stuck somewhere on the line between Middlesbrough and here.'

'Yes, the weather could be a consideration, if it's early in the year. That's a good thought, Dorothy.'

'One idea that I have, Andrew,' says Freda, 'would be to visit other farms while we are here — see dairy herds, for example, and see how they work, or sheep farms that have different breeds that we don't have down in Yorkshire. Of course the farmers would need to be in agreement.'

'I can't see that being a problem. Most farmers would welcome the chance to show off their stock.'

Netta laughs. 'Maybe not if they know it's women who are planning on taking up farming!'

Freda looks at Netta with a frown. 'Do they not like the idea of women working on the land? At school the farm was as popular with the lasses as with the lads.'

'Oh, it's only one farmer that we know of who's not so keen. But I think he's coming round, thanks to his family. And they have a flock of Border Leicester sheep, which is a breed you may not have seen. We get on well with James, his son, so I could have a word with him and get you a visit.'

293

Netta grins at Andrew but he declines to return her smile.

'And Billy Black has a flock of Cheviots in the farm over yonder, and there are several dairy herds between here and Lanark. Beef cattle too,' adds Finlay. 'I've rubbed shoulders with a good number of the farmers here in the last thirty years.'

'Good. We'll make some arrangements. Meanwhile there's a hundred and fifty sheep over there still to get through before dinner. And after dinner it will be your turn, girls, so you need to eat well, to give you the energy to get through the afternoon. And when all the sheep are clipped, there will be lambs to get ready for market, dozens of them, no' all in the best of shape but that's the weather for you and I guess everyone else's will be similar to ours. We have to make the most of what we have.'

★ ★ ★

James responds favourably to the suggestion that the girls visit the farm.

'I'll have to check with the old man, of course, and you know what he's like about women and farming. But if I do it at breakfast, when Mother's around, he'll no' have so much to say! Bring them over one day next week,' he says to Andrew, 'and make sure that Netta comes as well, just to get the old man really churned up!'

Andrew is not sure that the reason for wanting Netta's presence at the meeting is to upset James's father. He thinks it more likely that it is James himself who wants to see her again, that he is harbouring designs on her and has been ever since the day of the ceilidh. Andrew struggles to suppress a twinge of jealousy. But it is not in his nature to interfere in affairs of the heart, even if it is his own that will suffer. If Netta decides that James is more desirable than himself, then so be it. Maybe this is how it is meant to be.

★　★　★

They set off to the McCanns' farm in the horse and cart at the beginning of the following week. Dorothy has taken a liking to the Clydesdale, having looked after the horse on her family farm, and she is allowed to take the reins and guide Princess out of the valley and onto the road. Truth to tell, the horse knows the way so well that she needs little guidance. Once on the road Andrew takes over and, with Netta at his side and the girls on seats at the back, they make their way to Roddie's farm. 'Are you sure you're all right with this?' Andrew questions Netta. 'I know how much he upset you at our first meeting.'

'That was a long time ago. Anyway, I think 'round one' went to me, and 'round two' as well. And his son's not a bit like him. We get on just fine.'

Andrew touches the horse's flanks with the whip to encourage her to a trot and proceeds in silence, his heart weighing heavy in his chest.

Catherine McCann has pushed the boat out to welcome the students. She has prepared a lavish tea for them for when they have finished their tour of the Border Leicesters. Andrew and Roddie

McCann come on ahead of the girls who, with Netta and James, have stayed behind to look at the ram lambs that will soon go to market.

'It's very good of you to allow the students to see your flock, Mr McCann. I want them to get as much knowledge as possible of the different sheep we have up here. I know we don't see eye to eye about women's involvement on the farm.'

'Aye, well.' Roddie glances at his wife, who is busily pouring tea and seemingly unaware of their conversation. 'I suppose we can always be made to change our way of thinking.'

Catherine hands Andrew a cup of tea and he steps back diplomatically and begins to peruse the photographs on the mantelpiece. One in particular catches his eye. It is a picture of a young man in the uniform of a First World War infantryman. He recognises the deep-set piercing eyes of the farmer standing at his side.

'Did you no' have exemption from the army, Roddie? I was given to understand that farmers' sons were exempt.'

'Elder sons were exempt but no' younger ones. That's no' me, that's my brother. We've a strong likeness, have we no'?'

'You have indeed. Is he a farmer?'

'He died in the war.'

'I'm sorry. I didnae realise.'

Roddie takes a deep breath and continues slowly. 'He was my wee brother. He would have escaped the fighting but then, in the April of the last year of the war, they announced that eighteen-year-olds had to enlist. And he was just eighteen. Even so, he made it to November. There were talks of peace. I thought he was safe. And then, in the first week of November he was shot in the back. They said he lasted a couple of days. He never made it home, my wee brother — he's buried out there. The last time I ever saw him was when he left for the war.' Roddie's teacup is trembling in its saucer and he puts it down on the table with a clatter.

The silence that follows Roddie's revelation is broken by the entrance of the girls with Netta and James.

'Andrew, can we come to market with you and see the lamb sales?' Freda says eagerly. 'We've been guessing how much they will fetch and I want to see if mine gets the highest price.'

'I'm no' so sure you'll still be here. Do you know when the sales are, Roddie?'

'What's that? The sheep sales? Aye. The Border Leicesters ram lamb sale is 17th September.'

'Just too late, I'm afraid. You'll be back home by then. But you'll catch the Blackface sale. That's the week before. Sorry, girls, but your parents will start to complain if we keep you away for too long!'

Freda makes a sad face. 'Then I'll just have to get my mum and dad to come up here to stay,' she says, looking round, 'and then I can go to watch it with them.'

★ ★ ★

The girls are delivered back to Ellen, Princess returned to her field and the cows milked. Andrew and Netta are walking through the valley to her cottage. Dusk is gathering in the hollows of the hills, the waterbirds' evening chorus is over and the air disturbed only by the occasional sharp bleat of a lamb searching for its mother. The call of a tawny owl flutes from the forest, behind which a full moon is rising, silent and majestic.

'It's good to stretch our legs after all that standing around,' Netta says to break the silence that has accompanied their progress along the road. 'It's been a successful day, don't you think?'

He turns to her. 'The girls seemed to enjoy it. You too, I think,' he says quietly.

'Yes, I did. I'm glad that Roddie McCann and I can be civil to one another.'

'And his son? Did you enjoy being with him?'

'Andrew! If I didn't know you better, I would think you were jealous.'

'And I thought I knew you well enough not to be jealous. Now I'm no' so sure.'

Netta stops in her tracks. 'Andrew Cameron! How dare you doubt me!

Haven't I told you often enough what I feel for you?' Andrew glances at her, thinking her remark a light-hearted one, but he can see from her face that she is furious. 'I am not so two-faced that I could fall for someone else and not tell you.

If this is what you think of me, perhaps we are not meant for one another.

I'll see myself home.' And Netta takes off along the road at a run.

By the time Andrew catches up with her, her breath is coming in gasping sobs. He spins her round to face him and steadies her with a hand on each shoulder. He lifts a hand and gently brushes the tears from her cheeks. 'I'm sorry, I'm sorry. I shouldn't have said that. I've told you before, I've no' had much experience of relationships. But the way I feel about you, I've never felt about anyone before. I don't want to lose you and I don't know what to do to stop you going.'

'You are silly. You don't need to do anything. I love you the way you are. You're so peaceful and gentle and caring . . . and so naive when it comes to men and women. I don't want you any different. I'm not going anywhere. I love *you*.'

Andrew envelops her in his arms and rests his chin gently on the crown of her head, staring at the moon as it gains the tops of the trees and looks down on them as though bestowing a blessing. He is aware of his heart beating rapidly.

Netta mumbles something into the front of his jacket.

'What was that you said?'

She pulls away from him a little. 'I said, this is where you are meant to ask if I will marry you,' she repeats.

His sudden burst of laughter reverberates from the surrounding hills.

'What a woman you are! One in a million. Netta, will you do me the honour of becoming my wife?'

'Andrew Cameron, of course I will. I thought you'd never ask.' She takes his hand and they run laughing and carefree down the track to Netta's cottage.

* * *

Ellen watches Andrew approaching the farmhouse, looking round as he does so, as if he doesn't want anyone to see him. She is at the door and opens it as he knocks.

'Andrew, is everything all right? You're not usually round at this time of day.'

'Aye, everything's fine.' He grins at her. 'May I come in?'

She stands back and follows him as he walks into the kitchen. He pulls out a chair and sits down. She copies him.

'How's Elizabeth?'

'Same as usual. She's having her afternoon nap.'

'Good.'

Ellen regards him quizzically. 'Was there anything in particular you wanted, Andrew?'

'Ah! Where shall I start? Well, last night I asked Netta to marry me . . . but I'm old-fashioned enough to believe that I should ask permission and, as she has neither father nor stepfather to ask, I'm asking you.'

Ellen's expression switches from delight to sadness before assuming a more measured smile. 'That's wonderful news! I'm so pleased for you both. When are you planning for it to be?'

'Och, we haven't got that far yet. Sometime in late autumn maybe. It will be a quiet wedding — maybe in the Quaker style. No fancy dress, no bridesmaids, no giving away of the bride, so you wouldn't need to worry on that score.'

Ellen smiles. 'I hadn't really thought of Netta being given away.

Knowing how forthright she is, she probably wouldn't agree to that anyway!'

'No, you're probably right.' Andrew pauses. 'Er, I'd rather you didn't let on that I've been to see you. Let her tell you in her own time.'

Ellen jumps up and, stepping over to Andrew, throws her arms around him. 'I really am very happy about this. Netta deserves something good in her life and she has a lot of love in her, just waiting for the right person to give it to. I couldn't be more pleased. And I will pretend ignorance when Netta comes to tell me!'

31

Friends

September 1947

'It's all arranged,' Freda announces, waving a letter in Andrew's direction. 'Instead of me catching the train home, my mother says that they will drive up here and find us somewhere to say in the village. That way we will be able to go to the Border Leicester sale and see how Mr McCann gets on with his sheep. Then Mother says she will drop Dorothy off at their farm in Yorkshire on our way home.'

Andrew looks up from his paperwork at Freda's excited face. 'I didnae realise you had written to your parents, but it will be good to meet them. When are they coming?'

'At the weekend. My father's not so well since his accident so, that way they'll have a day to rest before the sale and after that we'll leave you in peace.'

'Well, if you're staying over the next few days, why don't you call in and see Mr McCann and ask if you can help him on the sale day? I'm just preparing to drive over to Lanark market as it happens. I could drop the two of yous off at Roddie's on the way and pick you up later. If he's not at home, we can arrange for me to take you maybe tomorrow.'

302

Freda goes off to find Dorothy and Andrew closes the accounts book with a snap, glad of the chance to be outside again. Finlay has been cutting corn in the only field suitable for growing it and Netta and the girls have been gathering it into stooks, in the hope that it will dry ready for gathering in a couple of weeks. It is a job with which Dorothy is familiar. On her father's farm, she says, they have acres of fields for growing crops. It takes days for harvesting to be completed. She seems to find the valley's small acreage suitable for crops amusing.

They set off in the early afternoon. Netta, who has been invited to go with them, has decided to stay and help her mother with Elizabeth who is becoming noticeably more confused. It is James who sees them approaching and walks over to the pickup to welcome them.

'What? Can you no' keep away? You obviously know a good farm when you see one! How can I help you?'

'They've come to offer *you* help.'

'Always welcome. Why don't you come in? My father's been having an after-lunch nap but he'll be ready for getting going again.'

'Do you mind if I leave them with you for a short while?' Andrew asks.

'I need to call at the market and I'm no' sure whether they might close earlier today.'

'Nae problem. Where's the lovely Netta today? Is she no' with you?'

'She's stayed behind to help her mother.'

'Ah, what a pity. It would have been nice — '

'Netta and Andrew are going to be married,'

303

Dorothy blurts out.

'Are they now? There goes my chance of happiness! I'm joking, pal. I could see the way the land lay. Well, congratulations to you. She's a woman in a million.' James clasps Andrew's shoulder and they shake hands warmly.

* * *

Freda tiptoes into the living room behind James. Roddie McCann is snoring gently in his armchair and starts when James taps him gently on the knee and calls his name.

'Visitors, Dad. Time to wake up. Here's Freda and Dorothy, come to offer help.'

'Help, you say?' He rubs his eyes, scratches his nose and eases himself upwards from his chair. 'You want to help me, do you?'

'Aye. We've arranged it so we can come and watch your sheep sale. Andrew suggested that we could offer to help you get the lambs ready. We helped with the Blackface sale last week. We were to go home but my mum says we can stop a day or two longer and they're coming up to fetch us.'

'Are they now? Well, I don't see any reason why you shouldn't help. You'll need to come in the day before, ken, and then be here very early on market day. Do you think you can manage that?'

'Of course. We've got quite good at getting up early, haven't we, Dorothy?'

'*You* have. I have to be persuaded.'

'You won't make a farmer then, if you can't get out of your bed.'

'I'm not sure I want to. I live on a farm, so I'm

304

used to a farming life but I'm not sure if it's for me long-term. I came here mostly to keep Freda company. She's the one who's keen.'

Roddie's wife, Catherine, comes in with a tea tray and a plateful of cakes.

The girls' eyes light up.

'Your parents are farmers then, Freda?' Catherine asks.

'No. They live in the middle of Manchester, in the big smoke. My dad was a teacher but he was injured when Manchester was bombed. He's not so well now and . . . well, he's recently had to retire.'

'So how come you're interested in farming?' Catherine pushes the plate of cakes in Freda's direction.

'The boarding school I go to has a small farm. I like helping there. I've learned a lot, and I want to carry on learning.'

'But why did your parents send you away to boarding school? It must have been hard for you being separated from them.'

'Well, my brother went there first. He's a few years older than me and when we came to England, he was being bullied in the local school. That's when my parents decided to move him.'

'You say he came to England. What was he doing abroad? Roddie asks.

'It's no' been a good time to be out of the country.'

'We were in Germany. We're German, you see, both of us. Our parents aren't our real parents. They adopted us.'

There's a pause. Roddie shifts in his chair.

His face has darkened at her words. 'So why did you come to England? Why no' stay in Germany, where you belong?' He glowers at Freda in a way that makes her want to shrink back in her seat. But she continues bravely.

'I don't remember much about it. I was only small. But my parents — my adoptive parents, that is — told me that our parents sent us to England because we would most likely have been killed by our own leaders. We have heard nothing from our parents back in Germany, so we believe now that they must have been killed. They were Jewish, you see.'

Roddie McCann is silent.

'There are good people in Germany and others not so good, just as we have found good people in England willing to help and others who are against us being here. I can see you are one of the good ones. You allow me to come and help on your farm.'

'Aye, well,' he mumbles. 'What can I say?'

'You don't need to say anything. We're just very grateful, aren't we, Dorothy?'

Dorothy, usually the voluble one, merely nods in agreement.

Roddie looks from one to the other. 'Right then. Be here early next Tuesday and we'll sort out the lambs. If you do a good job, I'll allow you in the ring with me the next morning and we'll see how we get on.'

★ ★ ★

306

Peter and Gwen arrive in the village at about four o'clock on a day of heavy rain. They have reserved a room at the coaching inn and straightaway they make their way to it. It is easy to find, a large building that must have seen busy times when horses and traps were the main means of conveyance but now sits quietly and somewhat faded in the centre of the long row of houses that makes up the village.

It has been a long journey and Peter is tired. Having been shown their room, he decides to have an hour's rest, so he is in good form to see Freda again and meet the people on the farm who have looked after her so well.

They have been invited to tea with them later. While he sleeps, Gwen settles on a walk to stretch her legs after the driving, which is her sole responsibility. Although Peter has made a partial recovery from his injury, the unpredictable fits and his compromised eyesight are enough to prevent him from getting behind the wheel of a car.

The rain has blown over at last but angry clouds are racing one another across the sky and sending shadows through a wide valley opposite the inn where they are staying. A small road leads off the main village street in the direction of the valley. She decides to follow it. It passes by means of a narrow bridge over the railway line. To the right of her is a station with, behind it, a row of railway cottages. Ahead, the road winds down to a large river, crosses a river bridge and disappears into the valley. She stands a minute to admire the scene, as it flicks from dark to light in the chasing shadows.

'That's the Clyde you're looking at. It's quite a sight, is it no'?'

Gwen turns to see a small elderly woman, comfortably proportioned and with curly white hair.

'It's a beautiful view.'

'I used to live along the valley when I was younger.' She chuckles. 'I'm sorry, I should introduce myself. I'm Margaret Simpson. Are you staying in the coaching inn? Aye, I thought so,' she says when Gwen nods.

'Our daughter has been helping on the farm in the valley. We've come to see what she's been up to in the last few weeks.'

'So you must be Dorothy's mother, or Freda's. I've met them a few times since their arrival.'

'Freda is mine. She's very keen on farming and by all accounts has enjoyed her time here.'

'And your husband is with you?'

'Yes, he's having a rest before we go down to see them. He's not too well, you see. He was injured during the war.'

'I lost my only son during the war,' Margaret says. 'The Great War, that is. I still miss him, all these years later. Where was your husband serving when he was injured.'

'He was working on the Home Front as an ambulance driver. There was an explosion . . .'

'I lost my husband near the end of the first war, soon after I lost my son. I think it was the shock of it that killed him. And I married again but I lost Duncan nearly five years ago — though we had more happy years together than we ever expected to have.'

'So you live on your own now?'

'Aye, but it's no' so bad. I have plenty to do and Ellen, my stepdaughter, is on the farm and is always popping in to see me. She brings Elizabeth — she was the farmer's wife. Her mind is going now and she takes a bit of looking after but Ellen's good at that. She's always had someone in the house to look after.'

Gwen, slightly confused with the introduction to so many names without being able to attach them to people nods and smiles. 'Well,' she says, 'I'd best be on my way. I was intending to stretch my legs after all that driving.'

'Enjoy yourselves tonight. They're a bonny pair, the two girls, though I would never have guessed that Freda was yours.'

Gwen smiles again and goes on her way.

* * *

Ellen is shocked to see Peter's face. Freda has told her of his injuries but she has no idea of their severity until she sees the scarring for herself and sees the struggle he has to see clearly with his remaining eye.

Freda dances attention on her parents, delighted to be able to show them off to Andrew and Netta and the rest of the family.

'And this is Finlay,' she says, taking him by the arm and encouraging him into the room. He has come in straight from the evening milking, which he had offered to do to give Netta the opportunity of chatting to Freda's parents, and is slightly embarrassed to be thrust into the centre of the room in his working clothes. 'We've been helping

Finlay with the harvesting and, before that, getting the lambs ready for market. Finlay's been here ever since the Great War, haven't you, Finlay? He helped to build the reservoir, didn't you, Finlay?' Finlay is about to reply but Freda continues. 'The reservoir's further up the valley. I don't think we'll have time to visit it but maybe we'll be invited again.' She looks expectantly at Ellen.

'I certainly hope you *will* come again. We'll be lost without you, won't we, Elizabeth?' Elizabeth is absorbed in the study of Peter's face. She has already twice made her way to his side and gently stroked the scarred flesh.

'Elizabeth has not had children of her own,' says Ellen. 'She was very good to me when I was wee and living here on the farm with my father.'

'No doubt you were very good for her as well,' says Peter. 'Freda won't mind me telling you that we adopted her and her brother. Gwen and I were never fortunate enough to have children of our own and when they arrived it was like a gift from God.'

'Your son — Freda tells me he is a musician,' continues Ellen.

'Sam? Yes, that's right. He attended the Royal Manchester College of Music. He has finished now and his ambition is to play the piano as a soloist in concert halls. It's a difficult field to get into but he is very determined. Meantime he has taken on pupils to teach piano. At the moment he is living at home with us but he will no doubt rent a house with his musician friends when they are all earning enough to do that.'

The sound of breaking china brings Ellen out

310

of the reverie induced by Peter's words. About to ask if his son has a favourite composer, instead she stares round vacantly, realises that Elizabeth has disappeared and hurries to the kitchen where Elizabeth has decided to make herself a cup of tea.

'Elizabeth! How many times must I tell you? You must ask me when you want a drink and I will make it for you. In fact, I must get a meal ready. We've invited everyone and so far I've offered them nothing.' And resisting the urge to ask Peter more about his son's music, she turns her hand to setting the table. Netta comes through to help her and she puts her arm around her mother's shoulders and hugs her.

'It is still very painful, isn't it, Mutti?'

Ellen tries to reply but a strangled sob is all that Netta hears.

★ ★ ★

Roddie McCann's lambs sell for a good sum, given the overall dip in prices that the earlier bad weather has brought in its wake. True to his word, he allows Dorothy and Freda into the ring and his son attributes their success in the sales to the presence of the two girls. There are whispered remarks among the tea-drinkers in the café afterwards about the change in attitude of the previously belligerent farmer.

'Pay us a visit when you are up this way again,' Roddie says to the girls when they are ready to go. They have introduced Freda's parents to the farmer and to James and are now returning to the valley for the night before making their way back to the north of England.

'I'm not sure whether we will be here again,' says Dorothy. 'After the holiday it's our exam year at school, so there'll be no time for anything else apart from work for a few months.'

'Unless Andrew and Netta will invite us to their wedding!' Freda says, looking at the pair expectantly.

Andrew puts his arm round Netta and smiles. 'We haven't decided when that will be yet. All these important things keep getting in the way. But we certainly won't forget you and, if your parents' invitation to visit you at Christmas still stands, we may see you then.'

* * *

'It's true what I said. All the important things that have been happening are getting in the way of the thing that is most important — when we are going to get married.'

Andrew and Netta are walking through the valley towards her cottage. Andrew has delivered the two girls safely back to the farmhouse. It is a dark clear night, even the myriad stars overhead unable to pierce the blackness. Netta clasps the collar of her coat tight against her neck as the wind keens down the valley, and Andrew draws her closer.

'Let's make it soon,' Netta says and Andrew looks at her in surprise.

'I thought you weren't in any hurry, sweetheart. What has changed your mind?'

'Oh, I'm getting older. And I want us to have

babies to care for and enjoy. And, yes, seeing Freda's parents so happy with her despite all the problems they have been through, I suppose that has made me hope that we can have a little bit of that too.'

'Our wedding can't come soon enough as far as I am concerned,' Andrew whispers, turning her to face him and tucking a strand of hair behind her ear. He kisses her tenderly and then nods towards the cottage, laughs. 'And it will put an end to this misery of separate beds!'

★ ★ ★

The following week Andrew and Netta make an appointment to see the minister in the village. They disclose a little of their past history to him — Andrew's association with the Quakers in Glasgow and his preference for a quiet simple ceremony, and Netta's traumatic losses of her sisters and stepfather when in Germany and the probability of those losses being highlighted on such an occasion as this. The minister is sympathetic and together they devise a simple yet meaningful ceremony to suit them both. It is planned for the end of October, when the sales will be done, the rams introduced to the sheep and left to do what they are so good at doing, and shepherds everywhere have a chance to draw breath and see to their own needs.

Two days before the wedding, the door into the milking parlour is flung open and Ellen enters in a turmoil of emotions.

'I'm so sorry, Netta. I'm so sorry.' Ellen's hair is

dishevelled and she is sobbing.

'Mutti! Whatever is the matter?'

'It's Elizabeth. She's dead. I've just found her dead in her bed.'

32
Will

October 1947

Ellen's distress is threefold. There is the shock of finding Elizabeth in this way. The old lady, although her mind was failing her, has ailed little physically, although her age must be eighty or more. Ellen has known that the death must come sometime but its suddenness is nevertheless upsetting. What makes her more upset, however, is the inevitability that Netta's wedding, which she and Netta have been anticipating eagerly, will now be spoiled and, in all likelihood, postponed. And the background anxiety looms suddenly large — the uncertainty of what will happen to the farm and to all of them who are living and working on it. It is an uncertainty that has never gone away despite Billy Black's assurances when Kenneth Douglas died. Until now it has lain dormant. Now it resurfaces and, as though a tidal wave is engulfing her, Ellen is struggling to keep afloat.

'Leave the milking to me, lass,' Finlay says quietly to Netta. 'You go with your mother.'

'Please come too,' Netta says, casting a despairing look at Andrew and he takes her hand as they hurry after Ellen who has disappeared back into the farmhouse.

It is as her mother has said. Elizabeth is lying,

as though asleep, in her bed. The coldness of her skin indicates that her death must have occurred some hours before.

'It is the best thing for Elizabeth,' says Netta. 'And for you too, Mutti. She would have become very difficult for you to look after, and I do not think she could have been happy as she was.'

'Yes, but for it to happen now, two days before your wedding.' Ellen puts her head in her hands and weeps. In all the horrific events of the past years Netta has rarely seen her mother give way to her emotions in this way.

'Don't worry about that,' Netta says stoically. 'We will talk to the minister and put it off for a week or two.' She turns from the bed and her face contorts in the effort not to cry. Andrew goes to put an arm around her but she pulls away from him. 'Don't!' she almost shouts. 'Leave me alone!'

Andrew steps back, shocked. 'I'm sorry,' he says quietly and leaves the room without another word.

* * *

When the two women enter the kitchen, they find Finlay. He has put the kettle on the range and is making a pot of tea.

'I thought we could all do with this,' he says.

'Where's Andrew?' Netta asks.

'He's driving to the village to tell the doctor. Then he's going to call on Billy Black.' Finlay gives a huge sigh. 'We were just saying while you were out of the room, we don't know what will happen now — about our jobs, that is. I'm sorry, I know this isn't the time to be saying it, with Elizabeth dead in her bed, but I can't help thinking it.'

'I know.' Ellen has recovered her composure. 'It is what we are all thinking.' She glances at Netta. 'But for now we must concentrate on one thing at a time. Elizabeth is our first concern. She has always looked after us. Now we must do her the honour of looking after her and giving her the burial that she deserves. At least she will be with Kenneth again. She found life gey difficult without him.'

'Aye. You're not wrong there.'

Netta has left the room and when Ellen finds her, she is staring out of the window into the distance, where two cars can be seen making their way through the valley. Behind her on the bed is the dress that Netta was to wear on her wedding day. Ellen puts her arm round her daughter's shoulder and Netta bursts into tears.

'I can't help it, Mutti. It's so unfair. I was so looking forward to my wedding day and now it has been ruined.' She glances out of the window. The pickup is nearing the farm, closely followed by Dr Ferguson's car.

'No, not ruined, my darling. You will have a lovely wedding. Perhaps it will be even better by having to wait an extra week or two.'

Netta pulls a face. 'I've already made Andrew wait longer than he would have liked. What with that and the way I spoke to him this morning, I would be surprised if he didn't change his mind altogether. But you may be right, Mutti. Perhaps it will be even better.' She pauses. 'We will have to contact Jack and Beth and Freda and her parents

317

and tell them the wedding is off. And, of course, we must talk to the minister.'

'Postponed, you mean.'

'Yes, postponed.'

* * *

The fact that Dr Ferguson has not seen Elizabeth for some months and the cause of her death is unknown means that it must be referred to the coroner.

'I don't like to put you through all this so soon after Kenneth's death but I have no alternative,' he says. 'I understand that Billy Black has been in charge of the farm since Kenneth's death and that he will be along directly.

I would leave any arrangements until he comes.' He walks to the door, then turns round. 'I do hope . . . that everything works out as far as the farm is concerned.' He nods, gives a half-smile and leaves the room. They stand in silence, looking at one another, uncertain what to say.

'I'll go,' says Andrew to Finlay. 'There are jobs that must be done and I'm not needed here.' Without a glance in Netta's direction, he leaves the room. With a heavy heart she watches him hurry down the path and out of sight. Glancing up, she sees Billy Black's pickup on the road.

Ellen opens the door to the farmer.

'Another sad day,' he begins. 'I didn't expect to be here again so soon.'

He follows Ellen into the living room and sits down. When Netta comes into the room, he asks her to sit with her mother and Finlay.

'I'll telephone for the undertaker when I get back to the village,' he begins. 'So you don't need to worry your heads about all that. As soon as the coroner has given his approval, I will go ahead and help you to arrange the funeral.' He pauses and looks at each in turn. 'I guess that what is concerning you most, once this sorry business is concluded, is what is going to happen to the farm and to your positions. As I said to you before, Ellen, you will all be well taken care of. I can't say more at the moment but please don't worry your heads about the future. As soon as is decently possible I will arrange a meeting with the solicitor at which I would like you all to be present. Netta, will you tell Andrew he is to come as well. Oh, by the way, Netta, Andrew has gone back out to the village to contact the minister and your friends who were to be at the wedding. I would like to say on behalf of Isobel and myself how sorry we are that your wedding can't go ahead as planned. Hopefully it will not be delayed too long.'

Netta attempts to reply to his kind words but she is unable to talk and merely shakes her head.

'Thank you, Billy. That's very kind,' says Ellen. 'We'll let you know as soon as we have set a new date.'

'Right. That's me away then. My first job is to contact the undertakers. They'll be here as soon as they are able.'

Ellen sees Billy to the door, then comes back in and sinks into a chair.

'What does he mean,' says Netta, "we'll all be taken care of"?'

'Maybe he's intending to buy the farm himself,'

319

suggests Finlay. 'After all, we are his next-door neighbours.'

Ellen brightens up. 'Yes, maybe that's it. I wouldn't mind if we were working for him. I only hope that someone like Roddie McCann's not buying it.'

'Even he's not as bad as he used to be,' says Netta, attempting a smile.

'And we have Freda and Dorothy to thank for that.'

* * *

Netta is exhausted. Looking after her mother, dealing with the visitors who have arrived on hearing of Elizabeth's death and the disappointment of her thwarted wedding plans have all taken their toll. She says goodnight to her mother, declining the invitation to stay the night at the farmhouse, although she knows that is what her mother would like. She needs the isolation of her own wee cottage near the reservoir, where she can nurse her thwarted hopes. She has a sickening feeling that her wedding will not take place at all, that it is not meant to be.

She walks past the barn, which is in darkness. She has not seen Andrew since early in the morning when she spoke harshly to him in her distress. If he has changed his mind about marrying her, she won't blame him. She is altogether too outspoken, too unkind for her own good. At the bridge she pauses, thinking of their previous loving words exchanged at this very spot. A bright full moon is reflected brokenly, like the jagged pieces of a jigsaw, in the water beneath her. With a feeling of doom weighing like a stone on her chest, she starts off along the road, the moon keeping her company as she walks and refusing to dim its brightness to match her mood.

At the cottage she opens the door but pauses, unwilling to relinquish the beauty all around her for the darkness within, looking back up the moonlit valley at the silver ribbon of water and the sheep dotted thickly up the slopes. Suddenly two arms encircle her waist. She cries out in alarm.

'Shh,' whispers Andrew in her ear. 'Don't spoil the magic.'

'Andrew!' she whispers back, swivelling to face him. 'You gave me such a fright! Where have you been?'

'Waiting here for you, of course. Where else would I be?'

Netta pauses. 'Andrew, I'm sorry. I never meant to speak like that to you.

I was . . . well, I was disappointed. I feel awful about it. I know I shouldn't feel like that.'

'Do you think that I feel good about it? Of course not. I'm as disappointed as you. But we can wait a wee bit longer, difficult though it is. Look, turn round and look by the river.'

Netta turns again and sees a family of rabbits playing at the water's edge, darting here and there, tails bobbing white in the moonlight.

'That will be our family in a few years' time,' he whispers in her ear.

'Not as many as that, I hope.'

He chuckles. 'Who knows?'

'Are you coming back indoors?' she says.

'There's nothing I would like better but I think, if I do, that our wedding night will happen before the ceremony has taken place.' He sighs. 'I have told our wedding guests that I will arrange another date just as soon as the funeral is past.'

'Suppose we lose our jobs on the farm? Billy has assured us we shouldn't worry but I can't help but worry for all of us.'

'There is nothing to worry about.' Andrew whispers in her ear and kisses the soft skin in front of it. 'There are sheep everywhere and where there are sheep, there will always be the need for shepherds. If we can't stay here, Scotland has a million other beautiful places. I shan't mind where I am looking after sheep, so long as you are there looking after them with me.' He turns her to face him, kisses her tenderly, hesitates . . . and sets off along the road at a run.

★ ★ ★

They are all there in Martin McCrae's office — Finlay, Ellen, Andrew and Netta, together with Billy Black, their neighbour and friend. It's been a week since Elizabeth's funeral and the first opportunity there has been for them to meet with her solicitor. There is a tenseness in the air, a concern that their lives may be about to change and not for the better.

'Thank you for coming,' the solicitor starts. 'I thought it best that everyone attends as the future of the farm affects you all. As I explained to Mrs Kessler when Kenneth Douglas passed away, the expressed wish of Mr Douglas was that Mr Black

322

administered the farm and you all continued to run the enterprise with Mrs Kessler looking after Elizabeth Douglas as her health began to decline. This you have all done to good effect over the last few difficult months.

'Mr Douglas also had the foresight to make provision for when his wife was no longer with us.' Martin McCrae looks round at each of them. 'I will read the relevant paragraph from his will:

> *'After the payment of all outstanding bills, I leave the farm, its farmhouse, outbuildings and livestock in trust to Mrs Ellen Kessler, on the understanding that in the event of her death, it passes to her family, namely Netta Fairclough, being the sole surviving member of said family, and to Netta's children, should she have them.'*

Ellen gasps. 'I can't be in charge,' she splutters. 'I have no idea how to run a farm.'

'You have no need to know, Mrs Kessler. Listen. The will continues:

> *'Mrs Kessler's father, Duncan Simpson, was shepherd at the farm all his working days. Through times of great personal and national difficulty he worked unstintingly, at the same time as raising single-handedly his young daughter. They were both a great comfort to me and my wife in our childless state. This arrangement is a token of our appreciation for all their help.*
>
> *'Mr Billy Black, my neighbour and good friend, will continue to apply his considerable knowledge to oversee the running of the farm. I*

wish Finlay Baird —who has, since 1918, been shepherd and latterly head shepherd on the farm — to be his assistant. They will receive a wage commensurate with their respective positions in the organisation.'

Finlay is awestruck. 'Me in a real position of authority!' he marvels. 'I never thought I'd see the day. But I cannae do it without Andrew here and Netta. They are as important as anyone.'

'Indeed,' says Martin McCrae. 'This will be a joint venture, dare I say it, the first of its kind in this area. Mr Black and yourself will take on employees as you think necessary. It ensures the safety of all of you as far as your jobs in the future are concerned.'

In a collective daze they leave the solicitor's office. Outside Billy Black shakes hands with each of them in turn. 'Congratulations. I told you there was no need to worry. What I suggest is that we have regular meetings to discuss ongoing development of the farm as well as sorting out any problems that arise. Are you all happy with that idea?'

'More than happy,' says Ellen. 'My only wish is to continue doing what I have always done. I will leave it to my knowledgeable daughter to help in the running of the business together with the men. She is more than capable of holding her own.'

'You were right, Andrew. There was no need to worry,' Netta says breathlessly, when they are out of earshot of the others. 'What a generous thing for Kenneth to do.'

'It certainly is. He must have thought a lot of

324

your mother and grandfather.' Andrew looks at Netta mischievously. 'So it looks as though it's up to us to carry on the family line.' He pauses and whispers in her ear, 'Maybe those rabbits can teach us a thing or two after all!'

33
Wedding

December 1947

The advantage of Andrew and Netta's wedding being postponed until well into December, at least as far as Dorothy and Freda are concerned, is that they have already started their school holidays and there is no necessity to take time off school at this critical time before the start of their exams. The disadvantage is uncertainty about the weather. In the event it is unseasonably warm and there is no snow or even rain. All their guests are able to be with them.

'I would like to invite your guests to stay here in the farmhouse,' Ellen had said, once the date had been arranged. 'There's so much room here now and only me rattling around in this great place.'

'Well,' Finlay had replied, 'if we take more would-be farmers for six-week courses or even six-month courses, you will need all the space you have, especially if they finish up bringing mothers and fathers and becoming life-long friends as the first students seem to be doing.'

With the help of Netta, Ellen has prepared food for her visitors. She has also decided to host the wedding reception and has enlisted the help, not only of Netta, but also the neighbouring farmers' wives. Cakes and other goodies have been arriving at regular intervals and Ellen has stored these in the big sideboard in the dining room.

Two days before the wedding day Ellen welcomes Peter and Gwen and the two girls. They have come early in order for Peter to rest before celebrations get underway. The next day Jack and Beth arrive. Andrew and Netta are outside the farmhouse chatting to Finlay as they draw up.

'Well,' says Jack, 'I understand now what you mean about this area being beautiful.' He shakes hands with Andrew and kisses Netta before opening the car door for Beth. She steps carefully out onto the uneven ground.

Netta gasps. 'You didn't tell us you were expecting a baby.'

'If you'd put back the date any further, you might have had an uninvited guest at the wedding,' her husband jokes.

It is a quiet ceremony that is planned, in front of a small gathering of friends, but Netta has relented to Dorothy and Freda's insistence that she needs bridesmaids. The two girls, already confident that they could get her to change her mind, have bought identical dresses and appear in them on the morning of the wedding.

'Andrew's going to get quite a shock when I arrive in the church with you.' Netta laughs.

'No, he's not,' Freda says. 'We told him our plan last night and he said he wouldn't be left out and he's asked Jack to be best man.'

'Not the quiet, no-fuss, Quaker-type service he was thinking of in that case.'

'Not really,' the girls giggle.

'Well, sweetheart,' Andrew says, as he drives the pickup through the valley.

'That was a lot more elaborate than I had in mind when I first asked you to marry me.'

'Did you not enjoy it?'

'Of course I did. I would have enjoyed it, even if we'd been married on a boat in the middle of the reservoir with all the residents of the county looking on, or if we'd climbed to the top of the hill over there and said our vows in an orange sunset with a congregation of sheep.'

'You're crazy, Andrew Cameron, do you know?'

'And you're beautiful, Mrs Cameron.'

'Hey, where are we going? The wedding breakfast is at the farm.' Netta has spent so much of the ride looking at her new husband that she has only now noticed that the car is past the turnoff to the farm and a fair distance along the road to the cottage.

'Is that right? Well, I have it on good authority that there is at least three-quarters of an hour's preparation to be done and we are not to arrive until everything is ready. Now we could go and milk the cows to save us a job later on, or we could make a round of the sheep to make sure that they are all behaving themselves. If you'd rather, we could get out the tractor and plough over the field before the snows come and we miss our chance to do it.' He turns the car onto the side road and steers carefully down the hill.

'Or we could make a preliminary inspection of the marital home to make sure everything is satisfactory.'

328

'We might be cold,' Netta says softly. 'I stayed with Mutti on the farm last night, remember, and the fire in the cottage will have gone out.'

'We're no' going to be cold, sweetheart, I promise.'

★ ★ ★

Ellen gets up from her seat and stands quietly. The room stills and people look at her expectantly.

'Ladies and Gentlemen,

'Netta had no-one to 'give her away' and, as I said to Andrew a while ago, she probably wouldn't have wanted it anyway. As many of you will have experienced, she is a young lady who knows her own mind. I should know that — I'm her mother! However, I am claiming the task of giving her away today, so no arguments! And it is a hard task because Netta has been to me the best daughter a mother could ever have and it's hard to give her away to anyone. This is not the occasion for talking of the problems we have had over the years but, without Netta, I don't know how I would have managed. She has been strong for both of us. She has kept me going when I was tempted to give up and cheerful when I would have wept.

'But there is one person I am happy to give her up to and that is Andrew. Over the time we have known him, he has been always helpful, considerate and patient. He has taught Netta much of what she knows about sheep farming and shown no prejudice against her because she is a woman. He tolerates her outbursts and her changes of heart. And I am sure there is one thing that will not change and that is her love for Andrew.

'Thank you, everyone, for your support since Netta and I arrived so unexpectedly two short years ago. Thank you too for coming to share Andrew and Netta's happiness today.'

Applause breaks out all around the room and Ellen sits down, suddenly flustered. Andrew goes up to her and kisses her on the cheek before turning to his guests.

'We never intended this to be a traditional wedding service but this is how it is turning out to be and I for one am very pleased.

'Thank you, Ellen, for your lovely words. I know I can turn to you if your daughter makes life difficult for me! But let me be serious for a minute. I first set eyes on Netta at Hogmanay two years ago. She was forthright then and she has been forthright ever since. That is one of the things I admire about her. Only the second day of meeting her I offered to escort her to the farmhouse and she told me she was quite capable of finding her own way! She is not afraid to say what she thinks. She is also not afraid to apologise when she has got something wrong. There are a lot of people who cannot do that. I knew that she was special that first time we met. I had come all the way from the west coast to meet Kenneth and Finlay but it was Netta I noticed when I arrived.

'I am so glad we have found one another so we can walk the way together. Thank you, Netta, for agreeing to be that person and thank you, Ellen, for parting with your daughter so that she and I can do that walk together.'

By four o'clock night is fast approaching. Andrew and Netta, who have said they want to make their way on foot back to the cottage, have changed into clothes more suitable for the walk. The guests are gathered in the hall to bid them goodbye.

'No honeymoon then, Andrew?' Moira Scott asks, as he shakes her hand.

'Yes, indeed — we are setting off on Monday morning to visit my uncle and cousins over on the west coast. They're farmers and no' able to leave everything and come here, so we thought we'd go there. It's a very beautiful part of Scotland — and it's no' too far away, should the weather take a turn for the worse.'

'Why don't you combine it with a trip south into England,' Gwen suggests. 'Manchester's not too far away either, and there's plenty to do and see there. Of course we're flitting shortly. We've found a small cottage in a village near Skipton in the Yorkshire Dales, away from the dirt and noise of the city, so Peter can breathe some clean air into his lungs. But if you come and see us straight after the visit to your relatives, we will still be in Manchester.'

'And there's always the North York Moors,' says Jack. 'You've already seen how beautiful that is. Though, on second thoughts, we might be a bit busy for a month or two after Christmas!'

'Steady on,' says Finlay. 'We'll no' be getting any work out of them by the time they've done a grand tour of the British Isles.'

There is a sudden loud knock on the door.

'Who can that be?' says Ellen. 'Whoever it is, they're a bit late for the party.' She opens the door and steps back in surprise. It is Roddie McCann and his wife.

'Excuse us butting in,' begins Roddie, 'only a certain young lady told us that she would be coming north for a wedding celebration. We wouldn't have known about the date but for her. We would like you to accept this wee present with thanks for sending Freda and Dorothy to help out, and with our good wishes and . . . ' Here, he glances at his wife. 'Well, apologies for the times we haven't seen eye to eye.' He glances down, embarrassed, as Catherine holds out a neatly wrapped parcel.

'This is very kind of you.' Netta steps forward to take the gift. 'Please do stay to have a drink. We are about to leave but you know most of the people here and my mother will introduce you to the rest, won't you, Mutti?'

'Of course. I would be only too pleased.'

★ ★ ★

'Well, who would have thought that Roddie and Catherine McCann would turn up on the doorstep,' Netta says, when they are away from the farm.

'It's all thanks to you, sweetheart. You are an example to us all of the good effects of speaking the truth!'

Netta laughs. 'It could have had the opposite effect and made us enemies for life.'

'I think Catherine is the power behind the throne there. You saw the way he glanced at his

332

wife before he gave his apology! I shall have to take lessons from them to make sure I keep on the right side of you!'

'Idiot! You don't need any lessons. Seriously though, everyone was very kind, the things they said about us.'

'And the offers of accommodation! What do you think, sweetheart? It would be lovely to venture into England for a few days after we've seen Uncle Stewart. We could call it 'The Grand Tour'. I would have to check with Finlay that he can manage but it's always quiet over Christmas with just the basics to do.'

'It would be fun. But do you think Mutti would be all right? She will be all alone. It will be hard for her.'

'It won't be for long, and she and Finlay already have an invitation to Billy and Isobel's for New Year. She will be in good hands. We'll call in tomorrow and see them. But before that, Mrs Cameron, we have fourteen hours or more to spend in each other's company. What are we possibly going to do?'

34
The Grand Tour

December 1947

Late Sunday morning Andrew and Netta walk back to the farmhouse to have dinner with Finlay and Ellen. Afterwards they enjoy opening the wedding presents that they were given the previous afternoon — a canteen of cutlery from Ellen, a clock from the Blacks, bed linen from the Scotts, a cookery book from Jack and Beth and a vase from Peter and Gwen. Roddie and Catherine have given them a teapot — maybe, Netta thinks, a hint that the pair would welcome an invitation to tea. Finlay gives them gardening equipment 'to make sure that they will always have something to do after the day's work is finished'.

The short winter day soon darkens towards evening and they take their leave. 'I'll be with you at seven in the morning,' says Finlay. 'Make sure you're not late. You've a long journey ahead of you.'

* * *

Since arriving in Scotland Netta has seen no more of it than the county town of Lanark and so every mile of the long and complicated journey to the place of Andrew's birth is exciting. At first the enjoyment of the train journey brings back bittersweet memories of leaving behind the land in which she grew up and which has retained the bodies of her dear family. But as the train steams west following the final stretches of the River Clyde, so much bigger now than at its beginnings near her home, she is entranced by the unfolding vista of the mountains and lochs. Finally they leave the train, hitch a lift with a friendly farmer and board the ferry at the Corran Narrows for the short journey across Loch Linnhe.

'*The North Argyll*,' Andrew says, leaning over the side and pointing to the name along the prow of the boat. 'This ferry brought me across the water two years ago. What a lot has happened in two years! Who would have thought that I would be standing here with my wife by my side.' He bends to kiss her. 'I'm a very lucky man.' Arms around each other, they stand in silence, watching the far shore draw closer.

The wind has got up while they have been travelling and buffets the boat, even during the short journey across the loch. It is the mirror image of Andrew's previous journey, his cousin Hughie leaning on the harbour wall watching the ferry come in and waving as they approach, just as he waved Andrew goodbye two short years ago.

'Andrew! Good to see you again.' He claps Andrew on the back.

'Hughie, Meet Netta. Netta, this is Hughie.' They shake hands formally.

'Come along to the pickup. We want to get back before nightfall and it'll no' be long in coming.'

Andrew sits next to his cousin, with Netta in

the back, and they set off along the narrow ribbon of road that winds into remote hills and past scattered farmhouses until it comes to an expanse of sea with, in the distance, the indistinct outline of an island. Here the road passes through a small village and follows the coast for several miles more until they stop at last at the farm that was Andrew's home for the earlier part of his life. The wind has risen still more while they have been driving and it catches Netta's dress and flicks the hair back from her face in salt-laden ferocity. They struggle across the farmyard to the back door.

It hasn't changed a bit. Fighting their way through a scattering of boots and over-trousers, they enter the kitchen and a scene of warm domesticity. Andrew's Aunt Lizzie is stirring a saucepan containing something delicious at the stove. His Uncle Stewart is sitting by an inviting fire, boots off, warming his toes. Cousin Stewie is nowhere to be seen.

Uncle Stewart turns at the sound of the latch and hauls himself out of the chair when he sees Netta. 'Andrew, my boy, good to see you again. And this must be Netta. Welcome to An Camas.'

Aunt Lizzie takes the saucepan off the heat and crosses the room, holding out her arms to embrace Andrew's wife. 'Welcome, my dear. We're so glad that Andrew has brought you to see us. You must be tired. Sit here by the fire and get warm. Andrew! It's been such a long time since we last saw you. You havenae changed a bit though — taller maybe and thinner but just as handsome as ever, don't you agree, Netta?'

'He's handsome, right enough, but I hope he's

not thinner. He's certainly been eating enough. It must be all the walking he has to do, and the extra work this year with the awful weather.'

'Has it been bad where you are?' asks his uncle. 'We lost a lot of stock with the snow earlier in the year.'

'The same with us. We're up in the hills where I am now and it's colder than here by the sea. But everyone's in the same boat. Like everyone else, we're hoping for better things next year.' Andrew looks round. 'Where's Stewie? He's no' still out working, is he?'

'No, lad. He's out courting. He'll be the next one married, I shouldn't wonder. He'll be in shortly. Anyway, Netta, lass, do as Lizzie says and come and sit by the fire and get yourself warm. It's a gey cold time of year to be honeymooning.'

Andrew laughs. 'As you well know, Uncle, you don't have much choice in the matter when you've over a thousand ewes to look after, as well as their lambs. Fortunately I'm not the head shepherd, so it's a bit easier to get away than might otherwise be the case.'

'That's a lot of sheep — many more than you had hereabouts. So what do you do on the farm, lass?' Stewart said, turning back to Netta.

'I'm learning the job of shepherd too,' Netta says proudly.

'Are you now! Well, good luck to you. There's a shepherdess over this way, looks after a flock all by herself. She never married and, when her father died, she just carried on. She's a fearsome lady. No-one dares get the wrong side of her.'

'A bit like Netta, then,' Andrew jokes. 'A breed

apart, lady shepherds!'

The latch of the door rattles and the wind catches the door and flings it against the wall with a crash, making them all jump. Stewie and his girlfriend step into the cosy room.

'Sorry about that! It's getting windy out there.' Stewie steps over to Andrew and holds out his hand. 'Good to see you again, cousin, and good to meet you, Netta.' He gives her a kiss on the cheek. 'Meet Shona. We are hoping to be married next year, just as long as your visit isn't a prelude to taking over the farm!'

'Now, now, you two,' says Uncle Stewart. 'Don't you start again.' Netta looks at them in confusion, making Stewie laugh.

'Don't worry. It's a family joke,' he says. 'Well, it is now, only it wasn't so much years back.' Stewie sits down in the one remaining chair and pulls Shona onto his lap. 'You see, Andrew came to live with us when he was only eleven. I ken that because he's a year older than me and I was just ten.

I got it into my head that he was going to take my place on the farm. The truth was, he'd lost his dad and then his mum, but at that age you only see what's in front of your eyes and my eyes were telling me I was going to lose my place in the scheme of things. All through the time he was with us it never left me, that thought. We fell out over it eventually and Andrew went off to Glasgow.'

'It's old history now.' Andrew smiles.

'No hard feelings then, cousin?'

'No hard feelings. Look at it this way, if I had stayed here and worked the farm with you all, I'd never have met Netta and what would my life be now?'

* * *

Netta wakes in the night to the sound of rain drumming on the roof tiles just above their heads. From time to time strong gusts of wind vibrate the walls. They are in Andrew's old bedroom in the attic of the farmhouse, his Uncle Stewart having explained with a wink and a nudge that he has replaced the narrow single bed with a much more comfortable bigger version.

Turning over towards her husband, Netta moulds herself to his back, sliding a hand around his waist. He murmurs, clasps her hand in his.

'Can't you sleep, sweetheart?'

'I *was* asleep but the storm's woken me. We won't be going far tomorrow if this carries on.'

'Suits me,' says her husband, turning slowly towards her. 'We'll stay here, keeping one another warm.'

'I think your Uncle Stewart would have something to say about that.'

'I think Uncle Stewart would turn a very discreet blind eye! Anyway, let's not worry about what Uncle Stewart thinks or says. Come here, Mrs Cameron. It's our honeymoon and it won't last long, so we need to make the most of it.'

* * *

An Camus, as its name suggests, is by the beach, located on a spit of land that forms the southern edge of a small bay. When Netta peers through the window the next morning, she can see what was impossible to see in the gathering darkness of the previous evening. The rain has eased and clouds are racing across a blue sky above the choppy waters of The Sound. The long coastline of an island stretches the full length of the view before her eyes. Towards its southern end the conical shape of a mountain pierces the sky, its apex covered with a sprinkling of snow.

'It's beautiful, Andrew.' She turns to him. He is lying back on the pillows, hands clasped behind his head watching her.

'It is indeed. It's the Isle of Mull.' Andrew swings his legs out of bed and comes over to see the view for himself, arms around her waist, chin resting on her shoulder as he scans the familiar view. 'And I never thought I would be standing here with my beautiful wife, the two of us looking at it together.'

'Shall we go across to the island?'

Andrew looks sceptical. 'I think we need to wait until the wind drops a bit. Look how rough the sea is at the moment, and there are strong currents in The Sound. No, we'll leave it till tomorrow and hopefully we'll get across then. I have an idea in my head of where I would like us to visit today but I need to check with my uncle that I can borrow some form of transport. It's too far to walk, even for you!'

After breakfast the two of them set off in the pickup. Auntie Lizzie has packed them some food, as Andrew has assured Netta that they will find nothing to eat where they are going. Their way retraces part of the previous evening's journey but after a while they turn off the road and take a track that winds its way through a wide valley, in the base of which snakes a loch.

The sides of the valley are covered in a mixture of pines and deciduous trees, the bare branches of the latter stark against the winter sky. Andrew pulls off the road and brings the car to a stop.'

'A wee bit of a walk,' he says, indicating a track leading uphill between the trees. They set off hand in hand, stopping now and then to catch their breath and see the loch sparkling in the winter sunshine. Whenever the trees thin, they see towering cliffs in the distance, their deep sides gouged over centuries by burns cascading their way downwards. At last the path leaves the trees behind them and they find themselves on the edge of a huge grassy concavity in the hillside, cliffs towering at its rear and, in front, the spectacular vista of the loch and the rounded hills on its further side.

Netta turns to Andrew and smiles. 'What a beautiful view.'

'It *is* beautiful,' he agrees, his face serious, 'but it holds a dark secret. Look across the hillside. What else can you see there?'

Netta casts her eyes over the amphitheatre in front of her and now she can see scattered ruins of houses — walls standing alone and broken, corners of rooms, ending in a jumble of stones, dwellings reverting to nature over the passage of years, stretching across the hillside. She looks quizzically at her husband.

'I don't know how much Scottish history you know, having spent most of your life in Germany,' he says. 'This is an awful part of *our* history, both locally and over much of the Highlands.' He nods towards the ruins. 'This is all that is left of the township of Inniemore. In the early 1800s fifteen farming families lived here. In 1824 the families, mostly Camerons, were evicted by the landowner to make room for his sheep. Husbands and wives, children, old people, all turned out of the only homes they had ever known, because of the greed of the man on whose land they farmed.'

'What happened to them?' Netta whispers.

Andrew shrugs. 'Nobody knows for sure. 'Some died. Many from here and the surrounding areas left on ships going to America or Australia.'

'And these were your ancestors?'

'Some of them would have been, certainly.'

'So it happens everywhere,' Netta says softly. 'The Jewish people in Germany are not alone in suffering at the hands of their neighbours.'

'I'm afraid not. It seems that greed and fear make people everywhere do dreadful things.'

They stand, Andrew's arm encircling Netta's shoulders, gazing at the deserted township, feeling the great sadness that has settled like a cloud over the village. Then they turn and in silence make their way down the winding path to the roadside.

They venture further along the road, following the side of the loch, into land even more remote than the way they have already travelled. From the vantage point of a raised headland, they see another loch cutting a meandering path deep into the interior, a land of hillocks and bogs, of inlets and bits of islands scattered across its waters. They spot deer, rustic on the far hillside, and a bright-eyed pine marten that darts across the path in front of them. Sea birds, foraging on the beaches, scream a warning. As the couple approach their own bay once more, they see, at the water's edge, an otter playing games with a tangle of seaweed.

By the next day the wind has dropped and the waters are calm. Some neighbouring fishermen are going out and agree to drop the newlyweds on the island and pick them up later. They bounce over the waves, Andrew looking anxiously at Netta to check that she isn't feeling unwell. But she is enjoying every minute of the experience. Dropped off at the island's capital, they wander up and down past fishing boats, moored along the lengthy harbour wall, stop to look at the fish being unloaded and enjoy fresh crab sandwiches.

'Look what we've been given for Christmas dinner,' Netta says, when they enter the farmhouse in the late afternoon. Andrew holds up a bucket, in the bottom of which are two very lively crabs.

'Well,' says Aunt Lizzie, 'that *is* a treat. I hope you know what to do with them!'

'We do indeed. We actually stood on the pier watching a guy with a brazier making crab sandwiches and also demonstrating how to make crab pâté.'

'Good,' says Uncle Stewart. The next thing is, how are you going to keep them fresh until tomorrow?'

'Mm. We could put them in the tin bath, perhaps. They wouldn't be able to climb out of that.'

'As long as no-one decides they want a bath tonight, that sounds like a good idea!'

On Christmas morning, therefore, Andrew and Netta contribute to the general, if low-key festivities by making crab pâté, which they serve with due ceremony and slices of bread for the first course of their Christmas dinner. Andrew's cousins are both there with his aunt and uncle, as is Stewie's girlfriend, Shona. Past rivalries having been laid to rest, as is usually possible when visitors are going to be soon on their way to other pastures, the group spend a relaxing day in each other's company. And when Andrew and Netta finally depart, it is with the promise that they will return the following year for a second family wedding.

*　*　*

A glance from the window of the train as it approaches Manchester is enough to illustrate to Netta that one big British city is much like the next. The depressing wartime damage and post-war greyness and delay in rebuilding is as obvious here as it was when they passed through Glasgow and two years earlier when she and her mother had been deposited in London on their exodus from Germany.

Andrew, perhaps because of his years spent living and working in Glasgow, is unfazed by the appearance and busyness of the northern city. Deciding, however, that they have spent more than enough hours travelling and have no wish to spend several more looking for Peter and Gwen's house, he finds the taxi rank outside the station and they travel the last miles in comfort. The taxi deposits them outside a terraced stone house with a small neat front garden.

Gwen opens the door to their knock.

'Andrew, Netta, come in. It's lovely to see you. I've been looking forward to your arrival.' She kisses Netta and turns to embrace Andrew.

'It's been a long journey,' Netta replies wearily, stepping into the hallway. 'Goodness, what's going on?' The hall is full of cardboard boxes and tea chests, stacked high against bare walls.

'I'm sorry about the mess. Our moving date has been brought forward. The new owners are needing to move in before the New Year. You know how it is — they have to move out of their accommodation and they have young children, so we couldn't see them on the streets. It's easier for us, now that the children are grown up. We would have let you know, in case you wanted to change your plans, but we didn't have the address of where you were staying. I hope you don't mind the mess.'

'Of course we don't, but it must not be at all convenient for you having to put us up when you are getting ready to move . . . unless, of course, we can help you.'

'Well, spending a honeymoon packing up someone else's belongings can't be anyone's idea of fun but, yes, I would actually be very glad of your help. Peter isn't able to do a lot and that upsets him, so he will feel a lot easier in his mind if he knows I don't have to do it all on my own. Come through and see him.' She ushers them through into the living room. Peter is sitting by the fire. He rises unsteadily from the chair, smiling his lopsided smile.

'Welcome, both of you. Come and sit by the fire. As you can see, we are upside down at the moment.'

'When do you move?'

'The day after tomorrow. The family need to be in by New Year's Day and of course there are no removal firms working on that day, so the move needs to be fitted in before that. Gwen will have told you that we had intended to let you know but of course you were on your travels by then.'

'It really isn't a problem, is it, Netta? We have had a good holiday with my uncle on the west coast with plenty of walking and talking. I for one am ready for some work — and Netta was getting restless even before we left!'

'He's right,' Netta agrees. 'It's always so busy on the farm that it's unusual to have nothing to do but enjoy ourselves.'

'I'm afraid you won't see Freda,' Peter continues. 'She has been here over Christmas but she's gone to stay with Dorothy on their farm now. The two of them are travelling back to school early, to prepare for their Higher School Certificate exams. She is dead set on becoming a farmer, especially since her stay with you. And Sam, he's away too. He is touring with an orchestra and playing his piano as a soloist for the first time.'

'You must be very proud of him,' Netta says.

Peter looks thoughtful. 'Well, it's all his own hard work that has got him where he is now. But, yes, we are delighted.'

'We are taking you out for a meal tonight,' Gwen says. 'At least that will be a small chance to relax and enjoy each other's company.'

346

'But what about helping with the packing?'

'Most of it is done. There is only what is in the study to pack and the rest of the kitchen cupboards. Tomorrow will be soon enough to finish it off.'

* * *

The bus takes them into the city centre, where Christmas lights are lending a modicum of cheer to the drab surroundings. It pulls up outside the hotel in which Gwen has booked a table. The restaurant is comfortable and relaxing, though both Andrew and Netta are somewhat in awe of the plush surroundings, having rarely dined out. They are escorted to their seats by an attentive waiter. Gwen smiles at their discomposure.

'This is a thank you for all you have done for our daughter and also for inviting us to your wedding. We very much enjoyed staying with you in that beautiful part of the country, didn't we, Peter?' Peter nods in agreement but doesn't speak. He looks unwell and grey. Gwen casts an anxious glance at him. 'Peter tires easily and it has been a hard couple of weeks, sorting through everything and packing. We have been in the house since we were married. Twenty-two years now. It's quite a wrench to leave it, though we are looking forward to a quiet village and a cottage that's easier to look after. And now Peter has officially retired from teaching, there is nothing to keep us here.'

In the middle of the meal — tender slices of beef served in onion gravy with assorted vegetables — Peter's knife clatters to the table. He has stopped eating and is staring ahead. Gwen grasps his wrist but he is unresponsive to his wife's questioning as to whether he feels all right. Suddenly his body falls sideways and he crashes to the floor. Gwen is by his side in an instant as his body stiffens, then begins to shake uncontrollably.

'It's a fit,' she says. 'Help me to roll him onto his side. There's nothing else to do but wait for it to pass.' Andrew and Netta have joined her on the floor and Andrew assists Gwen while Netta looks helplessly on. Two waiters have rushed over to the group and one of them asks if he should call an ambulance.

'I think so, yes,' Gwen replies calmly. 'He has these from time to time, ever since his accident,' she adds, as the waiter hurries off to the telephone. 'He'll be confused when he comes round and difficult to handle, but he'll be all right once he is over it. There is nothing to do but wait.' They sit on the floor, meal forgotten, while the other diners look on, a mixture of concern or embarrassment on their faces.

The ambulance men know Peter. They have been called out several times when he has been taken ill, and one of them, Gordon, was working on the night that Peter received his injury and has remained friends with the couple.

'Na' then, old buddy. What's been 'appening?' he addresses Peter. 'Has he been poorly, Gwen?'

'Tired, rather than poorly. I think that's what has brought this on. I don't think he needs hospital.'

'Best get him checked in Casualty first — make sure there's nothing we're missing and give him time to come round. Then, if all's well, we'll bring him home. Are you coming with us, Gwen?'

Gwen looks at her visitors. 'You go, Gwen,' says Andrew. 'Give us the house key and we'll let ourselves in — put the lights on ready for you coming back.'

'I'm sorry. We wanted to give you a nice evening and it's all gone wrong.'

'Please don't worry.' Netta puts an arm round Gwen's shoulders. 'It's Peter who's most important.' Gwen nods. Her eyes shine with tears.

* * *

'I have suggested that Peter stays in bed for a while.' Gwen says to the newlyweds when they enter the kitchen the following morning. 'He needs to rest. He is very upset about this happening. We wanted to give you a couple of days you wouldn't forget but not in this way!'

'Well, as we said last night, we have had enough of sitting around, so you must keep us occupied,' Netta replies.

'Come and have some breakfast. You must be starving. None of us had a chance to finish last night's meal.'

'How often does Peter have fits?'

'Three or four times a year, probably, but I've noticed before how if he's tired or unwell, one may be triggered. It's the main reason we are moving out into the countryside — to give him some peace and quiet. He takes medicine, of course, which helps to keep them under control. It was his accident during the war that caused the problem.'

349

Netta shudders. 'Freda told us about how he was injured.'

'Yes, I'm glad she wasn't here last night. It upsets her to see him like that. The doctors don't know whether it's because his brain was injured by the blast or whether there is material from the blast left embedded in his brain. Either way, there's nothing they can do except treat the problems when they occur. Strange when you think about it, he got a lot of criticism for his decision not to fight and here he is, with the self-same kind of injury that soldiers got on the front line.'

After breakfast they set to work on packing the remainder of the kitchen equipment, keeping out just enough to provide them with the means of preparing food for the evening meal and breakfast the following morning. After lunch Andrew volunteers to go for a gentle stroll with Peter. The day is cold but sunny and he suggests that the fresh air will do them good. While they are away, Gwen and Netta take boxes upstairs to pack the books and a few remaining pictures from the study.

'This was always the study before we had the children,' Gwen begins.

'But with the arrival of two children, we were short of rooms and had to turn this one into a bedroom for Sam. It's not really big enough but we had no choice and he never complained.'

Netta climbs on a chair and begins to hand down books to Gwen, stirring up a cloud of dust as she does so. 'Oh dear. This is really showing up my lack of housekeeping skills!' Gwen laughs, as Netta climbs down, moves the chair along and climbs again. 'Tell me if I'm being nosy,' she continues, 'but are you and Andrew planning to have children?'

'Oh, yes. We want to very much and we hope it will be soon. Both of us are into our thirties already and we don't want to be too old when they are growing up.' She stops, remembering too late how Freda had told her how that she and her brother were adopted.

'It's all right, Netta. I know what you're thinking. We waited and waited for our own children and then, when Sam and Freda came along, it was a miracle. Even if we were nearly old enough to be their grandparents!' There is a knock at the front door. 'That'll be Peter and Andrew. Peter always forgets his keys. Excuse me a minute.'

'I'll carry on here. These won't take long to pack,' Netta says. She closes the lid on a full box and looks at the shelves. She loves books. Her mind travels back to their home in Freiburg and the small collection of books ranged across the shelf in her bedroom. They were a collection started from her first days in Germany. When their home had been bombed, the books, like everything else she owned, disappeared beneath the rubble. And when she and her mother arrived in Britain, they brought nothing — had nothing — except a few tattered clothes in a battered suitcase. But of their few material possessions, it was the loss of her books that saddened her the most.

She reaches for the last handful of volumes from the end of the shelf. There is a clatter and a small framed photo that had been lying on top of the row of books falls onto the shelf. She picks it up. It is a picture in black and white of a young man at a piano. She studies it: his slim build, the serious face and curly brown hair, the long fingers stretched over the notes.

'Is the last box ready? If so, I'll take it down.'

Netta wheels round startled, almost falling off the chair.

'Steady on! I'm sorry, I didn't mean to make you jump. What have you got there?' Netta hands down the photograph. 'Oh, that's our Sam. Only last year, that was, when he had finished his studies. A handsome boy, don't you think?'

'Yes . . . yes, he is. But I would never have thought that he and Freda were brother and sister. They don't look at all alike.'

'Oh, that's Freda for you, the way she talks about him! They arrived in England on the same train and we took the two of them together but they're not actually brother and sister.'

* * *

Peter chats happily over tea that evening. His walk with Andrew has done him good and he is looking forward to the move the next day. From time to time Andrew glances anxiously at Netta.

'Are you all right, sweetheart?' he asks. 'You are very quiet.'

'I'm sorry,' says Gwen. 'We were talking about babies. I think I may have made her broody.'

Andrew laughs. 'All to the good,' he says. 'Though I'm no' sure what Finlay would say if we have to tell him there's one less to help with the lambing next year!'

352

Netta undresses, gets silently into bed and turns away from Andrew with her face to the wall. Andrew frowns. He looks at his face in the bathroom mirror while he is cleaning his teeth, trying to recall whether he might have said anything to upset his wife. But he can think of nothing.

He climbs into bed and runs his hand across her shoulders but she does not respond.

'Netta, there is something the matter. What is it? Have I said or done something to upset you?'

'No, nothing. There is nothing.'

'I can tell there is something. Come on, I am your husband. You know you can tell me anything. Was it Gwen talking about babies? Are you worried you might not be able to have a baby?'

She turns around slowly to face him. 'Of course not, silly.' She pauses, frowning. 'Andrew, you know how you have always said we must have no secrets?'

Andrew's heart sinks at what unknown revelation may be coming his way. 'Yes,' he says carefully.

'There are things that Mutti says are in the past and it is better to leave them in the past.'

'And is that what you think?'

'No.' Netta bites her lip. 'I do not like secrets but I have always respected her wish.'

'And now?'

'Now I think it is best to tell you.'

So she does.

35

A Change of Plan

December 1947

'We have a good idea,' Andrew says the next morning.

They have all risen early and are having a hasty breakfast of toast and marmalade before the removal men arrive.

'Please say if you don't agree with us, but we wondered if you would like us to travel up with you in your car and help you to sort out your cottage when your furniture catches up with you. It will be a lot for you to do and Peter should be resting after being ill the other evening. I've looked on our road atlas and there's a train station not far from you. We can pick up a train to Carlisle there and then one that takes us directly to the village with no need to go near Glasgow. What do you think?'

'What do I think? I think that would be marvellous. Are you happy with that, Peter?'

'More than happy, although I'm conscious that this is still meant to be your honeymoon and you've done nothing but help us, rather than enjoying yourselves.'

'We are enjoying ourselves. I'm married to this wonderful woman. What more could I want?' Netta leans towards Andrew and he puts his arm around her.

'Yes,' she agrees. 'We would love to help.'

A sharp rap on the door heralds the arrival of the removal men. The physical accumulation of twenty-two years of married life is packed into the van and Gwen sets off with Peter by her side and her helpful guests in the back of the car, in the hope that she will have the cottage unlocked and ready for the appearance of the van at their new dwelling.

The Dales are brownish-green, clear as yet of the threat of snow. Sheep graze the indifferent grass, hemmed in by innumerable limestone walls that criss-cross the winter fields. Andrew and Netta sit close, looking at the view as it unfolds before them. Andrew has her hand in his, his thumb gently stroking the back of her hand. From time to time she looks at him in bewilderment. Gone is the brittleness with which she has so often hidden her emotions in the past. She is quiet, wrapped in thoughts of a world he cannot fully comprehend. But there is a tenderness, which was absent before. She needs him close and she is not afraid to show it. Her defences are down.

Her gaze flicks over the passing hills before she turns to look at him, eyes glistening with tears.

'I love you,' she says.

'I know.'

'What am I going to do?'

'I really don't know.'

* * *

355

The village towards which they are making their way lies a few miles west of the town of Skipton, a journey of about fifty miles. They arrive before the van and Andrew and Netta go in search of a grocer's shop to buy lunch for everyone, arriving back to find the removal van outside the front gate and the men sitting on packing cases in the living room eating their sandwiches and chatting to Peter and Gwen. Even at this inclement time of the year it is a beautiful and tranquil location. A small river runs through the village and a larger canal to the side of it. The houses are of pale stone and the roads are edged with trees, boughs skeletal at present but bearing the promise of life in the months to come. Comparison with the dirt and noise of Manchester could not be greater.

Over the next two and a half days Andrew and Netta help Gwen to unpack. The cottage is small, though with the same number of rooms as their old house.

'It may be a squeeze when both the children are home but we will manage fine,' Gwen says, surveying the rooms with pleasure. 'And now that Sam is playing in concert halls, he is as likely to be in the south of England as the north. Who knows, he may even play in Scotland one day!'

They celebrate New Year together. In the morning they drive into Skipton and walk around the town with its castle dominating the view. In the evening they dine quietly, raising a toast to success in the new surroundings, success on the farm, and good health and happiness to their families, present ones and those still to come.

And the following day Andrew and Netta say

their goodbyes and catch the train bound for Scotland and home.

* * *

They leave their luggage at the station to collect the next day. They have told no-one exactly when they will be back and are walking home. The last few days have been tiring, both physically and mentally, and they want nothing more than to stretch their legs and enjoy the peace of the valley and of their own wee cottage near the reservoir. But it seems that other people have different ideas.

They are nearly home when they hear a car behind them. Finlay is in the driving seat. Andrew gives Netta a resigned look and they stop as the car draws near.

'Happy New Year, Finlay! I thought we wouldn't be able to sneak home without being seen.'

'I'm afraid not. We're having a late New Year's party to welcome you back. No backing out of it so don't try!'

'It will be lovely to see everyone again.'

'Well, it won't be everyone. That was yesterday's party. But there will be someone who may surprise you. We'll expect you at six. Shall I come and pick you up?'

'No, thanks, Finlay. I'm sure we'll manage. Unless there's anything needs done on the farm.'

'Nothing at all.'

'I'll see you later then.'

Andrew unlocks the door of the cottage. Although the weather is mild, it is cold and damp inside, the fire not having been lit for nearly a fortnight.

'Don't worry. I'll soon have it snug and warm again,' Andrew says, kneeling down to the fire.

Netta kneels down beside him and puts her arm around his shoulders. 'I think I like this being married,' she says. 'I'd make you a cup of tea if we could only boil the water!'

'I love you, Mrs Cameron,' Andrew replies to her teasing. 'And if you stay there with your arm around me, I will never get the fire made!'

'What time did Finlay say they wanted us?'

'Six o'clock, I think.'

'Good. That means we've at least an hour to get reacquainted with the house before we need to set out again.'

★ ★ ★

'I wonder who Finlay's surprise is,' Netta ponders as they retrace their steps.

'Perhaps he has found someone to keep him company after so many years on his own.'

'Mm, maybe.' Netta is quiet for a minute before giving a deep sigh. 'Andrew, you are sure that we should say nothing to Mutti?'

'Let us wait and see, that's all I'm saying. Things have a way of working themselves out. Remember the saying 'Fools rush in where angels fear to tread'? It's angels' feet that are needed here. Wait a bit, my darling.'

★ ★ ★

Margaret opens the door.

'Hello, Margaret. I didn't know you would be here tonight. How lovely to see you.'

'Hello, Netta. We're all waiting for you. Did you have a good holiday?'

'Wonderful, thank you. We'll tell you all about it.'

Ellen emerges from the kitchen and hugs her daughter, holding her at arm's length and studying her. 'Yes, I can see that married life is suiting you,' she says, noting the sparkle in Netta's eyes, deceptively like tears. 'Andrew, how are you?' She lets go of her daughter and Andrew steps forward and kisses his mother-in-law.

'Come through to the living room, both of you. Billy and Isobel are in here with Finlay.' There is much kissing and slapping on the back and general bonhomie before they are all seated with a drink.

Andrew looks pointedly round at the guests before turning to Finlay. 'So where is the surprise, Finlay? It's lovely to see everyone but I'm not surprised by anyone!'

'I think he means me,' says Margaret. 'You see, while you were away Ellen invited me to come and live here with her in the farmhouse.'

'Oh, that's lovely.' Netta jumps up, clapping her hands, and hugs Margaret warmly. 'I mean, I love your wee railway cottage but it's lonely up there for you, all on your own. Much better for you to be here with us.

And we all know what a good baker you are!'

'Part of the reason why we invited Billy and Isobel to come this evening is that Billy has done everything legally and gone to see the solicitor. This means that Margaret is now officially living in the farmhouse.'

Finlay turns to Andrew. 'So how about you bringing Netta to live in your old cottage? It's sitting empty now.'

'I don't think so, Finlay,' Andrew says slowly. 'I don't think I would be able to persuade Netta to move, even if I wanted. We both like to get away at the end of the day to enjoy the peace on our own. Apart from that, it's good for someone to keep an eye on that end of our patch. And, who knows, with all the comings and goings of recent months we are bound to get someone who's interested in staying there. I suggest we leave it as it is for now.'

'So did you have a peaceful holiday?' asks Ellen.

The pair burst out laughing. 'Nothing could be further from the truth,' says Andrew. 'A busy time spent with all my relatives for the first few days and then helping Peter and Gwen to flit from Manchester to Skipton just before New Year.'

'Oh, I didn't realise that was planned.'

'It wasnae planned. The family who were buying their house needed a roof over their heads for New Year, so Peter and Gwen, out of the goodness of their hearts, decided to put things into motion several days early. It took its toll on Peter. He has no' been so well. But now he's settling in the cottage, he's much happier.'

'And how's the farm?' asks Netta. 'Has anything exciting happened while we've been away?'

'Nothing at all. The weather has been kind, the sheep have been quiet and the cows are being well

360

behaved,' Finlay summarises. 'All we need is for this weather to continue over the next few months to give us a good lambing.'

★ ★ ★

The honeymoon is over. The early months of the New Year bring gales and rain but the majority of the sheep seem immune to these conditions. Finlay looks forward cautiously to the year's lambing. Ellen is enjoying Margaret's company, her stepmother being now happily settled in the farmhouse. Andrew and Netta seem blissfully happy in their marital isolation in the cottage by the reservoir.

And then one evening, when Andrew and Netta arrive back from their work, there on the doormat is a letter.

36
Concert

March 1948

Monday 22nd February

Dear Andrew and Netta,

I hope this letter finds you both well and happy. We are enjoying our Yorkshire cottage and thank you once again for making our move so much easier than it could have been. Peter especially is finding life much simpler here and, as a consequence, is feeling stronger.

I am writing with good news and an invitation. Sam is to play in a Beethoven concert at St Andrew's Hall, Glasgow, on Saturday, 13th March. As a token of our thanks for all your help, including your help with Freda, we are enclosing three tickets for the concert, one for each of you and one for your mother. We do hope you are free to come. We will be going up to Glasgow in advance of the performance, picking up Freda on the way, so we will see you at the concert.

With our love and very best wishes,
Peter and Gwen

★ ★ ★

Ellen is sitting in the front seat of the car, restless with excitement.

'It's years since I went to Glasgow. The last time, I think, was when your father was in hospital there, Netta. In fact you came with me when we went to fetch him home after his operation. So many years ago. I don't suppose it has changed much, certainly not for the better with all the wartime bombing.' Ellen sits back and there is silence, broken only by the engine of the pickup as it makes its way through the towns that skirt the city.

'I wonder what Sam will play. I can remember when I first went to hear Josef play at a concert in Freiburg. *He* played a piece by Beethoven — he was his favourite composer, you know. I remember how proud of him I was. I'm sure Peter and Gwen will feel the same about their son.' Ellen pauses. 'It will be very strange going to a concert again. I hope I won't find it too difficult.'

Andrew looks in the rear-view mirror and catches Netta's eye.

'We will be there with you, Mutti,' Netta says, leaning forward and putting a hand on her mother's shoulder. 'You mustn't worry.'

★ ★ ★

The concert hall is filling rapidly. They find their seats, only five rows from the front, and Ellen opens the programme to find Sam's name. And there it is: 'Appassionata' by Ludwig van Beethoven, played by Sam Halliwell'.

Ellen gasps. 'He's playing 'Appassionata'.' Her voice falters. 'That was Josef's favourite. He used

to play it for me. He said it was our love song —
our *Liebeslied*. How strange that I'm going to hear
it again tonight.'

'Maybe not so strange, Mutti. Sometimes these
things are meant to be.'

On the stage the orchestra are assembling.
Netta looks round the audience in an attempt to
locate Peter and Gwen. It is packed now and difficult to make out individuals. But then she looks
up and there they are, seated with Freda in one of
the boxes. With them is a distinguished-looking
man in a dress suit. They are listening attentively
to what he is saying. They nod, smiling, as the
man rises and leaves the box through the curtains
at the back.

Five minutes later the lights are dimmed, the
orchestra's tuning up comes to an end and clapping begins as the conductor walks onto the stage
between the violinists. It is the same man whom
Netta has seen talking to Peter and Gwen. The
concert starts with the 'Egmont Overture'. Netta
senses her mother relaxing into her seat as the
music begins. She feels Andrew's hand squeeze
her arm reassuringly and he leans towards her
and whispers in her ear.

There is prolonged applause when the first
piece of music comes to an end. The conductor
leaves the stage and, after a brief pause, reappears
escorting the pianist. He is young, much younger
than most of the musicians, and his light brown
curls and blue eyes enhance his boyish appearance. He walks up to the piano and sits with a
quiet confidence. After a pause of a few seconds,
the first notes drop into the silence.

Netta is rigid in her seat, scarcely able to breathe. As though from afar she feels her husband's comforting hand still resting on her arm. On her other side Ellen has sat forward at the young man's appearance on stage. Netta watches her out of the corner of her eye. Her mother is staring fixedly at him. He begins to play. Her mother gives a small cry, tries to rise from her seat but Netta takes hold of her arm, gently pulling her back down. 'Not now, Mutti. Afterwards. We'll go and find him afterwards.'

Ellen continues in a loud whisper. 'But he looks like Samuel. Can it be Samuel? Netta, do you think it is Samuel?'

From the row behind them, people are muttering for them to be quiet. 'Mutti, you are upsetting the audience. Be quiet for now. We will go and see him as soon as the music is finished. Sit still now and listen.' Netta puts an arm round Ellen's shoulder and hugs her tightly in an attempt to still the violent shivering of her mother's body.

The piece comes to a tumultuous ending and the pianist stands and bows to thunderous applause before leaving the stage. Before he has disappeared Ellen is on her feet and pushing her way to the end of the row, closely followed by Netta and Andrew. The pianist returns to the front of the stage and bows again, noting as he straightens the commotion in the rows in front of him. He sees a middle-aged woman supported by a younger one. The older woman raises her head and looks him straight in the eye. Momentarily he freezes and then his look of shock slowly turns to one of joy. 'Mutti,' he mouths and then, conscious

365

of the conductor's appearance at his side, turns and walks rapidly from the stage.

* * *

The management are reluctant to allow this distressed middle-aged woman into the dressing rooms but their remonstrations are brought to an abrupt halt by the sound of hurried steps and the appearance of the pianist in the corridor behind them. He comes rapidly towards the group and comes to a stop in front of them, staring at Ellen.

'Mutti? Is it really you?' His gaze swivels to the side. 'And Netta — my sister Netta. I cannot believe it. I thought you must all be dead.'

Ellen steps forward uncertainly and puts a hand up to his cheek. 'My boy.

So grown up — and so like your father. I did not believe I would ever see you again.' She throws her arms around him and he holds her tight. Netta runs up to them and they all three embrace as the opening bars of the 'Pastoral Symphony' waft towards them from the stage.

Andrew, looking on from the sidelines, turns at the approach of footsteps.

It is Peter and Gwen and their daughter. Andrew makes his way down the corridor towards them.

'Andrew, what is going on?' Gwen says anxiously. 'We saw the commotion and Ellen struggling to leave. Is she feeling ill? I don't understand.'

'No, she's not ill. Come over here and sit down a minute and I'll explain.' He glances anxiously at Peter and begins very slowly to explain. 'Ellen is Sam's mother — his real mother. I know it

366

seems incredible but it's true. We discovered it when we were helping you to move. Netta found that picture in the study, the one of Sam playing the piano. She thought it was her brother but she wasn't sure. After all, it is nine years since she saw him. He was still a child. Now he's a man, so changed from how she remembers him. We didn't want to cause an upset if she was mistaken. So we decided to do nothing, preferring to wait a bit and consider the best way forward. And then your letter arrived and that was a sign, if sign were needed, that powers outside of our control were working. We knew that if Netta was right, then her mother would certainly recognise him. And if she was mistaken, then no harm had been done, no false hopes raised.'

'So Sam has his mother back,' Freda says quietly. 'I wonder whether mine might still be alive.'

'Sam's mother is British, his sister too. That is how they managed to survive when thousands didn't.' Andrew's voice is gentle.

Freda turns to her parents. Peter has his arm around his wife's shoulders. 'It's all right,' says Freda. 'I have the best parents anyone could wish for. More might make life complicated.' Sam, hearing them laugh, comes over, holding Ellen's hand.

'Mother, Father. Meet my first mum, Ellen, and my sister, Netta! This is the most amazing coincidence.'

'Coincidence, maybe,' says Peter, 'but you could say that the last few years have been working up to this point.' He looks round at the corridor and the empty dressing rooms. 'Why don't we all go back

367

to the hotel, where we can talk properly? After all, there's a lot of catching up to do.'

* * *

While the rest of the party are seated in a circle in the lounge drinking tea, Sam — or rather, Samuel — takes Ellen aside.

'Mother, before we join the others — '

Ellen interrupts. 'I know what you are about to ask, Samuel, and I was about to tell you. You want to know why your father and your other sisters are not with us.'

'They are dead, aren't they?' Sam says in a strangled voice, struggling to hold back his emotion. 'I knew they must be. I thought you were all dead. I had to learn to live with that. And now, it is wonderful that you and Netta are here alive . . . but my father and Eva and Anna — can they be alive as well?'

'No, Samuel, they are dead.' Ellen sees her son's shoulders sag, the flash of hope on his face turn to one of despair. She takes his hand. 'Your father was arrested and taken to Dachau concentration camp. He never returned. I found out later that he died there in 1942. Your sisters . . . your sisters were killed by the soldiers.'

There is a long silence before Samuel turns to his mother, bleak eyes devoid of tears. 'I understood long ago that this must be so. I had come to believe that all my family were gone.' He pauses. 'If only Eva and Anna could have come with me to England . . .'

'They were too old to be allowed to travel with

368

the Kindertransport. Netta, of course, has no Jewish blood in her. There would have been trouble if she had been shot, though it could so easily have happened.'

'It is a miracle to find out that you and Netta have been spared. I had given up hope of any of you being alive.'

'Netta and I were kept in an internment camp because we were British, and allowed to leave Germany when the war was over.'

'So you did not get the letters that I sent to our house in Freiburg?'

'Our house was bombed before we were interred. We had no news of you or of your father. We went back to Freiburg after the war and it was there that we eventually found out that Father was dead. That was when we decided to come back to Scotland.'

'But you did not try to find me?'

'There was nothing I wanted to do more. But six years had gone by. You were a boy when you left. By the time we came back you were a man. You had a life that you were living and I did not feel it was right to interfere with that life. I did not even know which country you had been sent to — it might have been Great Britain but it could have been America. One boy among so many millions. It would have been impossible to find you. Netta tried to persuade me to try but I honestly thought it was better for you — and your new family — this way. You must believe me when I say that it has been the hardest thing in the world for me to give up a child. Any mother would say the same.' Ellen looks across at Gwen and Peter. 'Tell me, how did you come to find your new parents?'

'Let us join them and they will tell you.' They cross the room and pull chairs into the circle. 'Mother wants to know how you found Freda and myself,' he says to his adoptive parents.

'I was arranging to pick up some of the Kinder-transport children who had been put on the train from London to Manchester,' Peter says. 'Some were to go to homes, the rest into a hostel. Gwen chose Freda, and Freda refused to go without Samuel. She called him her brother, and that is what they have come to be — brother and sister.'

Gwen takes a deep breath. 'Peter and I are both very grateful to have had such a wonderful son and daughter, when we had given up hope of having any.'

'You still have us,' Sam says quickly. You don't stop being my parents because I have found my real mother. It is because of you that I have been playing here this evening. This would not have happened but for you. Think how happy my real father would be if he knew I was following in his footsteps.'

'You looked so like your father when you walked onto the stage and began to play.' Ellen runs her hand through his soft curls. 'It was the music he first played for me when I had helped him back to health all those years ago in Scotland.'

'And he played it often for you at home in Germany. I knew it was his own special code, that beautiful slow movement in the heart of the piece. I determined then and there that when I was old enough I would learn to play it.'

Sam goes over to where Freda is standing next

to Netta. 'And now I have my two sisters — my sister Freda who, I suspect, was often fed up with my practising when I was home from school, and now my sister Netta. She of course was much older than me and used to boss me around terribly! I shall never forget the family I have lost but it is wonderful to have found my mother and my sister again. And also I am grateful to find that I have a brother-in-law, so now Netta will be able to order him around, rather than me!'

'She already does that!' Andrew says to more laughter. He looks around at the elated but tired faces. 'I suggest that we draw the evening to a close.

It has been a long and emotional one. Some of us have jobs to go to very early in the morning. Why don't we all meet up at the farm tomorrow? Sam, will you be free or are you playing tomorrow?'

'I'm not playing tomorrow. In fact I was planning to travel down to Yorkshire with Peter and Gwen to see the new cottage. Maybe I could come back to the farm with you tonight and spend a few hours with Mother in the morning and Peter and Gwen could pick me up on their way south. Oh dear, I can see that this sudden excess of parents is going to be confusing, not to say time-consuming. There will soon be no time for work!'

★   ★   ★

It is very late when Andrew climbs into bed and takes Netta in his arms.

'You must be tired, poor darling,' he says, kissing her gently on the lips.

371

'Not as exhausted as Mutti, I think. I mean, I already had my suspicions. All of this was completely new for her. She didn't suspect a thing. My biggest worry was how she would react when she first saw him. Was it a cruel thing to let her find out like that?'

'We could have arranged it for them to meet before the concert but suppose you had been wrong. It would have led to distress all round. As it was, you handled everything as well as it was possible to do. It could have been a lot more tricky than it turned out to be.'

'He's so like my stepfather. Not just in his looks but in his character too. Josef was gentle and thoughtful and all the things that I am not. I am much more my father's child, if what Mutti says about him is true.'

'So who will our child be like, I wonder?'

'Now that will be a well-kept secret, at least until the end of September.'

'The only secret, I hope.'

'The only secret. I promise.'

Epilogue

November 1948

The fog of early morning had cleared, leaving only the tops of the highest hills wrapped in mist. Elsewhere a pale autumn sun washed the farm and its outbuildings and a stream of cars that was making its way slowly through the valley.

Finlay drove the first car. He pulled to a stop, stepped out and opened the passenger door for Ellen, Margaret and Freda to emerge. Next came a car driven by Gwen, with her husband Peter by her side. In the back sat Samuel and, with him, a slim, fair-haired young woman called Sarah, who was looking in awe at the imposing hills unfolding before them. The third car contained Andrew and Netta and a baby boy only ten weeks old, who had, only half an hour before, been baptised Joseph, and was now — worn out with all the fuss and commotion — sleeping peacefully.

Samuel stepped from the car and held out his hand to Sarah who was trying but not succeeding to avoid the mud that was everywhere around.

'We'll join you in a minute,' Samuel called back as he and Sarah, still hand in hand, ran up to the shepherd's cottage. Gwen and Ellen gave each other a look and smiled.

'He wants to show her his cottage,' Gwen said laughing. 'I think that's the last of them we'll see for a while!'

'I think it's so lovely that he has the cottage,' Freda said. 'It means I'll be able to come over and see him whenever he's playing in Glasgow and comes here to stay.'

'You'll be able to give us a helping hand on the farm as well, when you're not busy at college,' Andrew added, coming up behind them. 'Sam might have a share in the family business now but I don't think those precious hands will be getting dirty with farming work. And Sarah too will have the excuse of her violin playing. So you, Freda, will have to do their dirty work for them!' He turned to Netta and gently peeled back the shawl to plant a kiss on the forehead of their precious son, before putting his arm around Netta's shoulders and directing her towards the farmhouse. 'Come along, sweetheart. You need to keep your strength up. Let's get to the food — if I may be allowed to escort you!'

Ellen lingered in the yard, watching the sunlight play on the surface of the fast-flowing river. Gingerly she put her hand deep in the pocket of her coat. Her fingers encountered the ragged edge of a piece of paper. On it, had she looked, were words written in pencil, fading with the passing of the years. A letter. She had no need to draw it out and read it. She knew it by heart. It was important that it was here, that *he* was here, on this day of all days, with all the family gathered in thankfulness and hope for the future.

Winter 1942

Liebe Ellen,

374

I am not so strong now and I do not have much time on this earth. I feel very much thankful to Frank for his kindness to take my letter to you. What would I do all these years without his help? My friend Asher died last week. I miss him very much. Also many others have died who I do not know so well.

My darling, how I miss you all these years and wish to be with you. You are my shining star in this dark world. Please look after Netta, Eva, Anna and Samuel. Tell Samuel to be a good boy and to care for his mother. I pray that this horror may soon be over and never return, so that we will live at peace with one another.
I have no strength to write more. May the God of our Fathers keep you safe in his care.

Your Josef

Acknowledgements

A huge thank you to all my farming friends for keeping me right on aspects of farming and sharing memories and knowledge of the influence of World War 2 on farming practice.

My continuing thanks to all the Aria team for their help and support in the writing of this book.

And to my lovely family, thank you for your faith in me and my writing.

We do hope that you have enjoyed
reading this large print book.

Did you know that all of our titles
are available for purchase?

We publish a wide range of high
quality large print books including:
Romances, Mysteries, Classics
General Fiction
Non Fiction and Westerns

Special interest titles available in
large print are:
The Little Oxford Dictionary
Music Book, Song Book
Hymn Book, Service Book

Also available from us courtesy of
Oxford University Press:
Young Readers' Dictionary
(large print edition)
Young Readers' Thesaurus
(large print edition)

For further information or a free
brochure, please contact us at:
Ulverscroft Large Print Books Ltd.,
The Green, Bradgate Road, Anstey,
Leicester, LE7 7FU, England.
Tel: (00 44) **0116 236 4325**
Fax: (00 44) **0116 234 0205**

GOD'S ACRE

Dee Yates

As the drums of war begin to beat louder on the continent, 17-year-old Jeannie McIver heads to the wilds of the Scottish Uplands to start life as a Land Girl. Jeannie soon falls in love with life on the busy Scottish hill farm. She even finds her interest piqued by the attractive Tam, the son of the neighbouring farmer. But even in the barren hills, they can't avoid the hell of war, and Jeannie's idyllic life starts to crumble.

A YORKSHIRE LASS

Dee Yates

York 1886. Sarah-Lou has just left school and is ready for adventure! A position in the city sounds perfect, but working all hours for the haughty Ackroyds leaves little time for fun, and when their troubled son, Gideon, shows too much interest in the junior maid, her days at the Big House are numbered. Sarah-Lou sees a bright future training as a nurse — but her dreams are shattered again. A little girl needs her and the streets of York are no place to bring up a child, so there is only one place to go — the Yorkshire village Sarah-Lou was so eager to leave behind . . .

THE RAILWAYMAN'S DAUGHTER

Dee Yates

In 1875 railwayman Tom Swales, with his wife and five daughters, takes the tiny end cottage in a terrace by the newly-built York-Doncaster railway track. Eldest daughter Mary becomes housemaid to the stationmaster, where she battles the grime from passing trains and the stationmaster's brutal, lustful nature — a fight she cannot win. Mary flees to York, and when she is taken in by the York Quakers her spirit is nearly broken. If she finds the strength to return to her family will they accept her — and will her first love, farmer's son Nathaniel, still be waiting?